THE ALPHA'S ORACLE

MERRY RAVENELL

9 SWORDS

The Alpha's Oracle

For David.

NIGHTMARE COMING

"We're wolves! You're my father, you're the Beta, you aren't going to do anything? You aren't going to make Alpha Jermain fight?"

My father shook his head. "Gianna, there's a great deal you don't know, that we've kept from you."

"I know we're wolves. That means we don't let other wolves take what's ours without a fight. I'm an Oracle, and I'm telling a warrior this?" Shadowless wasn't a tiny pack. We were a large pack, a strong pack, and we didn't tuck our tails because another Alpha growled at us.

"Mind your mouth, Gianna," he snapped.

His authority as First Beta meant nothing now. He was a warrior who wouldn't fight. He was a male who'd tuck his tail and cower, and worse, he'd let his Alpha cower. This brief exchange dissolved all his power and prestige over me. He should have been growling a challenge at his Alpha. Instead he turned his snarl on me.

Alpha Gabel of IronMoon. Angry or not, the name still sent cold shivers through me.

Three years ago the IronMoon had been a small pack living

in the cold, northern forests. Nothing but a bunch of punks who fought amongst themselves and usually killed each other before they hurt anyone else. Then Alpha Gabel had appeared. He trained his warriors to be brutal and fierce. Under his leadership IronMoon had consumed all the small packs in the region, then moved on to bigger and bigger prey.

He didn't kill the packs he conquered.

The IronMoon tortured their victims.

The IronMoon broke their victims.

But Alpha Gabel made it easy to avoid his wrath, and the inevitable indignity of begging for mercy. Surrender, swear allegiance, and pay annual tribute to the IronMoon. That was all he seemed to want, and he otherwise left his liege-packs to rule themselves and manage their own affairs. It wasn't such a bad deal if you could get past being leashed like a dog.

Now the weakest packs surrendered before Gabel got around to menacing them. Shadowless had become one of those packs. There would be no fight. Alpha Jermain of Shadowless would surrender to Alpha Gabel of IronMoon without so much as a growl.

Gabel had never explained why he collected packs like hunters collected trophies. The rumor was he intended to crown himself King-Alpha. In public people scoffed at the idea, and Gabel didn't do much to support the rumors. He didn't maintain any kind of court, he didn't dissolve and annex the packs he conquered, he didn't even style himself as Lord-Alpha. His IronMoon stormed out of their heart in the north like locusts every few weeks, swept over their target, Gabel got his promise of tribute, and they went home. Not very much the conquering monarch.

The last of the King-Alphas had killed themselves off five hundred years earlier. The war had shattered our culture and almost extinguished our species. The kings had died, their kingdoms had fallen, and werewolves had moved on. Monarchies were dead in the modern, human-dominated world.

King-Alpha ambitions or just collecting packs to be a herd of milk-cows, Gabel's IronMoon had graduated to devouring packs Shadowless' size in the past year. He had already taken GleamingFang to our south and MarchMoon to our east. A fight with IronMoon had been inevitable.

At least that's what I had thought until this evening.

"Gianna." My father tried to take a stern tone with me. "This is how it's going to be. You don't know as much as you think you do."

"I am not a child," I snapped. "I stopped being a child four years ago." Other twenty-year-old females struggled for respect and position within a pack and were excluded from much of the pack's management, but I was a Seer: a female wolf blessed with visions and whispers from the Moon. I had finished my training at sixteen and graduated to adulthood as an Oracle. Shadowless' concerns and business weren't much of a mystery to me, no matter how hard my father tried to keep me in the dark. No one expects Oracles to be courageous in the face of battle. We aren't warriors. But weak, timid Seers don't survive to become Oracles. They get lost on the Tides, drown in the Moon's Eye, or go insane from the whispers and visions. I also came from a long line of warriors, and courage had been bred into my bones. I couldn't accept Alpha Jermain kneeling in front of Alpha Gabel unless—and until—Gabel ripped out his hamstrings.

Before a fight my father was all jumping muscle and fire, barking orders at the pack. Now he sighed, all the fight and strength fled from him. "I'm sorry, Gianna."

"Don't be sorry, just fight him. If Shadowless doesn't fight, it'll just embolden him! We have a responsibility! Even Gleaming-Fang and MarchMoon fought him!" The MarchMoon had fought until Gabel's forces had eviscerated most of their warriors. The GleamingFang had also fought, but with a little less gusto after seeing how MarchMoon had fared, and Alpha Anders had surrendered sooner than later

Anders was sort of gutless. He was more politician than warrior. But even he had fought.

"Gabel has sent his demands. He'll be here in the morning. He wants all the young, unmated she-wolves presented—"

I gasped.

"Gabel is unmated. He's been doing this with all the other packs. It's part of our deal with him."

"Part of the deal!" I exclaimed. "You're trading in females now?"

He kept talking like he didn't hear me. "Gia, he didn't ask about you. He's interested in Amber. I hope you can understand this is for the good of the pack."

No, I didn't understand. We didn't just let other wolves take what was ours without a fight, especially not our packmates and kin. We didn't just line up females for perusal because another Alpha demanded it.

Not a single growl or drop of blood before surrender. Tears welled up as the betrayal sank into me. "We aren't worth fighting for? You aren't even going to make him pay a drop of blood for us?"

He gripped my arm. "Gianna, listen to me. This is the deal we have. You don't know everything. Jermain hasn't told you everything. We've seen how fighting IronMoon has gone for GleamingFang, MarchMoon, and the others. They end up broken and bloody. It doesn't work. We have to be smarter."

"Smarter sounds a lot like cowardice," I spat. "What are you going to do if he chooses one of us?"

"I don't think he will, and if he does," a long pause, "casualties are inevitable."

The one for the many... So instead of asking the warriors to bleed, the pack would surrender. Gabel would waltz in, humiliate us all, and then we'd go back to our normal lives trying to pretend it hadn't happened.

"If you're going to trade a female, offer me to him as an Oracle. IronMoon doesn't have one. Don't line up everyone else to be humiliated by him," I said.

"That's not what he wants. Be ready at ten, Gianna."

This was what Gabel did to those who even considered opposing him.

He destroyed them on promise alone.

―――――

Romero shifted, sniffing the air drifting from the house five miles in the distance. He waited on a small hill just level with the tree line. The hill provided a clear vantage of the house, brightly illuminated by the swelling moon overhead, and the lights framing each of the doors. How nice of the Shadowless to make it easy to find the points of entry. "They do not even realize we are here."

"They do," Alpha Gabel answered, "but Jermain has already agreed to greet me on his knees."

Romero growled deep in his throat. "We should kill him for that alone."

"No. Surrender is surrender. If they show us their throats and swear fealty, the matter is concluded."

"Without bloodshed?" Romero snarled. "There is no honor in that. There is no honor in becoming King without conquest."

Gabel snarled back, the moon reflecting off the dilated pupils that nearly engulfed his ocean-blue eyes. Only a faint ring of blue remained, as if the Moon Herself clutched the blackness to constrain it.

Romero growled to himself and backed up a step, head

bowed to his left shoulder. "You temper yourself. We used to descend onto these miserable packs like Hounds and tear into them, and the stink of fear and blood and death until they wailed for surrender, but now! Now it is politics and phone calls."

Gabel ran his tongue over his front teeth as the blackness twinged in his blood and the teeth sharpened a touch. He poked one then the other until his tongue bled just a drop. Romero was right. He had not had to sink his claws into more than the occasional defiant IronMoon for a while now. Packs dropped to their knees when he glanced their way. Their pathetic warriors, fat and happy and fed a diet of easy prestige and good manners, dissolved like cotton candy on the tongue.

Cotton candy. Spun sugar. Such a strange thing. Not nearly as magical as it looked. Disappointing in every possible way.

"Let's make them bleed," Romero urged.

The other warriors didn't dare speak but shifted to show their approval.

Gabel rubbed the dents on his tongue, driving one a little deeper on the hungry tip of his elongated tooth. "No. That is not the agreement."

"Bah!" Romero threw up his hands. "We are warriors. We fight. We hunger for death and blood."

"Then you will remain hungry a while longer." Gabel flexed his left hand. The wind shifted directions. He inhaled, and his senses focused, sharp and perked. "Females."

"No shit. That's what you ordered," Romero said sourly.

"And you don't think it will gall them to have to line up their women for me to inspect? You are a fine warrior, Romero, but you still don't grasp that the most violent attacks are against the soul. That is pain. It is disgusting that they would surrender their women without so much as a drop of blood shed."

"And you won't demand they do so?"

"Why should I? They can live with the dishonor and shame. It will hurt that much more." He inhaled again.

"So that's why you do this?"

"I don't have any use for a mate right now," Gabel said. "One day I will. One day I will need heirs. But for now it terrifies the packs to think what I might do to one of their beloved daughters."

He inhaled again and walked forward a few steps, senses straining. There were two scents that played over his nerves and down the veins of his neck, strummed his spinal cord inside its bone armor. Like the scent of blood, it excited his instincts, ignited his nerves, made his lips curl back over his teeth. The scent. He had caught those scents before. They all varied, but each one came with the same shock, more or less. The scent of a potential mate, a female with a soul compatible with his own.

Now there were two lure-scents at Shadowless. One reminded him of pine needles and autumn, the other of the Moon, and under that, something fainter and more exotic: the night-blooming cereus, a flower that bloomed for a single night once a year

The Moon sailed overhead, silent, observing. He had never smelled the Moon before, never really thought of the Moon as having a scent, but he could smell the Moon on the wind. It was faint, weaker than the one of pine and autumn. How intriguing.

And distracting.

The wind shifted, this time blowing toward the house.

"But you never choose one. There are other things we could do that are less... permanent. For us," Romero said.

Gabel focused on him. "No. No rape, Second Beta."

"That would put terror in them."

"A female is no match for any of us. There is no good use in defiling a female, just like there's no purpose in killing pups. It breeds needless hatred."

Romero grumbled. Gabel ignored him. The Second Beta was violent and depraved, and left to his own devices, would have devolved into a hulking, stupid monstrosity who couldn't see beyond the end of his claws. Skin got numb after it was hit often enough. Pain was an art. Fear was an art. Cruelty was an art. Pushing a wolf beyond caring was failure. Once they stopped caring, and either died inside, or rebelled since no fate was worse than the one they currently endured, was when control was lost. It all had to be just within the limits of endurance. Just enough to keep them disarmed. Just enough to keep them focused on the glimmer of light. Pain without the promise of relief was pointless. A battle without the risk of loss was nothing.

Which was exactly why Romero was, and would remain, Second Beta. Just a cudgel. First Beta Hix had better understanding.

The scent from the house teased Gabel again. The Moon's scent had changed, carrying with it fear and anticipation and resolve.

The one who smelled like night-blooming cereus had smelled him.

She knew he was coming.

Gabel grinned.

ALL THESE WRONGS

There were eight unmated she-wolves of an appropriate age for Gabel, but we hid them in the basement, for all the good it would do if he demanded to see them. Only Amber and I would face him.

Amber squeezed my hand. "Ready?"

"Of course not," I whispered.

She smiled, and her lips trembled a bit at the corners.

Amber had every reason to be scared. Gabel would choose Amber if she had even a whiff of lure-scent on her. Amber was a rare female warrior, and she was destined to be a Luna somewhere. The word "statuesque" had been created just for her.

My only remarkable physical feature was my pale skin that didn't tan. The Moon-touched skin marked all Oracles. Gabel, if he knew anything, would recognize Amber as a warrior and myself as an Oracle, and not ask questions about the barely-grown females hiding under our feet.

Alpha Jermain stood like he still had some dignity. He was confused. Gabel had taken it all from the other end of a phone.

First there were footsteps on the porch outside, then shadows moving across the frosted windows. Scents wafted under the door just as it opened. Six males, and one stood apart. A musky scent of power, prestige, and authority, but with a very faint acrid edge.

One of the male tones cut over the others, and matched the strong scent. It was deep and dark and reminded me of rocks grinding across each other. All the little hairs down my spine shot straight up on end, and ice needles of fear jabbed through my belly.

Alpha Gabel.

Even Amber's eyes widened and glazed with fear.

The scent of a male wolf's power is a combination of his physical strength, the force of his will, and his intention to use both. Even in my visions, the ones more nightmare than anything else, there hadn't been a wolf's scent like his.

"And here they are, waiting as requested," the deep-toned rock-voice said as a shape blotted out the spring sunlight.

Gabel's appearance didn't match his smoldering, charred-wood scent. He was tall and broad, and while his tanned complexion was flawless, the back of his hands were scabbed and the skin leathery and worn. His wrists were the thickness of my ankle. The muscles under the back of his hands flexed and shifted like iron cables.

His face was handsome, with a square, strong jaw and a sharp nose to match his raw, high cheekbones. His eyes were a churning sea-blue-green so vivid they almost didn't seem real. His hair was a tawny blond that curled just a little bit, cut quite short. Where most wolves would have shown up in jeans, he wore pants and a button-down in a vibrant shade of plumb that barely contained his biceps. He was also barefoot.

He was glorious, and he could have snapped my legs like twigs with those hands of his.

His scent said he'd do just that if provoked.

That scent curled down my spine like the grasp of two

hands. Unmistakable prestige mixed with that peculiar scent of ash.

He was glorious. And as much as my brain did not want him: I wanted him.

The rest of me was only trying to decide if Gabel was more terrible than he was glorious.

Terrible was winning, but only by a narrow fraction.

What made other males cower to him, and other females crumble, made me stupid enough to want him. She-wolves are attracted to power, strength, prestige. It's how we're made. That scent stroked my nerves and breasts and slid between my thighs like a calloused caress.

Gabel ignored all the Shadowless and went straight to Amber. She squared up and met his gaze. He grinned in return. She sniffed, disdainful of his obvious glory, but her nipples perked against her tank top.

Gabel took her left hand in his own, and as gallant as a nobleman, brought her wrist to his nose, his eyes never leaving hers. She made a sound of disgust but didn't fight him, and after a few seconds, he drew back.

This close to him his scent of power and the aura of commanding prestige were suffocating.

Very gently, he took my left hand in his, as he had with Amber. The tender skin of my wrist prickled at the softness of his breath and the warmth of his touch. Responding warmth pooled between my thighs. He flicked his gaze at me, and inhaled again.

It shouldn't have been like this, without invitation or consent. I bit the inside of my cheek and tried not to squirm around the rogue warmth between my thighs.

Females couldn't smell the lure-scent, and since a female could have a number of potential mates, males had to court her and convince her he was the one. Werewolves mated for life, and the Bond couldn't be broken except by death. Smart females were choosy.

Gabel drew back. "An Oracle. You didn't tell me you had an Oracle, Jermain."

"I assumed you knew." Jermain's voice still had some authority in it, but the strength of his command meant nothing to me.

"Who is this?" Gabel asked Jermain.

"Gianna. She is my First Beta's daughter."

He inhaled the scent rising off my wrist once more. This time his lips met my wrist. I jumped and drew in a sharp breath, only to get a nose full of his dizzying power and strength.

Then the very tip of his tongue darted between his lips and grazed my skin.

Mental discipline from years of training as an Oracle shored up my nerves, and built buffers around my reactions. I wasn't the first female he had tormented this way, I wasn't special, and this wasn't remarkable. He wanted it to be those things. I wouldn't take the bait.

He dropped my wrist and looked around. "I smell more young females. Where are they?"

"There are only these two," Jermain said.

Gabel looked at him out of the corner of his eye. "No. There are more. I instructed they all be here. Not just your two best offerings."

"There are only these two." Jermain's voice tightened.

Gabel growled at him. "This was not the agreement."

Behind Gabel the wolves grinned and shifted, and one of them nodded. "Get ready, wolves."

Jermain ducked his head between his shoulders in submission. Gah! Coward! I glanced at Amber, but she nodded curtly to me to say nothing.

Jermain just rolled up like a bug, and everyone was going to let him.

Gabel's scent of ash intensified. "Bring them here. Now."

Jermain withered like summer grass and he started to gesture to my father to do as demanded.

I said, "They're barely grown. What use do you have for overgrown girls?"

Gabel's attention swung back to me, and his anger receded like water pulling back from the shore. "I gave an order they be presented, Oracle. That is my use for them."

"The six of them are barely old enough to be considered adults," I said quickly, before my courage ran out. "If you had been here a month ago two of them wouldn't even presented. If you want to smell some girls, then we'll bring them to you, but surely that's not what you want?"

The anger receded even further back, but I didn't trust it for an instant. "So Shadowless does not grow strong she-wolves, does it? You two are exceptions?"

Amber didn't respond to the trick question. If we asserted Shadowless did grow strong she-wolves, he'd demand to see them. If we didn't, it'd add some more humiliation to this fiasco. Considering how degrading and humiliating all this was, digging deeper didn't matter.

"They're coddled," I answered, because like hell I cared at this point.

He ignored me. His attention was back on Amber. He smelled her wrist again, smiling as his gaze traveled up and down her body and came to rest on the outline of her nipples.

Gabel released Amber's wrist and moved back to me. As before he lifted my wrist to his nose and inhaled, then lingered. He released me. He trailed the back of his fingers along my left bicep with a farce of tenderness.

"No," Amber breathed.

Gabel wouldn't dare. He might take me with him, he'd inform me I was his Oracle, he might try to play some sick courtship game, but he'd never Mark me. Blasphemy aside, it was stupid. A Bond was permanent. A mate was a big liability for a wolf who accumulated enemies like a corpse accumulated maggots.

His hand turned, and his fingernails raked my skin, gently. Shocks of delight lashed over my skin, into my core, as my mind shrieked. The Moon spun in my awareness, waiting, waiting, waiting, and the world stopped as the future itself hung on Gabel's next action.

I couldn't breathe. I couldn't speak.

His fingers elongated and darkened. His fingernails extended into putrid yellow claws. Most males could only partially shift one time: when they Marked their mates. Realization slammed into me. "No! Don't!"

He raked one claw oh-so-gently over my skin. My flesh stung as if with acid. Was I supposed to beg? Be silent? What did he want? He already had my terror. I'd never give him my consent.

"No?" He traced a pattern on my skin, peeling up the first layer of flesh.

"No. I do not consent," I snapped.

"Not even for your pack?" He pressed a little harder.

"That's not what you want, and I'm not what you want. You just want fear. You just want to prove a point. Fine. You've proven it."

"But you smell of moonlight," he said softly.

"So wha—"

His claw pierced my skin.

My spin arched and I opened my mouth to scream, but every fiber yanked tight. My soul burned and melted and sloughed off my bones and pooled somewhere else.

No!

Moon Goddess, no!

A burst of blue-white strength fractured the ritual's hold on me. I yanked away and stumbled backward. "No!"

He lunged at me and seized my other arm. I shrieked. His transformed hand snaked out, and he raked his claws down my bicep. Three ribbons of flesh peeled away and flopped to the ground.

The first strike of the Mark is suffocating agony, then pure, ice-like numbness, followed by exquisite pleasure. Under my ruined skin my soul melted and slid off my bones, congealing into a mass that mixed with something else. The pleasure suffused my entire being as my soul blended with his.

The melting sensation eased, and my mind staggered forward. His breathing came faster, his eyes bright and a little glassy, pupils dilated, and there was a quiver in how he held me, like he knew he was holding too tight and needed to let go, and the full magnitude of what he had just done had slammed into his arrogant brain.

Blood dripped down his own bicep.

No.

The ritual created a matching Mark on the male. My lure-scent was gone, his ability to smell lure-scents removed, and our matching Marks a symbol to everyone, no matter our form, that we shared the same life, the same soul, and the same fate.

The neonate Bond, the place where our souls had been grafted together, shifted like a delicate spiderweb, breathing, exchanging emotions and awareness.

"What have you done?"

THE MONSTER WHO EATS FEAR

I t was anathema. Forbidden. A crime, a sin, blasphemy, and a lot of other words for things that just weren't done. Even Gabel's own men cringed, and his top lieutenant spat in disgust.

There would be no private moment while my chosen mate lovingly etching a pattern into my arm, inspired by the power of the ritual and the Moon guiding his claw, as the same pattern appeared on his own, burning through his skin with Her white-blue light, creating a pattern just for us.

Instead we each had three crude rake marks slashed into our skin.

The Marking was Pain, for all couples had to endure pain.

The Consummation was Pleasure, where two bodies joined to complete the connection between souls.

The Vows were Affirmation, where the two mates announced to their pack, and the Moon, their love for each other.

But the Mark was like humans getting engaged, setting the date, and hiring the planner all at once. Marking was never done on the first meeting. Many males claimed they knew "the one" when they met her, but because females had to take him at his word, he had to spend a great deal of time courting and convincing her, her family, and maybe even her pack.

Gabel had just swooped in and taken me like a seagull stole a bag of chips.

"You know exactly what I've done," he retorted, slightly hunched and twitching as his own soul reformed and adjusted to the presence of mine.

"You have no idea what you've done. You're insane!"

He smirked, swollen on his own smugness. "I've been accused of that before."

"The Bond works both ways, you idiot. You should have chosen a she-wolf as depraved as you are."

"It's too late for suggestions." He flicked blood off his fingers.

"I said no. What part of 'no' did you not understand?"

"The 'no' part."

Amber reached for me and put her arms around me.

Gabel turned to Jermain. "We have no more business. I have what I came for. The tribute of an Oracle and a potential mate will fulfill your obligations to IronMoon for the next twelve moons."

Potential! He thought this was something he could get out of? I laughed in misery. Idiot. Many thought a first-stage Bond could be broken by saying a few words under the new moon and jumping over a dead fire.

That ritual worked *just* often enough to keep the belief alive, and only if it was performed in the very earliest days.

Amber squeezed me tight and shuddered with silent sobs.

"Say your goodbyes, Gianna," Gabel told me. "We aren't going to linger here."

He went outside with his men to wait.

"It'll fester," Amber whispered to me. "I know it will, and

you'll be free of him. The Moon won't abandon you. Not you, Gianna."

Blood dripped onto the tiles from my ripped skin, although I felt nothing through the ritual's numbing venom.

She squeezed my uninjured arm. Her eyes were bright with tears. "I'll help you pack. Oh, Gianna. I'm so sorry."

A pang of guilt flashed over her face. She had thought Gabel would take her, if Gabel took anyone.

I smoothed her hair and touched my forehead to hers. "At least it was one of us, and not one of the others. That's what we wanted, isn't it?"

I didn't have much to take. Just two duffel bags, one of clothes, and one of my precious scrying bowls, orbs, and rune-stones. An IronMoon male, a tall, swarthy type with a scowl and curled upper lip, stood in the doorway, impatiently waiting for me. He yanked my bags from me and took them to a waiting car.

"It will fester," Amber whispered again. "We'll come for you. I promise, we won't abandon you to him. I promise. Don't lose hope."

The second step—consummation—sealed everything, and the third step was little more than a formality. Gabel couldn't force me to do either, but he might not need to. The Bond wanted to be final and complete. It'd make us do stupid things. It was a living thing, like lungs, and lungs wanted to breathe.

No matter how hard someone might try, they couldn't force themself to *not* breathe. Eventually their most basic instincts would kick in, and their body would force them to take a big deep breath.

Even if whatever they breathed in would kill them.

Bonds sometimes died of inexplicable natural causes, just like love between humans died. Sometimes that one ritual would work. In the case of bitter betrayal, one mate could repudiate another, and the Moon would fracture the Bond, although the wound it caused to the soul often resulted in death for both wolves.

Most of the time the Bond lived on no matter how much either partner regretted it.

In the car, Gabel ignored me. Suited me just fine. Crazy sadist with delusions of grandeur now had his claws in my soul.

After two hours of silence, he prodded, "You aren't going to ask?"

"Ask what?" I didn't look at him, but being civil seemed prudent for the time being.

"Buttercup, don't play coy."

Buttercup? When had I gotten a pet name? I didn't want a pet name. Especially not that one. "Why did you Mark me? You've given me power over you and you don't even know who I am."

He smirked. "I realized I needed a fresh challenge. I want to see if I can resist the Bond's song."

Confirmed: crazy.

The Bond worked both ways. If I died, he'd probably die. If Gabel enjoyed dalliances with other females that was over. The Bond would punish him, if not render him impotent. He had given me power and authority over his pack. The Bond chained me to him, but it chained him to me. His pleasure would become mine, and vice versa.

Some less stars-in-their-eyes wolves had described the Bond like a parasite that punished the hosts.

"So torturing dozens of packs isn't a challenge. You wanted to step up to souls," I said, disgust covering up my growing horror.

"It's gotten a little too easy. As you can see. I just picked up my phone," he put his phone to his ear like a toddler playing with a toy telephone, "and called Jermain to say I was on my way."

I turned away from him.

"Don't you want to know about you and I, buttercup?"

"No." I ignored the sensation of a sore tooth deep within me.

He kept talking. "We'll let everyone think you will be my Luna. So you can get comfortable in case the Bond wins."

"The Bond will win, you fool!" I shouted.

"Yes, the odds are considerably in its favor." He granted after a thoughtful pause.

"Then why take the chance?"

Another grin. This one turned my blood to ice.

His grin widened at my terror. The Bond passed me the particles of his pleasure. It entered my bloodstream like a tingling, pleasing poison.

His smile was like honey pouring over his perfect lips. "That's what makes it fun, buttercup. A fight you know you'll win isn't interesting. I smelled the lure-scent on you. I've smelled it at least a dozen times before, and ignored it. But you're an Oracle, and now you are my Oracle."

"You could have just demanded I serve IronMoon." My voice shook.

"What's the fun in that? Now I will have a fresh challenge, maybe a Luna, but always an Oracle. You will serve IronMoon as my Oracle, and perhaps my mate."

"You have no idea what you've done!"

He slid towards me. I scrunched myself up against the car door. He seized my chin in his fingers. "Exactly. I don't have a clue, but so far I'm enjoying it. You enjoyed it too, the scent of pleasure on your wrist when I tasted you, I could smell the heat between your thighs and on your neck. I drowned in the wracking of our two souls."

"Get away from me," I rasped, even as my skin tingled from his touch.

"That's not very nice." His eyes darkened to a burning green-blue shade and his violent intentions burned through the Bond.

He hesitated, and cocked his head as if he had heard something. Then his attention shifted back to me, and he chuckled low in his throat. "So that is the Bond. Interesting. You feel my malevolence. I feel your terror. Do you think it is the same sort of terror others feel, or is it different?"

Tears poured down my cheeks, and my throat shook, his scent glory, prestige, and edged in burning ash. "What are you?"

"A werewolf, like you."

"You are nothing like me," I rasped.

He pushed his finger into one of the open wounds on my arm. The flesh squished. "Are you sure we're nothing alike, buttercup? You don't strike me as the dainty innocent type, so it's not the attraction of opposites."

"Get away from me!" My voice cracked, and fat tears escaped down my cheeks.

He laughed and slid back to his side of the car.

I spent the remainder of the six-hour trip crushed up against my door, fighting for every shred of daylight between us. He found that entertaining, and a tiny part of me enjoyed pleasing him.

Please your partner, please yourself. Sounded great, probably was great, unless your partner was a monster who savored pain.

After a few hours, the Mark throbbed as the ice-venom wore off, then the pain spread until it was all I was aware of, except when a jolt in the road sent a stab of agony through my whole body. A feverish chill settled under my skin, with my blood burning hot, and my skin so cold my teeth would have chattered if I had had the strength.

We arrived at IronMoon's heart after dark, but the vast

house was well-lit, with floodlights sending light up the walls, illuminating the manicured grounds and extravagant building.

A mansion in the middle of the forest sounded appropriate for an aspiring King-Alpha. A castle was too obvious. Probably would announce a little too loudly that all the rumors of his actual, ultimate ambitions were completely true. Serious intentions might result in a serious response from the most powerful packs.

This way he could gnaw on them one rib at a time, and by the time they realized the rumor was truth, it'd be too late. Gabel would snap his claws shut around any remaining throats.

Gabel came around to my side of the car. "Wake up call, buttercup."

"I'm not sleeping," I muttered.

He bent down to get a look at my arm. I shoved at him with my good arm, but the pain made me dizzy and nauseous, and the world blurred. He grabbed at my shirt and snatched the collar. His wrist twitched, and the fabric ripped.

"Hey!" I protested.

"I'm not going to ravish you." He tugged again, splitting the shirt further along the sleeve to expose the wound on my arm. His own arm had dried brown and sticky hours ago.

Being ravished was the least of my worries. If he wanted to resist the Bond's song, he wouldn't touch me. I managed a weak laugh at the absurdity of it all. "Modesty."

He ripped my shirt the rest of the way and my plain, nude-colored bra flashed the world. "Modesty is an irritating human concept."

The rake marks on my bicep had swollen into purple, crusted lumps. The bruising traveled up to my shoulder. Good. Hopefully it had started to fester, and I'd wake up from this nightmare. I'd still be the IronMoon Oracle, but I'd have my soul back.

Gabel slipped his arms under me and lifted me out of the car. I squirmed weakly. He ignored my struggles and told one of his goons, "Get the doctor."

He didn't bark or snap, just matter-of-factly demanded his will be done. Feet crunched on the pea gravel as someone rushed to comply. Most Alphas needed to bark or shout orders before anyone scurried away that quickly.

As if I were nothing and his own arm was not carved up like a fancy roast he carried me over the drive, up the stairs and down long brick walk to the house, and across the threshold into the brightly lit foyer.

There was nothing romantic at all about it.

"Put me down," I said.

"I will not drop you."

"You could. Right down these stairs. On my head. Please."

"Then what would people say?"

He bore me up the two flights of stairs that wound around the wall of the foyer, giving me a panoramic view of its castle-like state. He stepped off at the second floor and carried me down a very long, very quiet hallway illuminated only by a few delicate wall sconces. The house itself seemed afraid to make a single noise.

He nudged the door at the end of the hall with his foot. "This is your room."

Best news all day. Gabel hopefully slept somewhere far, far away. Like the other side of the world.

He set me down on the bed, then flipped on the lights. I opened my eyes to see the walls were a pale cream-grey color like the harvest moon, and on the far wall was a beautiful painting of the ocean.

Gabel backed away, out of my sight, but did not leave.

The pack doctor was a man old enough to be my grandfather, with the bushiest sideburns I had ever seen, and he was disgusted at having been summoned at such a late hour. He twisted my arm to get a good look. "This is a mess."

His powers of observation were top-notch. IronMoon could clearly command the best sort of talent.

"No permanent damage," the doctor said, not caring about why my Mark was hideous and disgusting, and clearly not referring to the permanent damage that had been done to my soul.

Gabel pulled off his shirt, ripping the crusted blood off his wound, and for the first time, examined the three rakes that had appeared on his own large bicep.

"Oh, I see," the doctor said, "didn't recognize it was a Mark at first."

Hard to fault his mistake. Marks were usually beautiful.

"Well, this sort of thing happens when the Mark is hasty." The doctor twisted my arm around to get a look at the bruising. "Rips up the female, but there's no permanent damage."

Yes, there was.

"I do not rip up females," Gabel said. The doctor ignored him.

Gabel seethed and turned to examine his scabs. "Interesting. I thought the Mark appearing on the male was not true."

I groaned at his ignorance. "You are an idiot."

The doctor shoved an unnaturally yellow liquid at me. It stank of acid and laundry detergent.

"What is it?" I asked.

"There's nothing I'm going to bother to do for a Mark. It'll be half-healed by morning. That will kill the pain and help you sleep."

It smelled like it'd kill just about anything. Sleeping off the awful day was worth the risk. I gulped it down. It tasted better than it smelled, but that wasn't saying much.

In five minutes I passed out cold.

A IS FOR APPLE, B IS FOR...

The next morning greeted me with a swollen arm and a mess of bruises. I reached across my breasts and touched my bicep. Scabs met my fingers. It was still tender, and the fevered feeling lingered, but physically the worst seemed to be over.

Dammit.

No hope of festering.

I dragged myself up into a sitting position and stared at my bedsheets. Not a dream. I groaned, rubbed my head, and forced myself to actually look at the hideous Mark.

Three four-inch long scabs crusted into my bicep.

"You fucking monster," I whispered. "You absolute fucking monster."

I pushed the blankets off my legs.

I was naked.

Not even panties! I patted myself. Nudity confirmed. "What the hell?! Please have been the doctor... please have been the doctor..."

And not Gabel.

But it had probably been Gabel.

I burned red with total mortification. I looked around for something to wear. Someone had laid out a blue silk robe, a pair of panties, a bra, and a pretty dress of pale blue on the foot of my bed.

I held the panties to my nose.

Gabel hadn't touched them. A female wolf had brought these clothes in.

I pulled on the robe, and took stock of my room. It was actually two rooms, the other room having its own couch, coffee table, and television on the wall. There was also an immense bathroom, with a tub so deep I could have drowned in it. The closet was completely empty.

My bowls, stones, orbs, and oils were nowhere to be found.

If Gabel wanted me to be his pet Oracle he needed to give them back.

"They're not gone," I assured myself as I showered, talking myself down off the ledge. I wouldn't panic, and I wouldn't grab for them if Gabel dangled them in front of me. "Don't fall for his games."

Time to find a meal instead. Think all this through. Come up with a plan.

The dress' straps showed my bruised upper body to the world.

How would I introduce myself when I bumped into an Iron-Moon wandering the hallway?

Oh, me? I'm nobody. Just the woman your crazy Alpha Marked yesterday because he was bored.

That sounded accurate and like a good conversation-stopper. I'd go with that.

Two large men stood on either side of the door to my room.

I looked between them. "Ah... am I a prisoner?"

The one on my left jumped forward with a quick reply. "No! No, you're not."

I inched between them and headed down the hallway.

They followed.

"What are you doing?" I asked.

They exchanged looks, and one said, "Keeping an eye on you?"

Gabel had given me some minders. Maybe then they could tell me where my tools were. "I came with two bags. Where are they?"

Another exchange of blank looks, then the one on my left confessed, "We don't know."

"Where's Alpha Gabel?" I demanded.

"In his office," the one on the right said.

"Take me to him."

"Maybe you'd like to get something to eat?" The other offered instead.

Storming around making a lot of bitchy demands might entertain or enrage Gabel, and doing either without a damn good reason sounded foolish. My bowls would have to wait another hour.

Goon A led me back down the long hallway and down the spiral staircase. It wrapped around the wall, affording a magnificent view of the vaulted ceiling that extended perhaps four stories, and massive windows that let the late spring sunlight pour through. In the center of the main foyer was a large, square, shallow fish pond inset into the marble, filled with waterlilies and fat koi.

What, no gold statue of Gabel? Must have been in the garden.

The kitchen, like everything else, was immense. A man in a chef's jacket with the name *Brian* monogrammed across his chest worked over several large pots on the stove. At the table under the window that overlooked the grounds sat two young women of about my age.

Both were pretty in the sort of way I would have fully expected of IronMoon females: clothes a little too tight, and just a little too much makeup. They were both blonds, but the dominant one was clearly the platinum one, and there was a sharp menace in her gaze. She reeked of floral perfume. Wolves almost never wore perfume; it masked our scent and our ability to smell clearly.

The platinum blonde zeroed in on my raked-up arm, and her lips curled into a snarl. Platinum there should have counted herself lucky she had avoided Gabel's affections. She didn't seem like the cruel sort of crazy that would want Gabel for what he really was, or recognize how dangerous he was until it was too late.

Brian offered me a sandwich. I took up a seat at the table with my two new... packmates.

They didn't introduce themselves, but Platinum sort of sneered, "So you're the one Alpha Gabel brought back."

"My name is Gianna."

She eyed my injury again, then stood up, almost knocking her drink over. "I'm going to go talk with Alpha Gabel about this."

I almost burst out laughing at her stupidity. My soul spasmed with a crush of pointless, unwelcome jealousy. Whatever entertainments Gabel had with Platinum were over now. Although if he wanted to fight his own soul, I wouldn't stop him. The more he paid attention to her, the less he'd bother me.

There had to be a way to free myself. Bonds did fade and die from time to time. That New Moon ritual occasionally worked. Mates could be repudiated if there was some gross offense. Murdering a Bond had to be possible, just like people who gnawed off their own arms.

"Don't do this," Brian said softly from the kitchen island. "Just eat your lunch."

Platinum turned on him. "Stay out of this, Brian!"

"She's his BondMate. Don't do this," Brian pled.

"No. I'm going to talk with Gabel about this."

Gesturing with my sandwich I said, "Tell him I'm fine going back to Shadowless if he's come to his senses this morning. You can have him."

If only it were that simple...

"You don't want him?" she scoffed.

"I don't even know him, and I didn't get a say in it. Fine with me if he's having second thoughts. I never had first thoughts." Each word caused the new membrane within me to twist, like skin threatening to rip. The thought of Gabel with this blond horror show twisted my throat into a growl, and I didn't even want the man.

"That's dangerous talk," Platinum informed me with sweet menace. "You chase him away, and what do you think is going to happen to an Alpha's left-overs?"

Fat chance of that happening, but if it did, I'd rejoice the rest of my days. Maybe other females would have been afraid of being in a new pack without protection or status, but I just curled my lip at her. "Absolutely nothing. I'm the IronMoon Oracle. I don't need this Mark. The Moon has touched my skin, and no one can take it away."

Her snide expression transformed into malevolence, melting and reshaping in a mask of hatred. Her sidekick almost trembled. "If that's what you think," she hissed, "you keep thinking that."

She stalked out with her companion and left me to my sandwich.

Brian braced his hands on the island and sighed. "Sorry about that."

"I don't care," I repeated, as much for him as for me.

"You've got nothing to worry about. Alpha Gabel is just

polite to the she-wolves, and sometimes, they get the wrong idea. He doesn't fraternize with them. The males he'll set down, but he's tolerant of the females."

"Right. Tolerant. The wrong idea. Sure."

Brian didn't argue with me further. I finished my sandwich and decided to prowl around the house so Platinum could have plenty of time to stomp and whine in front of Gabel. I rubbed my bruised Mark. If he tried to touch her, would I feel it? Probably. Even the thought of her with him sent an angry throb along our shared souls.

Not fair.

The house was bigger than I had originally estimated. It sprawled across the top of a forested bluff. In every direction there was nothing but thick woods and various outbuildings nestled amongst the trees. A single wide road led to the base of the hill. The air smelled of late spring, but there was also a fetid scent. Dead deer in the woods, perhaps.

IronMoon was supposedly a large pack, but the house echoed with emptiness. Customarily most of the pack's leadership lived in the same house, or at least in the same general community, with the rest of the pack not far away. There seemed to be no one in the house at all. "Who lives here?"

"Many live in the outlying barracks, or some live in town," the ever-present Goon B supplied. "Only a few of the ranked pack members live here, and a few others, like Cook."

Or like Platinum.

So Gabel kept only a chosen few close to his den, just like the King-Alphas of old.

After the interior of the house, they showed me the grounds. A lavish pool and patio, spectacular gardens, and beyond that, well trimmed grass, and a vast dirt arena for training that had been carved out of the forest. Perhaps about thirty males, in a mix of human and wolf form, exercised and sparred in groups of two or three while everyone else observed.

I drifted toward them. My goons didn't stop me.

I had seen training before, but this wasn't training... it was combat. Blood and fur flew everywhere. An older man in a plaid kilt, stood on a little wooden crate. Nothing missed his gaze, and he barked corrections and instructions constantly. He was about forty, huge, and even from a distance, intimidating.

"Master of Arms Flint," Goon A murmured to me.

Master of Arms. So Gabel had even gone for the traditional titles, too.

"Stop!" Flint bellowed.

Everything stopped moving. Even the bugs in the air. Even my heart, I think.

Flint raised one huge arm and pointed straight at me. As one the warriors spun around to face me, Goon A and Goon B snapped to attention.

The Master of Arms jumped down from his box with the nimble grace of a deer. Flint marched toward me, the hem of his kilt swirling around his massive knees. He had a couple of bruises on his body and a few healing scratches. He also looked fresh as a daisy and ready to go beat every single one of these warriors with one hand tied behind his back.

Flint's entire right arm, shoulder, chest, and trailing in a point along his torso an intricate tangle of old-order tattoos in blue-black ink. I recognized some of the symbols, but others I didn't, and the arrangement was one I hadn't seen before. As the sunlight slid over the curves and lines of his body, the black ink shone radiant, metallic blue.

Blue-gloss tattoos. Someone somewhere still knew how to make the blessed ink and apply it, and the blue-gloss had taken hold, just like my own skin's silvery paleness.

He snapped one hand behind his back, like he was going to

rip off his kilt and strangle me with it. Instead, he bowed. "The warriors of IronMoon bid you welcome, Lady Gianna."

What.

The.

F-

He straightened, then spun on his bare heels to face the assembled warriors. "As you can see, we train hard."

"Ah... yes." I found my tongue lodged somewhere in my throat. The runes extended to his back. One was the sacred rune for a man who dedicated his blood to the Moon's service. A few others for death, victory, memory, and family. "Yes, this is... impressive."

He nodded solemnly. "They may make something."

They looked like something already.

"Wolves!" he shouted to them, "This is Lady Gianna, Alpha Gabel's Bonded, and a Seer blessed by the Moon Goddess. Show her the proper respect!"

As one, the wolves threw their heads back and howled the pack's greeting to a returning female of high rank. It was slightly different than the howl greeting an absent Luna, but only just. It had never been sung for me. My Goons and Flint howled as well.

The song echoed over the forests and birds cawed and flooded into the sky. Flint laughed and spun around to me, his eyes a little too bright for comfort. I stretched an uncertain smile over my face. "Thank you, Master of Arms," I managed. "That was most um... fervent."

"Of course, Lady Gianna." He bowed low once again. "Allow the two strongest students present to demonstrate their ferocity for you."

Where the hell was I? Fifteenth century Europe? A bard wielding a lute might jump out of the bushes next. Playing along seemed the wisest course of action.

The wolves broke formation, and two moved to the center of the big dirt ring. They started in human form and were completely naked. That meant they intended to shift forms during the fight—indicating a very high level of control and endurance to be able to shift repeatedly and quickly enough for combat.

The wolves were big in their human forms. Easily over six feet, sleek muscles cut like fine diamonds, but they weren't very bulky. Big muscles looked great but they were impractical, inflexible, and robbed endurance. The men were tanned and already filthy and sweaty from training before I got there, but were all grins and eager to get started.

Flint had been very specific: the two best students he had *right then*. That meant there were wolves better than these.

"These are just our younger recruits," Flint said to me before they began. "So forgive them if they're a little unpolished."

My throat was too dry to respond.

The wolves slammed into each other. They punched, kicked and wrestled each other, then tumbled into the dirt. One shifted as he tumbled into a dark brown-red wolf, and bit into the human shoulder of the other. The other's transformation was just a few heartbeats later, into a tawny timber-wolf pelt. They slammed back together, snarling and scratching at each other. Once again they tumbled, one shifting to human form and throwing the wolf off him with his arms, then the other one rolled twice and shifted to war-form as if it were the easiest thing in the world to do.

The dark red one elected to remain in wolf, charged and leapt at the one in war-form, dodged a swipe with a massive arm, and bit into his thigh. He dropped between the other's legs, rolled a few times in the dirt, and sprang again, but this time he got slapped backwards like a fly. He sailed through the air, his form enlarging and shifting in mid-flight.

Oh by the Moon Goddess! He could shift into war-form sailing through the damn air?

"Very impressive, Master Flint." Impressive, and sickening. Shadowless had nothing like this. Even these wolves Master Flint said were raw and unpolished were stronger than Shadowless.

Flint smiled and nodded to me, crisp and formal. His tattoos shone with sweat and sunlight. He bowed once more. "Thank you, Lady Gianna."

If these were Gabel's weaklings, I couldn't fathom what strength was—or how powerful Gabel was to hold all their leads. I had thought combat shifting was something rare and special, and this rotten, soul-stealing monster had it in spades.

Time to find Alpha Gabel, my bowls, and my explanations.

INTO GABEL'S BED

My reluctant goons took me down the hallway, past the staircase, and to a small set of doors that opened onto a slightly narrower corridor and set of stairs. His office was on a protected mezzanine level of the house overlooking the training fields. The office was a huge, two-story room, but the second story was only a wrap-around balcony that gave access to walls lined with nothing but books.

The first level was more shelves, mostly books, but also featured antique werewolf weaponry: claw cuffs, collars, greaves, all for wolf and war-forms. On a standing easel by the huge window was a large map marked with pins and strings. His desk was a huge dark cherry wood affair with clawed feet. The rug under my feet was thin and bright red, and had once been exquisite. Now its beauty was a little faded in deference to its extraordinary age.

Everything about the office was vast, huge, and heavy. It would have devoured any other single person, but Gabel carried it well.

He was there with two other wolves, one of them the male who had taken my bags from me the day before, and the scent of fury hung thick in the air. There was also the scent of Platinum's perfume under all of it, but she was absent.

"Buttercup." Gabel greeted me as I walked in, flicking a pen through the fingers of his left hand, over and over again. "You are awake and fed, I have been told."

It wasn't a gentle greeting of affectionate pleasure, only a matter-of-fact acknowledgment I was not face-down in two inches of bathwater. In the light of a beautiful late spring day, wearing pants and another button-down, shaven and groomed, surrounded by paperwork, art, and books he seemed...

Normal.

"This is Second Beta Romero, and one of the warriors, Eroth." Gabel gestured to the wolf I recognized.

Romero had the seedy, smarmy look that fit the IronMoon reputation. Eroth was less seedy, and younger, and there was something hard and cold about him.

"Where are my bowls?"

"They're safe."

That's what adults told children when they had put something up out of reach. "Where is this safe place?"

"Our room." His tone conveyed the words as a very delicate barb.

Nervous heat formed under my breastbone. There was a *my* room. I did not know there was an *our* room.

Gabel smiled as he waited for a response. That civil exterior was a ruse. No civilized man did what he had done, and I hungered to plunge my claws right into his crotch. "I need my tools."

"Right now?"

"I want to know they're undisturbed and haven't been contaminated by your ham-handed handling."

Romero scowled. "Mind your tone, female."

I snapped, "I have a name."

Gabel held up a hand to silence Romero and said, "I removed them from their bag, left their wrappings intact, and put them in our closet. This is adequate, yes?"

Dammit, yes, it was adequate. His blue-green eyes took on an amused gleam as he sampled the hot gush of anger between us.

No, no childish tantrums about wanting my things now. "Yes, that should work."

Gabel turned to the other wolves. "Step out."

"Alpha," Romero said, "we have—"

"We can finish later," Gabel said with mild command.

Eroth headed out without further comment. Romero shook his head and snorted, then stalked out.

"I saw you outside." Gabel slipped around me and put his hand at the small of my back, and his fingertips pressed gently into my clothes. He guided me to the window that overlooked the training grounds. "You met Flint."

"Yes."

"You were properly impressed?"

Hell, yes, antique blue-gloss tattoos were impressive. Someone, somewhere, still knew how to make the ink, consecrate it, and apply it correctly to an appropriate male. Gabel certainly had an interesting collection. If Gabel didn't know what the blue-gloss was, then he could stay ignorant. "You don't care what I think, Gabel, you've made it clear I'm here as entertainment."

"There's always a possibility I will succumb to your charms. I wouldn't want you to be disapproving of your army." His fingertips traced a spiral on my spine.

I shivered all over. "I don't want an army."

"No? What do you want?" His voice lowered to a purr.

He had the audacity to ask me so blithely what I wanted? "I want what you took from me!"

He cocked his head a degree. "I took nothing from you."

He had taken my choices, my family, my home, even challenged my faith, and he thought he hadn't taken anything from me? "Fine. You gave me a parasite."

"I gave you myself," he said.

"You arrogant dog. I don't want you, and you don't want me! You just want a damn toy. You said so, so own it. I'm too highly trained to fall for mind games. Visions play games with Oracles all the time. You're an amateur with a cheap advantage."

He circled in front of me. I warily stepped back, and he matched it step for step, until I stopped and held my ground. This close his eyes were like the tropical sea, all shifting greens and azure tones. Warmth swirled around us, and he admired me from toes to hair. "You look lovely in that dress. Like a Luna should look."

This is a game, and you are his toy. Remember that. Don't get lost in the vision.

He studied my neck with those eyes, leaning close. He reached up and lifted the thin strap of my dress. My skin caught on fire, and I gasped. He needed to pull the strap over my arm and down, expose my breast to his turquoise gaze, cradle my flesh in his chapped, raw hands—

I yanked my head to the side and blinked on the blinding daylight outside the window. "How large is your army?"

He clicked his teeth once in annoyance. He rested his fingers against my collarbone, with the strap of my dress captured in the crevice of his fingers. He told me the number.

I looked back at him in disbelief. "All combat shifters?"

"Almost all. The others have skills that offset not being a combat shifter."

"How did you find so many?" There couldn't have been that many in all the world, much less in this small part of the world. It couldn't be. He had to be lying. Gabel was from somewhere else, he had brought forces with him, that had to be it.

Gabel chuckled. It sounded like bones crackling. "What other packs throw out as garbage I pick up. You call them rogues, criminals, or unwanted. I call them lost souls. Some beyond redemption but many only needed a second chance. I gave them that chance." His cruel smile turned my blood to frosty slush. "Now they are loyal without question."

He caressed my collarbone. Nerves quickened with rising panic, like the first time the Tides had threatened to sweep me away. "All of them?"

He breathed in my scent. "No, not all. Some are recruits. Shadowless had nothing I wanted, so I didn't make the offer. It's ironic. So often the older, so-called stronger packs have such unremarkable warriors. Being fat on rank and glory has dulled their fangs."

"SableFur won't be so easy," I whispered. The ancient SableFur, where I had finished my training and earned my bowls, rarely came out from beyond their mountain stronghold, but they'd swat Gabel's ambitions.

"I have no interest in SableFur." Gabel titled his head and examined the crusted scabs on my bicep. "How is your arm?"

Lies. Any aspiring King-Alpha had to have an interest in SableFur. "It'll be fine."

He drew the back of his fingers over the slashes on my exposed arm, sending a rush of warmth over me, and he inhaled again, drinking in the commingled scent of fear and desire. "I am glad to hear it. Since you are recovered, you will join me in my bed tonight."

"I have my own bed."

His bland tone betrayed him. "Of course. For when you don't feel well. But since you said you are recovered, you will sleep with me."

"Don't you have that platinum blonde and every other female in this mansion to do that?"

"Who?"

"The platinum blonde. I can smell her perfume. She was in here having a fit about me."

"Gardenia. Her name is Gardenia."

"She's no flower," I muttered.

That cold smirk again. This one came with a little gleam of victory and the curling sensation of a snake's deadly coils. "I may have a certain reputation from my earlier days, but I have found it very unwise for an Alpha to have any dalliances."

"Bullshit, don't lie to me. You've got a damned harem. Admit it."

He pulled his lips over his teeth, and his front canines elongated a tad. The coils constricted tighter around me, accompanied by a vicious, gleeful gleam. "Are you jealous, buttercup?"

"Like hell I'm jealous. I hate being lied to." I despised the truth-that-wasn't. My favorite food had once been strawberry shortcake, but one bout of food poisoning had ruined that. Logically my brain knew not to blame the shortcake, but something deeper refused to let me eat it again. Gabel had done that to me: on the surface Platinum was meaningless. Deep down, in a place I couldn't control, she was the enemy.

Gabel's tone lightened with laughter. "I'm not lying, but believe whatever suits you. I'll see you at dinner."

"And my bowls," I said.

"My room has become your room. Your bowls have only been waiting for you. Go find them if you like. Goodbye, Gianna. I have work to do, unless you would like to keep me company?"

Not a chance. "No."

"Pity. Remember. My bed. This evening. Do not make me come get you."

NAKED FOR GABEL

There were about thirty people at dinner, split between two long tables in the festive and brightly lit dining room. Gabel sat at the head of one table, and I had to sit at his left hand, across from his First Beta, Hix. Hix had dusky skin, dark eyes, and smooth, dark hair. He spoke with an interesting accent. I later learned he was Turkish, and when his pack had driven him out for challenging the Alpha, he had come to the west and been one of Gabel's first recruits.

"Have you met Gianna?" Gabel asked Hix.

"Just now."

"What do you think?"

I wasn't a new car or a new pet or painting! It didn't matter what the Beta thought of me. Gabel ignored my dirty look and savored needling me.

Hix studied me, expression bland. "A very fine selection, Alpha. An Oracle with spirit. She will make strong pups."

Strong pups, indeed!

Gabel clapped Hix on the shoulder. He was dead serious about milking this for all the entertainment it was worth. He cast a grin my way, mocking my anger and daring me to do something about it. I almost threw my drink on him. He stood. Dinner conversation and eating stopped. All attention turned to him. He gestured to the room. "Wolves of Iron-Moon. As you know, Alpha Jermain of Shadowless agreed to our terms."

Applause.

More like Alpha Jermain dropped to his knees and offered up all his she-wolves for Gabel to choose from.

"And," he twitched his fingers at me, "while Shadowless had little to offer us, they did have a treasure I could not possibly leave without."

I dug up a smile and obeyed his unspoken command to stand. Gabel gripped my hand. His touch sent shocks through my body that invoked the sensation of his claws raking my flesh. In my memory, the parting of my skin and the melting of my soul was raw, wracking pleasure. Dazed briefly, I searched out his face to make sure it wasn't buried once again in my neck.

He had the same shocked expression on his face. He recovered swiftly. "This is Gianna. She is an Oracle, and we have begun the mating process."

There had been no *we* involved.

Applause and howls from the crowd. Master Of Arms Flint stood and offered me the howl of greeting again, which was met with tremendous applause. Most of the group was single males, although there were a few single females. Gardenia clustered with her thralls at the end of the second table. The males present made up for their lack of enthusiasm.

Gabel's smile could melt lead. Inside was a monster, but he could turn on the charm like a faucet when it suited him.

After dinner my Goons (I still did not know their names) escorted me to the other side of the mansion to the master wing: Gabel's quarters.

Resisting Gabel's demand would have been pointless. It'd

have given him exactly what he wanted: me squealing and kicking like an affronted, helpless piglet.

It might have been noble resistance to fight him and see if the Bond would let him beat me to a pulp every night. The problem was no one in IronMoon would care if he did, everyone would mock my foolishness, and if Gabel *did* succeed in abusing me, he'd get the entertainment he craved. His sick pleasure might also infect me.

I shuddered. One time feeding his pleasure with my pain, and it pleasuring me in turn, was enough.

I had expected his room to be a mini Versailles, but it was disappointingly subdued. Stormy blue and dark polished woods, with cream rugs and trim. Everything simple, functional, and quietly refined. The only odd feature was there were no windows, and only the single door in or out.

The closet was full of clothing, both male and female. I ignored the clothes in favor of finding my tools. They were in the lowest of the built-in drawers. Everything still wrapped in silk and velvet, and the scent clinging to the velvet was faint, and only Gabel's. I ran my hand around the lip of my favorite bowl, feeling the hard obsidian edge through its velvet wrappings. Gabel knowing anything caused nervous flutters in my stomach, him giving me my bowls back so easily doubled the nerves.

I tucked the bowl back into its drawer and examined the rest of the closet. So many clothes. I brushed my hand along the fabric, bewildered. In the closet was a tall, built-in set of drawers. I yanked one open, and closed it just as quickly: men's boxers.

Not that I cared what sort of underwear Gabel wore, or if he wore any at all.

I pulled open another drawer. Women's panties. Silks and cottons in an array of colors. Skimpy to barely-there.

I slammed the drawer shut.

I tore through the closet. Most of my clothing wasn't there. The only thing that was mine were some socks. Someone had unpacked my stuff, inventoried it, and intentionally discarded most of it. It hadn't been lost, misplaced, or put somewhere for safe keeping.

"Jerk!" I shouted at the ceiling. "You hear me, Gabel?"

"Of the many things I've been called," his voice said from beyond the closet, "that's one of the least offensive."

I jumped backward.

He sauntered to the closet and leaned against the door frame. "Hello, buttercup."

"Don't call me that. I'm not your buttercup. I'm your war-prize."

He flicked his brows and dismissed my accusation with disappointment. "Don't be dramatic. No blood was spilled to win you."

The anger kept rising, laced with wild grief. "Oh, I know."

Gabel shifted slightly, deceptively casual. "They didn't think you were worth dying for, but I would have spilled quite a bit of blood to get you."

"You'd have spilled that blood anyway," I spat.

"Likely. You found your bowls, hmm?"

"Where are the rest of my things?"

"I don't know. Garbage, I suppose. I told Violet to take care of it."

Violet ran the household, an older, sweet (as far as I could tell) she-wolf. At least it had been her who sorted my things.

Gabel came into the closet, casual as you please, and pulled his shirt off with one smooth motion.

His skin was a glorious, subtle bronze, except where it was laced with pale scars, and under the smooth skin, his muscles flowed like water. Three ragged scabs took up half his upper arm, immense and unmistakable and hideous.

"Master Of Arms Flint likes you," he said casually, his strong back to me. "That is a large mark in your favor."

"I'm an Oracle. I don't need your pack's approval, or yours, or Flint's."

His voice was warm with pleasure. An Oracle made his game more challenging than any other she-wolf could make it. "Exactly. And about that. I need you to do some work for me in the morning."

"What kind of work?"

"An Oracle's work." He glanced over his shoulder at me. "I've had another room in the house, west facing, prepared for you. As best I could. I know you need to do most of the consecration rituals yourself."

Spooked by his knowledge of such things, I flung back. "A pond would be best. Can I have the foyer?"

"That would be inconvenient. See how the room in the west wing suits you. If it doesn't, we can talk about the foyer."

He was being too damn civilized again.

"Are you refusing?" He asked my silence.

He was still my Alpha, and I was still his Oracle. My duty and vows demanded I obey the request. Those rules governing us worked both ways, and if I refused to comply, he could punish me justly, and my Oracle sisters would not intercede, and the Moon might not succor me. "Of course I'm not refusing. You just didn't tell me what I'm supposed to look for."

He turned to me, blue-green gaze searching for a weakness in my armor. "One of my packs is being evasive. I want you to see what you can see. I will give you pictures and names in the morning."

"You still haven't said what I'm looking for."

"Anything." He took off his belt and hung it neatly on a

hook with twenty others.

"Oracles aren't spies. I will probably not see anything absent a specific request."

"No?"

"No. I need a specific question," I said irritably. "Or specific problem. There has to be an intent to focus my gifts upon. Visions are like dreams. They have to be interpreted. It's not like watching a security camera."

The muscles of Gabel's shoulders tightened and twitched. "I see. Then I will think of a specific question."

He unzipped his pants and stepped out of them.

What... was he doing?

Then he took off his boxers.

I made a terrified sound.

He turned around. "What?"

My eyes yanked downward in their sockets to his... you know. Manly bits.

No! Don't look at that!

I tore my eyes up to his ocean-like gaze.

"What are you doing?" I squeaked.

He wasn't going to touch me. That'd be surrender to the Bond, so he had no reason to be naked. He stood there like being naked was no big deal. It wasn't, normally, except we were in private, alone, the two of us...

"Going to bed."

"Naked?" I wheezed.

"I sleep naked."

I prayed for the floor to open up and swallow me right there.

"As will you," he informed me.

"Hell no!" My composure cracked. I'd sleep in the same bed with him if I absolutely had to, but naked was one step too far. "No!"

One of his scars traced the length of his left hip, like

someone had tried to saw his leg off. "Yes, you will. It will make it more... interesting."

"This is interesting enough. No."

"Am I the first man you've seen naked, buttercup? Up close? Personal? Hmm?"

"Shut up! Don't call me that. Don't!" I finally covered my face with my hands and looked away. "Put some damn pants on or something."

"We're all naked under our clothes, buttercup. We can talk about this in bed."

"No! I'm not sleeping next to you naked."

"You are. Or I'm going to rip your clothes off you."

"Don't you dare."

He advanced toward me.

I plastered myself against the drawers. "No!"

"Yes." He grabbed my dress, his hand darkening and fingers elongating, and his fingernails extending into threatening claws between my breast. "Last warning, buttercup."

He could partially shift outside of the ritual! I scrunched myself back, but the drawers wouldn't yield further, and his claws grazed my flesh.

What are you?

"Pity. It does suit you." He snapped the thin strap at one shoulder with a twitch of his half-shifted claws.

"No!" I shrieked and struck him. My fist hit his chest, he didn't notice and snapped the other strap. I struck again. He grabbed the fabric between my breasts and yanked the dress down, and off my hips.

The silk drifted to the ground.

I snapped my knee up to nail him in his naked crotch. He blocked it with a muscled thigh.

"Don't do that." He leaned over me, growling deep in his throat, pressing me back with with his body, his human voice twisted up in his throat as human speech mixed with something feral and very, very dangerous.

My terror didn't stop him or even cause him to hesitate. The Bond flailed like bridge cables in a high wind. It sang with distress but he seemed deaf to it. "This is how your challenge yourself?"

"Then take your own damn clothes off," he growled at me.

"No!"

"Yes. This isn't how I like to get a woman out of her bra and panties."

"But you have before?" My voice shook so hard it bounced back and forth in my throat.

"I have never taken a woman against her will, and I'm not going to start with you. Just. Get. Undressed. My pack doesn't pretend to be modest like a bunch of humans. I won't have my Queen blushing like a stupid girl every time she sees a naked man. Get over yourself. It's just a penis. You'd think it was a machine gun the way you're squealing. It's not like you haven't seen more on male wolves in wolf form."

My tears dripped onto my collarbone. It was different in human form, in private, with this creature that shared my soul.

He stepped back one stride and glared at me.

Tearfully, I unhooked my bra and dropped it. I pushed off my panties before my courage failed.

Miserable, violated, shaking, I turned my head from him.

He left the closet. "Come to bed."

My tears punished him like he drank burning liquid that seared all his guts. His response was to pick up a book.

I cried for a long time.

The only small morsel of satisfaction was I did not sleep most of the night—and despite whatever sick enjoyment he might get from my pain, neither did he.

THE EYE OF THE MOON

I said nothing at breakfast and just moved my oatmeal around in its bowl. Gabel murmured to Hix I was going to scry later, and best if I ate little, which was true, but not the cause. Each mouthful I managed to swallow flopped into the hollow within me.

After breakfast he took me out onto the stone veranda overlooking the gardens. I stood as far away from him as I could manage. The day was already hot and the air humid, and little gnats buzzed around my face.

He ignored my misery. "I've thought of the question."

"What is it?"

"Yes or no questions are best, right?"

"Usually. The more specific, the better." He needed to hurry up with this so I could get away from him.

"Is Alpha Anders of Gleaming Fang disloyal."

"That's the question?"

"That's the question."

No putting this off another hour to force him to do more thinking. "Do you have a picture of Anders?"

I was powerful enough I didn't need a name to focus on,

much less a picture or personal effect, but Gabel didn't deserve any special effort.

Gabel nodded. "Yes, and a letter he sent me."

Not even a tiny smirk or barb that morning. In his office he matter-of-factly handed over the picture and letter, then dismissed me with a flick of his hand.

The room he had set aside had windows along the far wall so the moon's light could stream in as it crossed the sky. A thick rug had been placed in the middle of the otherwise bare room. There were no curtains on the windows and no other furniture. Everything had been scrubbed from top to bottom with harsh, natural soap.

"It'll do." I looked at Goon A. "I need salt. Rough salt. Like sea salt. And candles. Undyed are best."

With luck, there would not be appropriate salt or candles in the house, and I could put off doing this.

But again, no such luck. The kitchen had rough, non-processed salt, and Cook had a stash of basic, tallow candles on hand. Gabel had been prepared.

"Let it never be said Alpha Gabel is not well educated. Except for not knowing how Bonds work." I took the candles from Goon B with a sigh. "Leave, and don't let anyone bother me. Even Gabel. I'll be done when I'm done."

Scrying was best done at night, but I was powerful enough that drawing curtains would be sufficient. This wasn't a difficult question. If the Eye of the Moon was closed I'd be forced to wait, but hopefully, I could get this over with.

I unpacked my stones and bowls with great care once the salt had been sprinkled all around the room's perimeter. I filled the bowl with water and set it aside, then contemplated my multitude of runestones. I chose the usual ones—*inquiry, pack, protection*—then one I almost never used: *traitor*.

I rubbed my thumb over the carving. After some contemplation, I cast it into the bowl as well, and sprinkled a little salt and then a tiny drop of frankincense oil into the water so it slid over the surface in a film. Normally I preferred jasmine oil, but jasmine oil had romantic overtones. I was afraid with my half-forged Bond it would cause problems.

I used one of the candles to pour wax onto the letter, then placed the candle over the folded letter and the print-out of Anders' photograph.

Already I could feel the Moon's gaze. I had half-hoped to be ignored, some evidence of Her anger with me to try to explain how I had found myself in Gabel's presence.

It was just not my day.

I resettled myself on my knees and bent over my bowl. The scent of the oil met my nose. I felt little bits of flame from the candles, the pull of the Moon like I was the ocean's tides. Slowly She tugged me out with Her, so I looked down into the bowl as She looked down upon us.

~*~ *The Vision In The Bowl* ~*~

The stone hallway stretched out before me. The stone was dark, granite-like bricks, with torches flickering the length of it. It smelled of earth and stone, and nothing else.

I turned around, but all that was behind me was a blank stone wall. No windows, just heavy stone doors set into grooves.

I set out down the hallway. Each of the stone doors had a rune carved into the door: balance, love, protection, pack. The fifth door had a rune on it I didn't recognize. I traced my finger-tips through the shape. It was warm and smooth, even though it looked rough-hewn. I touched the other four runes, and they were the same: *warm and smooth, although rough in appearance. I rubbed them to try to figure out how they had been made.*

Melting, perhaps? Yes, perhaps like a brand or stamp, and not like a carving.

At the end of the hallway the stone shimmered and dissolved into mist. I stepped through the mist, which was hot and painful, onto a shadowy stone perch overlooking a large stone box.

Within the box were many clusters of wolves. At the center was Alpha Anders, the largest of the pack.

He moved amongst his pack in wolf form. The rest of his pack mates were hidden, like they had been blurred. Around Anders' neck were four collars, each made of a different color leather, and each one had multiple iron rings on it for multiple leashes. He seemed strong and healthy, but frustrated.

He moved throughout his pack, as a wolf going through his life, day after day. Sometimes the blue collar tugged hard at his throat, and he used a hind claw to scratch it. Other times, the red collar tugged, and he scratched that one, too. Occasionally, the green collar tightened, until he bowed his head and coughed. Just once the black collar twisted around his neck, and the iron loops moved as if a hand sorted through them trying to decide the best place to attach another leash.

———

It was dark outside by the time my awareness returned fully to my body. Time to go give Gabel his answer.

Goon A pushed open the door to Gabel's office. The scent of rage hit me, and the sounds of footsteps pacing back and forth across the ancient carpet. Romero, Gabel, and Hix held court in the center of the room.

Romero turned his baleful look onto me. "This doesn't involve you, Oracle."

Hix glared at him. "She is Alpha Gabel's intended. It is for him to say what involves her, not you."

"She is his toy," Romero spat. "I was there, you weren't—"

"She outranks you," Hix said.

"The hell she does!"

"She has my Mark," Gabel interjected calmly, although his dark rage simmered underneath his civilized exterior. "You were saying, Second Beta."

Romero snorted through both nostrils, disgusted at my presence, and ignored me as he spoke. "Forget this little farce. It just makes you look weak. We need to turn our attention to RedWater, not waste time scouting what already belongs to us."

"Making sure that the SableFur are on their side of the pass and not having dinner with Anders is a good idea." Hix said.

"The SableFur are always on their side of the pass. It'd be a compliment if they felt like they needed to come across the mountains to deal with us." Romero barred his teeth at Hix.

"Reminding who Anders' loyalty belongs to is also a good idea." Hix stated, unruffled.

"Bah, lapdog." Romero flung up his hands.

"RedWater is geographically challenging," Gabel said calmly. "It is as large as Shadowless, perhaps larger, and isn't isolated yet. Holden can fall to the south or east."

"So what? We'll chase him," Romero insisted.

Gabel shook his head, a cruel smile playing over his lips. "Patience, Second Beta. Alpha Holden still has his pride."

"So let's go down there and make him choke on it!"

"No, we'll let it swell a bit more," Gabel disagreed, dark and pleased with the idea. "Dough has to rise before you punch it down. Let Holden make himself into a good challenge. You've been wanting one."

Romero grumbled an affirmative. Gabel's smile didn't

change, but the scent of power and ash around him intensified. He glanced at me. "Have you done what I asked?"

"Yes."

"What did you see on the Tides?" he asked.

"It is for your ears alone, Alpha. Visions are only for the one who asked. You can tell them later if you wish, but they will not hear it from me."

Gabel nodded and beckoned for the two Betas to leave. Hix obeyed without question, but Romero threw up his hands and muttered about things that could wait. Gabel's smile turned into an amused smirk, and he shook his head like an indulgent parent before turning back to me. "So what did you see?"

"I was in a large stone corridor set with five doors. The door were marked with runes: *balance, protection, love, pack,* and one I do not recognize."

"If you don't recognize it, how do you know it was a rune? Perhaps it was a Hunter's pictograph."

"I know all the standard Hunter pictographs. It's required for Oracles. It might have been some other sort of sigil or symbol, like an old pack sigil from when those were used. I feel it was a rune."

He retrieved a pad and piece of paper from his desk, and shoved them at me. "Draw it."

I sketched the mark for him. He examined it, turning the pad over and over in his hand, then tossed it back onto his desk. "And then what?"

"At the end of the corridor, the wall dissolved, and I stood over Anders in his wolf form, going about his normal life. He wore four leather collars. One blue, one green, one black, one red. The collars had iron rings around them like to attach a leash to, but I saw no leashes. As I watched, the blue and red would tug at him and he would scratch. The black one turned around his neck as if a hand were trying to choose where to clip a lead.

And the green would twist on his neck as if to strangle him. He would cough when this happened."

"And?"

"That was the vision. There was nothing else."

Gabel's eyes darkened like a stormy sea. "That's it. That's not an answer. I gave you a simple question to ask. Yes or no. Not collars and colors."

I flinched. "You decide what the vision means. Its your question."

"You have had many visions. What should I make of this, Oracle?"

I looked out the window to avoid looking at him. "Collars are usually symbols of a master or obligation. They own us, restrain us, or compel us."

"And all the collars were the same except for the color."

"Yes, and how they affected him was different."

Gabel scowled as he thought. Finally, he seemed to actually see me. "You look tired. Go to bed. I will be in in a few hours. I have work to do."

As I reached the door, his voice told my back, "Remember. Naked. I do not want to rip your clothes off you again."

Threat or no threat, I defied him and wore a tee-shirt and panties to bed. When he got into bed, I hoped he would turn over and leave me alone in the darkness.

Instead his fingertips grazed my back.

I tensed at the unexpected caress. The light touch sent my skin alight at first, until his fingers seized my shirt.

"I told you," he snarled, "naked!"

He surged across the bed. His silhouette was darker than the lightless room, and he yanked me onto my back. I scrunched back into the pillows, sheer terror choking me.

He's going to kill me.

The violent fury smashed through my soul. His silhouette

loomed over me, his fingers cranked into my arms.

Stop it! Stop it! You can't do this!

"Did I not warn you?" he growled.

How are you doing this? The Bond shouldn't let this happen!

"It's just a shirt," I gasped.

His fingers tore at my panties. "And these."

The lace of the panties raked my skin, and his anger suffocated me. "Let me go. You're hurting me!"

He damn well knew how badly his grip hurt, how his fingers dug into my half-healed Mark. He bent over me, and his breath pulsed into my face, but a rictus shook him, and he cringed as it caught him by surprise. His fury slammed into me again, and I stifled a scream.

"You have five seconds to take this off, or I will rip it off you. Again, and again, and we will do it every.single.damn.night!"

He abruptly released me and rocked back on his heels, his own nudity obscured by the darkness. Dazed, I pulled off my shirt and squirmed out of my panties. He grabbed both and flung them away.

"I told you." He slunk back to his corner of the bed, like a beast slinking back into its shadows. "We do not stand on human modesty here. It's stupid. You defying me just to prove you have the will to do so is even more stupid. Pick something that matters."

Ten seconds. My defiance had lasted all of ten seconds. I curled into a ball and wept. There was no point holding back the tears. He sensed my misery like I sensed his angry resolve to not care. He was the Alpha, and I had defied him. He was the Alpha, and I wasn't the Luna.

He didn't tell me to stop crying. His resolve to withhold comforting me—if he even knew how—and to resist my tears churned like iron machinery.

I laughed in my misery. Fool. We were already lost.

SPARRING SESSION

My Goons still hadn't introduced themselves by name, and considering I knew so few names of the IronMoon, it didn't seem like asking was appropriate at this point. The IronMoon didn't seem to deal in names, or even much in the way of conversation.

I sniffed the early summer air. My two goons were nervous in their large wolf-forms next to me. They weren't bad company, as far as such things went: polite, respectful, and not my jailers. They followed me around and made sure I didn't get lost, and also pointed out where I could find things so I didn't flail around like an idiot.

"Take me down to the road," I told them, pointing my snout at the main driveway that twisted down the hillside. *"It's that way, isn't it?"*

Goon A, a typical grey wolf with tawny highlights, reluctantly trotted out ahead of me, while Goon B, a darker brown, stayed at my shoulder. The driveway was steeper than I remembered, and much longer, winding down the steep southern face of the bluff. Most of it twisted through thick woods that would have afforded excellent cover for an attacker, except for the ever-present IronMoon scouts.

The driveway flattened out, stretched over a wide, deep creek, and then emptied onto a narrow two-lane country road stretching east to west. Across the way was more forest and rough terrain, and the trees stretched their branches overhead, creating a sun-dappled avenue. No mailbox, and no street markers to tell me where I was on a map. I inhaled the summer air again: no humans or other structures on the breeze.

"Which way is town?" I asked Goon A.

He indicated west with his snout. *"About twenty miles."*

I sat down and my tail thumped on the asphalt. Running away had a certain romantic appeal to it. It'd also be stupid: I wasn't a Hunter or a warrior, and while I had been on my share of hunts, I didn't know the art of tracking like the professionals did. I didn't know how to cover my trail. Gabel's Hunters would find me within days, if not hours. I could run a hundred, two hundred, maybe even three hundred miles in any direction and still be in IronMoon territory.

"We shouldn't linger down here," Goon B said, nervous.

"Why not?"

"It's not safe."

Safe from Gabel, he meant. I sighed. Fine. My Goons would catch it if Gabel thought I tried to run away, and they had helped me. I let them take me back up the bluff, where an irate Platinum sat on the front step, wilting in the sunlight and sweating under her makeup. Still doused in perfume. The chemical-floral scent flooded my snout. Goon B coughed.

"Alpha Gabel wants to see you."

"Why?"

"I don't know, and I don't care." She smirked. "He wasn't much for talking to me, if you get my drift."

Liar. Despite the haze of her perfume she reeked of aggravation, not sex, or even arousal. The aggravation intensified to hot jealousy as her eyes rested on my Mark, cut into my shoulder, and burned into my pelt.

Gabel had summoned me, but I decided on a shower first. He could wait.

He wasn't, however, in his office. That time of the afternoon he was down in the training ring. The Goons left me in his office and closed the door behind me.

I wandered around while I waited, examining his impressive collection of art and ancient weaponry, and his even more impressive library. On a large easel by the window was an immense map of the region, covered in pins and markers and multi-colored threads. I eased over to it.

IronMoon's heart—where I was—sat to the northern edge of the territory. The outline of IronMoon's reach was in black thread, wrapped and stretched neatly by pins tracing the pack boundary lines. More pins and notes marked human cities—places to be wary of—and more pins and thread denoting the packs in that part of the world. To the west the mountains created a natural boundary between IronMoon's ambitions and the ancient SableFur, to the east sat the ocean, and to the north were the forests where no packs lived.

The door opened and Gabel walked in, freshly showered. "Admiring my domain?"

Admiring? No. More like taking in the scope of it. It was worse than I had realized back in Shadowless. "The rumors are true, aren't they. You want to be King-Alpha. That's what all this is about."

"I trust my secret is safe with you, buttercup," he replied, chuckling.

Time to change the subject. "Gardenia said you wanted to see me." I remembered to use her proper name and not *Plat-*

inum, so he wouldn't know how much I loathed her. The less he had to use against me, the better.

"Are you two friends yet? She seems quite popular."

Right. More like domineering to the handful of females, and popular with males for a very particular reason. "Not yet."

Gabel's smirk warmed. "Perhaps if you gave her a chance, buttercup."

"Perhaps." There were some she-wolves who would never get along, and Platinum and I were two such she-wolves. I didn't want to get along with the painted whore.

Gabel inhaled, paused on whatever scent he caught, then asked, "Did you enjoy your jaunt down to the road?"

"It was hot."

"So why did you go down there?"

"I want to see the entire heart. Is that not allowed? You didn't inform me I was a prisoner in addition to your toy."

"You're not my prisoner. Just a reminder, Gianna, that you are also here as my Oracle, and you were taken as an offering from your pack to mine as terms of surrender. Abandoning your place here would violate the terms of Shadowless' surrender."

As an Oracle, I could leave and go to another pack, claiming the Moon had summoned me elsewhere. But as a she-wolf, Shadowless had offered me to Gabel as a condition of their surrender. Gabel had both claws into me: I had offered myself as an Oracle, and Shadowless had offered me as a female. I couldn't leave.

Gabel stated it without any menace at all: just a simple statement of the facts, and his ocean-colored gaze waiting for me to acknowledge it.

I said with dignity, "Running away wouldn't solve anything. We'd still be Bound. Just remember that abusing me violates the Oracle-Alpha rules, and I can still leave if you do that."

"Have I broken those rules? As I understand them I cannot

prohibit other wolves from petitioning you, I cannot demand you give up the secrets you keep for other wolves, and I may not deprive you of your tools. Did I break one of those?"

"Not yet, you haven't," I retorted, despising his civil, patronizing tone.

"And I won't."

"Says the wolf who broke one of the biggest rules of all."

"You were offered to me. I took what was offered."

"That didn't give you the right to Mark me!" I shouted. "Stop trying to justify what you did! You just wanted a toy."

His tone remained maddeningly calm. "Are you having a difficult time accepting that your precious Moon hasn't rotted that Mark off your arm? Beautiful Moon-touched Oracle that you are, with that Mark you resent so much cut into your flesh. If She objected so strongly and thought I had committed such a vile sin, your arm should be washed clean."

I stiffened, and my gorge rose. No. I wouldn't play this game with him. I wouldn't let him chip at my faith. The Moon didn't prevent us from mistakes, and She didn't punish us the instant we sinned. Our sins were counted when our lives ended, not before. An Oracle who broke her vows didn't always lose her Moon-touched skin, or even her Gift. There was a reason the Bond had taken hold, and my skin hadn't rotted, but that didn't make what Gabel had done right.

"Is there something you wanted?" My voice sounded raw and strained. "Or am I just here so you can play with me?"

"Anders' collars. In the vision. Are the colors symbolic?"

I chewed on my tongue so I wouldn't tell him to go screw himself. Mixing the duties of an Oracle with the nightmare of my Mark: clever. Trying to trick me into breaking one of the rules. Gabel did seem to love his rules, and bending them until they just about broke. I had been on offer to him for exactly the purpose he cut into my arm. There was no mortal rule that said he couldn't do what he had done, just the Moon's decrees, and Gabel didn't follow those rules.

No, Gianna. What he did was wrong. A normal wolf wouldn't need to be told not to take another's soul.

Although Gabel had thought it was a little less permanent than it was.

Stop it. Stop trying to justify or excuse it. There is no excuse.

When he stood there, all civilized and groomed, and reasonable and balanced and his scent of strength and authority in every breath I took, and his power on offer, pressing into me and the tiny little voice within me that whispered this is yours, this magnificent, terrible wolf is yours.

I shored up my mental walls, imagining myself within a clear box, where the Tides pressed around me, but I was safe on rock and behind strong, thick walls. "If the colors mean something to you, then yes, it is likely the Moon showed me those colors for a reason. If not, then it was just so that I could see there were four collars easier."

"Hmm." Gabel walked behind his desk and tapped some papers there, frowning down at them. "That is not helpful, either. The black collar with no lead attached to it troubles me the most."

Like I cared.

"But he's also a male with a mate, and pups, and a pack, and his own concerns, so it's possible he's just pulled in many directions," Gabel mused. "I think it's time to summon him for a visit so I can get a look at those collars myself."

THIS GOES BOTH WAYS

Planning the fete for Anders' arrival was left to Brian and the other she-wolves. Gabel told me not to trouble myself with it, even though with his Mark, it was sort of my responsibility to oversee such things.

"Leave it to the others," Gabel told me. "It doesn't concern you."

It did concern me, and I didn't care for how he told me it didn't. He waited, and I chewed on my suspicions of what he was up to. What if everything ended up a mess, and he planned on laying it at my feet because I hadn't overseen it? But he told me once more to leave it alone, and went as far as to summon Gardenia up to his office.

"You'll work with your cousin," Gabel told her, "Gianna has other things to do. Anders' arrival is on you."

Gardenia smirked at him. "You won't be disappointed, Alpha."

"I know," Gabel replied. He bid her leave and told me, "Buttercup, the scent of jealousy."

"I'm not jealous." I snapped, although I was, because that

damn little voice in the back of my head told me I should care about Platinum.

In bed, as long as I was naked, he didn't touch me, or even glance at me, and I sensed only the barest interest from him. His presence, though, was unavoidable. I got out of bed, I dressed, I showered, I ate. He always watched. Watching, watching, watching, waiting for—weakness? A flinch? A question? He would refresh my drinks, serve me food from large platters as males did for their mates, and offer me the best of everything IronMoon had to offer.

Every morning he told me I looked lovely and complimented something about me, which lured Platinum to him like a bee to honey.

She found every excuse to be around Gabel, or talk to him about the most trivial detail of Anders' visit, and although the house always seemed choked with echoes of her perfume, Cook seemed to be right: Gabel was just courteous to the she-wolves, like he had no idea how to tell them when they were behaving badly or crossing boundaries.

It was like living with an alligator. He drifted in the river waiting for some stupid zebra to come along, and then he'd strike. And I was the zebra.

My only escape was my scrying room, but the Moon rebuffed me. She wasn't ignoring me, but She kept Her Eye closed. Oracles couldn't scry for themselves, because the future was always in flux, and any vision we got would be instantly rendered useless, but we could meditate and invite wisdom. But a week of being gently ignored, and stalked by a river gator wore thin.

I bumped into Platinum on the stairs the day before Anders' arrival.

She smirked at me. "Alpha Anders will be here tomorrow."

"I know."

"Alpha Gabel has asked me to be at his side," she said oh-so-sweetly.

What?

Had I missed Gabel's betrayal and deluded myself? Was pain such deranged nectar to him that no rules made sense? Had he been standing there acting so calm because he did not care and was so flagrant? I should have sensed the Bond fighting and howling at him, but there hadn't been anything. I should have sensed his pleasure. I had sensed both before, in the car.

Gabel would humiliate me with Platinum in public. Forget private betrayals and sacrilege. My arm would match his, but he'd be hand in hand with Platinum.

The alligator had struck. I laughed at my own stupidity. Gabel had just been playing with his prey.

Then a new pain came along. Sharp, intense, the sort of pain that will kill. The sort of pain that you can't endure, that you have to find help, or die from the source.

When he came to bed, he told me, "Anders will be here at ten. I expect you there."

I lay on my side, staring at the wall and counting each little nub of texture, praying for the sharp pain to ease. "Fine."

"We will see what collars he is wearing."

Indeed.

"Have you met Anders before?"

"No." The mild-toned conversation gnawed on my control. My soul leaked pain into his, but I had to hold it out of his grasp. He wanted rage, a fight, something, and whatever that something was, I couldn't give it to him. I needed space to breathe, and there wasn't any, no matter how hard I pushed back against the crushing pain, it overwhelmed me like an avalanche.

He had Marked me against my will and now threw me aside like it meant nothing.

"Any questions about how we do things here?"

"No."

"No questions at all?" he pressed, daring me to say something. "You seem upset."

"I am not upset." Maybe if I told myself often enough I wasn't upset, my soul would start to believe it.

"Gardenia told you she was going to be on my arm?"

"Of course. She could not wait to inform me of the good news."

"Good news?"

Stupid, stupid girl. She was off having a triumphant giggle like a little fool, not realizing she was his toy as much as I was, and he'd turn on her too. They deserved each other. "By all means. Inflict yourself upon her and spare me. She gets you, and I don't have to deal with you. I consider that good news."

He withdrew a degree, and the pain backed off a bit, freeing up my brain for a little more thinking and a little less enduring. If he hadn't had any faith and didn't believe, I'd have understood his desire to test Her power. But he did believe, and he had just asked me ride the Tides for him, and he still spit on Her gift to us? Worse, he'd do it with that... thing. He'd humiliate and debase his whole pack in front of another Alpha he believed wasn't behaving according to the rules.

Hypocrite.

Contempt widened the space around me. My contempt for how he had just swaggered in and chosen me like a cow at market. My contempt for how he thought he was going to be the King-Alpha. My contempt for how he thought he could bring me to my knees. My contempt for how he thought he owned my soul, and the right to bring me pleasure or pain when it suited him to do either. That he thought something sacred could be his toy.

I flipped over onto my back. He tensed in response.

I owned Gabel as much as he owned me.

Everyone else in that pack he could boss around, punish, frighten, terrify. He could do those things to me, too. I couldn't change the soul I shared with him, the connection that forced me to want him, but he didn't own my feelings. He owned my instincts. No amount of force or brutality would get me to feel less contempt for him. I could fear him, but I didn't have to respect him.

He could gag me, cut out my tongue, lock me in that horrible basement, but that parasite we shared, that double-ended worm latched into our souls, meant he couldn't silence me.

"Goodnight, Gabel. Enjoy your dalliance."

AN UNEXPECTED, UNWANTED ALLY

As we got dressed in preparation for Anders' arrival, I focused once more on feeling utter contempt for Gabel's cheap games.

"Will you be ready on time, buttercup?" He intruded on my silence as I brushed my hair.

"Yes. I will not miss this for the world," I told him.

"No?"

"Miss the mighty Alpha Gabel of IronMoon revealing what a small, pathetic hypocrite he is?" I asked his reflection. "You'll parade it for all the world to see. I want to be there and remember it."

He snarled.

I spun around and faced him. "You are pathetic, Gabel. You brought Anders here because you think he's disloyal and has broken his promises to you. And what are you doing? You're betraying me." I pointed at my arm. "You're only doing this to prove you can, and it's pathetic. The King-Alphas of old who built kingdoms that lasted didn't treat their Queens like garbage. Those Kings led by example. They were the wolves everyone else wanted to be like, and they built Kingdoms that wolves wanted to be part of. The others rotted into the ground within a generation. Your Kingdom will crumble and rot the instant you are too feeble to growl."

My insides seared me as his rage built, but I didn't care. Good. I'd hit a nerve. I'd hit it again! I wanted to be free, and if stoking his hatred was what I had to do, and I had to endure humiliation and Platinum, then I'd endure it. The Bond howled at both of us. He grit his teeth, and I held onto the counter behind me like it was the railing of a boat.

I smirked through pain. "You better put a shirt on. One with sleeves to hide your shame."

"I am not ashamed," Gabel growled.

"Then you are an idiot." I shoved past him.

I yanked open the door to our room, and Platinum was on the other side, dressed and coiffed to perfection in a delicate purple sundress. "Oh, good morning!"

Rage stabbed into my bones, but I schooled it into disgust for an Alpha who would abuse a sacred, holy promise just for his own amusement, and for a King-Alpha who would humiliate his Queen with such a cheap, tawdry female. At least Gabel could have better taste and be less obvious about it. Stupid, clod-headed, crotch-governed male.

My dark blue satin dress showed off my pale skin, and the obvious Mark on my arm. Platinum's eyes zeroed in on it, and her brows drew together in a little scowl.

Those collars weren't around Anders' neck, they were around Gabel's, and this was all the Moon's trap. She was about to tug that black collar.

I could have warned him, but he wouldn't have listened—and I didn't want to.

This was utter, raw, public humiliation, and nothing would

ever ease the pain of it. On the surface I had control of roiling instincts, and that was what mattered, and that was what infuriated Gabel. He seethed, aware of the water of my pain and the oil of my scorn. He could stop the pain, and maybe if he acted decently, he'd disarm my scorn, but he wouldn't do either.

That would be admitting defeat.

"He's almost ready," I told Platinum. "I'm sure he'll be out in good time."

"Then I'll sit on the bed and wait for him," she sneered back.

If Gabel was going to let her sit on my bed, in my own den, go right ahead! Just another mark of disrespect and how pathetic he was. His Kingdom would be dust and bones before the generation was out. Moon spare me from ever producing pups by him! "If that's what he wants, fine."

Mental discipline had its benefits, and Gabel didn't have an Oracle's training.

I brushed past her and went down into the kitchen, where the ranked members of the pack had gathered. Flint, present with Beta Hix and a few others, asked me, "Where is Alpha Gabel?"

"Upstairs," I replied.

"He didn't come down with you?" Flint asked.

"No. Gardenia is going on his arm," I said with pride and satisfaction because my voice didn't tremble. "I am going on my own. As the Alpha's Oracle."

Because I could, because fuck Gabel. I still had my own rank without him, and I was going to stand there in sunlight with my pale skin and Marked arm, and drink in the entire damn sight of him demonstrating what a small little creature he was, and how powerless he was to stop me.

Flint frowned, and Beta Hix's cruel face shifted into something I think was disapproval. I soaked in the awkwardness.

"You should go as the Alpha's BondMate," Flint finally said in the strained silence.

Not a chance. I smiled. "Alpha Gabel is the one who decided he would rather take Gardenia."

Flint folded his arms across his chest and pondered me as if he understood my game, but the others looked extremely uncomfortable. The Master of Arms nodded once. "If that is his wish."

"Indeed." I agreed. "I'm certain he has his reasons. Gardenia made it quite clear to me yesterday who he preferred for the task."

The Bond snapped at me, and I kicked it back into its corner.

My smug satisfaction almost failed when Gabel appeared with Gardenia, hand in hand. Not even arm and arm. Hand in hand, fingers tenderly entwined.

Part of me withered and died, like a single petal falling off a rose.

I snatched the rest of me close and dismissed the dead part in anger. I must not have needed that part of me. There was plenty left.

Flint flicked Gardenia off Gabel's arm, and half-dragged the Alpha aside to whisper to him in intense, disapproving hisses. I told myself to relish it. Gabel ignored Flint's advice and Hix's furious glare, and no one else dared move, question, or speak.

"This is inappropriate," Flint risked saying as Gabel returned to Platinum, "and very unwise."

"This is what I have chosen," Gabel retorted.

"Lady Gianna?" Flint asked.

I managed a shrug. "He Marked me without my consent. I'm not going to fight for him. They deserve each other."

We filed out into the sunlight to greet Anders. The plan was to do a formal greeting, then the two Alphas would break to discuss business somewhere of Gabel's choosing—perhaps with Platinum present, perhaps not—and then reconvene for dinner. After dinner the GleamingFang would leave.

I took my place at the very end of the line between two unranked warriors.

They shifted like nervous horses.

You will regret this, Gabel, but I won't. Not one damn bit.

It hurt. I embraced it. Pain meant the Bond was dying. Pain meant I was that much closer to freedom. If I couldn't breathe, it was freedom. If my heart screamed, it was freedom. If my legs wanted to run and fling Platinum into the koi pond, it meant freedom was that much closer.

Alpha Anders had already arrived. Gabel had kept him waiting on the patio, which didn't seem a smart move. There was a fine line between power games and being downright insulting. But it wasn't the first stupid decision Gabel had made that day.

Anders was a handsome wolf, older than Gabel. He struck me as capable but worried. Very worried. With him were a dozen strong, younger warriors who I already knew by scent were no match for anything Gabel had.

Gabel introduced the ranked members of his pack, then Gardenia, and did not introduce me.

The Mighty Alpha Gabel, would-be King, playing the games reserved for adolescents.

The meeting lasted some time. Gabel would hold Platinum's hand, release it to emphasize some point of conversation with an artful gesture, then reclaim it.

Every time he touched Gardenia, a twinge of pain crossed between us, and I began to recognize the shift in his jaw, and the flicker of hesitation in his hands, or the slight pause in his words. He marched and clawed over the pain and dragged it forward with him until it fell away.

So that's what pain was to him. He didn't enjoy pain, he enjoyed his control over it. The harder I fought him, the better he liked it. He loved the fight, but he didn't love my burning scorn and disgust for his antics.

The realization almost made me laugh out loud.

He actually turned his head toward me and looked, his face dark, but everyone else just wondered why he had done it, as I had not moved.

Platinum giggled and fluttered with glee at being included in the conversation and having a center stage seat. There I was, my Mark thumping into my skin demanding I go over there and punch Platinum in the face and Gabel in the balls, at the end of the line. But I saw it all clearly now. Weeks of praying and pleading with Her to show me something, and finally, it was here.

It wasn't over between Gabel and I. The simple attacks of stealing me, trying to spook me, then terrifying me ripping off my clothing were only openers.

Gabel brushed a kiss along Platinum's fingertips at something funny she said, and brought her wrist to his nose to inhale the stench of her perfume. I caught myself before I lunged at both of them. Hix and Flint twitched, though. I think the whole line flinched, and eyes darted to me before darting back to the proceedings, and even Anders noticed it.

Every shred of my training went into remaining calm.

You will regret this for a very, very, very long time, Gabel. What you have done here today cannot be undone.

The Moon turned in the back of my mind, and for an instant, Her light brushed over my skin despite the sunlight, a cool rush like water.

"Will we be expecting a Bond announcement soon?" Anders asked in a dry tone of voice that carried to my ears and his warriors some steps away.

"Perhaps," Gabel told Anders.

The shock that went down the line was not lost on Anders. "So this is the first your pack as heard of it."

"Indeed," Gabel said, Platinum's wrist to his nose again, his own Mark covered by the long sleeve of his shirt.

The Tides seemed to be around my legs, up to my knees, churning and flooding inward.

Remember this moment, Gabel. You will regret it for the rest of your life.

Afterward, I holed myself up in my scrying room. I could mandate nobody bother me there. Not even Gabel.

I wept.

It all hurt, more than anything else had ever hurt. He had taken what didn't belong to him and what I hadn't wanted to give him, and mangled it for his own demented pleasure—and it was only going to get worse.

A knock on the door.

I ignored it.

Another knock on the door. Louder this time.

I untangled myself, went to the door and pulled it open a crack. "What? It's not time for dinner yet."

Beta Hix informed me, "I need to speak with you."

"I am busy."

"So am I."

He shoved his booted foot in the door.

"Fine. But do not wander around." I opened the door for him, and I slammed it shut behind him. "Don't step in the salt circle."

He looked around the spartan room. Then back at me. I didn't try to wipe away the tears or pretend like I hadn't been sobbing. "What do you want, Hix? Gabel sending his favorite toady to bring me missives now?"

"No, Gabel does not know I am here."

I rubbed the worthless Mark on my arm.

"I came to apologize for how you were treated today."

A pang hit me. "Oh."

"I did not think it would be appropriate to speak out in front of Alpha Anders and risk Gabel's dominance over GleamingFang."

"Couldn't risk Gabel's empire of blood and spit, could you? Get out of my sight. That's exactly why Alphas like Gabel behave like they do. Because no one has the balls to stand up to them."

Hix's eyes trailed over my Mark. He frowned as if he was going to say something. Then his dark eyes went to me. He was quite close, close enough I smelled the force of some emotion I couldn't define. Conviction, maybe, and old regret.

His eyes were dark. Dark as my favorite scrying bowl, and in their currents were unspoken words and buried memories. "I've stood up to an Alpha before, Lady Gianna, and it's always more complicated than that."

"There is nothing complicated about what happened today," I retorted. "But I don't care. I don't want to be with your Alpha, and if he can somehow get hard and fuck that slut through the Bond's punishment, good. I want this Bond dead, and I want to be free, and I will endure any pain I have to to make it happen. So you run back to him and tell him that like the good little toad you are."

"I see no reason to tell him that," Hix said. "I do not believe he is actually doing anything with her besides—"

"I don't care." I lied to both of us.

"I am sorry, Lady Gianna. I am very, very sorry."

"Is she with him and Anders?"

Hix's face darkened. "Yes, he is."

"We all have to play our parts, don't we?" I asked bitterly.

He looked away.

"Get out," I snapped, tears erupting. "Get out, you gutless Beta!"

"As you say, Lady Gianna." He half-bowed, then left my room.

A WORTHY ADVERSARY

At dinner, Platinum occupied my place next to Gabel. My new seat was across from Romero at one of the lower tables, surrounded by his favorite pets. The room snickered when I entered. Platinum raised her drink to me and asked sweetly, "Finally joining us, Oracle?"

"It suits the Moon that I be here." I had changed into something that covered my Mark, since I didn't want the questions or Anders' curious look. Platinum's beautiful face twisted into a scowl at my statement, but Gabel tapped her shoulder, sending shocks of electrical pain through both of us.

Romero grinned at me. "Gianna."

"Second Beta," I replied. "I take it this state of affairs suits you?"

"Completely." Romero grinned wider, and his wolves chuckled.

"If it was purely up to me, I'd willingly leave on my own four paws, and you'd never see me again." I poured my own drink and took what portions were left. Didn't matter they had left me scraps. I wasn't hungry, and the insult meant nothing after that afternoon.

"Don't say that too loudly, Gianna. Anders might get the wrong idea." Romero flicked his fork in my direction.

Anders was too busy being disgusted by Gabel kissing a delicate tattoo of kisses along Platinum's wrist. My stomach snapped like a cobra with each one. "And what idea do you think he's going to get if the truth comes out?"

"That Alpha Gabel does what suits him, when it suits him," Romero said. "Maybe you should be asking yourself what happens to you when he's done with you, Oracle."

Sniggers from my tablemates. I took another look back at Gabel and Platinum, then back at Romero. "Looks like he already is, but I'm still eating his food."

The Mark, however, was still intact.

After Anders left, I retreated to my bedroom. Gabel could sleep by himself, unless he wasn't, and I wasn't going to walk in on that.

A soft knock on my door. I groaned and peeked around the door. Violet said softly, "Alpha Gabel expects you in your quarters."

"Is he alone?"

Violet sighed. "Gardenia was sent away after dinner."

"So not how she or I planned to spend our evenings, I guess."

"Please go," Violet pleaded. "He'll come drag you out if you don't."

"After today, maybe he should." Maybe I should make Gabel drag me down the hallway by my hair. But Violet pleaded, so I got out of my tee-shirt and panties and put on a robe instead. I knew the drill: naked.

He was already in bed reading and didn't say a single word to me, or even look at me. He still reeked of her perfume and the scent of her flesh mingled with his scent of ash. Disgusting. Just what had he been doing with her while convincing Anders— and maybe Platinum herself—she was the one he had chosen?

I pushed the thought into a deep hole. I'd just torture myself, and he'd enjoy it. Me not *caring* pissed him off.

The next day was subdued in the house. Platinum pouted at Gabel and glared at me with pure malice the entire day. She even followed him out into the summer sunlight to watch him train, clapping and jumping around like a cheerleader. I watched from the kitchen. It didn't afford the best view because of hedges and courtyard gardens, but her almost ice-white hair bouncing around was unmistakable.

Afterward he summoned me up to his office. "I need you to look at Anders again."

"Nothing's changed." Except everything had changed. His antics would have consequences for years to come.

He tilted his head to the side. "No?"

"If some simple encounter will change the determined course of events, the Eye is closed. Outcomes are normally the result of many previous choices. It is very rare some trivial action will change them. You bringing Anders here for a civil meal changed nothing." Except perhaps teaching one of his lieges what bad taste in women he had. Just wait until Anders found out the truth.

I refused to give him the satisfaction of pointing any of this out. If he wanted to discuss how badly he'd behaved, he'd have to bring it up.

He paced from his windows overlooking the training ground to stand before me. The sunlight shone through his hair, illuminating the tips in gold. I inhaled reactively and got a noseful of his peculiar, ashen scent.

I summoned the memory of his antics, and it rewarded me with a pulse of fury that shot down our joined soul.

It hit like a drum, reverberating with anguish, and more importantly, disgust.

Gabel jerked his head to the side, his gaze going back to the window. His strong jaw ticked as his muscles clenched. "Meaning the Moon foresaw me attacking Anders, and it changes nothing."

"That would be likely," I said blandly.

"And what use are your powers, then, Oracle, if they do not show me what I can change?"

I laughed at him. "You criticize the Moon? She's not your servant and only humors your inquiry. Obviously the situation with Anders requires more than a blunt object, a peacock's tail, and roar of fury."

Gabel growled to himself.

"So why does Anders upset you so much? He's a wisp of an Alpha. Alpha Marcus of MarchMoon still growls your name," I needled him.

"Exactly. Marcus paces at the end of his chain. Anders' body bends in all the right ways, and the right words come out of his mouth, but his scent is scorn, and his eyes jaded." Gabel stopped speaking, then his eyes rested on my Mark.

He touched it with his fingertips, tracing the three slashes. His eyes unfocused, and his face softened in contemplation.

"Maybe he wasn't impressed with your choice of females." I brushed his hand off me. He captured my fingers in his grip. I shivered in pleasure but kept my tone bland. "Gardenia matches the IronMoon reputation. She doesn't impress. She just confirms what everyone already knows."

Gabel didn't release my hand, but his grip did stay gentle. "Which is what?"

"That you're a common, unthinking brute of no lasting importance." I schooled my tone into utter school-marm neutrality, but mostly failed. "If only your lieges knew the truth. That you value your own sick pleasure in an even sicker game over your duty to the pack. You are so obsessed with proving a point to yourself that you refuse to obey any basic standard of good behavior. The Moon saw what you did yesterday. She noted it. You will rue it the rest of your life, and I will be chained to your soul to witness it."

So much for my plan to not talk about it. Annoyed, I yanked my hand out of his grip. He let me go, but his fingers returned to my Mark.

"Don't touch me." My voice trembled.

Gabel's fingers brushed higher on my collar, up to my neck, under my jaw. His ocean-green eyes focused on me, his finger-tips tracing the outline of my cheek, neck, jaw, collarbone, shoulder, like an artist tracing an outline. It was like he saw me for the first time, and I was real, not just some trophy he had randomly acquired on his quest to be King-Alpha.

"Stop," I whispered.

"Your skin does not want me to stop." His fingers moved under my jaw. He held me still with that one finger and bent his lips to mine.

A feeling like moonlight poured through my skin and veins, soothing and cool and content. It was bliss. Like I had been starving for weeks, dying, and now I had been served a plate of divine food.

His lips moved over mine, so gentle and slow. It seemed impossible to me Gabel could have any artistry and delicacy in him. His tongue grazed my lips, and tentatively, mine sought to join his.

Platinum.

The vision of her dangling on his arm, their fingers entwined together, Gabel kissing her fingers as if the most elegant of courtiers. The metallic *clang!* that had gone over my nerves every time he had kissed her.

I shoved him away. "No!"

Gabel fell back a step.

Desire throbbed alongside my fury. No way Gabel would get the satisfaction of me exploding with jealousy at him. I gulped and said, "I'm your Oracle. If you need me to scry for you, you can't distract my flesh."

There. Make it about being an Oracle. Not about that blond horror show.

Gabel's face darkened as if a cloud was passing across it. "Ah. I thought it was something else bothering you."

"Whatever else could there be?" The bastard wanted my admission. Bonus points if it brought me to my knees, and I blubbered tears like a damn fountain.

Instead I asked sweetly, "Do you still want me to petition the Moon about Anders?"

He said, barely above a mutter, "If you say it will serve no purpose, then I won't waste your strength."

"May I go?"

"So eager to get away from me, buttercup?"

He expected something else after the way he had been treating me? He still wanted that confession. I glanced out the window and spotted my escape. "No, Flint is expecting me."

"That seems like a lie."

"Does it?" I asked innocently. "Well, you can watch out the window if you like."

Gabel turned back to his desk. "Have fun with whatever mischief you're up to, buttercup. For your sake, I hope Flint is expecting you."

IMPROVING ONE'S SELF

Flint's morning session was just mopping up, and now the midday session, with the sun at its highest, would begin. The bodies moved and shifted as wolves picked up kilts and shoes and dignity, and other wolves arrived. Beta Hix stood talking to Flint and scowling at some new recruits.

Midday sessions were for the most raw recruits—the ones who'd get killed sparring with the morning or afternoon groups. Wolves like me.

"Lady Gianna," Flint greeted me as I approached him and Hix.

"Master of Arms, may I speak with you a quick moment? Alone?" I asked.

Hix went to stand near the new recruits and wither them with his baleful stare.

I lowered my voice so only Flint would hear. If he didn't agree to my request, I was screwed. Gabel's watchful ire sat like a coal within me, and no doubt if I turned around his silhouette would be watching from his office window. "Master of Arms, may I train with this group? Now?"

"You are an Oracle, Lady Gianna, not a warrior," Flint said.

"Oh, I don't want to be a warrior." I rubbed the Mark on my arm and looked around. "I guess I just... think I should know more than I do."

It wasn't like any of the IronMoon wanted my services as an Oracle, and no one from outside the pack was brave enough to come to the house and petition me. I was the only Oracle within a thousand miles, and I was used to having more petitioners than I could handle, not being the private pet of a single Alpha.

"No quarters given, Lady Gianna. I am not gentle," Flint warned.

Hix had wandered back over. "This isn't appropriate. She is the Alpha's intended. She does not need to protect herself, and common wolves shouldn't have their paws on her."

"I didn't ask for your opinion," I snapped.

Flint, naked except for a kilt around his torso, rubbed his chin. "If Lady Gianna wants to train, I don't see a problem."

"The problem is she is the Alpha's intended. What does it say about us that she feels the need to defend herself? Not to mention that the idea of lesser wolves putting their paws on her is offensive."

"I think it says a great deal for a future Queen who wants to be a strong match for her King," Flint said.

"Gabel will not approve. It isn't necessary."

Nope, Gabel wouldn't approve at all. Bingo. Hix was so clever.

"If it upsets you so much thinking common wolves will be touching her, then you can be her training partner."

Hix jerked like someone had yanked his collar. "Me?"

Flint ignored Hix's reaction. "Lady Gianna wants to improve herself. I will never stand in the way of a wolf who wants to improve themself."

And with that, he walked away, and I hurried to the edge of the ring before anyone could change his mind.

"This is not needed," Hix hissed..

"Yes, it is," I hissed back.

"This is a borderline scandal."

"You've never met a female warrior before?"

"You are not a warrior! You are an Oracle, and we will protect you!"

"Fine job you're doing."

That shut up him.

Some of the wolves from the other sessions had drifted out of the house to watch my inevitable embarrassment. Even Platinum came along, smirking and laughing with two of her little friends. Interesting choice that she was down here instead of racing up to Gabel's office to rub her scent all over him.

This might have been a better choice of evasions than I'd originally realized. If Miss Gardenia and I ever had more than words, I'd be the winner. It'd be dangerously pathetic if I somehow became the IronMoon Luna and couldn't manage to smack the snot out of a she-wolf like her.

Soon enough it was my turn, timed exactly as the sun was at its highest.

Hix paced around me. He had on just a kilt, having already been training before I showed up, and there were half-healed red scratches raked into his dusky skin. He had several much older scars on his torso. One looked like it had been caused by a silver-acid burn. "I will be gentle with you."

"If you think Alpha Gabel is gentle with me, you insult me."

This made Hix scowl something fierce.

A big, strong Alpha wouldn't abuse a little, weak wolf. Weak wolves abused other weak wolves, trying to make themselves feel big.

"*I* will be gentle with you," Hix informed me, angry and insulted.

"If that's what you think is best." I made sure my hair was tied back tight.

Like all wolves, I had learned the basics of self-defense as a pup. When my Seer abilities manifested themselves, the time for training had been switched to my talents. I had only continued to do a very little bit, and compared to the strength of Gabel's forces, I was a joke.

Hitting Hix's broad palms with my own fists felt like hitting broad, flat stones. Hitting his carved abdomen was also like hitting a stone. In fact, hitting any part of him was like hitting a stone. And getting hit by him was like being hit with a stone. Wrestling him was like wrestling a giant hot magma flow.

He grabbed my hand, yanked me to him. It felt like I had gotten shoved into a wall. Or the wall had shoved itself at me. I choked on breath. His fingers dug into my wrist, his other hand slid over my shoulder and behind my head. He pushed my head down and into his chest. The other kept control of my wrist, curling into me. My bones creaked, and my fingers went numb from the pressure.

"Quit," he growled.

I almost whimpered about the pain in my hand, and my neck being cranked into his skin. He smelled of sweat and something that reminded me of an expensive cigar. It was not unpleasant. I squirmed, forcing him to hold me tighter.

I visualized Gabel watching from his glass window, feeling my pain, how I was trapped, and overwhelmed, and helpless. All those feelings that he would never tolerate. That feeling he had never felt. That feeling he inflicted on everyone else. Now he couldn't escape or prevent or do anything about because it was happening to me and not to him!

A surge of rage and strength shot through me. I yanked my right knee up and stomped Hix's foot. He twitched, then I kicked him as hard as I could on the inside of his leg. The shock —it's a little muscle and easy to hurt, but most males instinctively think you've caught them in the jewels until they realize you haven't—caused him to loosen his grip just enough that I was able to duck out of the neck crank.

He spun me around by the arm and flipped me onto my back. The impact knocked the wind out of me. He ducked over me, faster than I could even blink, and that huge forearm clamped under my neck. He released my hand to grab my hair and forced my head forward over his arm.

Gabel's window was in my sight even as my vision started to dim. I couldn't breathe. I couldn't even gag. His fingers in my hair hurt. Stones boring their way into my skull.

I hoped Gabel could feel my consciousness waning, my throat struggling to remain open, the blood not reaching my brain, my lungs burning and struggling for air. I hoped he felt completely powerless to prevent it, stop it, or fight against it. There'd be no triumph. I was weak.

The instant before I lost consciousness, I tapped.

The ultimate humiliation for Gabel: I had quit.

And so had he.

With a curse Hix released me and shot to his feet. I slumped forward and gagged a few times.

Master Of Arms Flint said, "Mind your tongue, Hix."

My neck buzzed, and my hand was completely numb except for the vague ache in every joint. I glanced towards the house. I was so exhausted I swayed on my feet, and my throat still felt like I was going to gag every breath.

Hix, lips twisted in a disgusted frown, threw a towel at me. He pulled one over his own body. He was sweating from the sun and fury, not effort. "You could not fight off a puppy."

"She is clever and tough," Flint corrected. "Those two things cannot be taught."

"Are we done with this farce now?" Hix demanded of both of us. "An Oracle *should* be clever and tough. This was pointless."

"No," Master Of Arms Flint said. "She wishes to improve. As long as she wishes that, you will work with her. Lady Gianna."

"Master of Arms." I inclined my head to him.

Flint walked away, barking orders for the rest of the moon-faced wolves. They drifted after Flint, looking back over their shoulders at me. Platinum stomped away with her toadies. Whatever she'd wanted to see I hadn't provided it.

In the mudroom, Hix threw our towels into the overflowing basket and scowled at me. He took my chin in his hands, jerked my head up to examine the abrasions on my neck, then the bruises forming on my wrist.

"Knock it off. I'm fine." I shook off his hands, or tried to.

"This is not necessary, Lady Gianna," he said.

Oh, it was *very* necessary. "You think I can't handle being sweaty? Get lost if you're going to insult me."

He snorted, spun on his heel, and stalked away. I went to shower.

Platinum rounded me up as soon as I emerged from the bedroom. Her face was so sour, lemons had probably been stuffed in her cheeks. "Alpha Gabel wants to see you. Now."

I smiled. "Not having the best day, Gardenia?"

"It's a fine day." She peered over my shoulder into our quarters.

"You are such a devoted little messenger. Gabel is so fortunate to have you." I slammed the door shut and pushed her out of my way.

Her growl stretched a huge grin over my face.

Gabel quickly wiped the smile off my face with a furious

look. The mantle of an enraged Alpha burned across his shoulders. He pointed at the window. "What the hell was *that*?"

I baked in my smugness. "That was your future Queen improving herself."

He titled is head to the side as if his chin were on a mechanical device. His jaw was uneven, his anger very real. I should have been afraid, but I was so pleased, I just had to gloat in my most reasonable tone. "Master of Arms Flint believes any wolf who wishes to improve herself should do it. Beta Hix will be my teacher and partner, since it would be very inappropriate for lesser wolves to touch me."

Gabel's tongue moved between his white teeth at the word "Queen", but he couldn't get any words out before I added, "Maybe you should speak to Master Flint?"

"I believe I will. I do not approve of this. It is not necessary for you, Gianna," he snapped, unwilling to confess his annoyance as much as I was unwilling to confess my jealousy.

When he said my name it stroked my entire body in pleasure. I shivered uncontrollably.

Gabel's hands moved over my face. Like Hix, he lifted my chin, saw the skin burns from where Hix's skin had rubbed mine raw. His fingertips were gentle, elegant, not rough. His fingers slid off my shoulders, and he bent, but not to kiss my lips: he pressed his lips to the abrasions on my neck, once, twice, thrice.

I breathed out without thinking.

His lips brushed mine, then pressed, and he kissed me slow and deep.

I dissolved into only one thought:

I wanted it.

His tongue against mine, his hands sliding over my bruised, tired body, the Mark throbbing like a second heart. The dark well of hurt inside me where our Bond bloomed.

I curled my arms around his shoulders. One of his hands pushed under my shirt along my side and cupped my breast in his palm. I could barely breathe. His other hand dug into the small of my back.

Then he yanked back.

Contact broken, the pulsing of my Mark stopped just as abruptly. His hand remained on my back. His hand remained on my breast. His blue eyes were wide with shock for a moment. Then he tore his hands back.

He turned away, dismissing everything with a shrug of his shoulders. "I'm going to speak with Flint about this."

Humiliation surged up my throat. I caught the words before they escaped.

His expression transformed into the more familiar one of smug victory. The Bond had slipped ahead of him for a moment, but he had regained control first.

I didn't have anything to say that wouldn't give him some more satisfaction, so I just told him I would see him at dinner and left his room.

The contact broken, my skin felt filthy. I could still feel his hands on me. His tongue against mine.

I knew he was laughing at me.

A HUNTIN' WE SHALL GO

I wasn't there for Gabel's encounter with Flint, but from the churning in my gut that slid outward like poison in my veins, it didn't go Gabel's way. A new sensation: Gabel had lost a fight. Twice in a day. Perhaps that was a new record.

Victory tasted sweet. I tucked it against my heart like a warm lantern in darkness.

Master Of Arms Flint seemed happy to see me when I showed up to my next lesson.

Beta Hix was less thrilled. "I still do not approve of this."

"Noted." Master Flint didn't care anymore that day than the previous day.

Hix grimaced. I wriggled my fingers and reminded myself it needed to hurt.

That night I had a bruise on my jaw. Hix had clipped me with an elbow, much to his horror. Gabel's look of fury when I came to dinner was all the reward I needed.

"I was too slow," I told Gabel as he turned on Hix, fork clutched in his hand like he'd plunge it into Hix's left eye, pop out the globe, and eat it like a grape. "It's not bad. Training doesn't count if it doesn't hurt a bit."

Hix and Gabel both gave me appalled looks.

"I will drink to that!" Master Flint declared at the other table. Fists pounded the table in agreement. "You remember that, runts. When I hurt your little paws, you just remember that!"

Chortles and laughter.

Hix and Gabel exchanged scowls. Romero made a noise of utter contempt.

Dinner tasted much better, and I devoured it with relish. I ate some off Gabel's plate, too, and he suffered my presumption in furious silence. Platinum practically howled her rage from a few tables over.

That night, a knock on our door pulled Gabel out of bed.

Gabel unerringly found his way through the complete darkness. Without a strip of clothing on he opened the door, light from the hallway sliding around his perfect silhouette. One of the young night-watch wolves was on the other side.

"Alpha," the wolf said, "Donovan brought this."

Gabel unfolded the piece of paper. "Is Donovan still here?"

"No. Left and gone."

"More cat than wolf," Gabel muttered. Then he growled, low and threatening. "Wake the First Beta."

He closed the door and flipped on the light, then put the piece of paper on the dresser as he headed into the closet to dress.

"Who is Donovan?" I had heard the name a few times since arriving.

"A Hunter." Gabel emerged from the closet still sashing a kilt around his hips. "Go back to sleep. This won't take long."

Once he was gone, I slid off the bed and retrieved the note. Donovan's handwriting was exquisite: educated and ornate script, like he wrote with a quill pen and ink well while out in the field. It also reeked of unwashed male and was covered in grimy fingerprints.

"Whew." I did not want to smell Donovan in person if I got that much from a note.

Beyond MarchMoon and to the south of GleamingFang was a large pack called RedWater. Back in Shadowless there had been speculation if Gabel would bid for Shadowless or RedWater first. With Shadowless having rolled over, it was only a matter of time before Gabel turned his attention to RedWater.

The note concerned RedWater, but the rest of it was written in pictograph scribbles I couldn't discern: the language of Hunters. Just like Oracles had their runes, Hunters had their own pictographs they'd scrawl onto rocks, trees, dirt, notes to communicate with other Hunters. The alphabet also contained about two dozen wild card pictographs that a Hunter would re-purpose to his pack's use, so he could communicate with his brethren in secret.

Mingled with the actual pack names were the standard pictographs—I recognized 'border'—but not much else. Gabel hadn't raced off or punched a hole in the wall or started howl-ing, so it couldn't be that bad. He also hadn't celebrated, so it couldn't be that good.

Gabel returned two hours later, chuckling with dark, violent amusement. I curled up under the blankets and prayed for dawn.

At breakfast Gabel tapped his fingers on his glass, glaring at me, then stood. "Wolves of IronMoon!"

All attention turned to him. Romero twisted over the back of his chair and winked at me. I shuddered.

Gabel raised his wine. "Tomorrow Beta Hix, myself, and some of our fine warriors," he gestured to the other tables, "will face the RedWater!"

Howls and cheers.

I hadn't seen any preparations for a war party with the news that had arrived. If Gabel really intended on attacking RedWater, surely he would put more planning into it. Gabel made no further statements and sat down to resume his meal. The wolves who had been chosen had already been informed.

That was it? Just that? I caught Romero grinning at me.

Later, in private, I asked, "You're going to RedWater?"

"We are not going to RedWater." His lips curled into a predatory smile. "The RedWater are coming to us."

"What?"

"Alpha Holden thinks he is being clever." Gabel sat down on the edge of the bed. He glanced at his phone, then looked at me. He enjoyed my bewildered expression. "You've told me there's no point focusing on Anders. Fair enough."

That's not what I had told him, but his vision had been for him, so if that's what he had taken from it, that was his business.

"RedWater is intending to hunt on IronMoon territory," Gabel elaborated.

"A formal hunt? How?" There were rituals to such a thing. That must have been what Donovan had seen: the preparations for a formal hunt, which explained why Gabel was moving so quickly.

"They're forming up on that narrow strip of unclaimed forest between RedWater and MarchMoon."

"Cheeky," I said for lack of anything else to say. There was a narrow strip of land—little wider than the interstate that was paved through it—that created a boundary between RedWater and MarchMoon. "And you don't think Alpha Marcus of MarchMoon knows about this?"

"Who do you think tipped Donovan off to it?" Gabel raised a brow.

I flushed at my stupidity. Holden of RedWater must have felt very powerful indeed to offer such an insult. They'd take deer, or goats, or rabbits, or whatever else there was, then leave marks on the trees to show they had been there, then gloat to the other packs about how they had taken IronMoon's prey right out from under us.

"It's cowardly of RedWater," I said. "Not big enough to come directly at us, just going to piss on some trees."

Gabel laughed. It startled me with how big and clear a laugh it was. "You do have some cute little fangs to you, don't you." He tapped me on the cheek, and his gaze trailed over my body. "Have I told you you look lovely today?"

"You always do," I said.

"You will come with me, buttercup," Gabel informed me. "You should see the southern perimeter anyway."

"What?" I had no business being on a war-hunt. Gabel wouldn't be satisfied with just chasing the RedWater onto their side of the border. This was going to get bloody, and if a single RedWater returned home alive, it would be impressive.

"You do know how to hunt, don't you?"

"Yes, but—"

"I would have my BondMate at my side. You will run with me, buttercup."

So I hadn't been good enough to be at his side of Anders, but I was supposed to be at his shoulder for a bloodbath. This was why Romero had been grinning at me. Everyone knew I'd have no business being there.

"A future Queen should know her domain," Gabel added. "You've been training with Flint, after all. You can't be completely useless in a fight."

"There's an easier way to get rid of me that wouldn't involve the disgrace of getting me killed," I snapped.

"I don't want to get rid of you, buttercup." He traced three fingers along the healed wounds of my Mark. His eyes trailed over my arm, down, over my breasts, lower, and then his heavy gaze met mine. He smelled of heat and salt and ash. "Be ready to go at dawn."

His words pressed downward, more resolve than predatory violence. I instinctively reached out and pushed my hand into his chest. He didn't budge, and neither did I.

My jealousy belonged to me, and so did my fear. I wouldn't lay them before him for him to add to his trophy case.

I pushed into his strong chest as he leaned into my hand. I met his blue-green gaze as if I were staring into an abyss. "As you wish, Alpha Gabel."

FLESH

Running through the woods at Gabel's side, the pack around us, the Bond between us singing with glee and joy, the scent of the hunt and wolves and earth all about, was exactly as things should be.

Except that it was all wrong.

All I had to do was think about Gabel's lips brushing Platinum's hand, and him declaring to Alpha Anders "perhaps," and the reality of things hit me full force. My soul wanted to believe. It was lungs that wanted to breathe, a heart that wanted to beat, a stomach that was starving, or a throat that was desperate for water.

Gabel was a large wolf with shaggy, rough-looking fur the color of charred iron. His bones were large, and there was a raw ugliness to his wolf form. It seemed like his skin was stretched a little too tight over his large frame. His fangs were large, but instead of gleaming white, were tinged yellow. His claws tore up huge clods of dirt as he moved. He reminded me of the stories of the Hounds that guarded the gates of Hell. When summoned by the Moon to take away a damned soul, they'd descend upon the soul in full cry, and hunt their quarry without pity, until finally they fell upon it and devoured it.

Raked onto his raw-boned shoulder in bright, pink proud-flesh lines, was his Mark. Cut into my Moon-silver fur was mine.

Matching Marks. He might be Alpha, but I wasn't going to be his Luna.

We ran through the woods in silence. No howls yet. No point in alerting the RedWater to our arrival.

The southern perimeter was rocky forest, where the ground was uneven and punctured with rocks, and covered with a thick carpet of rotting leaves. The pack slowed, and Gabel directed one of the scouting wolves to go find us a path.

The wind blew the scent of unfamiliar wolves toward my snout. I lifted my muzzle and sniffed deep. Many male wolves, but it was hard to tell much more than that. They were still a mile or so away.

Gabel moved over to a tree to sniff it, then pushed his snout into the ground cover. To my left, Beta Hix waited with his group of warriors. He met my gaze, and his amber eyes drifted to Gabel, then back toward the wind's direction. He was a large wolf in a jet-black pelt and had large ears that flopped forward when not perked.

It would have been cute, except it was Beta Hix, and nothing about Hix was cute.

His back leg was missing a large patch of fur. He also had a few patches of missing fur on his shoulder and spine.

We waited until the scout returned.

"*Come,*" Gabel told us after conferring with the scout. He nodded to Hix. The plan was for Gabel's small group to sweep around behind the RedWater and drive them back to Hix and his team.

"*Lady Gianna should stay here,*" Hix protested as Gabel moved off after the scout.

"*Her place is at my side.*"

Hix slicked his ears back, and his tail lowered, even as his spine stiffened. "*She is not a warrior. She has no business being in the front assault group. She should remain here under protection.*"

Gabel's displeasure with Hix was both scent and sensation for me. He growled. "*She is coming with me, Beta. Her place is at my side!*"

It was hard to fathom Gabel was actually trying to get me killed. That would be cowardly, and that would be surrender. His goal was something else.

Perhaps just to scare the shit out of me. if I could silently punish him with contempt, then he could punish me with fear.

Good luck with that. I was not going to give up. I had nothing to lose. He had already gone as far as he could possibly go. He'd stolen my soul and stomped all over it.

No orders were given for any males to keep an eye on me. I fell back off Gabel's shoulder into the greater pack. At his side didn't have to mean literally at his side.

The scout led us down a twisting hillside. Just as they wolves came into view below us, Gabel howled a war cry.

It grabbed my spine and twisted it with fear.

Ahead of us were half a dozen RedWater males. They broke off their track, and their cries sent the birds out of the trees. I fell back even farther into the sea of IronMoon warriors as Gabel's raw-boned form plowed forward.

The tide of wolves pulled me forward into the fray. The pack took over.

One of the RedWater lunged at me. I flung myself left and hit one of my own wolves. Another warrior surged forward and grabbed the RedWater. Gabel was several wolves deep making short, violent work of two RedWater.

A new wolf impacted me. I rolled into the leaves, scrambled to my paws, and squirmed to the left. The plan was to herd the RedWater toward Hix, so staying behind Gabel seemed the smart thing to do.

Another RedWater lunged at me. I yipped and scrambled past him, and he chomped down on my tail. I yipped again and pulled free.

Panic knocked on my brain. I couldn't panic! I'd die if I panicked. I'd panic later. The sea of bodies and claws and howls and barks felt like the Tides, churning and tossing me everywhere as I tried to ride the waves.

Gabel's glee surged under my panic, and his laughter echoed in my breast.

I hate you, Gabel!

Panic and laughter mingled into pure rancid hatred. Gabel's form loomed huge in the middle of the fray and then the scent of blood hit my snout.

Then some actual physical blood followed it.

Hot and coppery and alive, it sprayed me and several wolves around me. No idea where it came from or who it belonged to. The IronMoon warrior next to me wrestled with a RedWater, and I instinctively snapped at the RedWater's foreleg. My panic shattered, and fury replaced it. The RedWater struck at me, I bounced back, then shot back in for another try.

The courage came from somewhere. Instinct, or perhaps Gabel's bloodlust and cruelty. He wanted to see me panic and scream?

I'd faced the abyss. I could face the Moon's own monsters. I bit down on the RedWater's flailing foreleg and heard a shriek of pain. The taste of blood ran over my tongue.

Beta Hix's team crested the hillside and coursed across the

leaves to us. His eyes burned amber even from a distance. He saw me and barked as he leapt over a log. Two wolves separated from the pack and charged toward me.

They wrestled me off the dying RedWater wolf. One grabbed my ruff in his teeth and hauled me back up the hillside, while the other pushed with his much larger body. Once a safe distance away from the fray, they stood guard over me while the IronMoon broke RedWater's collective spine.

Then it became still as all the surviving RedWater pressed together in defeat.

The world seemed to stop to observe the outcome.

The IronMoon milled around, tails wagging, yipping and barking. One threw his head back in a victory howl. Hix barked for him to be silent.

Eight of the RedWater had survived. The rest lay in the leaves and dirt. None of the IronMoon had been killed, or even seriously injured. Gabel stood in front of the survivors, hairless, rat-like tail up and spine taut, reeking of power and glory and cruelty.

The IronMoon wolves settled down in a circle around the RedWater.

Gabel wasn't one for speeches. He ordered the highest ranked RedWater to come forward. The ranked RedWater came forward, his tail up in a gesture of disrespect, ears back. Gabel wagged his own tail, entertained.

Gabel advanced on him, sniffed him, then withdrew. *"Who is in command?"*

The wolf indicated one of the broken bodies.

Gabel's discontent churned in my own belly, the most awful, cruel desire yet. The courage of the wolf in front of Gabel failed, and he curled onto himself, tail pressed between his legs and head bowed.

"Pah!" Gabel spat. *"Coward!"*

His right foreleg snapped forward, and he raked his claws across the RedWater's wolf's face. Skin peeled up, and blood welled to the skin, strips of fur and flesh dangling. The RedWater whimpered, but that was his only response.

Gabel shoved his paw back into the dirt. *"Run, little RedWaters. Run. I will give you a chance to survive. Your dead can rot here."*

The IronMoon jumped up, tails wagging, yipping, eager.

What? No! What was Gabel trying to do? Wolves didn't abandon their dying!

Gabel threw his head back and howled.

The RedWater bolted, leaving behind their dead and dying like cowards, as half the IronMoon chased after them in full cry.

I stared in disbelief at the receding tails.

Gabel grunted and spat on the ground to show his contempt.

Two of the Red Water bodies, too injured to run, were still alive. Their sides heaved and shuddered on each ragged breath.

I broke from my guards and trotted down the slope to the closest one. It was a large male. His belly was split open, and pink loops of intestines spilled out onto the leaves under him. I lowered my head to his.

He rolled one amber eye to me, his breath shallow and sweet on my nose. He knew he was dying. But that was nothing to the awful truth that his pack had abandoned him.

"I am here," I whispered.

"Gianna!" Gabel barked.

I yanked my head up. Gabel had moved a distance away. *"He is suffering."*

"So?" Gabel growled. *"Let him die there."*

"Respect costs nothing." It would take hours for the wolf to die. Maybe days. His family had abandoned him to die. Death would be a mercy to him. *"This wolf has done you no*

wrong to suffer such a death! End his life and we'll be done with it."

The RedWater had come to hunt on IronMoon land and offered grave insult. But no IronMoon had been injured, no game had been taken. There was no reason for them to die like this.

Behind me I heard the IronMoon in full cry, pursuing the cowardly RedWater. Oh, those RedWater deserved what horrible death they were about to receive. They had abandoned their packmates to die without even a glance.

"Pah." Gabel spat again. *"They do not deserve respect."*

"Would you see IronMoon wolves left like this?"

"If they died to weaklings like the RedWater? Yes."

"These wolves will die because of IronMoon." So Gabel would not honor the wolves who had fallen under the paws of IronMoon warriors? It was almost an insult to the IronMoon warriors. *"You cannot leave them here to die like this! It is cruel. It is wrong."*

Gabel shrugged his raw-boned shoulders. Some of the wolves walked with him. Some others hesitated, glancing between the both of us.

"Let them suffer," Gabel said. *"Let the RedWater know their warriors are cowards who leave their fallen to die."*

"But these *have not fled. The IronMoon cannot spare even a shred of dignity for a fallen warrior? The IronMoon warriors didn't finish them off. You are so scant on remaining strength you cannot spare them a swipe of your paw?"*

"I cannot bother getting my paws dirty on that trash."

"If you cannot give his death meaning, you can give it dignity. His pack has abandoned him to die. He has done us no wrong to suffer like this."

Gabel turned his back to me and ambled away.

This punishment did not fit the crime. This was a cruel,

cruel way to die. This was not the death I would have thought appropriate had they been my warriors. This was not how warriors should be treated. There had to be mutual respect.

The ones who had ran could run straight on to hell.

The other IronMoon wolves melted behind Gabel, one after the other. This was how Gabel acted. This was what he did. The IronMoon would return to the house, knowing that out in the forest, two wolves lay dying, abandoned by everyone but the Moon.

I could bark and bark, and it wouldn't matter.

Hix was one of the last ones to leave. His eyes were full of apology as he turned away. This was the IronMoon way, and the Alpha had ordered the dying be left to die.

Gabel thought the Bond left him with choices, and as much as I prayed for freedom, chances of that were slim. Responsibility pressed down on my shoulders. This was not the kind of Queen I would want to be. This was not the reputation I wanted. I would not let Gabel turn me into a cruel monster, or a weakling too cowed to do what was right. I would not be the Queen who permitted punishments to exceed the crime committed.

The wolf under me whimpered a soft plea.

Moon, give me strength.

I lowered my head and took the throat of the wolf in my maw. He stretched his head back to fully expose the soft tissues. I closed my eyes. He smelled of peace, and calm, and a deep, deep gratitude.

The Mark, long since healed, pounded on my shoulder.

I bit down.

UNDERESTIMATED

S plattered with the blood of multiple wolves and with the taste of more blood in my mouth, and the scent of grief and blood and thanks in my snout, I loped up the hillside in pursuit of the IronMoon.

Gabel would have left me there to prove a point: that the wolves didn't matter, and my choice to deal in mercy didn't matter, either.

Gabel looked more like a Hound than ever with blood clumping his ugly, oily fur. He turned one amber eye to acknowledge me as I fell into place by his shoulder. He did not slow his pace, but increased it.

I'd tell you I didn't remember finishing those wolves off, and that my mind hid it from me behind a dreamy veil. But that would be a lie. I remembered all of it, as if the Moon had etched it into my brain. I would never forgot even the smallest detail of what I did in the forest that day. The only thing that kept it from eating my mind was that it had been the right thing to do. The thing I would have wanted for myself, or for any wolf from my pack.

I also hoped the IronMoon hunters found those cowardly RedWater runners and tore them into a thousand shreds.

Late that night Gabel left our bed for an hour, then returned. "The hunters are back."

I had laid awake until that time, unable to sleep. "Success?"

"Yes."

At least something had gone right, and the hunters had punished the cowards who had abandoned their packmates. I hugged my pillow and hoped their insides were hanging from trees.

In the morning at breakfast the hunters were acknowledged for their success. Gabel raised his cup to them all, and Master of Arms Flint led the howl that celebrated returning, victorious warriors.

"We shall send this," Gabel raised a cloth bag filled with many small objects, "to the RedWater! So that Alpha Holden knows not only is he an arrogant fool, but his warriors are cowards."

More howls.

The hunters had pulled the cowards' canines. Pulling a wolf's canine teeth was a desecration of the corpse. A final humiliation and exactly what those cowards had deserved.

But there seemed to be more teeth in that bag than there should have been.

Only six wolves had fled and abandoned their dying packmates.

Gabel held up the bag and showed it around so everyone could see it, his face alight with a wide, handsome grin. The wolves cheered and applauded, a few made noises of contempt.

Then, noticing that I wasn't cheering our warriors, he turned his gaze to me. "You are not pleased, Lady Gianna?"

Sudden silence.

"Why are you not pleased, Lady Gianna?" Romero asked me. "No taste for blood?"

"Shut up," Hix growled at him.

"But you aren't pleased." Gabel's pointed menace pricked my insides.

In my mind I saw Amber's beautiful wolf form lying dead on that forest floor, with her canines pulled.

There were rules to war and combat. There were rules, and it was about damn time someone made Gabel obey them.

If you're going to pick a fight, pick a fight over something that matters.

For just a second Gabel's eyes flickered with doubt, then a painful shudder between our souls where my disapproval and resolve ignited into a fire.

I stood. The silence deepened. Gabel's lips twitched—oh, was he glad he'd finally have an excuse to kill me? He wouldn't have to admit to crawling away from the Bond. He wouldn't even have to admit defeat to himself.

I wasn't going to live or die as his puppet. If I was going to have to be his Queen, then I would live and die as a Queen.

He could get Platinum for sock doll duties.

"May I see these trophies?" I held out my hand.

Refusal to let me examine his triumph was against the rules, and with the whole pack watching, he was forced to give me the bag.

The smell hit me first. Not the best smell in the morning. Inside were many more than twelve fangs. "The hunters pulled fangs from all the RedWater wolves."

"Yes."

"But only six died as cowards," I said in as mild and querying tone as I could manage.

The silence did not move, nor shift.

"Who cares?" Romero scoffed. "They are all fools and

idiots. Send the teeth back to Alpha Holden so he knows better!"

Hoots and fists pounding on the table. Many of these wolves were outcasts, rogues and criminals from other packs. But not all of them. Beta Hix watched me, and Flint leaned back in his chair, arms crossed, observed out of the corner of his green eyes.

Gabel said, "Your point being?"

"My point is that I care."

"Why do you care about some dregs?" Gabel snatched the bag from me. "They're mongrels sent like cowards to hunt on our land because they were too afraid to face us!"

Howls of approval that made my skin prickle. Gabel grinned at me, and his triumph and mocking of my paltry little attempt to resist him rubbed up against me.

With the majority of the pack weighing in on Gabel's side, I didn't have a way to get all the fangs back. I didn't know which were the runners that deserved to be de-fanged and which died in the fight. But I could get four fangs back, and two souls. It wouldn't change the desecration of their corpses or the matter of their souls, but it was something. I flicked my hair back and gave him my best imperious look. "I know the manner in which two of those wolves died, because I killed them. Their canines belong to me. They died bravely. You cannot desecrate them with the rest of the cowards."

Romero's chair scraped on the floor as he stood. "You didn't kill anything, Gianna."

"*Lady* Gianna," Hix corrected.

"She is not a warrior. She killed nothing!" Romero shouted.

"I ended the suffering of two wolves left behind to rot and die of their injuries!" I shouted. "Those are my souls. Not Gabel's, not yours, not IronMoon's. They didn't die as cowards. Or are you afraid of an Oracle who has fangs and the will to use them?"

"You killed the dying."

"I tasted their life and their death."

Gabel scowled, and his shoulders bunched under his shirt. I spun back to him and snarled. "You sent back one of your wolves to desecrate my kills? You said they weren't worth the swipe of an IronMoon paw. How dare you!"

"*Giannnnna,*" he growled, voice twisting into something not human.

"Dog!" I spat back. "You self-serving, petty, cowardly, low-bred piece of garbage!"

The flash of his extended front canines matched the violence that coursed through me.

How dare he flash fangs at me like I was some common male that needed discipline! I swiped at his face with my right hand.

Utter silence.

I didn't make contact. The gesture was enough.

Glasses and plates vibrated with growls.

These low-bred mongrels, and Gabel among them! If this was where I died, I was ready. "There is nothing you can do to me that will ever equal what you've already done. Do whatever you want to me, Alpha of IronMoon. You chose me because I can fight you, and now you are angry that I dare? I will fight you until there is not a piece of me!"

I waited for the violent crush of his fury or the crash of his hand across my face.

Instead he churned and smoldered, and terrifying, contemplative fury weighed my words.

Flint, in the hot quiet, said, "If Lady Gianna says those wolves died bravely under her fangs, then they died bravely."

"What would an Oracle know of bravery?" Romero shouted.

"She-wolves have a different sort of courage than males,"

Flint's voice said matter-of-factly. "Their courage is in their hearts. A male's courage is in his balls. You can castrate a male to make him worthless, but you have to kill a female to stop her. If she says she will fight until there is nothing left of her, she will."

I shoved my hand at Gabel. "Give me the fangs, you loathsome, small-minded, petty, disgraceful, hypocritical, pathetic excuse for a tyrant."

"And if I don't?"

"I will take them from you or die trying."

Gabel paused, contemplating the sensation that passed over his soul. It might have been defeat. It was so unfamiliar he could not categorize it. Thoughtful, he handed me the bag, and observed my next move.

I picked out the four fangs by smell, and clutched them in my hand. "These are mine. The others I care nothing for. Let Alpha Holden see what I think of his pathetic little attempt at intimidation."

I tossed the bag onto Gabel's plate instead of handing it back to him, and, clutching the fangs in my palm, retreated up to my workroom.

Getting them from Gabel had been symbolic, nothing more. For some reason I felt compelled to wash them, bury them in salt, and set them before the Moon.

Maybe I was just riddled with guilt, afraid that if I threw them out, someone might find them and think they belonged to cowards.

Gabel was pensive when he came to bed that night. When he lifted the blankets, his churning presence drew my attention. Normally he was like a swinging sword, moving with sharp, active purpose. Or a cloud of rage tumbling down a mountain consuming everything before it.

Not this thoughtful, contemplative stillness.

"I think I underestimated you, buttercup."

I looked sideways at him.

He smiled and slid closer to me. My book tumbled from my hands. His naked skin slid along mine.

Out of habit I contemplated the Bond between us for clues. I didn't sense anything remarkable.

His smile thrilled me, and it frightened me. It was his most typical smile, the one full of amusement and cunning.

Dazed, his blue eyes captured mine, and his fingers slid over my neck to cup my chin. I couldn't breathe. He felt so warm, his skin soft. My heart throbbed, and I could barely breathe. The Bond howled its pleasure, my mind couldn't think over its sound, but part of me scratched and clawed to not fall into the Bond's swirling clutches.

Gabel's lips pressed to mine. The now-familiar rictus of pleasure shook my body from skull to spine. My skin felt alive. I felt every inch of my flesh, every drop of blood. The Bond's howling increased.

He pulled back. "Yes," he restated, "I think I did."

WHAT YOU WANT, WHAT YOU DESERVE

Gabel may have underestimated me, but I never underestimated him. I could not figure out if he was cruel, insane, or misguided. Perhaps he was all of those things. But I never dismissed him.

"What's this?" I asked a few mornings later.

"A phone." He gave me a look like an explanation would only confirm my stupidity, and walked away.

I shuffled through the phone's contents. There wasn't much I hadn't expected. The only thing that seemed out of place was the large list of contacts. As I scrolled through them, an uncomfortable feeling took up residence in my belly.

Alpha Jermain. My father. Alpha Anders. Alpha Travis. Hix. Flint. Even Platinum. Dozens of other names I didn't know.

It had to be a trap. Gabel had to be testing my loyalty. This was all I would ever need to betray IronMoon.

Of course I could have just stabbed Gabel in his sleep if I wanted to betray him. Why go small-time?

I pocketed the phone. Flint didn't suffer anyone being late, and I needed to stay on his good side. The two hours a day I got to spend under his eye were two hours a day Gabel didn't expect me decorating his office.

And Gabel watched every session.

I'd infuriated him, and now I fascinated him. I wasn't thrilled with the upgrade. Things were less dangerous when I'd held the status of plaything. Being Gabel's adversary was akin to being his prey.

It would have been much easier to put on my fairy princess hat and assure myself he wasn't such a bad guy. That there must have been some dark thing in his past, like his pack getting slaughtered or his goldfish grilled and eaten in front of him, and he was just misunderstood and his love for me would redeem him.

Right. I rolled my eyes at myself, and instead told Hix, "You look grouchy today."

His face compressed into a scowl. "Hello, Lady Gianna."

I smiled at the ritual. I showed up, he glared. I told him he looked grouchy, he glared more. The burning, late-summer heat didn't help his disposition much. Hix actually trained with Gabel and the elite warriors but suffered this extra time with the idiots for my sake. The punishing summer sunlight made them puke and collapse while he barely broke a sweat, and he did not hide his contempt for them.

I'd stopped training so young I'd never amount to much, but Flint always praised my warrior's heart, and said that would take me farther than any talent. I'd started to enjoy the scratching and clawing and triumph, along with the largely inevitable defeat. It gave me a perverse kind of pleasure.

Unless that was Gabel's violent nature corrupting me.

So I told myself it was that it made me feel powerful, and it was something I chose. I would not have chosen this pack, but at least now, I got to carve out a little corner for myself and piss off Gabel in the process.

Still hurt when Hix popped me in the nose.

I sneezed out some blood.

"Shake it off!" Flint shouted. He wasn't talking to me.

Hix ignored Flint's command, stood back, and glared at me while I sneezed again

"Come on!" I shouted. Every time he landed a good shot on me, he fell back instead of pressing his advantage. He stood back like a surly donkey until Flint yelled at both of us.

Hix grumbled something.

Anger bubbled up from inside me. A bop on the nose and a little blood were love-taps, and I didn't need stupid love-taps. "I've got to scry later. Will you just get on with it? This is how I clear my damn mind these days."

Hix sighed. "Have you tried meditation?"

"Don't tell me how to do my job." And of course I had, except I had a pet parasite living inside my soul, and it was pretty damn comfy. We were almost on speaking terms, but I didn't want to be on speaking terms with it.

Before we could clash again a commotion by the house drew everyone's attention. Hix grunted, and his dark eyes left me for the house. "They're back."

Six young men that I presumed were IronMoon warriors came along the back of the house.

The warriors had not gone in the front, nor through the kitchen entrance, but instead through the little-used side porch. That opened onto a large mudroom. Nobody went in that way unless they were bleeding or covered in filth.

Flint barked at us to get back to it.

I became aware of an intense roiling within me. At first I thought I was going to be sick because I had worked too hard, or Hix had punched me too many times.

I dropped to my knees and panted. I fell forward onto my

palms and struggled with the sick feeling. Swear poured down my scalp, between my eyes, and off my nose.

Gabel was angry.

Mysteriously, furiously angry.

"You're done," Hix informed me. He nodded to Master Flint and exited the circle.

He was always so worried about hurting me in training but left me gagging and panting on the grass? Jerk.

Master of Arms Flint pulled me back to my feet. "More cardio for you, Lady Gianna."

Gabel's rage built and built, magma pouring from a chamber and overwhelming me. How could anyone be so angry? So malevolent?

His anger was like the Tides.

But unlike the Tides, this anger wasn't meant to be ridden. It wanted to consume and burn.

Flint gave my forearm a final squeeze, then spun around. The hem of his kilt brushed my legs. "Back to it, wolves! You don't want to crawl home like those pups!"

The tattoos on his back clenched and rippled, shining with sunlight and sweat. The blue-gloss hypnotized me for a second.

Where had Gabel found him... and why did Flint, who had commended his body to the Moon's service, stay with Gabel?

The house was silent, but Gabel's anger still churned against my awareness. I couldn't save the wolves from Gabel's rage—and I probably didn't want to—but what had driven the man I slept with to such fury?

The stench of bloodied, humiliated warrior led me to the drawing room at the far end of the first floor.

I expected shouting. I *wanted* to hear shouting.

Instead I walked into a room filled with Gabel's hot, silent fury with six warriors on their knees.

Gabel jerked his head to face me. "What are you doing here, Gianna?"

Gianna. I had always been *buttercup*.

"Come to see our returning warriors." I stepped up to him with caution. Hix stood to the side and wore a more intense version of his usual scowl.

"Warriors? These aren't warriors. These... things..." He growled, unable to form coherent words.

"They smell terrible." I ventured a truthful observation.

Gabel's laugh ran all over my skin as if his claws had raked me to the bone. It was a huge, horrible, awful laugh from the maw of a dark moon.

Gabel's hand shot forward toward me. I squeaked. His huge palm caressed my cheek gently. "It isn't so much what they did, my dear buttercup."

"No?" My voice trembled.

"No." He spoke tenderly, but there was a crazed look in his eyes. "No. It's what they didn't do. They failed. They failed the pack, they failed me, they failed you."

"What do I have to do with this?"

"You don't remember them? I suppose you wouldn't." He caressed my Mark. I shuddered. "You remember *this* from that day. Not these... *insects*. These insects I left behind in Shadowless to scout the territory. Make certain everyone knew the new order of things."

A wave of homesickness hit me, followed by a crunch of grief, then anger. He'd been checking up on his newest vassal and enjoying the northern outpost that gave him a border with SableFur. "It looks like they got into a fight."

Gabel snarled. "They were exploring the border with SableFur and crossed paths with a SableFur scout party."

The northern ridgeline, where some foothills of the natural mountain boundary between the southern part of Shadowless met the barren, empty tundra that comprised most of SableFur's northern reaches. The SableFur didn't normally scout or hunt that area, but after Gabel had claimed it for himself, Alpha Magnes and Luna Adrianna may have taken notice.

Gabel paced a few steps, growling under his breath. "They didn't fight. The SableFur ran them right back home. Did you even stop long enough to breathe, or did you run until your paws bled you were so frightened?"

Gabel's pulse visibly throbbed in the large artery of his neck.

"They outnumbered us," the lead warrior croaked. "They were hostile and—"

"You were in your own territory!" Gabel shouted. "You didn't defend it! You turned and fled like cowards, and let the SableFur run all over it!"

The room swelled around his fury like a pounding heart about to explode. Mortification coursed through his rage. "I don't believe that's what happened," Gabel snarled, "but I can't think what lie you'd be trying to cover up worse than this."

He jerked his head toward Hix. "Take them to the basement. I'll deal with them later."

There was nothing in the basement except an old, broken grandfather clock and boxes of holiday decorations. It was dusty and musty and dark, and certainly didn't have anything in it suitable to confine werewolves.

"Alpha." Hix saluted him with a crisp snap of his arm.

Hix and another warrior barked commands at the wolves and herded them single-file out of Gabel's office.

"Gianna." Gabel's low, slow growl crept toward me like something from a nightmare.

I licked my lips, and my voice shook, although at the same time, I had developed a very special hatred for runners. "Gabel."

"Tomorrow, you will ask the Moon the same question before. Is Alpha Anders working against me."

Anders? Not Magnes? Not SableFur? Not Shadowless?

Didn't matter, didn't care, I wasn't going to argue with him. I murmured obedience and fled into the hallway.

I gasped several deep breaths of the cool, clear air.

SableFur. SableFur on the IronMoon side of the mountains.

The SableFur were an ancient, vast, powerful pack that holed up in a territory naturally protected on the south and west by mountains. The north was a vast, flat tundra, and another range of mountains protected about half of SableFur's eastern border. The Shadowless and some more northern packs had shared that boundary.

It had made sense when IronMoon annexed Shadowless. A wide-open staging point for an eventual move against SableFur. Except Gabel wasn't that stupid. The tundra was barren and empty, with no roads or places to hide. The actual heart of SableFur sat farther to the south. They'd see a force of any particular size from a hundred miles. The scouts doomed to patrol SableFur's north were pairs of unfortunate youngsters. A couple of barely-grown SableFur weren't going to send six Iron-Moon warriors running.

I'd lived two years in SableFur completing my training. The pack was insular and disinterested in the affairs outside their territory.

Did Gabel know I'd trained at SableFur? It wasn't a secret. I worried my lower lip. This encounter with the scouts might not be as random as it appeared.

Or perhaps SableFur didn't like Gabel having an Oracle of his own. Maybe they didn't like him having a *SableFur* trained Oracle. Perhaps they took issue with Shadowless turning me over, or were stepping up patrols of that border. Gabel also had control of GleamingFang, and the GleamingFang Pass: a four-lane highway that lead straight into SableFur's heart. Hence, perhaps, his ongoing interest with Anders?

Or maybe...just maybe...my last teacher, Elder Oracle Anita, had appealed to Magnes to help me.

My spine weakened. Hope coursed through me like a cold drug. Amber's promise to come for me had never materialized (of course), but perhaps...

Down the hallway something large slammed against something immovable. A shudder moved over the wall. I jumped, shaking, heard more thuds, the scrambling of claws on tile and floor, growls and snarls, an agonized yip, and then a hair-raising howl.

Gabel stormed out of the drawing room and nearly trampled me.

Glass shattered. More howls. Splashing water.

I rushed to the stairway landing, grabbed the railing, and peered into the chaos below. The front doors lay in splinters. The koi pond's surface churned. Water and blood smeared the marble floor. Broken vases.

Gabel lunged through the shattered remains of the doors. Four of the wolves previously in his office cowered along the wall.

I hurried down the steps and jumped over the remains of the door.

Gabel grabbed me and yanked me against him. "IronMoon hunts. Stay close, buttercup."

"Hunts *what*?" I exclaimed. "What happened?"

Howls echoed from behind the house. In two lines all the IronMoon wolves streamed from either side of the property, forming into two dark lines. Their howls struck the sky. The lines converged on a single point: Hix's dark wolf-form running toward the horizon.

I looked back at the four wolves cowering along the wall, did quick math. There had been *six* wolves.

"Those two ran!" I exclaimed in disbelief.

Hix's dark form leapt, shifted into his massive war-form, and crushed one of the fleeing wolves. Screams, yelps, yips, snarls. They tumbled over and over again, and the IronMoon pack converged on the other wolf, swarming over him so I could not see him.

Gabel held me against him, his fingers tight against my skin. Not to prevent me from running, but to prevent himself from moving.

"I would kill them," he growled as he gripped me, "and that would be a shame."

The sea of warriors dragged the wolves up before Gabel and I. Master of Arms Flint, who was a glorious, tawny-gold wolf with his hair balded in the pattern of his tattoos, shifted back to human form and knelt. He crushed the ruff of the first wolf traitor into the dirt with one huge arm.

His tattoos shone as he bent over one knee.

Next to him, Hix stood with one paw on the other wolf's tender throat.

Nobody moved. The other warriors waited in a semicircle of wolves and humans, breathing in one heavy rhythm. Gabel released me, but held my hand in his, crushing my knuckles in his grip.

His eyes sank into Hix, then Flint. "Eroth! Bring collars!"

The wolves shifted, the pulse of their combined breathing twitched.

Eroth, one of the higher placed, unranked wolves, broke from the circle after a moment of hesitation.

"Take them," Gabel directed Hix and Flint. He pointed at the woods.

The pack murmured again, restless, and some growls rose to the surface.

Hix's captive had a broken foreleg. White bone poked through the skin.

Gabel offered me his elbow. His smile was too genuine for me to feel safe. "Come, Lady Gianna."

"Where?" I faltered.

He seized my hand and pressed the flat of my palm to his lips. My skin surged with sick pleasure. "Discipline, of course."

He then placed my hand on his forearm. Patted my fingers.

"I should get Gardenia." I tugged my hand, but he held it onto his wrist. "She attends all these official functions with you!"

"Why, buttercup, are you still jealous?"

Jealous—why yes, yes I was, but only because he'd forced it on me, forced me to care about this, be a part of it, and worse, he'd ruined me so I'd never go back and look at any other male like I looked at him again. "No, I don't want to do the dirty work. I guess she's too pretty and gutless to watch you butcher your own kind."

"You *are* jealous. How adorable."

The Bond lashed me and clutched my throat with a ghostly hand. It hurt, I groaned, and Gabel's eyes twinkled as he shuddered in pain. I wheezed, "I hate you."

"Ah, if only that were true. If only."

We arrived in a large, open dirt circle cut into the forest. Sunlight shone through the trees, the birds chirped, and it was a beautiful day. In the center of this extremely large circle were four thick iron posts twice my height. Various iron rings had been welded along their lengths. Loops of chain and clamps hung over a re-purposed bicycle rack to the side.

Those were not Maypoles for pretty dances involving chains.

Flint, back in his human form, bowed to me. "Lady Gianna. Your presence reminds us that males must always be courageous in the face of difficult circumstances, as females do not question their own lives being imperiled to give birth to the next generation."

What the hell did I have to do with this? I dared not ask.

Eroth returned with a large knapsack that jangled in time to his gait. He presented it to Gabel. The grove fell quiet. The rowdy anticipation of a bloody circus disappeared and transmuted into distinctly un-IronMoon sobriety.

Gabel pulled a heavy leather and metal collar from the bag. The leather was thick and stiff, and it had steel prongs placed along its length. The prongs were double-ended and long enough to extend beyond the collar's leather. The tips of the prongs were not sharp; they were pea-sized metal balls.

Gabel extended the strange device so I could get a good look at it. I didn't see anything exceptionally barbaric about it, but I could smell silver, and that was barbaric enough for most.

He took the first collar to the wolf with the broken leg. He slipped the loop of leather over the wolf's head and tightened it with the leather tug. The wolf whimpered and whined and pleaded.

Then the true horror of the collar became apparent: the prongs prevented the head from dropping forward or to the side. The wolf could lower his head to sleep, but the silver balls would press into his skin top and bottom. Silver was a soft metal, so the balls would deform to the shape of the body and sink perfectly into the skin.

It would burn and sting, and the flesh would start to die. His skin would slough off, and the wolf would die a slow, horrible death from exhaustion and necrosis.

If the Moon had more pity on him than IronMoon did, the compound leg fracture would finish him first.

Gabel fitted a second collar to the other wolf.

"Chain them." Gabel gestured to the posts.

"They should run! That's how they disgraced us. We are owed!" Romero shouted.

"Run them down!" Another wolf somewhere howled. A few more shouts.

"We are owed!" Romero pointed at Gabel. "SableFur will think we are cowards! That we are weak and will not face them! We want a Hunt! Let us chase them straight to SableFur and leave their bodies there!"

Howls of agreement.

Gabel returned to my side. He nodded to Eroth. "Chain them."

Romero shot Hix, the First Beta, a burning look, then Flint, then glared at me, his lips curling and his teeth glinting in the afternoon sunlight. He spat on the ground and turned to go. "I have no time for this!"

"No stomach for death's slow approach?" Gabel inquired.

"No patience for it. You have gotten soft, Gabel!"

Gabel ignored the blatant disrespect. He gestured to the posts, and a few wolves moved forward to manipulate the chains. Romero paced back and forth a few times before he accepted he wasn't getting a Hunt.

Within minutes the wolves were chained between the posts. They could not move left nor right, and chained up so high, they dared not try to lay down. They could only sit or stand. A wrong move, and the silver would push into their throats. They twisted and keened and yelped for their packmates to aid them.

Romero spit at them. The wolves began to disperse.

Then they yowled at me. "Lady Gianna!" The one with the four good legs pled. "Pity! Mercy!"

Gabel smiled and turned his head slowly to me.

"You cruel bastard," I whispered.

"Shall they suffer, buttercup? Or shall I release them?"

"Pity! Mercy!" The wolves howled. "Pity, mercy, Lady Gianna!"

"You do not deserve mercy!" I snapped, thinking of the wolves I had put down because they had been abandoned by everyone, including Gabel. Those wolves had deserved pity. These wolves did not. These wolves had shown Shadowless and SableFur that IronMoon warriors were weak. Weakness was death. "You had four good legs, and you used them to flee. Enjoy this time, dog. Because what the Moon will do to you for your sins is far worse than this."

Rage clouded my mind. Fire licked at my brain. I shouted, "You joined IronMoon knowing how things are done! You joined knowing what your Alpha demands of his warriors! You knew, and you joined, and you think you can flee his orders? You think you can beg for mercy? This was the choice you made. This is what you wanted.

"Why should I help you? You were garbage no other pack wanted, and this pack gave you a chance to prove you had some value. And you proved you have no value. You got what you wanted, so now you get what you deserve!"

My heart swelled, then cracked on bitterness and sadness and despair and fury. Before my tears erupted, I spun, dropped to wolf form, and bolted back to the house.

FLINT'S SONG

The wolves howled all night. The howls pled for the Alpha's forgiveness, for his mercy. They cried for him to excuse their weakness and take them back.

"Don't cry for them, buttercup," Gabel told my tears. He didn't sound angry, nor regretful. Just matter-of-fact.

I knew I shouldn't, but the howls still pulled at my heart. Couldn't I weep for what had been lost? Mourn what might have been? I didn't even know why I was crying, exactly. I didn't disagree with what had happened. I didn't even want to get all snotty and headachey over wolves like this.

"Your last Alpha did not punish idiots and weaklings?" Gabel asked.

"Of course he did."

The sheets shifted. His presence moved closer. "Then why are you sad?"

"I don't know. I don't think it's about them at all."

His rough fingertips brushed the small of my back. I jumped and squeaked. My skin also jumped, but for an entirely different reason. The Bond caught fire.

His fingertips trailed over my spine, up and down, a tender

sweeping motion. Every touch left light trails on my skin. "You should not care." His voice heavy with contemplation. "They proved to be worth nothing."

"I know," I whispered through my tight throat. I knew, and it broke my heart that I *knew*.

He traced a pattern over my shoulders, one way, then the next. I did not think his hands were capable of anything gentle, but this was a delicate whisper that made my skin quiver.

"Is that the pattern you would have given me?" I asked.

"I think so," he said softly, contemplating the pattern his index finger created. "Strange, how I can still sense its outline when I touch you."

It felt like it would have been beautiful coils and loops and strong lines. Instead there was just three rakes torn into my skin and soul.

"Does it feel beautiful? I think it would have been beautiful," he mused.

"How do you expect me to respond to that?" He'd taken me against my will, degraded me, humiliated me, terrified me... and still our souls fit together like this. Why did the Moon even let it happen?

His other hand moved over the dip of my waist and pulled me the few inches across the sheets to him.

His naked body. His very, very, very naked, very male body pressed right against mine, every inch and dip and curve. I arched in surprise and unbidden pleasure. My ears pounded. My skin trembled as if his hand raked delicate metal bristles all over me. Wrapped in warmth and strength, I even felt the raised ridge of the brutal scar over his hip and the rise and fall of his breathing.

He nipped my collar. I whimpered and arched against his hands, shivering all over with exquisite pleasure.

His hand pushed up along my ribs and over my breast. I

made a small sound and squirmed against him. His lips met mine, his tongue against mine. My soul sighed as my skin bloomed, and his fingers very gently pinched my nipple. His palm pressed into my breast, lifting, fondling. I gasped.

This is wrong. This is so wrong.

The sad howls echoed my ears.

He broke off the kiss, kissed under my jaw, down my throat. His teeth raked my skin.

Teeth.

I opened my eyes.

Teeth.

He would have left those RedWater wolves to die. He would have thrown their teeth away just out of petty hatred.

I yanked against his hands and kicked. My heel impacted his shin. It hurt me more than it hurt him. "No!"

His silhouette loomed over me. Hot breath pulsed against my cheek.

Fear slid in to replace my fury. The Bond squirmed and whined, thrashing back and forth, punishing both of us.

"No." The courage came from somewhere. "We can't do this! Don't give in to the song."

My soul constricted in protest, and I arched in pain, and he cringed over me, a rictus moving over his arms. He kissed me anyway. His tongue dipped between my lips, and I seized his face, but instead of pushing, I pulled him close. The constriction in my chest eased.

His caress so exquisite, so perfect, his chapped hand running over my breast, down my side, over my thigh, and that dizzying, deep, hungry kiss! The warmth and beauty of the place where our souls joined—

What am I doing?

I shoved him away again, and swam above the spell he'd

wove, like fighting the Tides. "No! No! Gabel, stop! It's the Bond's song."

This time his eyes focused on me and he heard what I was saying.

"Oh, Moon," I breathed. "It's instinct, Gabel. Stop!"

Wordlessly, he slid back to his side of the bed.

The Bond had gotten ahead of him—of both of us. I flipped over as well and slid down under the covers. This was not good. This was not good at all. I had heard about the Bond wanting feeding, that it wanted to be consummated and be complete, and it'd drive pairs to do just that. The Bond whined under my anxiety, and the flushed hunger between my thighs pestered me.

Neither of us slept much that night.

In my scrying room, I turned my attention to his question: Anders.

I selected my runes with care: *protection, inquiry, pack*. I hesitated over the one I had chosen the first time: *traitor*. Gabel hadn't asked if Anders was loyal, just if he was moving against him. Having met Anders, *traitor* might have been too cut and dry.

Wisdom held Oracles should choose runes that offered the most narrow focus. They were guides and anchors on the Tides.

But if Anders truly believed he was working for the good of his pack, or IronMoon, or the wolves as a species, then he might not have been a traitor. He likely was doing things Gabel wouldn't have approved of, but hadn't committed treason... not in his own mind, at least.

Oracles avoided *truth* for the same reason. Truth and facts weren't always the same thing.

I sighed and pawed through my runes. I preferred my other set, but this one was the bigger of the two. I'd told the stone-carver who had made this set that I wanted every rune possible, and I'd ended up with some spectacularly useless runes like *waterfall* and *leather*. I discarded *duty* and *justice* and *loyalty* as not right, but *balance* caught my eye. One of those archaic runes nobody had ever found a consistent use for.

Balance could mean literal balance, figurative balance, service, or justice. Everything in its place. The point on which light and dark turned.

And that was the reason nobody ever used it: its meaning was clear as mud.

But for my purposes it seemed like a good nexus point between *duty*, *justice*, *vow*, *loyalty*, *alpha*, and *traitor*.

I cast the rune into the bowl.

The ripples of water pulled me toward them, into them, passing through watery curtains into the Tides.

~*~ *The Vision In The Bowl* ~*~

I saw myself.

I immediately startled. The Tides sloshed around me. I caught my reaction and forced my mind to settle and still. Drift with the Currents until things became more clear.

But I still saw myself.

The watery curtains evaporated, and the rest of the vision came into focus. I stood on a large, old, stone platform overlooking mountainous jungles. The rocks were smooth and softened with age. Moss had taken over the grooves between stones, and tendrils of vines crept up from the edges.

The sky hung dark and grey, the air humid, and the wind constant. I couldn't see anything below except the tops of trees. The sides of the platform angled outward, with a set of stone stairs carved into each face of the rectangular-shaped structure.

Some kind of pyramid, then. With the pointed top shorn off to this flat expanse.

The other me stood off on the eastern-pointing side, wrapped in sheer white fabric that fluttered in the breeze. Around her— my?—neck were loop after loop of a necklace. I crept closer. The necklace was made entirely of fangs, one after the other, tied at the widest part by a loop in a single long, thin piece of twine. The tail of the twine ran down her back and off the edge of the structure to the forest below.

At her feet were three of my runes: balance, courage and love. Several runes translated to some type of love. This one was love of pack and family, the love of the living whole. Not romantic love or parental love.

A snuffling sound got my attention. In the center of the platform were two wolves, sniffing the stones. They were oddly unaware of each other. One was Gabel, one was a smoky grey stranger.

Beyond them, on the western edge of the platform, were two men. I couldn't quite see but knew one was Alpha Anders, still wearing his collars, and the other dressed in a long, hooded cloak of a nondescript shade of grey.

To my right was a small raised platform, well-worn and abused. On it sat Hix. His wolf form was large and dark, black as ink, and his fur ruffled in the breeze. His amber eyes were riveted to Gabel and the wolf beside him.

I followed his gaze and looked at what Gabel and the unknown wolf were sniffing.

Flint's dead body.

The Tide churned as I swallowed down a scream.

Flint. His body a bright, tawny-gold spot on the cold stones.

Gabel looked up. His skin had blackened and shrunk against his skull like a corpse baked by sunlight. He had no eyes. Just traces of ears and his lips long gone, so his fangs gleamed in the dull light.

I almost screamed again, then realized his gaze went beyond me to the other me. The me that was... not me? But it was me. I looked back at myself. No, at her.

I yanked my attention back to Flint's body. The tattoo marked with the sacred rune to the Moon's service shone upwards to the dead sky. He had been dead for a long, long time, but his body had not decomposed.

"Flint." I whispered his name, tears on my eyes.

No obvious injuries, simply dead.

I couldn't get distracted. I needed to hear what Anders and the other man were saying.

Was that a human Anders was talking to? I couldn't be sure. But if Anders had betrayed us to a human, that should have shown up the first time I had asked this question.

The man in the cloak slipped away down the side of the structure before I got halfway there. Anders shifted into a wolf and headed along the long side of the structure. He slunk along the edge, head twisted toward Gabel and the grey wolf.

Gabel moved his death's head from watching the other me, and both wolves froze. Gabel snarled. The sound rasped and rattled in his throat.

Flint jumped up.

He shook himself from nose to tail, threw his head back, and howled the song of greeting to the Moon. His fur seemed to shine. My heart lifted within the vision. Then he sang another song I had never heard, but thanks to the vision, I knew: the ancient call crying a female leader to battle.

Flint snapped at the unknown grey wolf, then Gabel. Gabel

whirled and growled, snapping at Flint's muzzle to silence him. Flint spun out of the way and bounded off across the stone plateau. Gabel sprang after him, howling a Hunt on Flint.

Hix jumped up on all fours, his amber eyes on Flint and his canine face hopeful. Gabel howled, but Hix didn't move. Flint came up to Anders, snapped and swiped at the Alpha, then sang the female's battle cry once more. He leapt in the air, head back, tail arched, more like a joyful spring, and sprinted downed the stairs. His song filled the sky.

Pebbles bounced down the long stairway into the jungle, but Flint was gone. Only his song remained. It bounced off the tree-tops like a bell tolling the hours.

Gabel's snarls spun me around again. Now he and the strange wolf fought over the same spot where Flint had lain, and Anders urged them on with a puppy's excited barks.

Then I realized I was no longer there at all.

THE NIGHTMARE OF HIS TOUCH

The Tides held me for two days. My nameless goons kept everyone from barging in. This had included enlisting Flint to impress upon Gabel that if he disturbed me during a vision, I might die.

Die might have been an exaggeration... sorta.

I half-crawled out of my room, head searing with pain, and my body bent from being still so long.

Flint stood guard with my goons. I stared up at him, brain replaying his song and the vision of him leaping in a joyful golden arc down the side of the structure.

"Lady Gianna," he stated as I collapsed into an undignified pile. My goons made some helpless noises. "I see you are back."

I stared up at him, mumbling and drooling.

Big hands slid between me and the floor. Flint scooped me up as though I were nothing. "Alpha Gabel will be relieved."

"Does he still have his balls?" I mumbled as Flint carried me down the hallway. My brain swam and sloshed.

"I have no reason to think they have been removed."

The other wolf. Who had been the other wolf? I moaned

and tried to escape Flint's arms. Where the hell was I going to go? I just had to...

Flint carried me to the second floor, to the room where I had spent my first night. I realized right away this was not the usual bed. Anxiety rattled my mind.

The connection of our souls twisted and gnawed. I should not be separate from him. I should not be here.

I whimpered as Flint set me down.

A punishingly jealous thought burned up from the depths: Platinum. Was she in in my bed with my BondMate? The slut! The bastard!

I whimpered again. I didn't want to hear it. I didn't want to feel it. The voice that I loathed. It wasn't fair or just or balanced. Faithless mongrel, let him have that whore and any others...

I fell asleep to Flint's song.

———

Most think riding the Tides is trivial. I have even heard some claim that Oracles feign their swooning dramatics to play to an audience.

If only.

Gabel waited impatiently for his answer.

When I finally woke up on the third morning my thoughts turned to what I'd tell him.

It had been his question, but the answer was complicated and not intended only for him. Me appearing in my own vision? Oracles couldn't scry for themselves, so they never saw themselves.

This had been no small vision. Three days was at the outer limits. The body started to wither after that. I already had large, deep bruises from kneeling. The top of my feet had turned to sores from the pressure. My muscles still ached.

I took the last piece of bacon from my breakfast tray and went downstairs.

Wolves in collars, wolves in the basement, wolves in my head.

I rubbed my arm. It ached and throbbed.

Gabel had to know I was awake now. Nothing happened in this house without him knowing.

I indulged myself in some bitter discontent.

"Buttercup."

My skin went hot, then cold. I turned, half afraid to look. I expected to see a deaths-head wolf attached to the voice.

But it was just Gabel, handsome and normal. He was alone, dripping sweat, and barely dressed, freshly come in from training in the summer heat.

"You are back." He held the ends of a towel looped behind his neck. A dirty kilt hung low and haphazard across his hips.

My brain stumbled under the memory of that body pressed against mine.

"Enjoying the view?"

His body was marked with bruises and scratches that wept blood. He enjoyed pain, he relished every scratch and mark. I understood more than I had ever wanted to about pain.

I ignored his comment. He knew the answer. He hadn't even asked how his Oracle had fared. I doubted Gabel could even feel those gentler emotions. Perhaps he could, and he didn't know how to act.

Perhaps the absence of malevolence was as cuddly as he got.

"Come, talk to me while I shower."

I followed him back upstairs, admiring the muscles of the small of his back as he walked ahead of me. I hated myself for doing it.

I prepared myself for Platinum's scent to assault my nose upon entering our room.

"Oh, I slept very much alone while you were indisposed." He tossed the towel casually over the bed's footboard.

"I wasn't thinking of her," I said.

"Of course you were. I can sense when she passes your mind." A pause, then he added, "Now that I'm listening."

"Listening?" I echoed without thought.

He pulled off his kilt and tossed it aside.

"I know you're territorial. Don't hide it. You can't."

I ignored the barb and sank down on my side of the bed. My mind still swam on the Tides.

"It isn't like I'd want a Queen without her pride."

He needed to shut up and stop poking me. "So you test it just to make sure I have enough spine to suit you?"

"Perhaps."

"Stop stroking your ego, Gabel." I was not in the mood for this. "I have enough Queenly pride to expect my King to have the manners to ask how his Oracle is feeling."

"Obviously you're fine." Gabel gestured to me. "You don't like anyone fussing over you. So I'm not fussing. Flint told me to stay away. So I stayed away."

I rolled my eyes and muttered something about having a headache. More like a brainache. My brain needed to stop swinging in the hammock it'd set up in my skull.

"What did you see on the Tides?" he asked with an easy charm that I might have found beguiling under different circumstances.

"Anders is still wearing his collars." I skipped to the part of the vision that I was sure I could reveal to him. "This time he was in human form, and I saw him speaking to a cloaked man. The man didn't hold a leash or touch him. I didn't see his face, and I didn't hear the conversation."

"No hands on the collars? No movement? Nothing?"

I shook my head. "Nothing useful. I only know it was a man."

"Were they arguing or agreeing?"

"I couldn't tell. They seemed to be just talking."

"But he is working with someone." Gabel felt along his jaw. He hadn't shaven yet.

I hadn't thought about it that way, but that's what made it his vision and not mine. How much more should I tell him? "It's your vision. It didn't seem to be a passing conversation. However—"

"However?"

"Sometimes in visions a cloaked person can be the person's internal self, and it represents being conflicted."

"Good enough."

Should I tell him the rest? I had never withheld a vision before. I had never even considered doing so until now.

"Problem?" Gabel asked.

"Just pondering."

"So you have no opinion."

"It was your vision." I felt helpless.

Gabel went to shower, and I sagged onto the bed.

Dealing with Gabel was exhausting.

Jealousy pricked me again. I didn't really believe he had been alone. He had toyed me with me too many other times. I slowly brought the pillow to my face and inhaled.

Nothing but Gabel's scent. Not a trace of Platinum or anyone else.

I inhaled again, just to be sure, but nothing. Not even a whiff.

I sobbed once. I was tired and weary. My Mark ached, and my head hurt. It was worse that Gabel hadn't had a whore in our bed, because now I couldn't even be angry at him.

Instinct wanted me to love him, to trust him, to accept him, surrender to him. He was part of my soul, now. The instant I surrendered he'd crush my heart in his paw to prove that he could, and the Bond would never defeat him.

Profound sadness washed over me.

"Buttercup."

I wiped my face and turned. Gabel stood with towel in hand, dripping water all over the floor, naked and glorious.

My eyes went south. Yes, his balls were still attached.

"Naughty, naughty, buttercup," he scolded me, but his tone rubbed me all over, painful but exquisite. "Here I thought you were upset, but all you wanted to do was lure me out here to oggle me."

"I did not!" Anger filled my energy reserves. How dare he mock my sadness. And how dare I be so easily distracted. I fumed at the cursed Bond.

"You can look, buttercup." He strode closer. "I don't mind. And to think how you squealed at first."

"I never said you weren't worth looking at."

"True, true." His smugness eroded as I pawed at a stray tear. I turned so he wouldn't see my tears and told him, "Finish your shower."

I ignored the vague sense of confusion from him. He didn't even know why he was there. He felt my sadness, and his soul whispered to him to be near me and fix the problem. He didn't understand sadness except that it was something he inflicted upon others.

Gabel lingered, brewing in his own confusion.

If he softened would I fall in love with him? Did I dare trust him?

"Are you still... sick, buttercup?" His tone sounded like the words all had a foreign taste to them.

"No. I'm just tired."

"Are you sure?"

My mind hurt. Something floated to the surface. "Gabel."

"Yes?"

"What happened to the wolves? The ones who ran. And the ones who didn't."

"They are not worth you caring about."

I half-agreed, but I still wanted to know their fate. "I like what knowing what's in my basement."

"Your basement?" He moved closer. "Well then, my Lady, the one with the broken leg succumbed two days ago. His companion will join him soon. The other four are below, as I was awaiting your return to question them."

By that he meant how much they would suffer before they died.

"There is no rush to punishment." He moved closer.

I was right at eye level with...

His fingers slipped into my hair. Prickles rose over my skin, and tension fled my muscles. Locks of my hair swirled around his fingertips like water currents. "Do you not trust me to punish them, buttercup?"

I wanted to close my eyes and savor the caress, drown in the waters of it. "I was only asking."

"Would you like to question them?"

"No."

"Are you sure? You take such an interest in so much else around here."

"As you said, your Queen is territorial." I could live with being called territorial. I resented being called jealous. Jealousy was for little girls and daytime talk shows. I would never scratch and claw to keep my teeth in some male.

"You seem so distracted. Am I too distracting? Should I put some clothes on?"

He moved closer. His thigh brushed mine.

I tried to avoid looking at the part of his body just about level with my eye.

He scooped up a large handful of my hair, pulled me back so my spine creaked, and leaned over me.

He smiled. He bent a little lower, pulled my head back a bit farther, fully exposing my throat. He kissed my windpipe. Out of the corner of my eye I could see just how much he was enjoying this.

"Tell me, buttercup," he whispered, his lips brushing my throat, "the rest of what you saw."

ESCALATION

My throat worked. A few sounds came out. None of them were words.

"Tell me what else you saw," he purred again.

My ears hummed. It was hard to breathe. I wheezed. "I didn't lie to you."

Pleasure shivered over my skin. My skin jolted with life as my brain stumbled from lack of air. Every sense seemed so sharp under the threat. Adrenaline coursed through me, burnishing everything, distilling everything. Even his voice came from somewhere under an ocean.

My addled brain sloshed, and the Bond pulled me deeper. He was there to meet me in the abyss.

"Oh I knew you didn't, buttercup. You just didn't tell me everything." He curled lower, reeking of hot desire. His body pressed against my thigh. I whispered a breathy sound. His teeth grazed my throat. My gasp wasn't protest.

I was wet.

His lips moved over my throat. I think I gasped a laugh. He could have ripped out my windpipe. Broken my spine. Tossed me around like a doll.

Dangerous and powerful and terrible, this cruel wolf shaped like a hound, this wolf who was mine as much as he could be anyone's. He would drown me in thick desire. He was a miasma, and I inhaled it, thick and hot. He was glorious in his own, dark, terrible way, and he was mine.

My brain hummed as the blood flow constricted further.

I slid deeper into the Bond, sliding into the waters, boneless, knowing. His lips on my skin. Now his free hand gripped one of my breasts. Harsh, rough in his touch. I wanted his mouth to go lower. Much, much lower.

I smelled the salt of the Tides and the horizon of my mind. I caught a whiff of jungle trees.

I swung one knee outward, then hooked it around his hamstring. With a quick buck of my hips, I shoved him backward.

All those hours grappling with Hix put to use.

I pushed Gabel onto his back. He still gripped my hair. I straddled him and pulled against his hand, but he didn't let go. The sharp pull on my scalp felt good, and so did his hot breath on my twisted throat. I hooked my heels under his thighs.

I breathed hard. It wasn't from the exertion.

He yanked my face down to his, eyes shifting in a stormy, blue-green sea. He grabbed my hip again and yanked me flush against him.

My body seared me. I had never felt so hot, begged so hard for clothing to not be there, resented wet satin so much. My skin pleaded and whispered to his. He was naked, I was the only one clothed, and those panties were so flimsy, so exquisitely flimsy...

"Buttercup," he growled, and I shuddered in pleasure at his tone, which sounded as thick and drunk as I felt, swirling about in a whirlpool. "You should have told me you liked being on top."

"Shut up, Gabel," I heard myself say.

My body begged for those panties to disintegrate. I arched against invisible hands. I should have been afraid. No matter how large he felt against me, how terrifying he was, how much I despised him, I knew all it would take would be a shift of my hips and those fragile panties being removed to feel him where every instinct told me he should be. We were kissing again, hot and deep. He held me against him, and my brain tried to shout over the din what was I doing.

I can't do this! It can't be undone!

The sound of the red ocean drowned out any thoughts.

His hand released my hip. I whimpered, but a second later, his hand shoved under my skirt and grabbed a handful of my rump. His fingers curled around my panties.

I moaned against his tongue. He held me pinned, rough, glorious. I drowned, tumbling in the hot ocean, pulled along the currents with him.

His hand raked through my hair, down my cheek, grabbed my other thigh, and lifted me higher on him. I mewled, and exquisite trembles grabbed me. The Bond leapt within us, lashing each of us forward.

The fabric of my panties cut into my skin when he yanked them off me. He tossed them away. Then he grabbed a handful of my dress and pulled upward. I curled backward, flowing forward like water, and the dress slipped over my head easily.

Maybe I ripped off my bra, maybe he did. It didn't matter. The only thing that mattered was that I was naked, free of suffocating clothes. Skin on skin, lips on lips, his length pressed between my wet petals.

The Moon hung in my mind, red-tinged, overlooking an angry, churning red ocean tossing back and forth.

His teeth sank into my left breast. I grabbed his hair, dug my fingers into his scalp, urged him on, yelped when the stinging pleasure of his bite shot through me.

The hand on my thigh moved between us.

It hurt.

Pain punched through me, through him, through us, ripped through my Mark, and I cried out. I clung to him as he sank deep, right to my core, all of him. The Bond anchored itself to us, metal claws grabbing and fusing our souls, burning melting iron.

His tongue found mine again. I raked his shoulders, pain on exquisite pain, feeling the hot lightening of my nails through him, hungry for him, for every movement, thrust, everything twisting the Bond tighter and tighter, burning white-hot forged iron.

Everything froze for one, exquisite, perfect moment.

Then the moment shattered, flung shards across the span between us, sparkling embers scattered as new stars.

My heartbeat slowed. My breathing eased. The burning heat ebbed.

The Bond cooled, white blazing hot dimming to smoldering shades of red.

I looked down at his sandy hair, his face pressed between my breasts, my fingernails dug into his thick shoulders. I reflexively lifted my fingers back. Trails of blood wept down them. Ten perfect crescents gouged into his skin.

He was still inside me, all of him, exquisitely painful, complete, filling me.

I yanked my fingers back with a gasp.

The wetness... down there... slippery, undeniable evidence of what we had so senselessly, thoughtlessly done, for those who didn't believe in Bonds.

Pain throbbed stronger and stronger with each heartbeat.

Gabel raised his head from my breasts, looked up at me.

We stared at each other, dumbfounded.

A RESTLESS SECRET

I recovered first and moved off him with great care. My body hurt, sharp and raw. I smelled sex and blood, and my thighs were streaked and smeared.

We didn't speak. We didn't say a word.

I went to the shower to wash.

It seemed like the thing to do. A necessary thing. I was bleeding and... slimy. And sticky as everything dried.

The Bond smoldered, fat and smug and gloating. A fat worm that attached both of us, binding us, latching into us like a cosmic, double-ended leech.

I started to cry.

I didn't want this. I didn't want him! This wasn't what I had chosen. He wasn't the one I would have chosen.

I sobbed under the water.

Stupid, arrogant monster. Pathetic mortal, manipulating the gift of a goddess for his own amusement.

All my sobs and tears from when this whole thing had started tumbled forth, and I just let myself weep.

Stupid.

Horrible.

Awful.

Monster!

Each thought punched the Bond. I cried with each blow, and I knew he felt it, too. He'd probably like it. If I went and punched him with my fists, he'd just laugh. This might get somewhere.

Stupid.

Horrible.

Monster!

I eventually got out of the shower, blinded by tears and steam. My Mark throbbed. My private parts stung and ached. My left breast was bruised and bitten.

Gabel's shoulders were ripped and clawed, blood drying across his back and chest. Except he hadn't acquired those because I'd fought him off.

He confronted me in the doorway, as cold as a blank slate.

Where was his arrogance now? His delight in this last challenge worth having? That no mortal could stop him, so he'd pit himself against the Moon's most powerful mandate?

He hadn't even held out half a year.

Before I could savor the contempt. Now I mourned the truth: I had fallen right along with him.

"No one can know," I blurted out.

He twitched all over with surprise. He'd been going to suggest it for a lot of obvious reasons, but I'd beaten him to it. "An Oracle saying that?"

"Shove your arrogance, Gabel. You lost."

His jaw ground.

"The final step is swearing it to the pack and Moon," I reminded him. "If no one knows that we... we..."

"Fucked."

"Then no one's going to try to get us to set the date. So. You keep screwing around, and I'll keep despising you, and nobody will think anything has changed."

A pulse of anger and betrayal. Somewhere in there I'd hit a nerve, but only Gabel could say which one. He shifted his weight between his feet. "You don't despise me. No matter how much you want to."

I growled. "Drop the arrogance. Has this taught you nothing? You lost. Am I not proof the Moon's power is real and you are not Her equal? You don't know anything about me, and you don't care, you never have. I've just been your damn toy."

He approached me. "Those things can't be true—"

"You have said them!"

"That does not make them true." He pushed two fingers into my Mark with one hand. With his other, he seized my hand and placed it on his own bicep, over his own Mark. "If those things were true, these would have festered and rotted like all animal wounds do."

"What's your point?" I rasped. Of course I couldn't hate all of him. He was all any she-wolf could want. Strong, powerful, clever, capable. Even smart, and apparently well educated. The Moon had fashioned us to covet those qualities in our mates.

Even, apparently, if they were balanced against an equal measure of cruelty.

"That is my point."

I laughed as the tears started again. "You don't even know what to do, do you? You just come in here and try to be the big wolf. Like you get any say in this anymore."

Gabel's fingertips pulled across my skin, over my breast, and his hand returned to his side. "Disbelief from an Oracle. A she-wolf finding a male's power attractive is no grounds for a Bond. There is more to it than that."

"You made it perfectly clear to me from the first moment

that is all it was to you. Let all the unspoken niceties you've trampled over remain unspoken."

He said nothing. This had ceased to be an amusement to him.

I couldn't even enjoy the perverse pleasure of seeing him caught in his own trap, because now I was in here with him, and there would be no escape.

He mulled it all over, and came up with. "So. A secret."

"There's no other option. I won't take those vows. You Marked me by force, but you can't make me say words I won't mean."

"How long will the secret keep?" He pondered.

"You want to take the vows?" I exclaimed.

"As I told you before. If there was no risk of failure, there's no point to a challenge." His smug arrogance wasn't there. He was frighteningly matter-of-fact.

Him acting normal seemed a trick unto itself. No more games, no ego, no flamboyance, no smirks. Suddenly I became the crazy and emotional one, while he set his usual cockiness aside to plan his next move.

"One day we're going to get asked what our plans are," Gabel continued, "or we'll get caught, or we'll find a way to separate. I do like having a plan."

"Get caught? This was a one-time deal, Gabel. I'm not fucking you again." Every time we had sex the Bond would strengthen.

He tilted his head a half-degree. "We also swore it would never happen at all."

I laughed bitterly. "I won't deny it when we're found out. But I won't take those vows. I swear on my Moon-touched skin, I won't take the vows."

He pondered this and nodded.

A thoughtful Gabel unnerved me more than the sadistic Gabel.

I could love a thoughtful Gabel. I could be won by a thinking Gabel.

I licked my lips. My tongue discovered a crack. He had nipped me in our passion. Was that what I called it? I had always thought of passion as a beautiful thing. A thing you wanted and welcomed. Not some sloppy, clawing, groping tangle of bodies and tongues.

Gabel picked at one of the gouges on his bloody shoulders. He rubbed the crumbling, drying blood between his fingers.

"Are you going to lie if we are discovered?" If he was going to lie, I wanted to be prepared for it. My fingers trailed over the raised ridges of my Mark.

"No. Will you?"

"I don't know." I pushed my finger into a sore spot and frowned.

"You should decide before the moment comes." He went to shower the blood off him.

THE COLD AND THE HEAT

I held out some hope that Gabel would have forgotten about the remainder of my vision, but of course, he hadn't. Why did I keep hoping Gabel would suddenly become the stupid, base, blunt instrument everyone wanted to believe cruel creatures to be? After breakfast he led me upstairs to his office. I took my usual place on the couch and winced, shifting my abused body, and trying my best to hate him.

He watched but said nothing until I stopped moving. "What else did you see?"

"What makes you think I saw something else?"

He raised one eyebrow. "My question, my vision, my answer."

Except how much of that vision had been for him? I hugged myself across my aching lower body. "Usually."

"Don't change the rules. Or are you trying to be sly?"

"I don't care about Anders or his games or your plans," I told him bitterly. "It was a large vision, and the Moon got a word or two in edgewise."

"Meaning?"

"I don't know." I shook my head. Had the Moon seen how

things would happen? Was that why I'd been wearing a neck-lace of souls? I shuddered.

Oracles almost never had mates. The only Oracle I knew who even had a relationship at all was the SableFur Oracle, Kiery. SableFur was so powerful and large they had three Oracles, making them a one-stop-shop for all your scrying needs. Kiery was first among them, and she had some kind of ongoing complicated mess of a relationship with their First Beta.

Anita, who had been Kiery's predecessor and now trained all the Oracles in this part of the world, had only had cryptic words for us about how we were *other* to our packs, although she'd never voiced disapproval or warned us.

The Bond had fused Gabel and I, burrowing into us like a two-ended parasite. This entwined our fates. Now he and I were on the same cosmic path, and I'd no longer be able to scry for him because I'd essentially be scrying for myself.

Limited utility to Gabel would end very, very badly.

Cold clenched my heart.

"What did you see?"

Automatically, I blurted, "Your balls."

"My balls? You saw my balls?"

Before I could answer, Gabel sprang across the floor and swept low over me. He shoved his face into mine, slammed his hands down on either side of the couch, and raked the slick fabric to show how easy it would be to rip my skin.

"My balls," he growled.

I wilted and shook all over. He growled, deeper, lower, looming. The couch cushions ripped. I didn't dare look down at his hands to see if the fingertips had extended to claws.

"Now I know you've seen all I have to offer from the very start, given how much you squealed over it, but you had a vision of them? Did you see what happened yesterday? Did you know what would happen?"

I yanked my head to the side and whimpered. Fury, anger, betrayal burned through me. The Bond writhed and thrashed.

So much for thinking the Bond might protect me from his murderous rage.

Shaking, I forced myself to meet his brilliant, sea-blue eyes. The rage built and built, the Bond swelled like a tick.

I had to be brave. I wouldn't show my throat.

I grasped for something in my mind, just like I would if the Tides had swept me under. I grabbed at the throbbing pain, the pounding in my arm that made my fingers numb.

You don't get to blame me for this!

It gave me a shred of courage, just enough to meet an Alpha's gaze.

He shook as well, eyes wide and bright. A vein crossed his forehead. His body shivered in rage and... pain.

"I can't scry for myself!" I gasped. "Don't you think if I'd have known, I'd have avoided you? I might have your spawn in my belly right now! You think I want that?"

His fury sparked my own into a fire. It burned away at my fear like it was paper. I shouted, "Your balls weren't even there! The Moon didn't even care about them. Your balls were missing!"

Gabel's anger melted, retreated, smoldered. He pulled back, eyes narrowed to contemplative slits, and frowned. "Missing."

"Castrated. You were castrated." Without my anger to keep me warm, I trembled violently.

"Go on."

I told him what I had seen of him and the second wolf, how both of them had been castrated, and instead of a head, he had had the leather death's skull, like one of the Hounds.

I almost told him the rest of it, but when I went to open my mouth, the words weren't there.

Gabel's expression grew increasingly perturbed. He reached down to make sure he was still intact.

"Yes, they're still there." I could see that clearly through his clothes. I'd also snuck a curious look when he'd gotten out of bed.

"Buttercup, a man likes to check."

"A man likes to touch himself," I muttered.

"That too." He sounded less cavalier than usual.

I suppose the Moon goddess suggesting an Alpha's balls were below Her concern (or She had removed them) could humble even Gabel.

"Was there a wound, or were they just..."

He couldn't bring himself to finish the sentence.

"Long healed." I took perverse pleasure in telling him.

He glared at me. "What were the other wolf and I arguing over?"

"Nothing I could make out."

He paced, stopped, said, "Interesting."

Interesting. Well, then. Fine by me if that's where he wanted to leave it. Further conversation might lead to him wanting to reassure himself his balls were still functional. The Bond would take that as a grand idea.

"What are you thinking?" I was suddenly suspicious of his pensive silence.

He unbuttoned one shift cuff and rolled it over his muscled forearm. He was divine to look at. I shifted on my battered body. He glanced my way, then moved to the other cuff.

I blushed. The Bond squirmed anyway.

Gabel leaned back over me. "I can smell your thoughts, buttercup."

"I'm not thinking." I protested.

He pressed his face to my neck and inhaled. "Such thoughts." He nipped my skin. I gasped, squirmed, dug my fingers into the couch so I wouldn't grab him. My fingers slid into rips and tears made by his own hands a few moments earlier.

"Do you enjoy what you see when you see my flesh?" he whispered.

I bit the split on my lip. Pain sparked, but it didn't do much to quell the torrent building between us. Somewhere my body whimpered about how much it would hurt for him to be inside me again. Instinct didn't care, and neither did the Bond.

"I know you do. You should just admit it," he purred.

"You like it." I managed to retort, but it felt as flat and lame as it sounded.

He kissed my lips, capturing the stinging bead of blood on his tongue.

I shuddered but don't know exactly why.

Somehow I managed to push him back, but just barely.

I told the Bond it was not going to get fed just then.

"I have to go downstairs, you should come with me."

"The basement?"

"Since your vision held nothing useful about them, I should go deal with them. You should come as well."

Gabel expected me to refuse. But I couldn't refuse—we were Bound, and my life as the IronMoon Luna... or Queen... would be awful if I was weak, or Gabel thought I was weak.

I needed to be strong enough to meet him on his terms. I could deal with watching his cruelty in action as he punished wolves who deserved it.

Was this the new game? He'd lost the first one, so now there was the second? Best two out of three?

"Should I... change?" I was in a dress and sandals.

"Buttercup, I'm not going to torture them. Blood thirsty minx." He clicked his teeth, and a swat of playful mischief reached me.

I pretended to ignore him as best I could.

Gabel held the door for me and circled behind me like a hungry beast.

My skin heated.

One foot in front of the other. Focus on the hallway. Walking down the hallway.

"Do you know the way, buttercup?" his voice rubbed me inside and out.

"Yes." I licked my lips. If I looked behind me, I knew his control would snap. He'd grab me, and push me against the wall and certainly someone would spot us at the worst possible moment, and I was sure whatever sounds my throat made wouldn't have been protests and I would—

"Whatever you are thinking, buttercup," his voice as hot and thick as the Bond, "you should stop."

I grabbed at a passing sober thought before it burned away entirely. "What are you going to do to them?"

A menacing chuckle. "Frighten them."

I kept walking. "To what end?"

"On the off chance they have something useful to say." He sounded bored.

"And then what? Execute them?"

"Probably."

I expected it to hit me harder than it did, but it all felt very matter-of-fact. Execution was an appropriate punishment for what these wolves had done. For IronMoon wolves.

He opened a small door off the little-used mudroom.

This was not "the basement" I had seen. The basement I had seen was the "cellar" in the house vernacular.

I stopped at the top of the cold, concrete steps. Gabel, a few steps farther down, seeming to glow in the murky darkness, gave me one of his most cruel, smug smiles.

I gathered the remains of my courage.

156   MERRY RAVENELL

The basement was a huge, smooth, grey concrete box. Blank floor, walls, even the ceiling was concrete. Air flowed through several circular fans set into the ceiling and walls. The floor angled downwards to a line of circulate drain gates. This was all reasonable construction for a basement.

Except this was a sarcophagus. A well-lit abyss where the Moon's eye could not or would not see.

I shuddered with the empty cold that felt along my skin, curious at this thing that had entered its otherwise consuming vacuum.

When a wolf was banished to eternal punishment, the Hounds came to take their soul to a place where the Moon's light did not reach. Not because it could not reach, but because She chose not to look upon them. She sent them to a place beyond Her concern.

Along the right wall were six small cages. The bars were iron rebar driven into raised slabs of cement and pushed into the ceiling, with more rebar in a grid across the top. Rebar wouldn't normally stop a determined war-form werewolf, except this rebar had thin, flat stripes of silver wound between the rebar threads.

Any wolf that tried to fight their way through the rebar lattice would be so sickened and burned they wouldn't get far.

On the left wall were two sets of three chains: one chain led to a collar, the remaining two to shackles.

Two of the rebar cages had occupants.

The place smelled of subterranean musk and dampness, but also of strong soap and bleach. It was terrifyingly clean. It would have been the envy of any hospital operating room. Along the wall behind me were freestanding cabinets. Cleaning supplies, perhaps. I didn't look. I didn't want to see if there was also an assortment of torture devices.

The two wolves who had survived cowered in wolf-form in the back of their cages.

Nobody needed sophisticated implements of torment when they had this unholy sarcophagus buried in the ground.

All the rumors about Gabel spoke of his cruelty. His *physical* cruelty. But oh, if it only stopped there! Gabel didn't merely break bodies; he tortured them. Tormented them. Made them suffer until even their spirits were broken, twisted things. I laughed at anyone who thought Gabel dealt in pulling off fingernails or pouring silver over the skin. If only Gabel stopped at the flesh.

I hugged myself without shame. I dug my fingers into my skin to hold onto it before the emptiness consumed me.

Hix and Flint waited for us. The First Beta retrieved a folding metal chair. He set it almost dead-center of the room and nodded to me.

Gabel took the first wolf from his cage and proceeded with the questions. Where had they been in Shadowless? How close to the boundary? How many SableFur? Who called the retreat? When he was finished he questioned the next one.

At first I wondered why Gabel asked all the same questions when the wolves had had a chance to get their stories straight, and could hear the answers. Then I realized all the answers varied. Closer to the boundary line than the previous, arguing over who had called the retreat, blaming the others for the retreat call.

Their answers didn't matter. It was the brightness in their eyes as they gabbled their answers, though. It was hope. They fawned and frothed to answer Gabel's questions, and he stood there like a wealthy businessman nodding to each answer like he cared. He spoke calmly, deliberately, reasonably. He periodically shifted his fingers, drawing attention to the sleeves rolled up over his forearms like he intended to do something, but their words kept his rage at bay.

These foolish wolves believed they might talk their way out of this. I caught Flint's gaze, and he nodded once to me with grave agreement. These wolves had fled their mission like cowards, then crawled on their bellies like shamed puppies instead of owning their weakness.

IronMoon had no other virtue in the eyes of the world except its unrelenting ferocity and capacity for violence, and these wolves had undermined it with cowardice.

Gabel's knuckles needed to crack across those unbruised, unmarred faces! He needed to—

"Buttercup," his voice echoed in the tomb, his back still to me. "Buttercup, such thoughts. Temper, temper."

Flint glanced at me, a twitch in one brow that I refused to acknowledge. Gabel would have thrown good fangs out with bad, but he was being gentle with these cowards. It wasn't just! His scales had tipped out of balance. I seethed. And he forced me to watch this? The sick, demented—

Gabel looked over his shoulder at me. "So angry. Would you like to come do this? I won't object."

"Stop playing with your prey, Gabel," I snapped. If he wanted to toy with them I couldn't stop him, but I didn't want to watch. The taste of blood washed over my tongue. A grateful dying wolf's breath touched my cheek.

Those RedWater wolves had died with more dignity and purpose than these. I was ashamed, ashamed of the IronMoon, and even a little ashamed of Gabel for bothering with this.

Flint, dressed only in a kilt, flexed one wrist. The joint crackled.

Gabel's focus swirled and shifted, then something like lock-pins slammed shut in my chest.

"Beta," Gabel told Hix, "brand these dogs and take them to the edge of our territory. Leave them."

I sat up straight.

"Alpha?" Hix's voice echoed my shock.

"Brand them," Gabel repeated, "and leave them outside our borders."

Hix coughed, Flint watched Gabel with a contemplative expression.

"Is there a problem?" Gabel asked his Beta.

"No, Alpha, there is not a problem."

"You're going to let them go?" I demanded. "You pulled the fangs on the RedWater wolves for less!"

"Are you accusing me of being gentle?" Gabel asked.

"I'm accusing you of avoiding disciplining your wolves because it's your fault they're even in this pack." Ultimately, the Alpha was responsible for the conduct of every wolf in his pack. When one of them failed so miserably, it was partly the Alpha's fault for not seeing the wolf's weakness, or flaws, or putting him to a task beyond him.

"Dangerous accusations." He smiled. "Hix, do it before midnight. Master of Arms, walk with the Lady and I."

"Ignoring me changes nothing," I growled at him once we were in sunlight again.

"You aren't wrong, buttercup, but I have a different use for them," he assured me with a gleam in his eye. "So feisty. Oracles are so very strong."

I shuddered.

Flint folded his arms in front of himself, and asked, "You have an additional task, Alpha?"

"Send a tracker to follow them," Gabel instructed. "At a far distance. Donovan, if you can find him."

"To what end?"

"To whatever end they come to. If there is nothing of interest, come home."

"You're still certain that one of your vassals is moving against you?" Flint asked.

"Of course," Gabel replied.

Flint saluted both of us and strode away, kilt swirling around his knees.

"You think they're stupid enough to try to approach another pack?" I asked. A wolf rejected from IronMoon wasn't even worth humoring. IronMoon took the rejects nobody else wanted. After IronMoon there was nowhere left to go. "They're stupid, Gabel, but do you think they're that stupid?"

"Anders was wearing quite a few collars." Gabel straightened the strap of my dress, his face thoughtful. "I don't think anything will come of it. Unless you think they should just be put down?"

"If I told you I think they should die, would you do it?"

"I prefer things to be useful until they are not. I want to know who Anders is talking to, Gianna. Perhaps these wolves can lead us to him, and if they've got a little meat left on their bones, it will whet all the right appetites."

"And perhaps you will get us all killed," I said.

"But that's the point, buttercup."

"Getting us killed?"

"What's the point of winning when you don't take the risk of losing?"

I snarled, "Haven't you learned anything, Gabel?" I lowered my voice and hissed, "I could have your bastard pup in my belly right now, and you're still flirting with this nonsense."

"It would not remain a bastard."

I curled my lip.

He brushed his thumb over my cheek. "You would have

enjoyed watching me bloody those wolves. I felt how badly you wanted me to hurt them."

"Don't change the subject."

He pushed his two fingers into my Mark again. "Before you, I would have just killed them. Before me, you would never have hungered for the blood of the weak."

My heart shriveled. "Then why didn't you do either?"

"Because this is better. This suits *us*."

ACCOUNTABILITY

A wolf was waiting for us after breakfast. More specifically, he was waiting for me.

The wolf was not from IronMoon but from one of the innumerable small packs that IronMoon had conquered or annexed. He was thin and more of a mouse than a wolf, in his thirties, and unremarkable in every possible way. Just the sort of easy prey that disgusted Gabel.

Gabel bade me remain in his office while Hix verified the visitor's request.

"This isn't how it's done," I told Gabel, aggravated. "He's a petitioner. He's here to see an Oracle."

"And he *will* see you, once I've determined that's all he's here for," Gabel said, irate.

"I dislike playing a living sculpture."

"Violet can run the house, and you should learn how to run your domain." He gestured to the room around us.

"I am not going to be your Luna or your Queen. I don't *need* a domain. Stop treating this like a game, Gabel. It's not a game!"

Gabel took note of the book I'd been reading. "Field survival? Planning on running away?"

"And where the hell could I run that you wouldn't find me?" I flung back, although a secret hope that perhaps this Petitioner was here because of Anita and SableFur nibbled my insides. Maybe they *were* going to get me out of here after all. If I couldn't be free of him, at least I could be safe from him in SableFur. I suppressed a smirk. That made sense if SableFur actually did move their bulk to retrieve me. If I was mated to Gabel, he'd never be able to Mark another female, and he'd remain unmated, without legitimate offspring, and his true mate having been captured from him, and him powerless to take her back.

I snickered silently to myself, and shoved my bitter glee down the Bond's gullet.

Gabel eyed me. "I sense you have somewhere in mind."

"Just entertaining the possibilities." I cursed the Bond again. Stupid snitching parasite.

Flint eventually appeared to inform Gabel, "He is who he says he is, and he is here for Lady Gianna."

Gabel scowled. "Send him away. She is otherwise occupied."

"She isn't Queen, nor your Luna," Flint stated. "Her duty as an Oracle still takes precedence over any matter you have for her."

Gabel paced behind his desk, aggravated. He wasn't the first Alpha in history to learn that Alphas didn't get pet Oracles. The room had been properly prepared, the candles, the salt, but he had ignored that he didn't have a monopoly.

That was why Oracles were trained to resist an Alpha's grasping authority. Now if only my training had included resisting my mate.

Gabel's irritation reduced to a simmer. His silent, possessive snarl sent a ripple of dark flattery through me.

I uncrossed my knees and stood up. "I'll meet him, Flint."

Gabel snarled a silent *no*. This time I was prepared with a mental hold on myself, and I gave him a sweet smile instead. Gabel practically gnashed his teeth. I didn't hide my eagerness.

I'll be with a strange male. All alone. And I won't tell you anything he says.

The Bond flopped and struck me like the slap of a wet hand.

"She will be well guarded." Flint pretended to think Gabel's reaction was something other than grabby-paws. "We can't have a guard in with her, but two will be just outside the door."

Gabel snapped a pencil in half but managed a bare nod. I winked at him as I turned to leave.

He snarled, and his jealous rage slammed into me hard enough I staggered. Flint caught me and steadied me while the Bond seared and punished me for even teasing.

Now you know how it feels to be a toy, Gabel.

"Lady?" Flint held my arm.

"I'm fine," I heard myself say in a light, laughing tone. "I just tripped over that rug."

Flint uttered something conciliatory before escorting me downstairs to the drawing room where the Petitioner waited. From here, habit took over. I entered the room alone, closed the doors, and faced him.

"No," I stopped him before he could introduce himself, "don't tell me your name."

Confused, he sank back on the couch. He told me he was from a very small pack to the south, just on the current edge of IronMoon's influence. Gabel had annexed them two years ago. One of his first conquests-by-phone. He had not given them a second thought since, save that he intended to expand his borders further, and that pack might make a good staging area. Gabel paid little attention to them. That meant they'd be perfect to traffic a message from the SableFur.

I sat down across from him, careful to keep my eagerness in

check. "No one can hear us. No one is listening. Why have you come to me?"

He fidgeted, glanced beyond my shoulder, then back at me. His eyes rested on my Marked arm, and he didn't hide the shudder at seeing the raw scars. He licked his dry lips, the scent of fear rising off him. "If I ask a question it's a secret, right? From everyone?"

"It is your question and your answer. You can tell anyone you wish, but I am bound by silence."

"To everyone," he whispered.

"To everyone," I affirmed, keeping my hope on a very, very tight chain as my heart swelled. At the other end of the Bond, Gabel rumbled like a storm in a deep chasm.

He moved his lips as if practicing his question before he spoke it. "Should the line in the forest be crossed?"

My hope intensified. Such a common question! It was a practical joke among Oracles. Cross a road or a river, jump into a lake, take a plunge. Always translating as Do The Big Thing Or Not. This wolf couldn't have come all the way to IronMoon and risked Gabel just to ask me that. I suppressed my relieved laughter. Anita or Kiery had sent him.

I waited for him to offer something else, but he didn't. Fine. If I needed to through the farce of the Tides for such a question, so be it. "Your question, your answer. I will go to the Tides this evening."

That evening I chose my runes with care and decided to include *balance* again. The point on which light and dark spun. My fingers trembled with eagerness, and it took a long time to quell my hope and to block out Gabel's increasing fury—he knew I was up to mischief.

The Tides waited for me.

~*~ The Vision In The Bowl ~*~

The forest. Alone. Wet leaves. Drizzle. Wolf form, leaves under my paws, the scent of everything in my nose.

The scent of blood.

Where the RedWater wolves had died.

Two piles of bodies waited. On the left the bodies were piled high, jaws snapped and canines removed. On the right were just two bodies, jaws also opened, teeth also removed, but their ruffs bloody from my life-ending bite.

Between the bodies sat a stone table with legs made of burned bones and a flat, granite top. Carved into the stone's face were four runes: balance, courage, love, and one I didn't recognize. The first three had been carved by a skilled hand. The forth had been created by something that had slammed the rock with such force, it had charred the stone itself and now glittered like it had been crusted with glass.

The Tides trembled under my feet. This wasn't the question. This wasn't the answer.

I backed away and the Tides trembled again, shaking all the eager mischief and glee and hope out of me like dust shaken off a carpet.

Behind me the Tides stretched out to the horizon. Before me was the forest, resting beyond the rocks and bodies.

The two RedWater wolves stirred, stumbled, got to their paws. The one with the gutted belly still had loops of intestines hanging free in the leaves, the other had his shattered hind leg and gashed face. Both greeted me with wagging tails and broken jaws, the lower mandible hanging slack, and their missing canines obvious.

"This..." I whispered, "this is not his question..."

I picked my way up the hillside, crouched low, and crawled over the ridgeline.

I tumbled down into a new, different forest. This one smelled like ocean and sand and seaweed, and there was sand and scrub mixed in with the forest underbrush. I shook the sand out of my fur and skulked deeper into the woods. Eventually I found two wolves in human form talking in low tones, separated by a line in the leaves. The wind carried their scent, and I had a good look at their faces. The only remarkable thing about either was the one to my left had a raw, red, dripping-blood piece of meat in his palm, and he offered this to the wolf on my right.

The MeatMan was tall, brown-haired, amber eyed, straight-shouldered. The air bent around him. The other wolf deferred to him. I squinted as my fur tingled. I'd never met or seen Alpha Magnes of SableFur. Was this him? Perhaps not, as he seemed a bit too young, but I might not be seeing him true-to-flesh. I crouched lower and squirmed closer. The other wolf didn't seem like a small coward; he had some authority, too. Another Alpha, likely, but a smaller Alpha.

Blood dripped between MeatMan's fingers, and my mouth watered at the scent rising off that fresh meat. I fought the urge to charge and snatch it from his hand.

The MeatMan urged the other man to take it.

The man shifted into wolf form and allowed the MeatMan to drop the meat into his waiting mouth. The line of the leaves pushed backward. Now the MeatTaker was on the MeatMan's side.

The MeatMan smiled, turned, and walked back east. The wolf gulped down his prize, then bounded back over the line and headed west.

JEALOUSY, LOYALTY, DECEPTION

S ableFur was not coming for me.
Even if that had been Alpha Magnes in the dream, the Petitioner's question was, more or less, real. The Moon had just put a few words in edgewise.

I sniffled and rubbed the back of my hand across my eyes.

"You shouldn't have gotten yourself hopeful, Gianna," I whispered to myself. I slid my bowl back into its velvet bag and put the runes in their pouches.

Nobody was coming for me. Not Shadowless, not my father, not SableFur, not my Oracle sisters.

The Petitioner was here for something else, and any first-year Seer would have recognized what the MeatMan part of that vision had been about. Betrayal brewing. Someone bribing someone else. And all this was some lousy trap. The Petitioner was a plant.

The Bond squirmed a little, and Gabel's rancid impatience waited at the other end like a fetid pool.

Stupid me. This was why Oracles rarely mated. I'd never thought about it. Now I did: my vows demanded my silence. I couldn't tell Gabel what I'd seen. There were no exceptions.

None.

No what-if-this or how-about-that or he-might-destroy-the-world-and-kill-everyone or someone's-pup-will-die. No exceptions.

This was how we were *other*. It wasn't our gifts or prestige bequeathed by a force beyond the Alpha. No, it was worse:

We couldn't be trusted. We put the privacy of a single wolf above the safety of an entire pack.

I sobbed quietly. My sisters weren't coming to get me. I had to keep a potential betrayal a secret. I'd betray my pack, my... mate. The betrayal could result in his death or harm to another pack. How would the Moon weigh me if one of those came to pass? I was the one who *could* tell Gabel look for an Alpha trading in flesh and blood.

I still had *balance* in my palm. "So which is it? The cardinal sin of betraying my mate and Alpha, or the cardinal sin of opening my mouth?"

I slept in my own room that night. Gabel didn't drag me to bed, but he came in at dawn. By that time I'd been pacing for an hour trying to figure out what to do.

"Buttercup, you seem... distressed."

Unprepared for his arrival, I couldn't respond.

His eyes narrowed. He slunk over to me. "Did that wolf bother you?"

I backed up a step. Gabel matched my stride. My fingers grazed the wall behind me. Gabel studied me up and down, looking for clues that I was not as he had left me. A deep sort of violence slid between us. "No." I gulped. "No, his question was just difficult."

All I wanted to do was weep. I should have been able to turn to my mate for comfort even if I couldn't tell him why. But I was completely alone with this wretched choice. I had to choose between loyalty to my de-facto mate or my integrity as an Oracle.

"Difficult?" Gabel prodded.

His scent made me dizzy. I saw the piles of dead wolves again, and my tongue tasted of blood. I couldn't breathe with him so close. "His question. His vision."

Gabel's hands seized my forearms. "But it upset you. Did he upset you? You seemed... very enthused... to meet him."

His voice held a low growl and a possessive snarl curling just under it.

I laughed, weak and bitter. "And you think that's why I slept alone? So I wouldn't bring his scent to our bed? A little wolf like that?"

"Why would you even waste the glance?" Gabel growled.

Such a foolish, pathetic question. Beneath him. "You know that wolf is no threat to you."

"You know Gardenia is no threat to you."

"I never gave a damn about Gardenia."

"Lies are beneath you."

"I have to go downstairs."

His grip didn't ease.

"He is waiting," I prodded softly.

"And I am here! Your Alpha, your—" He stumbled on the word. Fury gnashed his teeth together.

"The sooner I take him his answer, the sooner he will be gone."

Gabel scowled but released me. He did want that wolf gone. "I do not like this. Something isn't right about this."

"Are you going to act like this every time someone petitions me?" I pushed around him. "You chose to Mark an Oracle. This is how it works."

"You are miserable. You were so pleased yesterday, like he

had brought you some forbidden delicacy. Now you are wracked by tears," he stated roughly.

"I told you, his vision was difficult."

And it was half mine, apparently.

Gabel followed me, practically stepping on my heels as we entered the hallway to the drawing room.

"Gabel, please! I can't think straight with you like this."

"I can't think straight when you're... upset."

"It was an upsetting vision." My voice cracked.

"I will wait here for you."

"In the middle of the hall?"

"Yes. Right here." He folded his arms and glared at me.

Confused, I continued down the hall to the double doors. Every few steps I glanced behind me, and Gabel would gesture for me to keep walking.

"Will you go away?" I hissed.

"No."

His presence cluttered up my mind. I stood at the doors of the drawing room, waiting for the instinct that would tell me which way to go, and nothing.

Screwing him had been such a mistake.

The Moon had made me Hers before I had ever been anything else. My fingernails dug into the wood, and I squeezed my eyes shut against tears. Gabel was a hot coal within me, a smoldering, sullen heartbeat that echoed my own.

The wolf inside the drawing room stood to greet me. The sharp gleam in his eyes struck me in an uncomfortable way.

A trap. This had all been a trap. For me? For Gabel? Iron-Moon? Some small local politics that didn't matter?

"Do you have my answer?" he pressed before I had even sat down.

I nodded, my emotions sliding under the familiar mask of an

Oracle. "Two wolves in human form in a forest. There was a line in the forest. The wolf on the far side of the line offered the wolf on the nearside a piece of fresh, raw meat. The other wolf took the meat. The line shifted so that that both wolves stood on the same side."

"And?"

"And nothing. That was the vision." My heart thundered under my ribs. That was all the vision for him. And I'd told him. Told him and not warned Gabel.

"But that wasn't the question."

I shook my head. "That was the answer given."

He glared at me. "That wasn't the question."

I stared at him a moment. Was I supposed to say something? Was he waiting—no, he was just plain angry. I stood. "Goodbye, wolf. I have nothing else for you."

"Wait! We aren't done."

I went to the drawing room doors and yanked them open. The air was no better out here. Here it smelled of Gabel. I coughed.

"We aren't done. Get back here!" The wolf snarled behind me.

Gabel's form sliced between him and I.

"Did I just hear you growl at her?" Gabel inquired.

"I—I—" the wolf gabbled, "I, no, I—"

The Mark throbbed and pounded.

Whatever he had been about to say withered and died under Gabel's anger.

"Leave," Gabel growled.

The wolf yipped some pathetic noise and bolted down the hallway.

I buried my face in my hands and shuddered. What had I done? Why did the Moon do this to me? Had Gabel taken me out of Her light, dragged me into his personal Hell-Kennel on earth?

Gabel's smoldering emotions slid over me and through me like tentacles. He lowered his head to my neck and inhaled my scent. A male assuring himself his mate was healthy and safe. An act meant to comfort and bring solace, that he cared, that it mattered to him.

I could not call what was within me just then as caring. Maybe in Gabel's own strange, twisted way it was a kind of caring.

Gabel clicked his teeth together. I jumped at the snap.

"Did he... disrespect... you, buttercup?"

"No." Instinct told me to confess everything I knew. An instinct almost as powerful as the Bond to obey my Alpha and to place the safety of the pack before anything else.

Gabel frowned. He sniffed my neck again, brushed his lips across my skin to taste me. What did this tell him? He coiled within me. I could not name a single emotion, just a dark tangle like some nightmare parasite embedded into every tissue and membrane. "You are lying, buttercup. He upset you."

"Not him. His question." Not even his question. The not-answer. The answer that told me no one was coming to save me. That I was truly, completely, totally alone with Gabel. "I cannot tell you, Gabel. His question, his vision, his answer."

Gabel's fingers slid under my chin and pulled my gaze up to his. His eyes were such beautiful blue-green, but his gaze hard and dark. All his doubts and anger were clear to me through the Bond, but there wasn't a rebuttal because they were justified.

They weren't coming. No one was coming. Not even the Moon. I was alone with him.

He tasted my anguish. An anguish he could not solve. Instinct gnawed on him to remedy it, but at the same time, pain and fear were things he conquered. He was not the master of this anguish, but he had to live with it.

"I do not like wolves coming here, taking your time, and

upsetting you, buttercup," he told me in a rough tone. "Especially not no-regard wolves from territories so small I do not
even remember conquering them. You and I will have to discuss
this later. When you are not upset."

"There is nothing to discuss. You knew what I was when
you Marked me."

"And I know what you are now," he snapped.

The Bond all but purred with the unspoken words.

Mate. Luna. Queen.

Gabel yanked his hands off me and stepped back, shoulders
tight and jaw clenched. His eyes burned blue.

I bit my lip so hard I tasted a drop of blood. He was glorious,
and I wanted him, even if I shouldn't, even if I knew—

He spun on his heel and stalked away before his hands
could betray him.

The air did not clear when he was gone. I covered my face
with my hands and sobbed once, twice.

Platinum melted out of the room downwind of the drawing
room.

I snarled. "Eavesdropping?"

She slid along the far side of the hallway in the direction
Gabel had gone. Her eyes dared me to challenge her.

"Hurry along," I told her through gritted teeth, tears welling
in my eyes. If only she'd do me the favor and get Gabel away
from me!

But she couldn't. She'd been my only real hope, and now it
was gone.

"Finally shedding a tear?" she asked suspiciously. I snapped
at her, and she slithered down into the shadows after Gabel.

Did she suspect? So what if she did? What would Gardenia
stand to gain if she knew Gabel and I had consummated the
Bond? If anything, she'd want to make sure nobody found out.

... right?

SMOLDERING

I did not want there to be an *us*.

I tried to work my frustration out with Hix and Flint, but after three days of wringing myself out, Flint demanded I take a day off. That meant I couldn't avoid Gabel during the day.

So here I was, back in his office again, so he didn't get the satisfaction of accusing me of avoiding him. And he didn't want to admit to avoiding me by coming to bed late.

Gabel stared at his map in utter silence, as he so often did.

It was marked in various colors and labeled with pack names, Alpha names and other markers showing encampments, outposts, and other information relevant to Gabel's quest to become King-Alpha. It was flanked with more pieces of paper containing various notes and diagrams. Gabel, already looking the part in dark pants and a button-down with the sleeves rolled over his muscled forearms, contemplated his domain.

He was too damn easy on the eyes.

I bit the inside of my cheek as I approached the map.

This would be easier if he wore grungy sweatpants and a stained wifebeater.

Gabel's blue gaze smoldered, and his attention churned as his gaze slid toward me.

Something about the map had always repulsed me. Gabel's ambitions were no secret to me, but just seeing the big swathes of his domain and being able to figure out his next target was too much to absorb. Now, for whatever reason, my curiosity was piqued. Probably because being curious about his ambition was safer than sitting on the couch and admiring his physique, trying not to think about what his hands felt like on my skin.

He shifted toward me, ducking his head slightly as if to kiss me, but catching himself just as he moved. The air between us felt like a hot wall, as if summer had suddenly taken up residence in the small space between us.

The IronMoon territory was huge. I had known it was large, but seeing it mapped out was chilling. Warmth forgotten, my eyes moved over the large, thick, green line of tape that marked the boundary of IronMoon's holdings. Smaller, thinner lines marked individual pack territories within the holdings.

Shadowless.

"I have done nothing to your birthpack." Gabel read my jolt of distress.

"Except conquer them." Except for the obvious insult of putting them on leads like good little doggies.

Gabel shifted with mild contempt. Conquer was a very strong word. Shadowless hadn't even fought.

Old conversation. I turned my attention back to the map and tried to figure out Gabel's next move, and when he'd be foolish enough to bid for SableFur.

SableFur. I gulped down some bitterness. I wasn't mad at them. I was mad at myself for being stupid enough to think they'd come save me.

At some point Gabel was also going to have to pick a fight with IceMaw who wouldn't roll over. Except that should have been Shadowless. Maybe their Alpha, Aaron, would fight back. Maybe he'd kneel down like all the others.

Why in the Moon's name did I want him to fail? I was Gabel's BondMate, and that meant I'd be first in line for abduction or death in a fight. Me wanting Gabel to get his tail handed to him in a fight didn't do much to keep me alive.

I rubbed my Mark. "There will be war."

Gabel pondered his map. "Probably."

Something in his voice caught my ear. "Wait, are you trying to *avoid* a war?"

"I don't think there is any way to avoid war," Gabel said thoughtfully.

"Then why not be content with what you have?" I asked, nonplussed. "Look at this, Gabel. Isn't it enough?"

"Would you stop scrying just because someone told you you had done it enough?" Gabel asked.

It would have been so much easier to dismiss Gabel if he had been stupid. An intelligent, thinking demon was far worse than a mindless flesh-render looking for its next meal. "Conquering packs is not the same as the Tides."

"No? You never know if you're going to come back. Or have you not realized the risks you take?" He turned his head just enough so that one of his sea-blue eyes met my gaze.

"It's still not the same thing."

"It is exactly the same thing. You don't *need* to scry. I do not *need* more territory. Did you become an Oracle because it gave you status? Glory? Attention? Power?"

"No."

"Exactly."

"So you're saying you are doing this because you have a geas?" I frowned. Gabel's wolf-form did look like a Hound...

There were plenty of legends about how the Moon would one day set Her Hounds upon the world to bring about the end

of days. There'd been plenty of cruel wolves in history that
stories likened to Hounds, but nobody had ever set himself up as
King, then justified his methods by saying he was a Hound sent
by the Moon.

Well, not that anyone remembered. There'd been plenty of
dark, shattered times in our history.

"You mean do I think I'm a divine instrument doing the
Moon's will?" Gabel asked.

"Ah, sure. That." My gut reaction was Gabel was nuts to
think that. But on the other hand there was a Master of Arms
with holy blue-gloss tattoos. The knowledge to make the sacred
ink for those tattoos had been lost centuries earlier in one of
those dark times.

Gabel chuckled. "No. I'm only drawing a comparison
between your calling and my compulsion."

"How can you compare my mandate to your ambition?" My
voice trembled a tiny bit.

"You know what I meant."

I grumbled. "So what? What if one day I want to take off my
mantle? You want me to. You don't like your little pet Oracle
scrying for anyone but you."

"Perhaps one day I will be satisfied with what I have and
feel no more need." He studied me with a pensive expression.

"What's your next move?" I didn't expect him to tell me.

"I was thinking of here." He pressed his fingertip to a small
territory southwest of the Shadowless borders. "But my instinct
is that is not a smart move."

"SableFur is probably still on the alert after the wolves,"
I said.

Gabel's lips drew into a line. "Yes, buttercup. My thought
was to go there to show the SableFur I'm not afraid of
them, but—"

"You actually are?" I prodded.

"You want me to go there and cause a war? Because it would be your precious birthpack that ate it first, when the SableFur finds out where you're from. I am not ready for SableFur."

My birthpack had abandoned me to Gabel. Traded me to him to buy their own safety. I could accept that, but they hadn't bled for me. Not even a single drop. That was the wound. My father hadn't even growled. Not once. Not even a trifle. Not even after Gabel had mauled me in front of him.

Gabel pointed to a tiny southern territory. "I think here, instead. Push south."

"Where was the wolf who petitioned me from? I was told the south."

Gabel pointed to a little shred of territory in the extreme southwest. "Here."

I squinted at the map. There was indeed a forest close to the ocean. I scanned the rest of the map looking for clues as to who the Alpha had been. That was a long way from SableFur. "Have you ever seen Alpha Magnes of SableFur?"

"No, why?"

"Just curious."

The door to the office opened, and the sounds of three pairs of footsteps followed. Hix, another warrior wolf, and a lanky wolf of about thirty. The lanky wolf was thin, filthy, his beard almost to his chest, and his hair hadn't been cut (nor brushed) in weeks.. His sharp, cruel eyes were those of a predator.

He saluted Gabel but eyed me, trying to decide if I was worth acknowledging.

I glared right back at him.

Hix punched him in the kidney and hissed my name in his ear. The hunter wolf just sort of oofed from the impact, but half-bowed to me to greet me, an excessively respectful greeting. My name would have sufficed.

"This is Donovan," Gabel told me, gesturing to the wild wolf. "He is our best hunter."

Donovan ran his filthy fingers through his equally filthy beard. "You howled, Alpha?"

Despite his squalor, he had a sophisticated voice and tone, like he should have been reading poetry or acting on stage.

"Change of task for you," Gabel said. "Pick up the trail of the wolf who petitioned Lady Gianna three days ago. Track him, find him, determine where he's been, where he's going, and everyone, human or wolf, he speaks to."

"What?" I exclaimed. "You can't do that, Gabel!"

"Alpha." Donovan half-bowed in dramatic fashion.

"No!" I shoved Gabel. "You can't do that!"

"Go." Gabel told Donovan.

Donovan ducked out the room, taking his stink with him. Hix followed.

I spun around and snarled at Gabel. "You can't do that!"

"Donovan won't be spotted," Gabel said. He returned his attention to the map.

"They'll think I betrayed them. You can't attack that pack, you can't hunt that petitioner," I shouted.

"Was there something I should know about either?"

"You know I can't tell you anything."

He rolled his eyes and smiled at me. "Fine, fine, buttercup. If it upsets you so much I'll attack someone else."

I pursed my lips. "How magnanimous of you."

He stepped behind me, and his amusement curled around me like smoke. One of his hands extended toward the map and caressed it, while he whispered in my ear, "Does it please you, this thing I have created?"

His other hand slid over my hip.

"It is not mine, and my pleasure doesn't matter," I rasped.

His palm slid along the line of my hip, fingertips grazing lower and lower. He kissed my neck, my ear.

"It impresses you," he whispered hoarsely. His other hand turned my chin, and he kissed me, slow and deep and hungry, and that hand slid down my neck to grasp my breast. I shuddered and whimpered, but none of it was a protest.

The Bond dug into both of us, envenoming us like a two-headed snake. Gabel's fingers slid lower, between my thighs, and I gasped as he touched me through my panties, his strong fingers rubbing and caressing, evoking memories that sent pleas through my whole body. My mind, paralyzed, watched, somehow convinced by the Bond's venom that this was either inevitable or a smart move.

His kiss. I could have drowned in it. His rigid body pushed against my back.

I couldn't tell where my thoughts ended and his began. He seemed to be everywhere, he was his own Tide, pulling me, drowning me, everywhere. His tongue chased mine, a low, wicked chuckle escaped him as my body dampened against his fingers. A moan escaped my lips. I didn't want him to stop, I should have wanted him to stop, but I didn't, I just arched against his hands.

"Still so ready for me," he whispered hoarsely.

"I hate you," I whimpered as his fingers slid under my panty hem and onto my wet skin. I was so wet.

"So pleasure for you, then my turn, hmm?"

"Gabel, we can't—"

"I can't resist you, buttercup. I don't want to." His fingers moved against me.

"Don't say that," I whispered.

"Alpha Gabel. Lady Gianna."

LEAKING SECRETS

Gabel and I yanked apart.

Master of Arms Flint didn't even blink.

"Another interruption," Gabel said. "Have you all lost the ability to *knock?*"

My heart thundered, my pulse throbbed. My thighs were raw and wet and aching with unfinished business.

Gabel did not flinch or shrivel before the Master of Arms, but his displeasure at being disturbed was plain.

"Lady Gianna," Flint addressed me. "I was looking for you."

It took a few more shallow breaths for me to find my voice and hope it wouldn't shake. It wasn't like my father had caught me.

It was so much worse.

"What do you need, Flint?" I asked, shaken by being caught, what it might mean, that I had fallen under the Bond's influence one more time.

Gabel turned and headed over to his desk, "You do not knock now, Master of Arms?"

I bit my lip and told my privates to settle down.

Flint only nodded to Gabel's question and didn't actually

answer it. He had his hands behind his back, but the small muscles of his shoulders flexed under his skin.

Gabel's hot silence was all the permission I needed to leave. Not much either of us could say. Just not speak about it. Pretend Flint hadn't caught us. Pretend it wasn't what it looked like. Pretend nothing was out of the ordinary, and my embarrassment was just maidenly horror at being caught with Gabel's hand in my panties.

"Let's speak in your workroom," Flint told me.

Even the cool, salted air of my workroom couldn't ease the squirming in my gut. "Do you have a question for me, Flint?"

"No." Flint stepped over to the windows. His tattoos shone and shifted over his muscled torso. He noted the little bowls of salt and candles and other evidence of my work. "I know you and Gabel have consummated the Bond."

I gulped down a wave of nausea. "Based on what?" I managed to choke out. "What you just saw?"

"He betrays it. To eyes who know the symptoms, it is plain."

"Symptoms? I know I have a soul parasite. Do share what the symptoms are."

"The way he watches you. The way his eye is always on you. The way his eye is on everyone else," Flint stated, deadpan. "Other things that betray the connection. Most don't recognize it, because there is rarely a gap between the Mark and the Pairing. You both try to hide it, but you don't know what you're trying to hide, so you do a very bad job."

The Bond poked and prodded, like an evil gaining power for having been named.

"You do not want the pack to know."

I didn't answer.

He stepped closer to me, his kilt twisting around his thighs, his tattoos very dark against his skin. Flint's hair was the same tawny color as his wolf, and his eyes a bright green, like jungle trees. He felt warm, even from a distance.

"Have you taken your suspicions to him?" I asked Flint.

Flint smiled. "You've grown some fangs, Lady Gianna. Gabel gave you those. No. I have not spoken with him. I am speaking with you. It would do no good to speak to him."

"I have no power over Gabel. Gabel takes what he wants, when it pleases him to do so."

"I don't think he was the only one in that room pleased." Flint raised both eyebrows.

I blushed.

"We both know what was going to happen if I had not walked in," Flint said.

"Not what you think." I lied to both of us.

"He is a male," Flint told me, "and while it may sound old-fashioned, he has less control than you do. That is how we are made."

"Why are you telling me this?"

"You won't succeed in keeping this a secret. The harder you fight, the harder the Bond fights back. It is still forming. It needs feeding."

"I don't want to feed it. Your Alpha Marked me against my will. I don't want to be here, and I want the Bond to die."

Flint looked at my arm, then sighed as if I were a willful child. "We both know it's too late for that. You must make peace with this—"

"Peace? Peace with what he did to me?" I spun away from him. "Peace with that monster who stole my soul? Who gave me this hideous Mark? Who turned me into his plaything because he was bored?"

"You are angry, and that anger is dangerous. It is fueled by Gabel. As long as you two both fight the Bond, it will think it is in danger. It will gnaw on both of you. He will pursue. You will slow. You will both go mad. It is that simple."

"I am an Oracle. I am trained to ride the Tides. If I were going to go mad from compulsion and delusion, it would have already happened."

"Your resolve might last longer than his, but eventually, you will both collapse. The pack will have its expectations."

"Then *help* me," I pleaded. "Tell me how to kill the Bond."

"Is that really what you want? You've both tortured it, abused it, poisoned it, and it is still alive and strong."

"Yes! I can't be bound to that monster. Why would the Moon fashion any soul to match his?"

"So you are horrified that any part of you could love part of him?"

"It's the balance of things, Flint. Yes, there are good, magnificent parts of him but...no, repudiation works. I know it does."

Flint gave me a piteous look. "It only works when there is a fulcrum to break the Bond over. You *want* that conviction. You don't have it. You wish you did. That is what hurts. You just don't want to look into the abyss. Perhaps Gabel did you a favor Marking you as he did. It spared you the pain of being wooed by him."

"Says the wolf who let him humiliate me in front of another Alpha," I said bitterly. "Stop making excuses for him. For yourself, and how you stood by and let him do this to me!"

Flint sighed and suddenly looked very, very old. The tattoos moved with the motion of his breathing and tension. "Some things simply have to play out, Lady Gianna."

Tears pooled in my eyes. "I won't be forced to take vows I don't mean. And I don't care if this pack understands that or not. And I don't care what the Bond or the Moon has to say about it!"

"The Moon is having Her say. The Bond will consume both of you. Eventually you will be caught in his embrace, or with his pups in your belly. The Tide is coming in because the Moon's motion has willed it to be so. You're not looking into the abyss, Oracle. You're afraid of what you're going to see. And then it will own you."

Flint half-bowed to me, and left my workroom.

ENSNARED

I didn't normally watch Gabel train.

The rings sat far back from the house itself and the window was more about providing an expansive view of the estate, not sparring practice. Still, I picked Gabel out from a distance, and in the late afternoon haze, easily identified other warriors. Names were a bit of a mystery yet, but faces and bodies and scents were familiar.

Gabel might have been pissed to find me in his office. He didn't like anyone in there without him being present (and even then, he didn't like intruders).

The map on the far wall accused me of my actual sin: withholding information from the Alpha. If I really wanted to make Gabel mad, I could just tell him *I know something you don't know*. If I really wanted to drive him into a fury. If I had the courage.

I toyed with it for a few minutes, like a sore tooth.

Yeah, that'd end well. He'd put me down in the basement, in that cement hellhole, where not even the Moon would see. The instant he broke me, he'd know what I knew, and he'd win. Then I'd have nothing left. Not even my place as an Oracle.

Gabel hadn't broken me yet, but I wasn't stupid enough to think he couldn't. I knew the dark pit of his heart better than anyone. Given the proper motivation he was capable of anything. For his next trick he'd probably try to Mark the Moon.

"Where did you come from, Gabel?" I asked the empty air of the room, my eyes moving over the map on the far wall with its markers and lines. Because he'd seemed to come out of nowhere a few years earlier. Flint? I hadn't heard of Flint *at all*, and Oracles would have noticed a golden wolf with jungle-green eyes and blue-gloss tattoos. He looked like he'd walked out of some old, dusty book.

Look into the abyss.

Flint had pretty much cuffed me and said, *there's more going on here. Pay attention!*

The burned-out rune in the MeatMan vision. What had it been?

The door to the office opened.

Second Beta Romero stepped inside, carrying envelopes in his hands.

"Lady Gianna," he said after a moment of startlement. "I was not expecting to see you in Alpha Gabel's office."

"Oh? I am often here," I reminded him.

"I meant alone."

The way he said *alone* curled off his tongue like the flicking hiss of a viper. Beta Romero and I had nothing to talk about. He could finish dropping off the mail like a good little pageboy and get out. If he wanted to tattle, fine. I'd deal with *that* monster and not this little ant.

The low-hanging clouds shifted in the sky, and some columns of sunlight peeked through them. It was late, lazy summer, but those clouds said autumn was coming. Had I already been here a full season? Different wolves were sparring now. Gabel's bronze form moved in a cluster of wolves. Perhaps he would soon be on his way up to the office.

The notion sent a shudder of unbidden pleasure through me, followed just as quickly by embarrassment.

Romero had taken up a place behind my right shoulder. He had no business lingering. I almost was getting used to the interruptions. Gardenia snooping, Romero skulking around, Flint just barging right in... although Flint had done us both a favor, embarrassing as it had been. "Do you need something else, Romero?"

He chuckled under his breath.

My blood froze in my veins.

"Don't pretend, Gianna," he told me in a mocking tone. "The lady-of-the-manor act might impress everyone else, but not me. Don't think I'm going to heel like a good little pup."

Romero had dropped off the mail. He could get lost now. "What do you want?"

Romero's fingers snatched a handful of my hair and yanked my head backward.

I squeaked and instinctively grabbed at his rough, iron-claw hand. My throat spasmed.

He leaned over my shoulder, his chest against my back. He grinned at me. "You have a neck like everyone else, Gianna. It is a very pretty neck. Gabel said you smelled like the Moon. Do you taste like the Moon?"

His fingers curled into my hair. My scalp burned and seared with pain. My heart punched against my ribs, but I couldn't move. Romero dragged his tongue along my throat. "No," he hissed in my ear, "you just taste like every other female."

"Get off me, dog!"

"I could snap your neck."

"What do you want?" I struggled and scratched at his hand, but every movement pulled shreds of my scalp off my skull.

What was he doing? Why was he doing this? I never had anything to do with Romero, and it wasn't like Gabel had suddenly become a weak, ineffectual Alpha since my arrival. Oh no, Gabel's balls were still firmly attached!

Romero shoved me forward. My balance shot over my toes, and I staggered into the windows. I caught myself, the panes rattled under my weight. I flipped around, but he closed the distance, pressing his entire body against mine.

The Bond howled and writhed, and Romero's touch seemed all the more nauseating.

Romero laughed at me. "All that training, improving yourself, and you're still pathetic."

I screamed when he licked my throat again. He yanked my shirt down, and his filthy, slimy tongue bathed my skin.

I shrieked, and every drop of my blood churned with revulsion. "Get off me!"

"Do you like this?" He gripped my left hand and pinned it back against the glass, his whole body pressing us both into the window. His tongue found the hollow of my throat, and he laughed as he toyed with it. "Gabel doesn't need you. Soon you'll be thrown to all the rest of us."

"No!" I tried to get my knee up to kick him where it counted, but he just laughed.

My entire body protested everything that was happening, my soul wanted to crawl out of my skin, the Bond screamed and fought. What the hell was the Bond fighting against? Didn't it know I was fighting? It needed to shut up already, and let me think!

Romero stank. He stank of lust, power, desire, something crazy and horrible, something far worse than I had ever smelled on Gabel. Just pure, sadistic cruelty mixed with weakness.

Weakness. Weakness?

He didn't seem weak to me! My nose was off the scent.

Didn't matter. Had to get him off me. Had to at least fight for all I was worth. No way he was going to get the satisfaction of me giving in! Gabel hadn't gotten it from me, and like hell Romero would. Gabel had my soul. Romero wasn't going to get my body or my dignity or whatever it was he had come for.

No.

Raw anger replaced my panic.

I raised my left knee again, just as much as I could with his body shoved against mine. I wasn't going going to kick, and he shifted, expecting it. I stomped down on his foot.

He yelped and shoved his face right in mine.

Dark hatred bubbled up inside me and curdled my blood. "Gabel isn't done with me, dog, so you'll have to keep begging for table scraps."

Out of the corner of my eye, movement. Gabel was on his way. Bronze and obsidian thunder with every footstep.. "There he is," I hissed at Romero. "He's coming. He knows you're here. Run while you can, little dog."

His eyes glanced over my shoulder.

Thunder with each footstep reverberating within me. "Or stay and face him. Let him catch you like this."

"You'll be scraps sooner than you expect, Gianna," he hissed.

He shoved off the glass and fled.

The heat of anger and panic faded away, and chilling cold replaced them. Shaking and shivers took over my body.

My knees knocked into each other, my hamstrings trembled, and I slid down the window glass onto the floor.

Had Romero been telling the truth? Had Gabel promised me to them when he was done with me?

The Bond shuddered and wept from the trauma of another male's touch.

The door shuddered on its hinges as Gabel stormed in.

He stopped dead, stared at me, face twisted in fury and bewilderment. His feet were still bare and filthy with mud, and he reeked of sweat, dirt, and wolf. I'd never seen him so paralyzed or bewildered.

"What's going on?" Gabel asked in a wary tone, stepping slowly toward me.

I closed my eyes. Tears swam, and I didn't want them to fall, but it was too hard to talk. I pointed at my neck. It still felt slick and gross, like it was covered in slime.

"It looks fine, Gianna," Gabel's fury clouded his voice and rattled my bones.

I jabbed my finger and managed to choke out, "Smell."

He crouched down next to me, his breath soft on my skin. I opened my eyes again and stared at the point over his desk, the opposite wall covered in books. The tears started.

His hands seized my arms, ran all over my body and thighs, then clapped behind the back of my neck. I resisted, but he pulled me forward. His anger churned another notch higher. How could he even breathe around that much rage?

I whimpered and flinched and swatted at his hand when his fingers touched the sore, tender spot on the back of my head.

He looked at his bloody fingertips as if he did not understand, then my neck, then growled deep in his throat.

"I'm bleeding?" I stared at my own blood.

"He pulled up a patch of scalp," Gabel stated. "It is minor."

Minor. Such a cold diagnosis from his lips. Tremors hit me again. Gabel couldn't honestly think I had let Romero do that. Gabel had to have known something was wrong, and he knew something was wrong now. He had to. As much as he might not want to, and might even be enjoying this, he had to know I was upset.

Gabel wiped his fingers on his kilt and crouched next to me. He was almost at eye level, his body coiled muscle, and his anger transmuting into something far darker, colder, and more terrifying than a burst of hot temper. My breath came quick and shallow.

"I swear I—" I started to say. I hadn't invited Romero to touch me!

"He dared to put himself upon you." Gabel's every muscle tight under his skin, his lips curled back over his teeth.

I faltered, confused and lost.

His teeth clicked together. "Am I correct?"

"Yes."

He growled.

"He... he said you promised me to them. When you were done with me."

Gabel barked a cruel laugh. "No. If they want their own females, they go out and get them for themselves. I do not provide whores for their pleasure, and I do not let them rape along with their pillaging. Romero has often disagreed with that."

Gabel rested his elbows on his knees and considered me. "How did you get away from him?"

"He wasn't expecting me to fight back. Foot stomp and..." I gestured pathetically to the window.

He clicked his teeth again and straightened. He lowered one hand to me. "Come on, buttercup. You reek of another male. I do not like it, and I am sure you despise it. You shower while I think of what I am going to do about Romero."

I gripped his hand. "Do something?"

"You do not want me to do anything about Romero?" Gabel's tone made it clear that wasn't an option.

"What are you going to do? I'm not your mate."

"You are mine."

"Right of blood belongs to mates," I whispered, "you can't claim right of vengeance."

"We can." He corrected darkly.

"Think about it for a minute." I trembled in absolute fear and cursed the Moon, and Flint, and everything else. *The pack will have expectations. You should decide before the time comes.* No! This would not be that time!

"Do not cut my balls off, Gianna," Gabel growled. "Romero needs to be dealt with. Be grateful I am not charging off and beating him into a bloody pulp in a fit of rage."

My Mark thumped, reminding me it existed, that it had not festered.

Gabel stood at the center of our room, kilt crooked on his hips, still barefoot and dirty, while I showered. I scrubbed my skin raw before emerging to stand naked and dripping wet and miserable before him. His anger built several more notches as he looked at my raw, bloody skin.

Gabel had Marked me. We'd consummated the Bond. The vows were a formality. A public acknowledgment of what had been settled privately between us. The final nail in the coffin. He could have claimed right of blood vengeance for what Romero had done. And if he did, it was as good as announcing our intentions, that I *was* the future Luna of IronMoon.

"You don't know what you're going to do," I realized.

Sharp annoyance from him. "No. Romero *wants* a confrontation, and it's what he expects. Romero has never managed to corner me until today." Gabel's tone hardened with each syllable, although doubt rattled around within him. "He is violent, and he is wily. He lost the First Beta position to Hix, and since, he has been eyeing me. I've avoided giving him the fight he wants."

"What fight does he want?" I asked.

He shrugged. "Any fight. He's like a dog chasing a car. No idea what to do if he catches it. Something has changed if he's become this bold."

My Mark thrummed. Romero had been disgusted with me from the moment Gabel had Marked me. He'd despised me when I'd challenged him. He'd resented me when Gabel allowed the traitorous IronMoon to be chained rather than hunted. He took sick enjoyment watching me humiliated in front of Anders, like that's where I'd belonged. "Me. I'm here. That's what changed."

Gabel looked at me directly, eyes bright, ocean-blue. "The *what* does not matter."

But it did. "Gabel, what color is his wolf form?"

"Pale, smoky grey."

"Is he about medium sized, rangy, but with big shoulders?"

"I would say so."

I seized his hand. "Gabel, he was the castrated wolf you were fighting with. In the jungle vision. Be careful of him."

"I thought Oracles did not interpret visions."

"I'm not interpreting anything. I'm recognizing he was the wolf you were fighting with."

He frowned. "Are you sure? It was him?"

"Yes, I'm sure. Yes, yes, I'm sure. So why were you two fighting over Flint's corpse?"

Gabel gripped my chin in his hand, his thumb and forefinger tightening into a squeeze. "My question, my vision, buttercup," he reminded me. His handsome face twisted with a dark light. "Now," he bent and kissed me very lightly, the tenderness of his lips balanced against the relentless vise of his fingers. "Let's go. I know what I have to do."

FROM THE MOON'S VOID

After Romero had finished with me, he had gone down to the training rings to wait for Gabel's response.

And Gabel was playing right into his plan for a big glorious confrontation with his Alpha.

"Be careful, Gabel." I tugged against his grip. "He used me to get to you."

"Of course he did, buttercup," Gabel snarled. "Can't fight the male, go for his female."

"I'm not yours!" I hissed. "Don't talk like that."

He ignored me and dragged me right to the edge of the ring.

I stopped, aware of all the IronMoon warriors around me, and how vulnerable I was. Gabel kept going into the ring, stopped halfway in, and pointed at Romero.

"Romero!"

The air shuddered. Everything stopped. Even a few birds burst out of the trees and fled into the sky.

Romero turned to face Gabel, rolling his shoulders. His face curled in a half-grin. "Gabel."

Gabel's back tightened at the casual address, and his voice

was as taut as his shoulders. "You put your hands on Lady Gianna. You put your tongue on her. Against her will."

Well, technically so had Gabel when he had Marked me. There was some uncomfortable irony to this.

But Romero and Gabel were not the same. Romero was a mongrel dog. Gabel was something else entirely. It didn't make things right, it just made things more complicated.

Hix shoved his way to the front of the training ring, and Flint stepped down off his box. Most of the wolves startled and shifted, exchanging nervous glances and looking at me. Their eyes pawed over me as if trying to guess what parts Romero had tasted. A small wave of them crept toward Romero's end of the ring, and the wolves around me pressed backward, creating a small and terrifying halo of emptiness. Romero had allies to compliment his bad intentions.

Hix snarled something, pushed wolves aside, and placed himself next to me. His dark bulk dwarfed me. "I will stand with you, Lady Gianna," he whispered.

"You said she tasted like the Moon," Romero told Gabel, "but she doesn't. She tastes like every other female."

"Mongrel!" I lashed out.

"Be quiet, female. Do not speak to me!"

Hix growled. Flint titled his head to indicate disapproval.

"She is not meant for you." Gabel's shoulders bunched with the effort of not pouncing on Romero and ripping his arms out of their sockets.

Romero held up his hands in a large, unapologetic shrug. "She's a female, Gabel, and I am a male."

"I have made it clear I do not tolerate this sort of behavior." Gabel's voice rattled the air.

"You demand too much and give us nothing but scraps in return! You *took* her for yourself but say we can't do the same!"

Gabel churned. The Bond was full of furious, confused

clots of emotion: anger, jealousy, violation, possession, fury. "You will apologize to Lady Gianna. On your knees. Beg her to excuse your actions. You will be stripped of all title and rank, but if she excuses your actions, I may let you keep your balls."

I tossed my hair. If Gabel was going to give me Romero's balls, I'd bronze them and wear them as a bracelet.

"Apologize for what? To her? You should apologize to us!" Romero pointed at Gabel.

"For what?" Gabel laughed at this absurdity.

Romero flung his arms out wide again, then paced back and forth, gesturing to the onlookers. "For what, our Alpha asks! He Marks her and brings her back here. She is weak, not beautiful, and a sorry example of a good mate. She does not respect her Alpha. She dares to come here and pretend she is worthy of training. She lets other males put their hands on her. She disobeys, she talks back, she fights with him and dares to question his authority. And he lets her! She demanded he give her teeth of worthless wolves because she thought they had died good deaths, and he did. She needs to be reminded of her place and be grateful to the males around her!"

Romero spat on the sand.

"And who was that mangy little wolf who dared come here and ask for visions? Gabel permitted that. He permitted that pathetic little wolf in this territory, this house!" Romero shouted, gesturing wildly. More than a few heads nodded. "Then he let her see the wolf alone! I would never let my woman be alone with another male. Never! She keeps secrets from him, and he tolerates this? He is supposed to be an Alpha."

Romero snarled to Gabel, "No more! I want an Alpha who is strong. Who lets us crush our enemies, show them who is mightier, stronger, better, not this Alpha who conquers like a human businessman. Once you let us put fear into them, now you don't hunger for blood. You're a lapdog who has forgotten what power and strength really are. It is just a matter of time before Gianna takes you to the groomers and has you nails painted and little bows put in your hair like a poodle!"

A number of heads nodded to Romero's wrath. The Iron-Moon was like no other pack. That's what they'd signed on for. Blood, glory, death, loot in the old style. Females used as weapons and commodities and breeding stock.

Gabel's grin suffused his face with dark glee.

I almost pitied the horrible end Romero was about to come to.

Gabel yanked off his kilt, flung it aside, and sprang at Romero.

His war-form was horrific. A thing from human nightmares. Oily, dark-grey-brown fur in shaggy patches over a dark, leathery hide, muscled limbs, eyes of burning yellow-blue, and a maw dripping acidic spittle between yellowed fangs the length of my fingers. His clawed feet tore up huge clods of dirt.

Romero screamed the challenge, and pale, ash-grey fur bloomed over him, his body swiftly reforming to meet Gabel's. The howl choked short as Gabel impacted him, and the two somersaulted head over head to the edge of the ring.

Gabel raised his right arm to strike, his claws yellowed bone, and snapped his arm down.

His claws cleaved into Romero's neck, piercing all the way through, the yellowed bone-tips peeking out the other side.

Gabel curled over Romero, maw open, spittle dripping onto Romero's shuddering face. Blood pooled under them and pulsed from around Gabel's claw tips. A clicking sound came from Gabel's throat.

"*Alpha.*" he growled in a tone that commanded me to drop to my knees. I remained on my feet, as did Flint, Hix bowed his shoulders, but many of the others dropped to the ground. Some were so frightened they shifted to wolf form and wriggled on their bellies, whining obedience.

It had been summoned like a beast from the Moon's darkest voids.

Romero gulped like a fish, gasping and dying by ounces and drops. Gabel's lips pulled back in a grin, and he twitched the hand holding Romero, eliciting some kind of gurgle of agony.

Gabel yanked his claw back. Blood surged out of the holes in Romero's neck, splattering the sand. Gabel got off him and walked toward me, yellow-blue eyes holding my gaze.

Alpha Gabel of IronMoon, with the form and fur of the Moon's monsters.

His fur melted away, his form shrinking as he walked. He swept low to retrieve his kilt as he passed it, then sashed it over his hips.

Hix did not look at Gabel and kept his head bowed, but I did not look away. I *couldn't.*

What are *you?*

"Clean that up when it is done dying," Gabel commanded the low-ranked warrior closest to my left. Then he turned to me, took my arm, and led me away.

THE NEW UNWRITTEN RULES

"Well, that was interesting."

"Interesting!" I exclaimed.

Gabel removed his much-abused kilt and tossed it in the general direction of the hamper. "What else could it have been?"

"A very bad ending."

"Buttercup, were you worried about me?"

I glared at him.

"You were worried." He came over to me and pulled me against him. "I am not sure if I should be insulted or flattered."

"You didn't notice some of the other wolves there *agreed* with him?" I tried not to look at the four deep, bloody rakes carved into his shoulder. He probably needed stitches but wouldn't get them. Just as easy to imagine them across his throat, and then Romero would have thrown me to the dregs.

Blood wept out of his shoulder, but he didn't notice it. "They are of no concern. Romero has been dealt with. He danced at the end of his line for a while, and I would have kept him there if not for you showing me how unwise that was."

Nauseating realization moved to the side as something

colder replaced it. I grabbed one of his hands and tried to pry him off me.

He held me firm. "Let me tell you about the vision, buttercup."

"Go on." I stopped trying to wrest myself free.

"You told me that the visions show the path we are currently on and the most likely outcome. I wasted my time squabbling over unimportant things with wolves who did not matter while the world turned. I ignored everything Flint taught me and lost my balls in the process to a similarly impotent wolf. Even when he shook off death to sing the queen's battle song, I didn't listen. I tried to silence him instead. A weak, foolish choice."

"Your question, your answer," I said warily. It didn't explain the souls I had wrapped around my neck, the runes I'd seen, or why Hix had looked on.

He lowered his face to mine, darkly amused. There was no tenderness in his tone. Just gentle mocking. "Well. Now I have heeded. What are you so afraid of, buttercup? I am alive, you are safe. I heeded the queen's song before it was too late."

I licked my dry lips. If that was how he saw it, then the future had changed. My guts crawled like they were full of ants. "I was there, too. Wearing a necklace of fangs. Thousands of fangs. A necklace of souls. Flint called *me* to war."

His handsome face broke out in a smile as bright as the setting sunlight from the jungle vision. His scent bloomed with hot pleasure. "Yes, I remembered you said that. It occurred to me when I chose this course of action."

I shivered. The vision had warned Gabel off his path, but it'd forged a harsher, crueler Gabel. Maybe one better suited to being King-Alpha. I yanked my brain to something less terrifying. "The IronMoon won't accept you and I."

Never in all of this had I considered that the IronMoon

would not accept me as Gabel's Luna. Gabel's hold over Iron-Moon was not as absolute and unquestioning as it seemed. For every wolf that was like Hix or Flint, there were half a dozen mongrels. Every pack had them, but IronMoon was *made* of them.

"I am the Alpha. You wear my Mark. That is all they need concern themselves with."

"You might have killed Romero, but you haven't defeated any of the problems this Mark has caused. You wanted a play-thing, well playtime is over."

Gabel's grip on me tightened to a soft, enjoyable pinch. The edge of his voice lay against my skin like a cool blade. "I don't need to concern myself with every wolf's individual complaints. Do not confuse me respecting my challengers with me being afraid of them."

"Even the ones not worthy of respect?"

"What you cannot plan for, you must be prepared for. You are an Oracle. You never truly know what you will see out on the Tides, but you are trained to manage. You and I are very alike."

He released me and looked down at the blood on his shoul-der. "Should I shower?"

I realized he had been holding me against him as filthy and bloody and smelly as he was. I hadn't even noticed, now I was grateful for the stench. "This is even a question? Yes, yes you should. Are you sure you don't want stitches in that?"

"You can bandage it for me. It is not so bad it will not close on its own, and if we send for the doctor, they will think Romero did real damage to me."

Blood smeared my shirt. Damage indeed.. I sighed and pulled it off. Perhaps if I soaked it in the sink I could salvage it.

"Buttercup, are you coming with me?" Gabel eyed me, a gleam sparkling in his eye, and a pulse of hot interest.

"I—I—no," I stammered as heat flushed my body, especially between my thighs, warmth washing down the Bond between us, and it suddenly constricted. "Just... I—Gabel, we can't..."

"Why not?" Half of Gabel's mouth curled in a taunting smile, cruel and predatory. I gulped as the Bond dilated and warmed, and it was impossible for my eyes not to be drawn to his swelling body. My resolve weakened more.

"You know why," I whispered, weak and faint. "Did you knock your head on a rock?"

"Come, buttercup. I'd like a real challenge." He held out a hand to me.

"What sort of challenge?"

"You, of course."

My knees turned to water. "It's not a challenge if you give in."

"I won't give in. You will. Romero's tongue was the last one on you. That will not do."

"I washed myself raw."

"That is not the same."

The Bond quivered, but there was a feral cruelty sliding between it as well. And pride, and possession, and jealousy, and ferocity, which all made my instincts sing with anticipation. Had Gabel devised a new way to play with the Bond that had bested him at every turn? I risked another glance at his swollen cock and licked my lips.

I reached up and slowly unhooked my bra, my eyes never leaving his. I threw it away, then pushed my skirt over my hips. The Bond snapped alert, and he took a step toward me.

I backed up. "No, you said you wouldn't give in."

The Bond smoldered and paced like a chained animal.

My fingers hooked over the edge of my panties. I gave a final thought to what I was doing, then pushed them down my hips and stepped out of them.

Gabel's lust and hunger howled, surging against the shackles of his will. But he took my wrist, his grip a little too rough, and pulled my after him into the bathroom.

He shoved me into the shower stall and turned on the water. Ice smashed into us. It didn't make a difference. He bit my shoulder hard enough to leave a mark, and I gasped. The water was so cold it hurt. Gabel's hands slid down my slick sides as he knelt in front of me, heedless of his torn shoulder. He kissed a trail along my ribs and belly as he slid onto the marble. I laughed at the heat of his lips, chasing the ice water away.

He kissed the inside of each thigh, the softest, most tender part.

"Gabel," I breathed his name.

"Patience."

I arched against the marble wall as his tongue slid over me, a single bright, hot spot in the water. My fingers tore at his hair. The Bond didn't have us in its clutches, but I didn't trust it wouldn't spring like a crazed beast. "You'll be in pain later."

"No, you'll just watch, buttercup. Now be silent, or I will figure out something to silence you with..."

NOT SO SIMPLE GESTURES

Romero didn't take long to die, and Flint supervised the cleaning up of the corpse and grooming of the sand ring. Dinner that night started as a subdued affair.

My guilty conscious prodded me. Romero had brought up the petitioner wolf, and Gabel not being privy to those meetings or questions. IronMoon had every reason to give that—and me— a hard look. It was also a question that was never going to go away until I made it go away.

Platinum picked at her dinner. Had Romero known that Oracles had vows of silence, or had Gardenia warned him that Gabel and I had argued in the hallway? She might have swung her allegiance to a different wolf once Gabel had stopped toying with her. She'd faded into the background. Tonight she seemed exceptionally wilted.

I felt wilted, too. No one was coming to save me. There was no escape. I couldn't seem to muster the willpower to repudiate Gabel, and IronMoon didn't want or trust me to be their Luna.

My expression must have telegraphed some of my thoughts, because Gabel's dinner fork tines hit his plate. I looked up at him, startled. His eyes shifted to Platinum, beyond my shoulder. His expression warned me, *that does not bear thinking about.*

"Have you given thought to a Second Beta?" Hix intruded on our silent exchange.

Gabel's tines hit the plate again. "I always have thoughts on such things. This is IronMoon."

Every wolf in the room chewed a little more quietly, and conversation dimmed to better enable eavesdropping.

Second Betas were pure warriors. The warrior's warrior. First Betas straddled the line between pack and warrior, able to step in for the Alpha. Second Betas concerned themselves with defense and combat. The First needed to be able to do the Second's job, but the reverse was not true.

"Do you have some suggestions?" Gabel asked Hix.

"A few."

"There is no stand-out in my mind for the job, and no one seemed to leap at the bone the second Romero dropped dead." Gabel glanced at the room with mild disappointment. "Perhaps trial by combat."

Hix grinned. "A good suggestion."

"Would trial by combat suit you, Gianna?" Gabel asked.

Hix sipped his drink as if asking me was a perfectly reasonable thing to do.

Gianna. Not *buttercup.*

Color crept onto my cheeks. Gabel involving me with the selection of the next Second Beta shocked more than just me. In a fashion, he had had to defend me that afternoon, when Romero had complained so bitterly about me, but he'd spun it as Romero violating pack law. Which was true. But if he'd wanted to *really* distance himself personally, he'd have asked Hix or Flint to be my champion.

I had no business being involved in the selection of a Beta. I might have his Mark, and the title of Lady, and I slept in his bed, but I'd been disrespected and insulted many times. I wasn't his BondMate. I was temporary. A dalliance. A toy. An amusement. Romero's biggest crime had been touching something that didn't belong to him.

Dammit, Gabel.

The press of sharp eyes into my back. Romero's allies would think I was presumptuous. I didn't want to give Gabel the direct answer he wanted. And I didn't want to act like I'd been scared into acting "proper." Romero was rotting in the woods, along with his stupidity, where it belonged.

I grasped for an answer that wouldn't suit Gabel. "As Master Flint says, Alpha, warriors *always* need to be prepared to prove themselves whenever and however is required."

Flint pounded both his fists into the table. "That is right, wolves!" He raised his drink. "A toast to being ready at any moment!"

A howl went up. Gabel gave me a sideways grin. I had dodged that one.

The atmosphere seemed much improved, and when the walls stopped quivering under the howls, conversation increased to the normal buzz.

Not that Flint supported the secret Gabel and I kept. But who wanted to get rumors started at dinner?

"Don't be angry, buttercup," he told me afterward, in the safety of our room.

"Don't be angry? Gabel, you just had Romero challenge you because of how you treat me. You *could* have delegated enforcing pack law to Flint or Hix, but you did it yourself! Tongues are going to be wagging enough as it is, and you ask *me* about the Second Beta?"

"I asked my Oracle."

"You called me by my name. You didn't even bother with that awful nickname."

"You are my buttercup."

"Where the hell did you get that pet name?" I scowled. "I don't want a pet name, and I don't want to be some damn flower."

He chortled. "I did it all to show the pack I don't care about Romero. He thought he could beat me and drum up support for a coup. He just wanted a legitimate excuse to growl at me because he was too much of a coward to do it plainly. That is how it is for males."

"I know how challenges work," I growled.

"Buttercup, it's not my first challenge. It won't be my last."

"Fine. But don't involve me in this any further," I told him.

"Of course you're involved. You'll be there for the trial."

"Take Platinum."

"You don't mean that."

"Maybe I do. You've done it before. You take her to the easy things, and I have to be there for blood and suffering. You want to call me buttercup, well her real name *is* a flower!"

Gabel dropped the book he was reading onto his chest. "Yes, that *wasn't* one of my better life choices."

That caught me off-guard, and I scrambled. "Presenting her to Anders instead of me? Suited me fine."

"Lies."

I glared at him, and almost spat something about since when had he cared about what I felt so long as I squirmed like a slug (or panted his name), but either he'd give me some answer that translated to *never have*, or he'd lay on a shocker that suddenly he did care. He didn't sound smug, either, just matter-of-fact. I considered saying I had been humiliated, but then he'd either apologize or not apologize, and either one was not what I wanted to hear.

I didn't know *what* I wanted to hear.

It made my stomach knot.

"Fine," I consented. "But remember. I'm not your Bond-Mate. I'm your Oracle."

"You are both."

"Not outside this room, doofus."

He grinned at me. "'Doofus'? Buttercup. The mouth on you. Tsk, tsk. Such language."

———

Hix and Gabel created a list of six wolves to compete for the Second Beta slot. Gabel insisted I be present for this conversation, which was absolutely not necessary for anyone but a Luna I growled my disapproval, but he refused to let it go. So I sat on the couch and ignored the conversation.

The challenge was set for that evening, in the training ring where Romero had met his end a day before.

"They're not given time to prepare?" I asked Gabel as we walked outside in the frigid late autumn evening. Lanterns danced in the trees. I had to give Gardenia credit: she had been charged with setting up the area appropriately, and she had done an amazing job on short notice. Paper lanterns in blue and pale moon-yellow danced in lines on the trees, there was a raised platform for the ranked wolves to observe from, and everything seemed to be like something out of a history book.

"You said they always needed to be ready. They were put on notice last night once we decided to do the trial."

"*You* decided," I hissed.

"I consulted my Oracle. She had the final vote."

"Then call me by my title, not my name," I reminded him in an angry whisper.

Most of the pack was already there, and all eyes were on us as we ascended to the platform to take our seats. I could practically hear their thoughts as eyes examined us to see how close

Gabel kept me at his side, if we moved together like lovers, if they could catch any scents that might give clues to the state of things between us.

"Alpha Gabel, Lady Gianna," Flint greeted us.

"Master of Arms, you are joining us this evening?" Gabel steadied my hand as I knelt on the cushion that served as a chair. I was freezing, and my pale skin seemed even more pale in the blue light of the lanterns.

"They are on their own before themselves and the Moon, Lady. I am observing the result of my training. I am on trial here, too."

Hix knelt down on my right side, and Flint took the place on Gabel's left. Gabel placed his hands on his knees, then raised one hand to signal the start. "Let the challenge for he who would be Second Beta, the warrior who speaks for all warriors, begin!"

Howls and stomps from the assembled crowds. A huge number of eyes gleamed in the dark. All the IronMoon from the surrounding area had made the trip for this.

Gabel had before him a small bowl with six stones. Each stone was a different color, and he drew two at random. The two warriors who had armbands of the corresponding colors stepped into the sand ring.

The point of these trials was not to fight to the death, or even serious injury. It was to force the other opponent to submit. Refusal to submit when one had obviously been bested was a significant mark against a wolf. Gabel, Hix or Flint could stop the match and determine the winner, and it was a loss of face for this to happen. A wolf who lost had to accept he lost.

When a wolf lost his stone was removed from the basket and thrown onto the ground before us.

"There is more to it than simply winning one round," Gabel told me as the third fight concluded. "A wolf has to win, but he has to have enough left to win the next round, and the next. It is not just blood and fur. It is strategy and knowing oneself as a warrior."

As far as I knew, Shadowless had trained its warriors in more practical terms. Not so much talk of honor and tradition and the old ways of doing things. Not all of the old ways were things I fancied, but the type of warriors Flint trained, and Gabel seemed to prefer, appealed to me. There was a weird sort of nobility to it all.

Gabel tossed two more stones to the ground, and now just two wolves were left. They were tired, exhausted, bloody and torn up, but still game to fight. The crowd cheered and howled for both of them.

"This is heart." Gabel held up the two stones between his fingers so the pack could see. They shook the sky with their howls, honoring the courage and heart of the warriors. "They are tired, bleeding and wounded. This last round is won on mental strength. The winner will be worthy to serve at my side as Second Beta!"

When it was over one wolf staggered to his feet to throw back his head and howl his victory to the Moon, while his vanquished opponent crawled to the edge of the ring. Then the winning wolf howled again to honor the wolf he had defeated.

Such was the custom.

Gabel threw the losing wolf's stone onto the ground, then tossed the winning wolf's stone at him to keep as a trinket of his victory.

The wolf shifted back to human form., One eye was already swollen shut, and blood crusted his face, but the stone lay clutched in his fist. In human form I recognized him: Eroth.

"Alpha Gabel," he said. "I greet you as Second Beta of Iron Moon."

Gabel rocked to his feet. He extended an open palm in my

direction. I stared at him like he was stupid. I was allowed to sit with him during this event, but I could not stand next to him to welcome the new Second Beta. So said tradition. Hix twitched, surprise rising off him like a mist, Flint's eyes warned me to be careful.

Gabel twitched his fingers impatiently.

The eyes in the dark turned to me like a swarm of fireflies, flickering with lantern light, and there was a hush.

What could I do? I couldn't refuse. I got to my feet but did not take Gabel's hand. I tried not to look as panicked as I felt standing before the whole of IronMoon at his side.

Gabel captured their attention with his voice. "Second Beta Eroth. Your victory is well earned. IronMoon Pack! Your new Second Beta. Greet him as he deserves!"

The IronMoon howl shook the sky, and nobody noticed my shaking.

HOW TO CATCH AN ALPHA

I dug out the four canines I had rescued from ill-earned disgrace. They had been buried in salt for long enough. I cupped them all in my palm, then transferred them to a small, velvet bag. Although I could discern the two pairs from the similarities between the teeth, it seemed more appropriate to keep them together. They had died together for the same reason and by the same fangs, so perhaps should stay together.

I placed the little bag with the rest of my tools. Maybe one day I'd have a use for them.

A sudden, hot, stabbing pain burst through my midsection.

I choked, clutched myself with one hand, and fell forward onto my runes, scattering them. My palm pressed into some of the runes. I panted, eyes wide. The pain receded a bit, just enough that I could squeeze out a few choking breaths. A hot twist yanked another gasp from me.

Calm, steady, calm.

My insides were so hot, but my body was so cold. I couldn't shiver. I needed to sweat, because I was burning inside along with the furious, stabbing pain all throughout my midsection, but my skin was cold stone.

Was this a bizarre vision? I had suffered pain before in my visions, but I wasn't in a vision.

Right?

The world wobbled within my mind for a terrifying moment. Where was I? Had I gotten lost on the Tides, and this —all of this—was an hallucination?

The pain within me ebbed, coalesced, and took the vague form of something I could understand and recognize.

Gabel.

Anger. Wherever he was, he was furiously, violently angry. And it had burst through the Bond with overwhelming force.

Air rushed into my lungs and helped cool the searing heat. A shiver coursed over my skin, sort of a strange relief. Just Gabel. Just Gabel's—

unholy

anger.

My insides felt seared, like they had been brushed with a light coating of acid. I stumbled a little going down the stairs and fought the urge to hold my belly as I went to his office. Flint had said there were symptoms that were obvious to those who knew. Me stumbling into his office clutching my belly saying I knew he had just busted a vein over something would have been a dead giveaway.

I tip-toed inside, expecting mayhem and carnage. Papers were scattered all around his desk, and shattered pencils lay in fragments on the floor. The room was full of the scent of his fury, and as I emerged from under the balcony that ran around the second level, I finally spotted him standing, stiff-backed and furious, in front of his map. His shirt struggled against the taut, clenched muscles of his shoulders and arms. His knuckles were raw and bleeding from whatever he had found to punch.

"Buttercup." His tone cut into me like a whip.

I made a small sound and backed up a step, reconsidering all my life choices. Especially the one to intrude on his anger.

"What are you doing here?"

"I... I came to see what has you so angry."

"Ah." His lips twisted. Annoyance. "I guess you would know, wouldn't you?"

"When you're this angry? Apparently." That's how it worked, or had he not figured that part out yet? I retreated to my usual couch.

"The SpringHide." Gabel growled at his map.

"SpringHide? Who are they? What kind of pack name is that?"

"Exactly." Gabel jabbed his finger at the tiny little section of map right smack in the middle of nowhere important. Gabel had taken my advice (if you could call it that) and turned his attention to the southeast of IronMoon. "I just called their Alpha. It was a brief conversation. He told me to fuck myself, and if I wanted his pack, I'd have to take it."

I frowned. "Gabel, you've had packs tell you to sod off before. Get over yourself."

He fumed and yanked himself away from the map to stalk over to me. "No. He's being stupid. That little pack? He doesn't have a chance against me, but now he has defied me, so I have to go myself, and I have to make a point. Make a point to a pack that can't even put up a good fight."

"You mean make an example of them," I corrected.

"Exactly."

"Some packs have pride." Shadowless hadn't had enough pride to even growl at Gabel. No, just line up all the females so he could select one he fancied.

"Pride, stupidity, which goes first? This Alpha practically dared me to come for him, and I'll have to lower myself to teach all the clever Alphas in that area to reconsider their own arrogance. What a waste of my time and their blood."

I worked my jaw. The MeatMan, perhaps. I stole a glance at the map, but there were no clues there; the MeatMan had been an Alpha of prestige and weight. The ruler of the little Spring-Hide couldn't be that Alpha. *SpringHide* sounded like something you'd name a herd of rabbits. "Do you think someone's been whispering in his ear?"

"Who would bother? The SpringHide are tiny. A speck. No value. They shouldn't be surprised I've finally gotten around to them." Gabel's voice was edged with venom and steel.

"So why bother with them at all?" I ventured.

"To feed the pack. The warriors are restless. They haven't had a proper fight since before Shadowless. Jermain didn't offer anything but his abject surrender, so I permitted nothing."

I tasted copper and bitterness.

"Romero often got to set the tone of things, but the thing about fear and cruelty is you have to do more and more of it. More blood, more death, more cruelty. If it is not necessary, it should not be used. Romero never understood that. He never wanted to. I despise wasting violence on packs like this."

He sat next to me. "Think about it, Gianna. We notice when the Moon is full, and when She is hidden. Ah, there is no moon tonight, ah, there is a full moon tonight. We pay little attention to waxing or waning crescents."

"Were you ever trained as an Oracle?" I asked, only half joking. The conversation about the Moon's many faces wasn't a new one, but I had rarely heard it spoken outside cleric circles. Given all the books on his shelves, it shouldn't have been a surprise, although it put me on my guard. Things could get twisted to justify anything.

"Of course not. As you well know I am male." He brushed my cheek with the back of his hand.

I withdrew from his impromptu caress. "That's what we're taught. The Moon can be dark and cruel, or bright and pure, but She is mostly everything in between. It's the visions of extremes that tend to stay with us, or the very strange ones."

"So you understand."

"Not really." I didn't understand Gabel's need to conquer or his ambitions. I just knew he had them, and he wasn't the stupid, mindless, violent, craven creature I had originally taken him for. It had been easy to despise him when I did not know him.

But the Moon loved Her Hounds. She had created them to serve a terrible but necessary purpose. She granted Oracles their gifts to serve a purpose.

I did not like where this led.

I understood Gabel Marking me for his amusement. I understood why he'd been cruel to me. This Gabel? The one who showed me his map, murmured his plans, answered my questions, confessed his frustrations? Now it seemed as though he intended to complete our mating.

Oh no. He wasn't going to trick me into thinking the Moon had a purpose for him, and all this was part of Her grand design.

If anyone was possible of spinning defeat into victory, it'd be Gabel.

Gabel pushed two fingers into the Mark on my arm. "Shadowless had its conflicts. You're no stranger to what warriors do or why they exist. Or does it just bother you that you aren't as bothered as you think you should be?"

I brushed his hand away and didn't answer. Gabel flashed a smug grin at me, then stalked back over to his map, anger rekindled after the brief diversion. He smoldered a few more moments. "I will have to go myself."

"You could send Hix."

"No. Now this requires my attention." He ran his hand over

his chin, slowly eyeing his map, and making whatever calculations a warrior makes when choosing their plan of attack. "There is something off about this, buttercup. Unless I'm starting to believe all the rumors about me. Shadowless should have put up a fight, but Jermain offered no resistance. This Alpha growled right away. He's an old dog, though, so perhaps he's growling over scraps."

My father hadn't even written me a letter.

Gabel clapped his hands together, and I jumped at the sudden sound, "If it is Alpha Gabel they are expecting, I shall not disappoint. And if they hope I no longer get my claws dirty..." Gabel grinned at me, and my blood ran cold, but my feral self panted eagerly. "Then they need an education."

He moved to go summon Hix and Eroth. I stood. "Gabel."

He stopped and raised his brows.

"Be careful."

"Buttercup, there you go. Worrying again. First you were jealous, and now you worry after me? What is a man to think?"

He laughed and continued on his way.

"That Alpha better not kill you before I have the chance to," I grumbled, although everything, including my very toes, tingled at his laughter.

HOW THINGS ARE SUPPOSED TO BE

G abel, having been challenged, wasted no time in leaving for SpringHide. There was no formal send-off for warriors. This was not glorious. It was clean-up duty. Just twenty of the IronMoon: a mix of newer wolves and reliable ones, with Gabel at the helm.

"Be careful," I warned him again as I stood on the brick stairs at the front of the house. Gabel stood one step below me, which put him at eye level.

"Did you see something, buttercup?"

"Not exactly. I just have an uncomfortable feeling. Don't get caught off-guard." I quelled my feeling of guilt, and bit my tongue before the Petitioner's vision escaped my mouth.

"You're lying, buttercup." He sniffed my neck.

"Don't ask me questions I can't answer," I whispered.

Gabel's brows drew together. He paused for a few breaths, then told me, "Romero is dead."

"His puppies aren't," I told him, meaning those who had agreed with him.

"Hix is here, and I've left him orders that you are his concern in my absence. If anyone gives you trouble, just use that charming wit of yours on them. You have your teeth in my thigh often enough I'm sure you can manage."

His attention and instincts were elsewhere. Either he was confident Hix could handle any trouble I might have, or he cared more about the hunt than me. Either way, he spun around on his heel and barked a command that it was time to go.

I watched the line of vehicles roll down the driveway. The cold winter wind tugged at my skirt, wrapping it around my ankles like a twining cat.

With Gabel gone it felt as though much of the turmoil had left my life. I hadn't realized what a source of confusion and conflict he was, even when he wasn't doing anything at all. The parasite between us squirmed incessantly.

I opted to spend time in deep mediation. While I couldn't ask the Moon specific questions about myself, I also didn't need a specific question to enter the Tides. Just deep meditation and letting the Tides carry an Oracle was an important part of an Oracle's work, and one I had been (understandably) neglecting.

Since I had no specific question, I chose *guidance* and *balance*, settled back on my heels, and welcomed the rush of the Tides.

~*~ *In Meditation* ~*~

A dark grotto. Water lapped against rocks. Purple darkness, the shine of the water, the matte velvet of the sky.

An unpleasant smell drifted from the darkness.

From behind me I heard the click of claws on stone. A wolf, ordinary tawny grey, although his shaggy coat carried a strange light around it that illuminated him but nothing else around him, padded next to me.

One of the RedWater wolves I had put down.

He wagged his tail once, twice, then pulled back his gums to reveal two missing canines before stepping ahead of me.

He led me deep into the grotto, deep enough the mouth disappeared and he was the only source of light, even though he illuminated nothing around him. The grotto could have been vast, or it could have been very tiny. There was no sound and no light, and only a hot breeze gave any sense of direction. The breeze itself had no scent.

The grotto opened up onto a burned-out house, illuminated by dim daylight, and the grotto behind me disappeared.

Everything in the house was ash and cinder. The place had been tossed as if someone had been looking for something before setting the whole thing on fire. Outside the broken windows were autumn woods, leaves thick on the ground, and the sky an overcast grey.

The house wasn't modern. The bed had been stuffed with straw, the furniture was all wood, and the window pane glass was the wavy, thickened type of something from long ago. Even the floor was rough-hewn and unpolished, and showed the scratches of many claws under the layer of ash and soot.

Someone had been looking for something, but they hadn't found it. The wolf wagged his tail to get my attention and led me across the rubble to a pile of debris. Together we dug through it until ash darkened us both, and we came up with a little metal box. Inside was a gold ring meant for a human woman's finger. It was a flat gold band, blasted sooty from -the fire, and inscribed with the entwined sigils for Luna and Mother. A pup-ring, the customary gift from an Alpha to his Luna to celebrate the birth of their first pup.

I studied the ring and its entwined symbols. The sigil for

Mother had been carved over and around the symbol for Luna—it had been added later. Not the proper order of things.

I turned the ring over in my fingers. On the inside of the band were three more runes: love, faith, and balance.

Directly under the Luna and Mother sigils was the same mark burned into the stone of the MeatMan vision.

No, the ring wasn't sooty from the fire. The ring had been blasted with that sigil, and it had somehow singed and charred the gold itself.

I put the ring down and pawed through more of the ash. The only other thing I found was a single piece of charred paper. On it was a single rune, somehow drawn in a waxy ink of many colors. The rune for Food. It could mean a successful hunt, a successful kill, but literally translated, it meant...

Meat.

Gabel and the warriors returned a few days later. One of the younger warriors had taken a bad bite to the thigh, but other than that, there weren't any real injuries.

I had greeted plenty of returning warriors before, but this was the first time I rounded up the house and had the howls sent up, and I wondered if it was at all appropriate for me to do. I wasn't the Luna, but Hix didn't seem inclined to do it.

A few of the wolves gave me a questioning look when I summoned them, and I agreed. Who the hell was I to be doing it? Presumptuous, little old me.

I didn't need a shovel; I seemed to be doing quite well digging myself into a hole with my own two paws.

It was customary that the Alpha congratulate the newly minted Beta on his first successful campaign, but Gabel only clapped Eroth on the shoulder as they came up the walk. Eroth

nodded, and as he passed me, inclined his head with a respectful, "Lady Gianna."

"Beta," I murmured back. Gabel brought a familiar sort of
hot turmoil, not unlike the air from my cave vision.

Gabel stood on the step below mine, his lips curled in a
frown. "It is done."

"No feting of the warriors?" Normally returning warriors
were given a fete at dinner, or if the victory had been note-
worthy enough, an entire party. Gabel didn't exactly seem in a
festive mood. I cursed asking the question. An Oracle wouldn't
have asked.

"No," Gabel muttered. "Nothing. It was worth nothing. Just
cleaning up."

He pointed at a few warriors carrying boxes into the house.
"Records from the SpringHide. Probably nothing there, but...
not now. There's no rush. Buttercup."

Only then did he take my wrist and lead me upstairs to
our room.

The Bond was glad to have him back, and it basked in his
return. It was a strange feeling of contented warmth, similar to
laying in front of a fire on a cold winter evening. One of my
favorite feelings in the world. I wasn't sure how I felt about
sharing it with the Bond

Gabel pulled off his shirt and his kilt. The lash marks on his
shoulders had ripped open and re-crusted with thick, black
blood. Gabel poked them with a fingertip.

"Don't do that," I said. It was creepy, gross, and it made the
cuts take longer to heal. "Did something go wrong at
SpringHide?"

"Not for us, but for that Alpha, something went
very wrong."

"Obviously, " I said, annoyed at his attitude. "We knew that
was going to happen."

"No, that's not what I meant. I meant the Alpha was surprised. They all seemed surprised when we fell onto the house. The Alpha, once I had my claws on him, said to me 'this isn't how it's supposed to be.'"

"Supposed to be like what?" I tilted my head to the side.

"I have no idea," Gabel said. "They were surprised, but not that I was there, just that something else was also supposed to happen that didn't."

My stomach started to churn. I licked my lips. "Are they all... dead?"

He shook his head, aggravated. "No. I confined the violence to the warriors. Some have to survive to spread my reputation."

Logically true, vaguely noble, and unsettling all at the same time. "What now?"

"Now I look through his records."

"For what?"

"Anything." Gabel shrugged. "You are very pale."

We were looking for the MeatMan. I could have put him onto the scent.

I licked my lips and swallowed the lump in my throat.

He cocked his head to the side. "It's late to try to convince me you don't have the stomach for this. You've invested in showing how much spine you have."

The ocean-blue eyes that looked at me were those of a predator, like we were two wolves that had met on a narrow mountain pass.

I could have told him I didn't have the spine for it, that I couldn't be a part of anything more with the IronMoon, that I was weak and fearful., and that I couldn't accept any of this.

Shadowless hadn't fought. Shadowless had decided sacrificing one daughter without asking the warriors to shed their blood for her was the logical course of action. My mind understood it. My heart didn't.

I raised my chin to him and shifted my shoulders back, assuming a posture of defiant courage.

I was still the only one who had any control and influence over Gabel, who was both his victim and the only one who could meaningfully harm him. It was too late for me to flinch now, even if he was taking me further and further into a dark grotto.

Gabel grinned. "I'll get changed for dinner, buttercup."

COMETS, SWORDS, SCISSORS, AND THE
ORACLES BOUND TO THEM

Mid-afternoon meant Flint would be in his rooms, at least for another twenty minutes. I hated to intrude, and but he was the only one in the pack who might know about the symbol on the underside of the ring, the same one blasted onto the stone. And he'd probably take the opportunity to give me a scolding if things were as obvious as Gabel seemed determined to make them.

Flint had quarters at the far end of the house on the first floor. After spending all day shouting orders and dealing with students, nobody blamed him for wanting a little peace and quiet to himself in his off time.

I knocked on the closed door. The house was always so damn quiet. Not just quiet, but empty.

A few moments, long enough that Flint had taken a second to decide if he actually would answer or not, and the door opened. He greeted me with surprise. "Lady Gianna."

"I'm sorry to intrude, but do you have a moment?"

"Always for you." Flint stepped aside.

Flint had a large front room with huge windows that over-looked the forest, then a narrow hallway off to the right, which led to the bathroom and bedroom. The front room was pale creams and tans with the occasional splash of bright red or green. It reminded me of classy Christmas decor. It suited him.

Flint was in a simple tee-shirt of heathered grey and a pair of jeans. I had never seen him in anything except a kilt, and now with just the tattoos on his forearms visible, he seemed like a different person to my eyes.

"Sit." He gestured to a chair. On the coffee table was an upside-down book. A cheesy mystery from the looks of it, with a well-worn spine. He caught me glancing at it and said, "Book roulette. I buy boxes of books for pennies at yard sales, flea markets, warehouses."

"You and Gabel are the same that way." Gabel seemed to read anything and everything, although I had never caught him reading a cheesy mystery.

Flint took a seat in a well-worn chair. "What can I do for you, Lady Gianna?"

"My name is Gianna, at least in private." I handed him a piece of paper on which I had sketched the unknown symbol from my vision. "Do you recognize this?"

"The paper or the drawing?"

"The drawing. I don't know that mark. I think I've seen it, but I can't place it. You know the old runes and sigils. I was hoping you'd be able to tell me what it is."

Flint turned the paper around, looking at it from each angle. His brow knitted together in ridges. Then he reached across the table and handed it back to me. "I know it. Where did you see it?"

"A few days ago, in a vision." I studied him carefully to see if there was any flicker of recognition, like this was something I was supposed to have found.

"An old rune. You'll see it on ancient shrines and talismans. It means 'comet.'"

"Comet. Those are the heralds of destruction in the old legends."

"For humans, too."

"But there's a rune for them?"

"I don't know if it's a rune that Oracles have ever used. I've only seen the sigil a few times, as I said."

He didn't seem to be playing coy. I frowned. "Of course a wolf wearing blue-gloss tattoos would know it."

He chuckled. "I'd hope so. The Comet was like you said. The symbol of the Moon's wrath, or Her vengeance. Moon and Mother always appear together, but the true greater meaning always depends on the other symbols present. It usually means destruction, sometimes literal, but often symbolic, like the Death card in Tarot."

"I didn't see the Moon rune." I shook my head. "I saw it on a pup-ring. The symbols for Luna and Mother were on top, then on the inside of the band, directly under those, was this symbol, blasted into the gold."

Flint leaned forward on his knees. "It was your vision, Gianna. The symbol for Luna and Moon are very close, of course. I doubt the Moon made a mistake if the symbol was Luna. Unless it was a literal ring you were looking at, and a mistake was made during the ring's manufacture."

"Or a conceit," I said.

"History has had its share of arrogant Alphas," Flint said.

"You seem to know more about what's going on here than you'd like me to know."

"I've known Gabel longer than you, and I am the Moon's Servant, no different from you," he said. "And I'm old enough to be your father. Conceit of age and seniority."

I sighed, but he didn't seem to be lying about any of that. "A Moon's Servant."

"A Moon's Servant. But that's obvious, isn't it?" He gestured to his tattoos.

Obvious? Maybe, but the tattoos were a mystery. I set it aside. He wasn't going to tell me where those blue-gloss tattoos had come from. "Flint, why the Comet? There's already a rune for destruction."

"The Comet is different. The Comet is the instrument of Her wrath. She sends the Comet to end what has offended Her. That's why the other runes are important ,so we know if it's Her blight, wiping something from view, or shattering something so something new can be built from what's left."

I folded the paper a few more times until it wouldn't bend further. "On the ring there was *faith, love,* and *balance. Mother* was present, but had been added later. It wasn't part of the original ring."

"Then are you sure it was a pup-ring?" Flint raised his brows.

"Then why add *mother* at all? Why not just have a proper pup-ring?"

"Perhaps there wasn't the ability to craft a second ring," Flint said.

I saw his meaning right away. So to honor his Luna, the Alpha had taken an existing ring from a happier time, and had the Mother symbol added later. A pre-Comet time, perhaps?

Flint's green eyes clouded. "Perhaps she died with an unborn pup, and he added it to a promise ring. Did you find it on a body?"

"No, in a mangled metal box."

"A trinket, then. A memento."

Whatever this ring and rune were, Flint was as bewildered as I was. "But why have it marked with *comet*?"

"It doesn't sound like the original maker is the one who

marked it. You said the *comet* had been blasted into the ring."

"But *comet* was original. The ring was charred," I said, increasingly frustrated, "but *mother* wasn't. It was added after *comet.*"

"It was your vision, Gianna. I am not an Oracle."

"Yes, but you've got your Service inked onto your shoulder."

Flint favored me with a little grin. "*Comet* was little-used even a thousand years ago. I think it was treated as bad luck to even suggest the Comet, and most chose to use *destruction* instead. What's the difference to a common man who is hungry when his fields are ash?"

I tucked the paper into my pocket.

"When will you two tell the pack?" Flint asked.

"Why ask?" I couldn't keep the sharp tone out of my voice. I hadn't come down here to talk to him about Gabel and I, and I didn't appreciate him shoving his snout into my business.

"We've had this conversation."

"And I don't see how it's your business," I snapped.

"This is a poorly kept secret. Why are you so resistant? He seems comfortable enough."

"I don't trust him."

"He was cruel to you in the beginning," Flint agreed. "Baiting you with Gardenia was petty. The matter with Alpha Anders was too far."

"*Baiting* me with Gardenia. I do not care what he did with Gardenia—"

"Yes, you do."

I snorted. "I don't want to care, so I am determined to not care."

"I am not making excuses for what he did," Flint said quite seriously, "but you should know Gabel has only ever tolerated Gardenia and her ambitions in this pack. She's only here for Cook's sake."

"You think it makes a difference what he did versus what he tried to convince me he did?" My throat tightened and felt thicker, and the Bond whimpered. "Baited me or actually did it, he just wanted to torment me. And that matter with Anders? He humiliated me to the whole, damn world. At the time I just knew him to be a disrespectful monster. Now I know he's something else, and it just makes what he did back then much worse. It was all beneath him!"

Flint wove his fingers together and his strong shoulders shifted forward, heavy with what I had just said. "You're worried you can't trust him. That you don't know his true face. He's shown you two different ones. Which one is the real one. That's the problem, isn't it?"

"It's one of the problems."

"Gabel is no gentle soul," Flint said. "Neither was Romero. Romero was weakness. A small, weak, petty excuse for a wolf, who saw violence as entertainment, not a tool. It's easy to be that way. It's intoxicating. It takes discipline to control all that into a weapon, and to understand the power it can be. The lump of steel versus the sword. A lump of steel will kill you, but it can also be a paperweight. A sword will kill you, its design and purpose is combat. It's difficult to make a sword and easy to break one through carelessness, laziness, or just throwing it back into the fire to melt. A good sword will last generations and be an object of terror and respect. Most steel will never be a sword. Most swords will invariably be ruined. All that are used will require the occasional repair, some more repair than others depending on how badly handled they are, and how lazy the wielder is."

"And how do you repair a sword?" I asked warily.

"There are many methods, but it usually involves a very hot forge and a very heavy hammer." Flint got to his feet and escorted me to the door. "You know the fastest way to dull a pair of scissors, yes?"

"No, I don't. What is it? Rock?" *Rock, paper, scissors,* and all.

He smiled and shook his head. "Cutting paper."

"Cutting paper?" I thought of how easily scissors minced through paper, even a long line of wrapping paper.

He pulled the door open. "Good afternoon, Lady Gianna. I hope I was of some help."

BOG, RIVER, THICKET

"I want to help."

Gabel waved the papers clutched in his hands at the boxes and crates. It looked like preparation for a lawsuit or a criminal investigation. Several wolves helped sort through things. "Pick a box."

"No, I'm looking for something else." I was on the hunt for MeatMan or MeatTaker's scent.

"What would that be?"

I ignored him and shrugged off my cardigan.

"Well, that is not the help I was expecting." He tossed down the papers. "You're not usually so aggressive, buttercup. I will hardly deny you if you—"

Yikes!

"I need to be in wolf-form!" I scurried up the stairs to the second floor of the office and pressed myself back into a little alcove between bookshelves. "Don't look!"

I felt how hard he had to fight to not charge up there and—

But, I wanted him to look, or the Bond did, and—

"Buttercup," He growled from downstairs

"Being naked isn't always about sex," I reminded him. "Remember what you told me about modesty."

I shimmied out of my clothing and into my wolf's-fur in a matter of moments, then trotted back down the steps to the main floor.

In this form Gabel was far more vivid, his scent telling me a thousand things about him. His usual, peculiar scent of ash and burning. Just little things, aside from the big thing of sexual provocation. The scent of scabbed blood from his shoulder, soap, shaving cream, his clothing, the laundry detergent, the faint scent of other wolves picked up from moving around the pack. All familiar and normal, just... I wasn't used to his scent being so intimate and close.

I spent the next two hours carefully sniffing every damn item in those boxes, but there was nothing. So I tried to imprint every unique wolf scent I picked up into my memory. Who knew? Perhaps I might brush up against a wolf in a place I wouldn't expect to find them, and it would provide a clue.

I was perilously close to breaking my vow of silence. Perilously. I needed to find MeatTaker or MeatMan, and then figure out how to put Gabel onto the scent.

"What were you looking for, buttercup?" Gabel asked as I descended the stairs, dressed as a human again.

"I don't know. Something familiar, I guess. But it wasn't there."

"There doesn't appear to be *anything* here." Gabel tossed aside a wad of papers. "Just ten years' worth of electric bills."

The door to the office opened. Hix, another warrior wolf, and Donovan. The Hunter gave me a quick, sharp look, then a cunning smirk.

"What have you brought, Hunter?" Gabel asked.

"Word of the prey," Donovan replied. "Followed the branded wolves just as you ordered. They tried to cover their tracks, but they're not good at it. They headed straight for RedWater, but only the edge. They stopped at a bar and a RedWater showed up to send them on their way."

"Do you think they had a connection there?" I asked.

"No, but I find it unusual the RedWater gave them safe passage and didn't kill them. IronMoon is not very popular in RedWater right now. Not that we ever were." He grinned.

Gabel's eyes narrowed. "And where did they go from there?"

Donovan's grin widened a notch. "IceMaw."

"IceMaw," I blurted.

Gabel stroked his chin. "Who did they meet there?"

"Again, no one. The IceMaw showed up almost instantly, marched them to the eastern border, and told them to keep going."

The only things to the east of IceMaw were the other, small packs Gabel was currently annexing, like SpringHide. Alpha Aaron of IceMaw had, more or less, sent them home.

Donovan shrugged. "The IceMaw Hunters are experts. I couldn't follow the trail closely. I can pick them back up again if you like but figured this would be of interest to you. They were shuffled from RedWater and IceMaw, yes, but they were not wandering. They were knocking on doors they had expected would be opened to them."

"Do the IceMaw have dealings with the SableFur?" Hix asked nobody in particular.

"The SableFur don't deal with anyone but themselves," I said. "I trained in SableFur. They're large, wealthy, and even have three Oracles."

"You spent time in SableFur?" Gabel asked.

I gave him a look like he was dumb. "All Oracles in this part of the world finish their training at SableFur. I didn't train close to the heart. I've lived in a few packs for training but finished in

SableFur. Aaron sent them on their way. Does Aaron deal with GleamingFang?"

"Hmmm." Gabel murmured.

Donovan said, "IceMaw has a direct path into SableFur through their southern pass, true, and does have dealings with GleamingFang, but SableFur is still on their side of things. Nothing that happens between IceMaw and SableFur doesn't also happen between GleamingFang and SableFur. Or GleamingFang and IceMaw. All the motions of those scouts are exactly the same, except for the increased northern patrols along the Shadowless ridgeline."

Gabel's hand stole a caress across the small of my back. I jumped. Donovan noted it with a sharp look. Not hostile. Sizing me up, reevaluating who I was in the order of IronMoon.

I wanted to tell him if he figured it out, he should share, because I had no idea.

Was the Bond slowly gnawing at my resistance? Was I just so tired I was slipping beneath the waves and didn't realize it?

Was it something else I dare not name?

Or was it just a glorious trap from Gabel, leading me to believe there was no fight left to have, that he had succumbed and drifted beneath the waves, and he'd burst from below and gulp me down at the final minute?

Because I could see him hitting me from below like a shark gobbling up an unsuspecting seal.

I didn't intend to die a seal.

Did Donovan see it? Did he smell it all those symptoms Flint swore betrayed Gabel and I? True hunters were so sharp.

Stop worrying about the hunter, Gianna. He'll see you're worried and then start looking for clues.

Gabel's hand slid across the small of my back once more.

I jumped, eyes widening, Hix caught the movement and reached for me before realizing I wasn't about to fall over. My cheeks burned with mortification and anxiety and pleasure. Gabel's hand was warm and strong across my back, and so, so pleasant. I wanted to just arch my back and purr like a silly kitten, even as Donovan stared at us.

"Can you go back?" Gabel asked the hunter.

"I can easily find their trail."

"No. IceMaw."

"Aaron's Hunters are sharp. Sharp as me. They caught my scent. No one is going to stay there as a spy without them knowing. Aaron has hunters and scouts all over his northern edges. You want me to pick up the wolves' trail again and see where they're going?"

"I'm sure I don't care at this point."

I bit my lower lip. The MeatMan might be very interested to find these wolves.

Gabel left my side to go to his desk. He opened one of the innumerable small drawers and pulled out a roll of bills secured with an elastic band. He threw it to the hunter. "Your payment. The women aren't on the menu. Go into town and pay for it if that's what you're after, but you know my feelings on it."

"Haven't forgotten." Donovan held up the little roll between two fingers. He brought it to his lips like it was a cigarette, and grinned. "Thank you, Alpha. *Lady* Gianna."

Gabel returned to me, and his hand on my back did as well. "The IceMaw."

He said this as if he didn't still have his arm around me, and his hand on my back, fingertips just a few inches from my rump, and there weren't still three wolves pawing through records and trying very hard to pretend like they weren't seeing anything. Or hearing it.

Was Gabel trying to sow the seeds of rumors? Or was he just oblivious to how he was acting, and he couldn't help it, like Flint had warned me?

"I know nothing about them," I said.

"I know very little. It is time to find out some more."

"Gabel, I told you. I'm not a security camera."

"Of course you aren't, buttercup. I meant old-fashioned spies and research. I don't have a specific question for the Moon anyway. Not on the IceMaw, at least." He caressed my cheek.

I wanted to believe him so badly it hurt. The Bond wanted to believe, and by now, the damn thing had slid its tentacles into every part of me. Those tentacles implored me to believe everything would be fine. Because love conquered all, and the Bond was sacred, and the Moon would not let anything happen. Have faith. Right? In movies and fairy tales, supposedly.

"I'll leave you to that, then." I looked at the boxes and saw the three wolves looking at us before snapping back to their work.

Crap.

"What I was looking for wasn't here anyway." I slipped out of his grasp. He tried to hold me for a moment, then released me. "I'll see you at dinner, Gabel."

By the time dinner rolled around, Donovan was scrubbed clean, his beard and hair trimmed, and even the dirt under his fingernails had disappeared. In jeans and an old flannel and workboots, he had plans to go twenty miles into town later that evening to spend his earnings. He was a member of IronMoon but rarely about, as Gabel had him in the field hunting and scouting prey.

Wolf or deer, Donovan didn't question and didn't care.

He was thin, not so tall, and except when he spoke, he was unremarkable. The sort of man who melted into his surroundings. Nobody noticed him. His voice had an educated timbre, though, and he spoke as a very learned man. He enjoyed ancient Greek tragedies, apparently.

Even though he told Hix, Eroth, Gabel and myself of what

he had seen in the south, I couldn't shake the feeling he watched Gabel and I for clues. I listened carefully, hoping he'd tell me something that would lead me to the MeatMan and MeatTaker. Even if he did tell me something, I still didn't know if I could tell Gabel. Would that be a betrayal of trust?

Oracles are supposed to forget the answers and the questions. We're not supposed to get cluttered up with other people's concerns. Like the visions in the bowl: there, then gone. On to the next one. Their question, their answer, not our concern.

But it had been my concern. It had started in my forest, with the RedWater wolves I had put down around me, and now I had had a subsequent vision with the specter of one of the RedWaters leading me to a many-color drawing of the Food rune.

Gabel, the two Betas, and a few of the other senior wolves went to talk after dinner. Gabel did not invite me, but if I had wanted to attend, I could have. Instead, I went on to bed.

~*~ *Dreaming* ~*~

The road was wide enough for a car. There were two tracks of dirt and a strip of grass running between. The road dipped and bobbed over the spine of a tall hill, affording me a view of the countryside on either side: trees in autumn colors, beautiful, silvery-grey morning sky, and little dots of buildings.

I was in human form with the two RedWater wolves, walking into town.

Their tails wagged. Each one was missing their canines, and their fur glowed with the luminescence I had seen in the grotto vision. A light that did not touch anything else around it, and seemed trapped within the shafts of their fur.

We came to a blind hill, and as we crested the top, the road stretched out flat and split three ways. The horizon suddenly became obscured by mist and low-hanging autumn clouds. One road led to a raspberry thicket so thick it would blot out all the sunlight. One road led to a thick, churning river dotted with a pattern of huge rocks. The third to a thick mud pit with a surface pocked by gurgles of air from below.

I tried to step off the side of the road to go across a hay field, but green mist obscured my vision. The wolves whined and herded me back to the road.

No going off the path. No way around. It was forward or back.

I inspected each option. The raspberry thicket was too dense to see through, and the thorns sliced my skin at the slightest touch. The rushing river thundered, but there were rocks that might have formed a series of jumps to the other side. My feet sank an inch or two into the muck, and the smaller RedWater wolves sank even more. There was nothing to grab onto if things went badly during the crossing.

All these choices seemed terrible. The wolves agreed.

I turned and walked back to the main road, determined to go back the other way and see what lay beyond where we had started.

My father stood in the middle of the road, and beyond him, the road had turned into a busy, old-time looking village of narrow, wood houses with orange firelight and gas lanterns illuminating thick-paned windows. Some of the human-form wolves who passed by us frowned at me in disapproval and hurried away, shielding themselves from the sight of me.

My father stood with his arms folded and his ankles spread,

staring at me with a stern expression, one I remembered from childhood. "There is no place for you here."

"Why? What have I done?" I frowned, not understanding my banishment from the town.

He pointed with three fingers to the three paths. "Go."

"There's no way through any of those."

"There is no place for you here." He frowned at my defiance.

"May I at least pass through to the other side?" I asked.

"No."

I resisted, not convinced I should do what my dream Father wanted me to do. There were tricks and tests in dreams. He had no authority over me. I looked past him, trying to spot a quick path through the village. If I shifted and bolted, I might be able to outrun the human-form wolves, who would need to squirm and wriggle out of their clothing.

Oh, I was naked.

That might explain the looks and disapproval.

"I'll put clothes on," I offered.

"We've burned them." My father grabbed me with both hands, his strength crushing my arms, splitting my flesh down to the bone, and he flung me backward into the dirt. My head snapped against a rock and red brambles cracked my vision.

"Donovan makes you nervous. Or are you just reading survival books for dinner conversation?"

I was doing reading on getting through thickets, across rivers, and across bogs of sucking mud. Understanding the real-world mechanics and connotations of whatever I saw in visions helped me understand the Moon's point. It also meant I acquired a large array of random and obscure knowledge.

"I had a dream last night," I told him. "Although yes, he makes me nervous."

"Why?"

"He was watching us. You are careless." I rubbed the back of my head where it had cracked against the dream rock. I obviously wasn't injured, but vivid dreams left an impression for a day or two.

"Careless?"

"You making me stand at your side for Eroth's victory, you putting your arm around me yesterday," I reminded him. I closed the book and put it back on the shelf, then went over to the balcony edge, gripped the railing, and leaned down to speak to him.

He stood in the center of the lower floor, arms akimbo. "He wasn't here for the victory, and you think he would care about me touching you?"

"That's not the point, Gabel. The point is you're careless. Donovan is a hunter, and they don't miss even the slightest things on a trail. All it will take is one innocent comment from him, and it'll put the whole pack on our scent."

Gabel frowned with thought.

"This is where you have some witty comment about playing with your prey."

"Are you sure you're not just feeling a little... paranoid? We notice things when we're aware of them."

"I have visions, not hallucinations."

"But Donovan was not here for Eroth, so I don't know why—"

"Flint figured it out," I interrupted Gabel. "He confronted me with it."

He titled his head with a sharp jerk to an inquiring angle. "Did he drag this out of you after he walked in on us?"

"I wish. When he caught us he took me aside to warn me

the symptoms are obvious, and it's a secret that won't keep. If Flint figured it out right away, you don't think a true hunter isn't going to piece it together in a matter of minutes?" My voice bordered on panic. I wasn't ready for whatever Gabel was going to say. I wasn't ready for all this to come apart.

Gabel didn't move or speak.

"Oh, by the Moon," I breathed. "You thought you had it under control. You really thought you were doing a wonderful job."

I gripped the railing, quivering from all the emotions clotting up within me. There was absolutely nothing Gabel could or would say that would bring me any comfort.

"Not exactly," Gabel finally said. "Don't look so ashen. I'm afraid you will faint and fall right over that railing."

"I'm not capable of such maidenly dramatics."

He broke from his position and headed for the stairs.

"Stay down there, Gabel. Don't come up here." I didn't want him anywhere near me. I didn't trust myself right then, feeling through the tangle of emotions, because the Bond was the most real, tenuous thing right then, and if Gabel was anywhere near me, I knew what would happen. I knew what I'd grab onto just to have something in the storm.

"My office, buttercup. I'll go where I want."

I backed up away from him as he approached.

"We'll just go in circles, buttercup." He gestured to the wrap-around balcony. "Stand still so I can talk to you."

"I don't want to talk."

"I'm not asking you to talk. I'm talking, you can listen. Then we trade. That's how it goes."

I didn't want to do that either, but I put my back to the wall of books and eyed him, steeled for whatever had to say.

Gabel's presence felt huge, looming over me, hot like the air from that grotto, inescapable. The Bond howled and struggled like a beast against its chains, surging forward, and I had a glimpse of what he had been fighting.

He didn't want to have this conversation anymore than I did. Small comforts.

"I'm not unaware of what I've been doing."

UNCERTAIN DESIRES

My whole body stiffened. My heart muscle included, so tight it could barely pump blood through my body.

His body was as tight as mine, his hands curled into fists, his jaw clenched. Anger, frustration, and raw intensity coursed through him.

This wasn't a conversation he had been expecting to have. This was not a time and place of his choosing.

A cornered Gabel was a dangerous man.

His whole body moved with one slow, careful breath.

"I know what I've been doing." Steel threads laced through his voice.

"Then why have you been doing it? You know what will happen. Your pack—"

"*Our* pack."

I breathed in through my nose. Yes. I was an IronMoon now, by right of Marking, by right of conquest, by right of kidnapping, by right of the Shadowless throwing me away, by right of tribute. Whatever method anyone cared to invoke, I was an IronMoon. "*Our* pack will expect the vows. They still think this was all serious. You and I are the only ones who know what really happened, and why you really Marked me."

The sour feelings bubbled up from within me, and I contain them before they leached into the Bond and mixed with his intensity.

"So is that it?" I pressed, not caring, not afraid of him. What could he do to me that he hadn't already done? Punish my flesh? There was so much worse than that. "You're just doing this to prove you can? That the pack can't make you do anything, and fuck expectations, you are Alpha Gabel of Iron Moon?"

"I have always told you the pleasure in any challenge is the risk of failure. It's not a challenge if you might not succeed."

"Gabel, I swear by the Moon, I am done with your games, and I'll castrate you in your sleep tonight if you don't speak plain."

He twitched. "Buttercup, you're so fierce under that pretty exterior of yours."

"Want a demonstration? Drop the pants." I snapped my teeth together.

"You are also so distracting. I thought you wanted to talk about a different kind of antics. But if—" he reached for the button of his pants.

I smacked his hands. "Stop it! It's not about sex. That's the Bond whispering in your ear, and you don't even realize it."

"I do know where I stop and the Bond begins," Gabel retorted.

"Then act like it."

"I am. Am I not allowed to contemplate if this is something I want?"

"Not without asking me first!" I screamed. "Not without asking me what I want!"

Gabel backed up two quick steps.

Anger poured through me, burned me, tears choked my throat, my heart twisted, and the Bond shrieked and writhed.

"Everything has been about what you want." The words bubbled with tears and mingled with the deep well of pain I had tried to bury. "You have not asked me one time what I want. Now you've decided you want to take those vows after all? Did you expect I'd swoon into your arms? The ends don't justify the means, so don't think just because the Mark didn't fester, and the Bond is alive, it makes what you've done acceptable. Where in this do I get to say I don't want to take them? Where do you even ask me what I want? Or do you assume because I'm the female I'd want to?"

Tears poured down my cheeks. The Bond wept and moaned, swinging back and forth like a hammock in a storm.

I'm sorry seemed like such a pathetic offering. A penny thrown into an empty fountain.

"I *hate* you!" I shouted. "I hate you! I hate myself for wanting you! I hate myself for what you did to me, what the Moon made me for, to fit into your soul like some fucking puzzle piece! I hate all of this, and I hate *you!*"

You want to hate me.

But he was smart enough not to say it.

I stood breathing hard, exhausted and spent, and grieving.

I *wanted* to hate him, and I *did* hate him.

Just not enough.

There wasn't a single thing I wanted to hear. Nothing that could ever be said could ever make this better.

Gabel asked me the question I dreaded most: "What do you want, Gianna?"

"I don't know anymore."

At first it had been easy: free myself.

He'd made it so easy at first to despise him.

Then it had become so complicated. It became so complicated as it seemed the monster he was was a form he assumed to serve some purpose. Was he a Hound? The Moon loved Her Hounds.

Was I in love with this four-form werewolf? What was I, then?

His resolve reached me through the storm of the Bond, the conviction and steel nerves required for him to confess: "Neither am I."

I pressed myself back against the books, but there was no escaping him. He clasped my cheeks in both of his hands, his face very close to mine, his body pressed against mine. The Bond sighed at how all our curves and angles fit together. How his touch on my skin was exactly what I craved, what made me feel most alive and most complete.

And still he could slip into that fourth form of his and mangle me worse than he ever had before.

"Then we should each figure it out, buttercup," Gabel whispered to me, "because I know time is against us. Hix suspects, Flint already knows, Donovan, if you're right, will spot it. I know what I've done. I've planted the seeds. It won't take much before they take take root."

"You think I can forget what you've done to me?" I whispered.

"If you told me you had, I would not believe you. Then you would not be Gianna. I would ask you where she is on the Tides, and I would go to find her myself. She and I have unfinished business."

"You would never find me if I were lost."

"I was arrogant enough to play with the MateBond," Gabel said. "I am arrogant enough to howl at the Moon to let me onto the Tides, and foolish enough to wade right in to find you."

I laughed weakly. "Gabel, I think that passes for romance in your mind."

"If it is roses and sonnets you are looking for, I'd need Flint to be my Cyrano."

"Roxanne was an idiot to be seduced by pretty words."

He smiled at me, that predatory light in his sea-blue eyes.

It would have been easy to be seduced by him, and to believe everything the Bond whispered to me. The Bond wanted to survive. It needed me to believe everything it said.

"May I kiss you?" He asked.

He asked, and he expected me to say yes.

"Only ever ask once," I told him, not liking him so well if he was going to suddenly start asking permission to breathe just to prove he could be coerced into proper behavior.

"Now I have asked. Remember how you answered."

His lips against mine seared my skin like salt water cleaning a wound. My fingernails dug into the back of his strong neck, his tongue entwined with mine.

It was different, not fighting the Bond, although it tugged against its lead, urging us onward.

His hands slid down my neck, over my breasts, lifting them, caressing, then slid lower to my hips, over my curves, to my rump.

I tugged free of him, breathing hard. "Gabel, stop."

"Why?" His fingers tightened.

Good question. Oh, yes, I had a good answer. "We can't get caught."

"I'll go lock the office door. Stay right here."

"No, Gabel, you think they're stupid? You hate being cornered, why do it to yourself? It's the Bond goading you—"

"Goading both of us." He kissed my throat.

That was true. I breathed out as his lips tasted my neck, his hands sliding under my skirt to grasp my flesh, skin on skin. "Not now," I breathed, voice hoarse. "Not now, Gabel. Later."

Later sounded better than someone storming in here and

catching us in the act. Or this office reeking of sex and desire, and this whole conversation about not knowing what we wanted being moot. I was the female. If Flint was right, I needed to be the voice of ahem... moderation. "Later," I told him again. "Go back downstairs, Gabel. We both have work to do."

"Later, buttercup. When only the Moon will see. Since it is no secret to Her what is between us."

IF WE HAD A SHOVEL...

The moon was almost full that night. Gabel and I stood in the courtyard after dinner.

"Almost a Solstice moon." I said. We were about a month away from true winter, although the air was already crisp and skin-burning cold. Snow was on the wind. Not much, and the sky was still mostly clear. Just a few strands of clouds that preceded the incoming front.

In the cold air Gardenia's perfume stood out like a sore thumb. She watched us from the kitchen window, where she helped Cook clean up the remains of dinner. The windows were cracked just a tad because the kitchen was a sweat house any time of the year. It gave her the perfect vantage point to spy on us, and the perfect excuse as to why she'd be within line of sight at all.

We moved deeper into the courtyard.

I tried to figure out how to ask what I wanted without sounding like I was being jealous or territorial. "Has she always been so... ambitious?"

"Yes," Gabel answered.

I reminded myself to not care. I would not get jealous. "Does she have any reason to think she'll ever get anywhere?"

"No."

"I meant more than you've already led her to believe." The sour words got out before I could stifle them.

There were moments when Gabel became like a dark centrifuge, and his emotions whirled away from the center as he spun them around, then let them settle back down. A pause while he chose his words. "I never told her anything except there would never be anything between us."

I stopped walking. "What? How does that work?"

"Gardenia has always been the way she is."

It all made sense, now that I knew Gabel better. I whispered, appalled, "You just let me believe it. You just let me fill in the blanks. Did you sneak into her room and dab yourself with her perfume, too? Don't answer that. I don't want to know. But just tell me one thing, Gabel. How did Anders happen if all the rest of it was just supposed to be a shitty, cruel illusion."

He had baited me. Laid a trap and I had walked right on in, fed my anxieties and suspicions. He'd toyed with me like I was some cat and he had tied tin cans to my tail. "You needed Gardenia to play along for Anders. How did you do that if you didn't lie to her?"

Gabel looked at me from the corner of his eye, wary that I might claw that same eye out at any moment. "I told her she would be on my arm for the meeting. I didn't explain, and she didn't ask. I was expecting you to fight and demand to take her place."

"Fight for you? Because you'd rather have had the company of that tramp? Never. If you want to slum, Gabel, you go right on and slum!"

"As I told you some time ago, not one of my finer moments."

I gnashed my teeth together. The Bond flailed, gagging on

my emotions. I almost bolted into the forests, wanting to crash through the woods and run away from all of this.

But there was nowhere to run. My violent death would likely kill him. It'd certainly cripple him for a time. His enemies would love to possess me for that reason alone.

I growled, "Is that when you realized you were no better than Romero? Just some common would-be king acting like every other petty tyrant in history? Some rusty old blade that still thinks it can cut down armies?"

He held very still under the Moon's light, the blue of his eyes illuminated by Her silvery gaze.

I ground it a little deeper. "Hix apologized to me for your behavior. A Beta apologizing for his Alpha's shitty behavior. You must be very proud of yourself."

A dark cauldron of emotions from him, stewing. Good. Somewhere in there was anger at himself, embarrassment, discomfort. No apology for me, but I'd take the shame and anger he felt. He had fallen into his own stupid trap.

He said, "I'm not. But you're right about being like Romero. It had all become too easy. I even told you that in the beginning.

"You were supposed to fight Gardenia. That's what I thought you'd do. Instead I had to go through with the whole, disgusting charade." He eyed me all over to make sure I wasn't holding any hidden weapons. "And then, yes, I took you on the hunt. And you challenged me there as well, and then again at dinner. I had underestimated you. A mistake I was stupid enough to make twice, and fortunate enough to survive. I will never make that mistake again."

The well of hurt inside of me didn't go away, and it probably never would completely disappear. I didn't want an apology. *I'm sorry* didn't touch what Gabel had done. *I'm sorry* is what children said to each other. But while I sensed many things from

Gabel—regret, disappointment, shame, anger—the *I'm sorry* wasn't in there.

"Is it an apology you are looking for?" Gabel asked, his tone warning me I wouldn't get one.

"No." He didn't want my forgiveness anyway. That worked to balance things out. I had met Gabel when his edges were dull from slicing through paper enemies. It didn't excuse anything he had done, but it did, perhaps, mean those things were firmly in the past.

I breathed in one last time, then it was time to shove this corpse into the grave. "I won't forgive it, Gabel. It was beneath you. I won't forgive the weakness, but I'll excuse it. *Once.*"

The Bond shifted and settled, rattled by all the anger and hurt and disgust being fed into it, and my burning contempt for Gabel's pettiness. Well, it would just have to suck it up for a little while. It hadn't been born in roses and sonnets while Gabel serenaded me under the stars.

Gabel turned his gaze to the moon. He stared at it for a long time, then said, " I am starting to think I did the right thing in the wrong manner for all the wrong reasons."

"That doesn't change that you didn't ask me," I muttered. "You just sliced me."

"Would you have refused?"

I rolled my eyes. "That's not the *point*. I wasn't in a position to say *no*. If you'd wanted me you'd have risked me refusing."

"True."

"It also fed Gardenia's ambitions. You strung her along. That was also cruel."

"You can handle her."

"That's not my point. You don't have the right to prey on her, either."

Gabel shrugged. "Gardenia was a thorn before you arrived. So what if I turned that thorn back on her? I told her one day she would be old and faded, and what would she be without her beauty? She snarled. *You* will still have your mind and gifts and dignity. She will have nothing to offer."

"But for right now it's enough?" I couldn't suppress another eye roll.

"Males like good looks, Gianna," Gabel said like it was a stupid, obvious point. "She is nice to look at from a distance. A far distance. She drowns herself in perfume so you can't smell the bad intentions."

"And to think, Gabel, another Alpha saw you with her on your arm, and he was looking at you like you were a fool. Seems like that thorn was a brier."

"I know." Gabel scowled.

His annoyance was so genuine I couldn't help but laugh. He'd played his part so perfectly, fawning over her fluttering, kissing her hand. And he had been acting because I hadn't played along! I told him, feeling malicious, "You deserved it, Gabel. I hope you gagged on her perfume. Anders thought I belonged to someone else. Hix, perhaps."

"Aren't we past these jealous games, buttercup?"

"Funny how you want to move past the jealous games when you're losing."

"I haven't made you move past training with Hix, which I know you enjoy."

"He does have a certain charm."

"Turnabout is fair play?" There was a twinkle in his eyes, but a jealous crinkle to the Bond, a warning that I was playing with something dangerous and primal, but that Gabel enjoyed it all the same.

"This is why you favor me. Like you said before, force has to be met with more force. Cruelty is always escalation. What can you do to me you haven't already done? I'm immune to all your charms."

Gabel laughed. He seized me by my arms and lowered his face to mine, his voice a hiss, "Truer words never fell on more grateful ears. Even if you say them to anger me."

"It's not my fault if the truth pisses you off."

"So we move on, buttercup, from the past. Does this mean we are taking the vows?"

"Does that mean you want to?" I tried to escape his grasp. He didn't let me go.

A long pause. Then a simple answer hit me with a thud. "Yes."

I needed to stop anticipating anything Gabel did or said. There was no pulse of warmth or affection with his affirmation. No softening of his expression. My arm throbbed. "I'll think about it."

He pulled me tight against him. The Bond churned, he shifted, and our lips met in a careful, uncertain kiss. But it was only tentative for a moment, then our tongues met, my fingers curled into his shirt, and I could not resist the roar of the Bond, just for a moment. Just one, brittle moment out in the cold courtyard.

The courtyard was silent. But a number of eyes watched us from the darkened windows of the house.

A SCORE TO SETTLE

I t was probably my paranoid imagination, but breakfast seemed quiet the next morning, with a lot of sideways looks and glances. Gardenia's eyes stabbing into my spine was not my imagination.

"We have some business to discuss, Alpha." Hix told Gabel as everyone milled about for last comments before heading out to their days.

Gabel nodded, then to me said, "Will you be joining us?"

Gabel still expected me to spend my days with him if I wasn't otherwise busy. It had been that way for as long as I had been with IronMoon, and it wasn't going to change anytime soon, especially if I became a permanent fixture. I also needed to finish my research on the *comet* rune—my working theory was perhaps it had cropped up in human history. There were books throughout the entire house (which now I knew to largely be the product of Flint's "Book Roulette" habit), but the ones I needed were in Gabel's library.

I told him I'd be along in about half an hour.

I took a fresh cup of coffee in one hand and headed up to my workroom for my morning tasks. Rotate bowls by the windows, make sure nothing had been disturbed during the night, dust out the corners. I twirled my finger in a bowl of sand as I mulled how much of a lie the vows would be.

At least a little bit.

The door opened.

"Hey," I snapped. "Knock!"

Gardenia slammed it shut behind her.

One of my favorite people in the world. "Don't touch anything."

"Oh, because it's your special little room?" She sneered.

"Yes, actually, exactly that."

She stomped across the floor, her socked feet disrupting the salt circle in the center of the room. She snickered and kicked a little bit of salt. The circle was easy enough to fix. Let her think she was actually damaging something important if it kept her away from what was important.

"What do you want, Gardenia?" I still had no interest in squabbling with her. That entire sordid era of history just needed to stay in its grave.

"I saw you in the courtyard last night. You think he's yours, don't you?" Gardenia sneered.

I groaned and looked at the ceiling. "Why are you here? I never wanted to have this stupid fight with you, and now we both know it was nothing but a bunch of smoke and mirrors."

She hissed, "Is that what he tells you? He's a liar, but he's *my* liar."

Whatever sympathy I might have had for Gardenia drained away. She would have gone along with those games just for a chance at him. Or any other wolf. A pack-climber. That's all she was. "I know you ran right to Romero about the Petitioner Wolf. Couldn't get Gabel or Hix, so you settled on Romero. You have any luck with him?"

"I have Gabel, why would I need Romero?" She paced close

to me, reeking of perfume. "The whole world outside IronMoon knows I'm the next Luna. You think Gabel and I were foolish enough to fuck in your bed? You've smelled my perfume on him. *You* are deluded, Oracle. You're blind to what's really happening."

"No." I circled her. "No, the trouble with Oracles is we're trained to see what is real, and what is a vision haunting us. *You* are a lie. Maybe Gabel touched you, maybe he didn't, but I know after Anders, he had no further use for you. So you hopped to Romero. You spied for him. How else would he have known Gabel dared to ask what the Petitioner Wolf's vision was —and that I refused to say?"

She curled her lip at me.

"It was you. Admit it. What did he promise you? His Mark on your arm and my head on a rope? Now he's dead, so you're back on Gabel."

"I never left him," she hissed. "He is still between my legs."

"He isn't between your legs," I whispered, "because he's between mine."

Her blue eyes widened into intense, gorgeous orbs.

"Shhh," I whispered. "The rest of the pack doesn't know. But I'll tell *you*. Some time ago. Months ago. I may have his pup in my belly now. He's asked me to take the vows, but that's still a secret too."

The secret was safe with her. Gardenia wasn't going to tell anyone in IronMoon *that*. Wouldn't fit into her plans.

"That's a lie!" She looked down at my belly, back at me. "You're a liar!"

The idea of having a pup in my belly scared the hell out of me, but I pressed ahead like all of this pleased me to no end. "He told you all you were was beauty, and one day that'd fade. You didn't listen. You were nothing but part of his strategy."

Gardenia's face sort of melted, and for a moment, I felt terrible. I tried to reach out to her. We'd both been Gabel's pawns, and—

Then her face reformed into something else entirely.

Everything she had told herself dissolved like a sandcastle in the tide. The truth knocked her backward a solid six steps.

She looked around, eyes sort of crazy and bright. Her cheeks burned with color. Fury and hatred overwhelmed her perfume. Her fingers snapped into fists, and she screeched, then whirled and bolted to the door. She yanked it open and spun around.

Jealous rage is a hell of a thing. Her blue eyes sparkled, pupils tiny little pinpoints. She looked around again and spotted the bowls on the shelf.

"No!" I barked and lunged.

She snatched the large, velvet pouch that held my obsidian scrying bowl from the nearby shelf, then threw it on the ground.

I gasped at the muffled shattering sound, then stared, struck dumb with horror.

Gardenia laughed and swept her arm across the shelf, shattering the smaller bowls, spilling salt everywhere, and scattering my runes over the floor. A few broke on impact. "Aren't so special now, are you, Oracle?"

My tools... destroyed, desecrated, shattered, ruined.

She cackled.

I jerked my head up to face her. "Start running, bitch."

Gardenia hesitated, but as I melted into wolf form, lips curled over fangs and ears slicked, she got the idea. Her eyes widened, and under her choking perfume, she stank of something that can only be described as:

oh shit.

This was IronMoon, and I was going to kill her. Nobody was going to stop me.

She shrieked and bolted down the stairs, melting into her own pale tawny-gold wolf form, struggling out of her clothing and barking for help. Help? Who was going to help her? I barked, lunged over the steps, and tackled her. She flattened on the stairs with a yelp. My teeth found some soft, large part of her (it turned out to be a shoulder), and we somersaulted end over end down the remainder of the stairs to the hallway floor below. We smashed into the opposite wall. I bit down on another part of her. She shrieked, squirmed out from under me, and bolted. I shook myself off and sprang after her.

She screamed like a terrified puppy.

She was also pretty fast. Faster than I was. Downright fleet.

She led me through the marble foyer, splashing through the pond, down the main hallway, through the mudroom. She plowed through the screen on the screen door. It tore and dangled in the breeze. I leapt through the hole. Hah! She was making a run for the training fields! Did she hope Flint would pull me off her?

She accelerated away from me, opening her lead stride by stride. I barked after her: I'd catch her eventually, she could just keep on running. She yipped, yipped, yipped, speeding toward the training ring barking for help.

She plowed right into the center of the sand ring, scattering the warriors in the center, and yowled for them to help her, that I was going to kill her, stop me before it was too late.

Stupid, she should have kept running. Five seconds later I caught up to her, lunged, and tumbled her into the sand.

She screamed. I bit down on her foreleg, and she shrieked and flailed. Blood bloomed on my tongue and splattered the sand.

The males all scattered back. Flint, on his box, simply held up his arms to keep all the males steady and silent. "Stay well clear when females fight, wolves!"

Gardenia wailed for help.

"*No one is going to save you!*" I snapped my teeth near her snout and peeled off a layer of skin.

She whimpered and flung her snout away from my teeth, exposing her throat, and she stayed that way, bloody, shaking, reeking of cheap human perfume and real fear. Her foreleg dangled unnaturally.

I backed off her and curled into human-form, which was considerably colder in the snow, as I was completely naked. My blood was still hot with fury. Gardenia whimpered and rolled around on the sand, blood pouring from her mangled foreleg, and tufts of fur bloodied and ripped.

I spat out a mouthful of her fur and blood.

One of the males tried to advance again.

"Stay out of it," Flint ordered him. "It is disturbing to watch females fight, I know, but when they decide they must, you must not interfere, or there will never be harmony within the pack."

"You shattered my bowls," I snarled at her.

I should kill you.

The dark thought whispered from my mind. I'd never been so angry I wanted to *kill* someone. I'd never even considered killing Gabel.

She slid back into human-form and whimpered over her broken arm. Her face needed some stitches, and she was battered and marked up.

I snorted at the hatred burning in her eyes. She could hate me all she wanted. She could sit and glare at me during meals, plot my demise, and whisper to her little cadre about what a rancid, stuck-up cow I was. That was the best she could do.

Violent rage seeped into my blood, something dark and cruel and malevolent.

Kill her.

No. Not over this. Not over *her*.

Instead, I told Flint, "I apologize for the interruption, Master of Arms. Excuse me, Alpha Gabel is expecting me."

Flint half-bowed to me. "Lady Gianna."

Gardenia could find her own way to the doctor.

SHARDS OF OBSIDIAN

I fished a piece of grass out of my hair and flicked it onto the mudroom floor.

Flint directed two of the warriors to take pity on Gardenia and drag her off to the doctor's small house a quarter mile down into the woods. Pathetic. She could have dragged herself down there, but no, she had cried and whimpered until two males carted her off.

And Gabel wanted me to be the Luna of *that*? No thank you.

I rubbed a bruise coming up on my hip.

Gabel and Hix almost collided with me in the narrow hallway from the mudroom to the main hall. They'd seen (and heard) the chaos, and now (being students of Flint) had come to see how the fight had ended. Gabel took one look at me, then glared at Hix. Hix coughed and looked somewhere other than my naked body.

"Oh stop," I told Gabel's surge of jealousy. "We're all naked under our clothes. They're just breasts and hips."

Gabel scowled at me.

"Are you going to ask me why I just walked naked around

half the warriors of IronMoon, or are you going to assume I'm up to no good?" After Gardenia smashed my precious tools, I was in no mood for Gabel's rage. Bond-fueled, possessive jealousy. He didn't even realize it was the Bond gnawing at him. Nobody out there had been ogling me, and if they had, fine. They couldn't have me any more than Gardenia could have him. " Jealousy doesn't suit you."

Hix coughed again, this time on laughter. Gabel growled at him again, with actual menace, before whirling back to me. He scowled, jaw churning as he looked me up and down, torn between jealousy and lust and the overpowering urge to remind me just who I belonged to.

Hix's presence was the only thing keeping Gabel in his own clothes.

"What..." Gabel's voice was rough, more like a growl, human speech having suddenly become difficult, "happened?"

"Gardenia smashed my tools." When I said it, my throat closed over in sadness, and despair washed over me. Each bowl, each rune, each item was special. Part of me. They were attuned specifically to me, extensions of my own powers.

Shattered. Broken.

"All of them?" Gabel asked. Hix tore his eyes from the ceiling and swung his dark attention onto me.

"Just cleared off my shelf." I swept my arm along an invisible plane and choked down another sob. "So I had to... deal with her."

"Did you kill her? You don't look bloody enough for that." Gabel took inventory of my dirty body.

"No, of course not," I snapped, guilty at the little voice from within the abyss that whispered *but I wanted to. I could have. I might have. I still might.*

"I see. Come on, you need to get some clothes on and—"

"I thought we didn't deal in silly human modesty." I shook

off his hand. Hix slid past me, careful to keep his eyes somewhere else, even though I caught the scent of his interest.

Gabel did too, and his eyes flickered at Hix's back as the
Beta moved to the mudroom. Gabel grabbed my bicep in his
hand, his fingers clenched down like stone. "Naughty, naughty,
buttercup."

I growled back. "So what if he knows I'm alive? You're the
one who has me."

"So true, so true." He grinned crazy-like. So the Bond had
defeated him, now he wrestled with the possibility my eye
might wander? This wolf was strange.

"I'm not in the mood." I yanked my arm away, still aching
from the loss of my tools. There was nothing sexy about dried
blood and dirt crusted onto my skin. "I had to tell that little
whore she was just a pawn in your game. That she was part of a
strategy. Being the scab she is, she didn't even ask. But it sure
infuriated her to hear she might have helped me. This is
your fault!"

I stomped upstairs to our room. He followed.

I stood under the hot shower water, scrubbing and peeling
at the dried blood, and wincing as soapy water found little
scratches and scrapes and bruises.

Gabel offered me a towel with one hand, and in the other,
held a fresh dress and dainties, as if he were some glorified valet.
Then he silently followed me up to my workroom to take stock
of the damage.

All my tools were stored in velvet or silk bags between
uses. The bags now held the smashed remains of the fragile
bowls. My upended two bags of runes and spilled their
contents all over the floor. Some of the runes had cracked and
broken upon impact. There was salt everywhere. Smashed
vials of oil created a mangled stench in the air. The only thing
that had been spared had been the small bowls on the

window ledges where I had been purifying other tools in salt or water.

I cradled the velvet bag that housed my favorite bowl. The large pieces made it lumpy and limp in my hands, like lifting a broken body. This piece of obsidian had spoken to me, chosen me. I had felt safe within it, even if it had taken me to scary places within the Tides. I sobbed once and scrubbed my eyes with the back of my arm. The bowl was broken and could never be repaired.

I reached inside the bag and removed a large, sharp-edged piece. Destroyed. Even the power imbued within it was broken.

"Can it be fixed?" Gabel inquired.

"No. It's dead."

"Dead?"

"They die. The power in them is broken. They can't be made whole again." I set the bag down gently and gathered up the scattered runestones.

Four runes had been broken, the ones for *safety*, *flight*, *waterfall* and *storm*.

"What of the runes?" he asked.

"The sets have to be complete and carved from the same stone or bones of the same prey. I can use an incomplete set, but it's less safe. Especially since *safety* has been broken. I'll have to be that much more careful now that I don't have access to these runes or their powers."

Gabel watched in pensive silence while I sniffled and picked up what I could.

Only when I was done placing the shattered bowl-bags into a pile to carry to the trash did he ask, "Can the bowls be replaced? Surely bowls and mirrors and tools break."

"It's a blemish on the Oracle." I tried to explain to him the shame of having to replace even one bowl, or having lost even one rune. Then I gave up trying. Only another Oracle would understand.

The oils were easy enough to replace, as were herbs and incense. I could keep using the runes, but my bowls? They were what was important.

"But they *can* be replaced. How?"

"I have to find chunks of obsidian that speak to me. Maybe clear quartz, or malachite, or jasper, but I've always worked best with obsidian. And it has to be large enough to be carved into a bowl."

"Not a mirror?"

I shuddered. "Most Oracles can't use mirrors. Even fewer *want* to use one."

"But can you?"

"If I have to, but it's dangerous. Mirrors are a flat raft on the Tides. Bowls are boats." I shuddered a second time. My one time with a mirror had been terrifying. I'd slid over the smooth surface as the Tides had bucked and tossed me about, spray in my face, the sensation of clinging to the sharp edges. I'd screamed myself hoarse and suffered a sharp headache for a week.

"What about a metal bowl? Don't some Oracles use iron or white gold?"

"Some do, but I've never been able to use metal."

"So it's specific to the Oracle. The tools you can use."

"Yes. And the chunk of rock, it has to speak to you. It has to be the *right* rock. And it has to be large enough and flawless enough to be carved. My favorite bowl was my initiation gift. Others I've collected, but you saw how many I had." I gestured to the four bags. "One large, the others were small. I used them mostly for purification or anchor bowls. The obsidian one was... the one."

"And when you find the chunk, can any craftsman do the carving?"

"Most any. Then the Oracle has to do all the rest of the work."

"So where exactly did you get these?"

"Elder Oracle Anita of SableFur. She was my last teacher. She collects possible stones, and all the Oracles in this part of the world go to her to...browse." My favorite bowl had been my gift, but the others I had had to pay for (or Shadowless had). The Elder Oracle had standing orders for stones that met certain requirements. SableFur paid a bounty on them and had craftsmen who could carve out the bowls as the Oracle wanted, then the Oracles (or their packs) paid a princely sum.

I explained all this to Gabel. I also explained how we couldn't ask Anita of SableFur for help. It was *my* fault (doubly my fault as the first-rank female) my tools were broken. If there was a pack who was going to destroy an Oracle's tools, everyone would say it would be IronMoon. It wouldn't do anything to improve our reputation as mindless barbarians. We might have plenty of mindless predators that were just teeth with legs attached, but IronMoon wasn't *run* by the rabble.

"Considering you ripped up Gardenia in public, probably won't stay a secret," Gabel said.

I scowled, hot, angry tears coming up anew. "Embarrassed by her. Again."

I let that barb sink right into Gabel. He felt it but didn't flinch.

"Then we'll need to figure out how to get you in front of chunks of obsidian," Gabel stated. "The SableFur can't have a monopoly on it. We'll find some, even if we have to wander around on volcanoes with a sledgehammer."

"I'd take a sledgehammer to Gardenia first."

"Buttercup, you've become so violent. I wouldn't stop you, in fact, I'm sure we have a sledgehammer around somewhere."

Platinum needed to learn she couldn't even wag that pretty little ass of hers without my permission. She didn't get to come after what was mine.

As if he could read my thoughts, Gabel said, "Her punishment doesn't fit her crimes, Gianna."

"You want me to decide her punishment?"

"Yes."

"Didn't I already do that?"

"No."

"You're the Alpha. Discipline is your job."

"She's a female."

"Oh no, Gabel. I'm not your Luna." I backed up a step.

"I'll tell the pack this is what you want, and I agreed to give you the justice you wanted. But between you and I, you name her punishment."

"It makes you uncomfortable," I gasped, realizing he didn't want to. He practically squirmed away from it.

"Females usually don't require rough handling. I don't like it when they do," Gabel said, annoyed. "I'll do it if I have to, though. This isn't behavior that can be tolerated, and if you think it can be—"

I cut him off with a sharp gesture. He waited, expecting something suitable to the IronMoon.

I couldn't believe I was about to so blithely mete out such a cruel punishment.

Maybe I should have killed her.

"Put her in the basement for a few days. Let's see how she feels when she gets thrown out like trash."

VICTORY AND DEFEAT

Gabel bent down and lifted a bag of shards. "May I have these?"

"I guess. Why would you want them?"

"I don't know. They might be useful. Why did you keep the canines of the RedWater wolves?"

"Why do you think I kept them? Maybe I threw them out."

"Of course you kept them. There's no way to properly bury them, so you kept them, and I don't believe you would have thrown them out after the fact. You fought too hard to make me give them to you."

I shrugged. "So what?"

"Exactly. So may I keep these?"

Gabel seemed to be able to find a use for things nobody else wanted, so he could do whatever he wanted with the dead shards.

Gabel slung the bags over his shoulder, the little silk cords hooked around the first joint of his right index finger. I winced at the scraping noises from the shards shifting and jostling. "So, buttercup. There's one more thing for this morning."

"One more thing? Isn't this enough?" I gestured helplessly to my destroyed room.

"Hix asked what our intentions are. Rather forcefully."

The words hit me hard enough to knock the wind out of me.

"He and I didn't get to have much of a conversation before two pretty she-wolves running across the yard distracted us, but he'll be back for more once Gardenia gets mopped up and put into a bucket. You and I won't evade him for long."

"You're the Alpha. Growl at him."

Gabel laughed. "One of the reasons I like Hix as First Beta is he growls back."

"Let's wait and see what he says," I said.

"You know what he'll say. In fact, I imagine if we put him off, he'll say that if you're not sure about me, he'll be pleased to make his case to you. It's far too late for that, of course, but I doubt that would stop him."

Twinges of hot jealousy laced with a peculiar, exquisite pleasure emanated from Gabel.

"Gabel, not right now! I can't right now." I gestured helplessly to the ruins.

"Yes, I suppose I am being a bit inappropriate."

"I'm going to go get a broom," I muttered.

Gardenia limped back to the house just before dinner. Her arm was heavily bandaged in a sling, and her face stitched, and she moved like her whole body hurt. If she felt that tumble down the stairs like I did, her whole body did hurt. Without makeup she looked completely different, although still very pretty.

When she arrived at the front door the wolf who greeted her made her wait. Then all the wolves in the house filed into the foyer, and Violet retrieved me from the bedroom to join Gabel on the stairs.

Gardenia seemed very small and frightened as she stood in front of all of us. This was not the sort of attention she wanted.

She looked up at me on the landing, and through the pain and humiliation, there was burning hatred.

Gardenia's spirit wasn't broken. She still wanted a fight.

Just as well Romero was dead. They would have been a perfect match, and had many stupid little puppies.

Platinum's little cadre of friends clustered in a frightened group, looking nervously between their leader and me. They wanted to go over to Platinum, coo over her injuries, stroke her hair, simper about what a terrible bitch I was. Because that's what little wolves like them did. Platinum had destroyed my tools in a fit of jealous rage, having a tantrum because she didn't have Gabel's Mark, and yet, self-defense had made me the ogre.

Gabel had the velvet bags with him. "Gardenia, this morning you entered Lady Gianna's sanctuary without invitation or permission. You did not leave when she ordered you to do so. Instead you desecrated the room and shattered her tools."

Gardenia looked at the pond.

"You attacked a wolf of higher prestige and challenged her status. That is acceptable in IronMoon. Lady Gianna answered the challenge. You, however, ran like a coward from the fight you started and you begged for someone to save you. Gardenia," Gabel moved down two steps, his voice lowering several notes. "Tsk tsk. You know that is not how things work here in IronMoon."

Gardenia shifted on her feet.

"The punishment for such things is death. As this pack knows from recent history." Gabel's voice warmed with cruel amusement, and it slid down the Bond between us, the memory of his triumph over Romero, how easy it had been. His authority and prestige shone brighter, the scent drifting through the room, commanding everyone to wilt before him. Except for me. I drank it, dined upon it, relished it.

"But Lady Gianna does not want you to die. She could have killed you for the offense you have given her. Do you not understand," Gabel moved one step lower, "that she outranks you?"

Oh Gabel, salting wounds.

Gabel turned to me, "Lady Gianna, having seen her standing here now, you have not changed your mind on the punishment you would see meted out? I think perhaps it is not harsh enough. She challenged your status, destroyed your tools, then dishonored this pack by fleeing like a coward."

"Oh, I think it's harsh enough," I said. "She craves attention. Put her where not even the Moon will pay her mind."

Gabel shrugged. "As you wish. Gardenia, you will spend three days and three nights in the basement."

"What? The basement? No!" Gardenia yelped, "Alpha Gabel, please, no, not that! Don't!"

Cook turned his head to the side, expression grieved.

"Please," Gardenia pled to Gabel, holding her good hand up in supplication.

"It is not me you should beg for forgiveness. It is Lady Gianna."

Gardenia yanked back, face washing over with shocked, horrified realization.

"Go quietly." I moved down one step. "Or I'll take your canines next and have them made into earrings."

Gabel grinned at me, his whole presence seeming to brighten another notch, feral hunger lacing it now.

Cook came forward and whispered to his cousin, pushing her out of the hallway while she whimpered and swore angrily. Cook gave me an apologetic look. Gardenia was always family to him, no matter how stupid she acted. Gardenia was probably the reason they had ended up in IronMoon, not Cook himself.

The show over, the rest of the pack moved away to sit for dinner. Hix said, "Alpha. We need to continue our conversation. Lady Gianna should be there as well."

"Master of Arms," Gabel told the lingering Flint, who had already figured out what we were going to talk about, "we won't be at dinner."

Flint nodded once, half-bowed to me, and left to oversee dinner.

Gabel ushered me to his office with Hix looming behind us.

Told you so, Gabel's glance said.

Hix waited until I was seated on the couch. Hix looked at the nasty gash on my shin and told me, "I suppose all that training I've endured with you went to some good use."

"Your generosity is astonishing," I said sarcastically.

In classic Hix fashion, he did not mince words. "When will you be taking the vows?"

Ton.

Of.

Bricks.

"We haven't talked about it." Gabel went for pure honesty.

Because we hadn't talked about it.

That didn't put Hix off, and Hix didn't take the hint even though he recognized there was a hint in there. "The Bond has obviously been consummated. You treat her as your Luna. I see no reason to delay. The pack is expecting the announcement soon. Late-night trysts in the courtyard don't go unnoticed."

"It wasn't a tryst. It was just a kiss! Since when is a kiss a tryst?"

"That's what everyone else might think. I am not an idiot. I understand if you wanted to keep it private for a short while before making the announcement, but with recent events, the time has simply come. Don't you agree?" He sounded like a school marm asking a basic rhetorical question.

We didn't answer.

Hix dragged us forward with his logic. "The Solstice Moon is three weeks away. It is the best time of year to do it, and since you two are ready, we should take advantage."

Ready? Who said anything about being ready?

Gabel was waiting for me to say something, I was waiting for him to say something, and neither of us had anything clever to say.

The Solstice Moon was the luckiest time of year to have a vow-taking, and many Alphas and Lunas planned their mating around it.

"That feels sudden..." I managed to mutter.

"It is not sudden at all. It is just a formality."

"I suppose..."

"Excuse us a moment." Gabel stepped between us. "You've caught us off-guard, Hix."

"How have I caught you off-guard?" Hix's low tone bordered on a growl.

"As you said, a great deal has happened recently. We haven't had time to speak about trivialities like this."

There was nothing trivial about it. But it got through to Hix. He nodded, gave each of us a meaningful look that said he'd wait exactly five minutes, then stepped outside.

Gabel said, "It would seem we have both lost to the Bond."

I touched the Mark still on my arm. It had not festered or rotted. The Bond between us had tightened and hungered. Even now, it hungered for Gabel, and his hands on my flesh. Did I love Gabel? Was I even fond of him? Would the vows be a lie? Would they be a truth I didn't want to speak even to myself?

Could I be a Luna and an Oracle?

I would never escape Gabel. There was nowhere to run. There was nowhere to hide. Even his authority and command didn't affect me. It just pleased me, and I drank it up, I basked in it.

There might be other Alphas like him, but they would kill me on sight. They wouldn't take me to their side. Even if I found another partner, I'd never bow to another Alpha.

"You could persuade me to try to break the Bond," I ventured, knowing it was a worthless suggestion.

"No. You say those things just to hear me refuse? Neither of us would survive. Even now, even fighting as we do, we are bound too tightly. Say those things if you just want to try on the words, but you know it's not an option."

I mumbled an agreement.

"Then there's only one thing left for us to do."

Perhaps, but there was one thing I wanted to know.

"How does defeat taste, Gabel?" I whispered.

He ran his thumb over a light scratch on my cheek. "It tastes of you, buttercup. There is no longer any reason to resist. Tonight, I am going to taste all of you. Again. And again. And again. We will see how tight that Bond will twist."

CLAIMED

The Bond pulsed like a soft heartbeat, warm and content, as if it had baked all night in the warmth of a fire.

It sort of had. A fire named Gabel, who burned hot and dark when determined to indulge his carnality.

And explore every corner of mine.

For the first time in... a long time... I did not feel torn apart.

My nervous shock, dismay, confusion and everything else that went with my impending nuptials was still present.

But the whole torn-apart-from-the-inside-feeling was absent.

"Why are there no windows in this room?" I always had to walk out into the hallway and look out the large windows overlooking the stairs to actually see what the weather was like. Considering there had been snow on the wind again, I wanted to know how to dress. When your mate preferred you in skirts and dresses, it mattered.

Gabel leaned over my back and kissed my shoulder blades in turn. "They make me nervous."

"You. Nervous."

"It is not a good den if anything can peer in. I have never

understood why anyone would want to sleep with windows open to the world."

He gently bit the point of my left shoulder blade, and his fingertips traced curling patterns along the back of my right thigh, teasing higher and and higher. I squirmed.

"The maidenly act doesn't suit you," he growled under his breath. "We both know your desires."

His fingers moved higher, teasing the softness of my inner thighs. I squirmed a little more and tried to turn over. He pressed me into the sheets with his chest and laughed, very softly. "Your mouth can lie all it wants, but your skin doesn't. Why do you make me work so hard to convince you that you want everything I can give you?" He moved across me and bit down gently on my shoulder. I gasped and squirmed, and yelped again as his fingers slipped to the apex of my thighs.

His words sent a tremor of pleasure so intense down the Bond that I mewled and my spine arched.

"If you are going to play the maiden," Gabel said as he inhaled my scent, a new growl in his voice, "I am going to play the lord who expects what he is entitled to."

Gabel's wandering hand clutched my hip and yanked me to him. I squeaked in shock, torn by old fear and desire. He growled in my ear, looming over me, moving faster than my not-so-well-rested-brain could process.

He took what he wanted, a crazed, carnal desire flooding through him. The Bond twisted tighter within us. As I drowned in the pleasure and panted as his rough hands held me delight-fully pinned, I wondered just how tightly a Bonded pair could be bound.

I swear our souls fused. Was that even possible? Was that how it worked?

Gabel's hands released me, and I crumbled, panting, sweaty, damp and flushed, back into our abused sheets.

I needed a shower.

I crawled out of bed.

Fresh wetness slid down my thigh, poking me with anxiety. "We should be more careful, Gabel."

"Why?" he asked, arm behind his head. He was magnificently naked on the sheets, not a stitch of cloth upon him. By the Moon, he was a creature of glory, especially with a thin sheen of sweat on his slightly bronze skin. Even when he said crazy things.

I ignored temptation and pointed out the obvious instead. "Why? You know how puppies get made, don't you?"

Gabel chuckled.

"Is this your new game? Get me pregnant as fast as you can?"

Gabel smirked. "Let the Moon sort it out."

"Now you surrender to the Moon? Or is this just an excuse to not use a condom every time?"

"A King needs his heirs," he said lazily.

"You're not a King, Gabel."

He sat up. "So you're saying I have to become a King before you will give me my heirs?"

"Your heirs? They are my children, too. I'm not your goddamn baby-mill."

Gabel's devilish smirk widened.

I sniffed, not interested in dancing on the end of the string that morning, "They don't have a crown to inherit, Gabel. Just a pack of questionably behaved mongrels."

Gabel's ocean-blue eyes ignited with a terrifying brilliance. "That sounds like a challenge laid at my feet."

I fled to the shower.

"You know, buttercup," Gabel said as he shaved, his reflection in the mirror eyeing me as I emerged from the shower, wrapped in a towel. "It might take me a little longer than is practical to achieve my goals. You may have to reconsider holding out on the pups."

I swear he did this just to see me cringe and pale and squirm. "Maybe I will. But not if you ever use them as a toy, Gabel. The pups aren't a toy for your games. You even nip them, and I will kill you. I will rip your throat out and eat it in one gulp."

I knew in that moment I not only would kill him, but that I *could*. All the maternal rage and snarls slid down the Bond, pouring into him, branding itself against him.

Gabel actually stopped shaving.

I curled my lips and growled at him.

Gabel broke eye contact first. "Noted."

We had an understanding on that, at least.

Breakfast was the usual affair. Hix had only told Flint and Eroth that we'd make the announcement that evening before dinner. Cook had been told to prepare something festive for dinner and dessert. Cook was resigned to his cousin's antics, which (as it turned out) was the entire reason they were in Iron-Moon, and he was grateful there was anywhere in the world that would put up with her.

I did admire his loyalty to his family, and I turned a blind eye when I saw him disappear while holding a plate of food.

"I don't approve," Gabel growled.

"You didn't say she couldn't have visitors or had to starve. Let Cook see his family."

"Are you going down there?"

"Why should I? I have other things to do."

Like the depressing work of purifying my work room. It kept me occupied until the early afternoon, and my mind firmly not on Gabel, the Bond, these vows I still wasn't sure about, and the life that was taking me with it.

But it was all too late now.

That evening the whole of IronMoon gathered in the expansive courtyard. Gabel had summoned them, and attendance was not optional.

There were so many of them. Even more than had been present at the trials for the Second Beta slot.

Gabel and I stood on the top patio. The night was freezing cold and clear, with only a tiny sliver of Moon in the sky. I licked my lips in the frigid air, wishing this announcement came under a brighter portent. Everyone knew what announcement was coming, and the anticipation was thick.

I better get used to standing in front of a sea of wolves. Lunas tended to do that.

Gabel was in just a kilt, and I wore a blue dress, with nothing under it. In the darkness of the near-moonless night the yellow light of the house gave his skin a dusky gleam, and the shadows seemed menacing and close. I expected to see the yellow-fire eyes of Hounds staring back at me, here to watch one of their own claim a mortal mate.

"Wolves of IronMoon!" Gabel raised his hands and the crowd settled. "For a pack such as this, you know I have searched long and carefully for a she-wolf worthy of being your Luna."

All eyes snapped to me.

"A she-wolf strong enough to suit my... tastes." Gabel's voice filled the air, smug and triumphant. "One wise enough to understand a Luna is not only a crown, one proud enough to bow to no insult, and one brave enough to run at my side on the Hunt."

He made it sound like everything up until now had been some kind of series of tests to prove to Gabel I was worthy of him and his pack.

No way, Gabel. Don't try to make yourself look so good.

"She has fought hard to show me how much contempt she has for all that I am, and that she would not be easily won over by a strong pack," he gestured to the IronMoon, "our wealth or our reputation. And why should an Oracle, who dares to venture into the Tides and enter the Court of the Moon, be easily impressed? Courting her has been my greatest challenge so far. But I have finally proven to her that not only am I her Alpha, but I am the one the Moon has chosen for her."

Leave it to Gabel to present defeat as victory. Gabel winked at me, then extended a hand. I balked one final moment.

If you do this, there is no undoing it.

There hadn't been any undoing anything from the start.

Gabel drew me up next to him, our hands raised. "Before the Moon and this pack, I claim Lady Gianna of IronMoon! Under the Solstice Moon we will make our vows, and we shall celebrate the IronMoon Luna, and our new future with her!"

Flint spun around and raised his arms, howling and encouraging all the warriors to sing louder to the Moon. A few shifted into wolf form and threw their heads back, howling, and several slipped into war-form, offering guttural, rage-filled howls that sent any remaining creatures plunging in a panic through the woods.

"My Luna," Gabel said to me, leaning very close so I could hear him over the thunder, "run with your pack."

"I am not Luna yet, Gabel." I chided his arrogance but put a finger over his lips anyway. He bit the tip, and I gasped. The howls rang in my skull, his scent consumed me. The tiny little crescent of the moon watched us from behind slitted eyes.

"To me you are." Gabel traded his teeth on my finger for biting my lower lip, his eyes hanging in my field of vision for a long second while my heartbeat increased its pace. "The vows are only a formality. You are mine, Gianna. I have Marked you, I have claimed you, before my pack and the Moon's Eye."

I seized his hair in my hands and yanked myself against him

for a fierce, long kiss. "Then, my Lord-Alpha," I panted around the sudden fervor the howls wove over me, "we should run."

Gabel spun around to his wolves, "Come! We shall run in full cry, then share food!"

He leapt forward, twisting out of his kilt as his body stretched and reshaped into his terrifying, leathery wolf form. He landed on the stones at the base of the steps, his claws cracking the flagstones, and turned his head to me, maw open and immense yellow fangs dripping spittle, his eyes yellow fire in the lamplight.

He waited for me, a guttural growl sliding through the howls and barks to summon me to his side.

I pulled my dress over my head, flung it away, and did as commanded.

He sniffed my silvery ruff. All Oracles were silvery-grey wolves with dark points, no matter our pedigrees or hair color. Cautiously, I sniffed the long, oily fur that clung around his neck where a full ruff should be, and smelled only Gabel, nothing more.

Hix and Eroth barked commands so we wouldn't trample each other on the run. Flint sat nearby, wagging his tail. His tawny-gold wolf form stood out like a miniature sun.

He extended one foreleg to me and bowed low.

Gabel flung his head back and howled the Alpha's song of summoning, and as one, we plunged off into the night in full cry.

OLD CUSTOMS

My heart lifted as we crashed into the underbrush of the forest. I howled to the sliver of moon, and the pack answered with their own yips and barks.

Master of Arms Flint ran easily to my left, and I ran on Gabel's left as he led us through the nearly-black forest.

One of the males behind us accelerated between Gabel and I, splitting us apart, and lunged at Gabel with a snarl.

I swerved and fell back a few paces while the two males snapped and snarled and swiped at each other as the run continued.

"*The old custom,*" Flint said.

Of course. Because IronMoon was all about the old customs: the claiming run. Silly me, I thought we had just been going for the typical celebration run. The other males of the pack honored the female by trying to "steal" her. It was an ancient custom, and the last "chance" for a male to stake a claim on a female. Gabel fought off the wolf, some fur and blood flew, and the male fell back into the pack.

The more males that attacked, and the more fiercely, the more desirable the female.

(And the more powerful the male when he vanquished each opponent, and the more prestige it granted him to have a mate that others desired)

Flint barked a little laugh at the tumbling. *"These are dangerous runs, Lady. Enjoy the blood offered to you!"*

Another male pounced, tumbling Gabel off his feet. Excited barks as the story made its way down the pack. Gabel fought off that male, and another, and another.

He threw off every wolf, laughing at them and summoning me to his side with a triumphant bark after each one.

We ran down a steep hillside and leapt into a clearing, splashed across a slushy, half-frozen creek.

Then another shadow moved in my vision, blotting out the faint starlight over Gabel's right shoulder. Fangs flashed, a snarl, and then Gabel went down like a ragdoll. His momentum carried him and the other wolf sliding across the terrain. He got to his feet, the other wolf pounced again, and they locked together, snarling and flailing. Blood splattered the snow-layered ground as claws met flesh, and the forward run became a thrashing, snarling fight.

I slowed, and Flint slowed with me. The pack poured around us to watch, giving the two wolves a wide circle. It was Gabel's leathery, nightmare form versus a large wolf with short, plush, dark fur: Hix.

The males broke apart, and Hix slunk sideways, circling Gabel, body crouched low, snarling and fangs bared. Gabel matched him, his talon-like claws ripping up huge clumps of the earth and snow, the starlight sliding off his oily hide.

"This can't be real," I whispered to Flint.

Flint shifted his shoulders in a shrug. *"Perhaps it is. Perhaps they are just honoring you with blood and fangs. As Shadowless did not."*

Gabel and Hix clashed together again. Hix snarled and

snaked forward, shoving Gabel back onto his hind legs, and with a sharp twist of his head, bit down on Gabel's shoulder. They struggled, blood dripping onto the ground from the bite wound, until Gabel managed to get Hix off balance and flung him to the ground. I couldn't hear what they were saying, but I heard wheezing and panting. I could feel Gabel's bubbling rage within me, his enjoyment of the fight and the blood.

He pressed Hix into the dirt by the throat. Hix struggled a few breaths, sides heaving, just to prove not even Gabel's fangs on his throat would compel his immediate obedience.

I leapt forward, *"Enough!"*

Movement stopped. Gabel growled in his throat. He turned his head to look at me with one yellow eye, dragging Hix a bit in the snow as his head moved.

"Blood has been spilled," I said. *"It is enough. It is more than my birth pack saw fit to do when one sought to claim me."*

Gabel spat out Hix's neck. Hix jumped to his feet, teeth still barred and hackles still raised. Gabel sniffed once and walked away, and Hix waited a heartbeat before he too went back to join the pack.

I wagged my tail at Gabel as he approached and licked his snout once. He swiped at me with his teeth, harmless, and growled, *"Well played, buttercup."*

"Would you really have killed him?"

"No, I would have made him submit." Gabel pivoted about to restart the run, despite deep bloody rakes in his shoulder to match the barely-healed wounds Romero had left.

"I didn't want to see that." I sniffed his shoulder wound carefully. He also smelled of exertion, pain, effort, the fight and rankled anger.

Roiling anger and jealousy, but mixed with enjoyment. *"I'll keep it in mind you favor him."*

"He is a good Beta."

"*Of course.*" He chortled. "*A Beta should have the Luna's favor. It is wise politics.*"

We bounded back into the darkness, Hix taking his place at Gabel's right shoulder for the balance of the run. A few miles from home, Gabel told me, "*Lead them home, buttercup.*"

"*Where are you going?*" I barked after him as he stretched his legs and accelerated away from us into the forest.

I had never led a run or a hunt before. I had rarely even been near the front of the line.

The path was easy enough, and since we were just running, I didn't really need to do anything besides not step in a hole and break my legs. I yipped to the pack, and all down the line came the barks and howls answering back. Higher toned, different calls because I was a female run leader.

I crested a final, short hill, and the groomed grounds of the house beckoned. I barked the command to slow and eased into a jog. In the lights of the patio, we milled around, panting, tails wagging, yipping and howling. Flint jumped up onto a planter and howled praises to the Moon for Her blessings, and we all howled with him.

The wolves parted as Gabel returned from the woods, something clutched in his jaws. I waited at the top of the steps, tail up, ears forward, half-expecting him to be carrying something horrible and violent. But all it was was a rabbit. A half-white winter hare.

He clicked up the flagstones, further shattering them under his claws, and then dropped the hare at my feet.

We were being traditional.

I picked up the hare, carried it backward one step to indicate my taking it for myself, then settled down and began to eat. Gabel sat opposite me, close enough he could have snatched it from me if he had wanted to. The IronMoon watched with more confusion than understanding of the ancient and long-forgotten ritual.

I gnawed on the delicious rabbit for several moments. Then I paused in my chewing, looked at him, thumped my tail exactly twice, whined once, and nudged the carcass toward him. He crouched down onto his forelegs, his claw tips touching mine, and gnawed on the rabbit with me. Flint started a song of celebration.

"You are traditional," I told Gabel under the song.

"Kings are traditional." He chomped off part of the rabbit and gulped it down whole.

"Where did you learn all this? Flint?"

"Some of it." He chomped off another leg. *"We've had our appetizers. Run as wolves, eat as humans. We can negotiate the form for what comes after the meal."*

"Human," I choked as if I had gotten a bone lodged in my throat. He couldn't seriously be suggesting something else.

"You object to a litter of lupines?" Gabel licked his chops.

Lupines were werewolves born as wolves, not humans. They had always been rare, and in modern society, virtually unheard of due to practical matters like birth certificates. They had always been difficult to integrate with human society, being feral. They reached physical maturity within two to three years but missed out on learning as human children do. By the same token, human-born werewolves could not fully integrate with wolf packs most of the time. We did lack a certain feral edge, and there was even a language gap. Our minds remained the same, not quite fully human, not quite fully wolf. But humans were more tolerant of eccentricities and aberrations, while wolves instantly distrusted such things that did not conform to expectations.

There was debate about whether or not wolves were wolves first, then gained a human-form, or if they were humans who had gained a wolf form, and which was the "intended" birth form for us.

"Now you're just watching me squirm."

Gabel actually wagged his tail twice, got to his feet, and melted upward into his human form, a smirk stretched across his lips. "You are still a little bashful, buttercup. I really must remove the maidenly blushing from you."

My eyes were drawn to Gabel's ripped up shoulder, the deep scratches across his torso, and a thin slice that had peeled up a strip of flesh from his left thigh. The burning pain only goaded his ego; the pain was laced with victory and triumph. He was still, unquestionably, the Alpha of IronMoon.

"Human it is." Gabel grinned, his lips still stained with rabbit blood. "Wolves of IronMoon. Now, we dine!"

Hix approached. He bled from his wounds. Gabel had bit down hard enough to puncture the skin and draw blood. A few centimeters more, and the punctures would have been fatal. Hix brought his arm across his torso and bowed to me. "My blood is always well-spent when spilled in your name, Lady Gianna."

Struck by his sincerity, I only managed, "Thank you, First Beta."

I turned to Gabel when Hix had left, noting the wounds that really did need stitches and proper dressing. "So was that little demonstration planned?"

"Not exactly."

"Not exactly?"

"He warned me. Something to the effect of I had won you by conquest without actually having conquered anything?" Gabel smirked, enjoying the challenge and conquest. He pulled at the strip of hanging skin on his thigh. He yanked it free and flung it away into the flowers.

"Sounds like it was planned, and perhaps you were unprepared."

"Buttercup, so fierce, so fierce. I almost felt that. Perhaps if you stuck your finger into my shoulder."

"Ug!" I recoiled, "Gabel!"

He laughed and gestured with his good arm for me to precede him to the festivities. "After you, my Luna. After you."

GLIMPSES

"Gabel, you need to start getting proper stitches."

"Do you object to scars?"

"No. I object to you bleeding all over the sheets, pillows, your shirts, and me." I slapped his hand away as he picked at a flake of blood.

"They will just think I had a virgin in my bed last night."

"They'll think you sacrificed a virgin," I retorted.

He glanced at the bloody sheets and pillowcases. "You are right, buttercup. I would not want Hix storming in here thinking I had been violent with your tender flesh."

The chortle on his voice and the cruel smugness slithering through the Bond made me roll my eyes. "You said you liked him as First Beta because he growls at you."

"He does more than growl."

Clearly, because I stood there trying to figure out what to salve and what to clean and how to wrap his shoulder. "You should have the doctor look at this."

"Is it infected?" Gabel turned his head to eye his pulpy shoulder.

"No, but I'm not a good nurse."

"I am not giving Hix any more of a victory that you stole from me," Gabel growled with sudden annoyance.

Stole from him? Because him riping Hix's throat out was a victory worth having. I sighed again. "This isn't about Hix, this is about your damned shoulder looking like a rabbit leg."

"He would have submitted. I would have made him."

"You can't make Hix do anything he doesn't agree with. That's why he is your First Beta."

Hix was an enemy Gabel couldn't afford to have. That's why Gabel liked him. That's why Hix liked Gabel.

But mix some masculine egos and the scent of a female, and all bets were off. Hix was probably stitching up himself for the same reasons Gabel didn't want to get the doctor involved.

Too bad for Gabel that he wasn't a bachelor with no one to look after him. Or decide it was simply time for professional help.

I hadn't seen the doctor since the night I'd arrived, and when he showed up, I remembered why I didn't like him. He was competent but had the bedside manner of a sadistic prison warden. He enjoyed his work a little too much.

While the doctor did what could be done, I ripped the sheets off the bed.

"You do not need to do that." Gabel told me.

Normally I didn't: Violet did. I ignored Gabel's mild tone of disapproval. Ripping sheets off a bed was not beneath anyone. "It took less than a minute. Now it's done."

"You should be watching. Learning."

The doctor had to cut out the edge of some of the slashes so that he could then sort of stitch and glue the edges together. Gabel refused anything to numb the skin, and it must have hurt like fire and stomach flu as the doctor cut the skin away and stitched everything shut. Gabel reveled in his victory over the pain. I did not enjoy it at all.

"Would you watch your own belly surgery too?" I asked, angry at having to watch it. If I didn't focus on being angry and annoyed, I was going to puke. It was one thing to see grisly sights in my visions, but the real, corporeal manifestation made me gag, and feeling the echoes of his physical trauma didn't improve anything.

"Quite likely."

If he really thought I was going to learn to stitch wounds just so he could avoid the pack knowing someone had dared damage his skin, he had another thing coming. "Flint is expecting me."

Master of Arms Flint held his own little combat court in his usual place, wearing one of his usual battered kilts and seem-ingly immune to the biting cold. How Flint didn't freeze to death standing in one place baffled me, even if he was shouting and gesturing every thirty seconds. How he maintained his tan in the dead of winter was another mystery. It didn't have the orange look of tan-in-a-can, and he never left the estate, as far as I knew. I wasn't aware of any tanning beds around, unless he had one in his rooms. Which was possible but seemed terribly frivolous for Flint.

I looked around for the First Beta, but he was nowhere to be seen. I hoped it was not him being too badly hurt, but it prob-ably was.

"Lady Gianna!" Flint shouted a greeting to me. He jumped down off his crate and bowed to me. All movement ceased, and all eyes turned to me, just like my first day at IronMoon.

If this was going to be how it was every morning I showed up, it would get old quickly. I hadn't made the promises to Gabel yet. I wasn't Luna yet.

"Hix is occupied elsewhere today. You will have to train with me."

"Ah..." I dared not refuse to utter a word of complaint: it was an honor to work with him, especially a little runt like me, who would probably never find herself in combat again. The wolves looking on scowled at my unearned privilege.

"Excellent!" Flint declared before I even made a sound. He spun around and jumped on his box. He flicked his fingers at a wolf standing nearby and pointed to the spot at his feet. That's where I was to wait until he was ready.

I waited, and waited, and waited. That wasn't unusual. I enjoyed watching the warriors train and Flint shout directions and ease drop on the wolves around me passing commentary between themselves. But knowing that I had to work out with Flint had some appointed hour made things a little different.

Finally, Flint ordered the ring cleared. I went to the center.

He bounced off his crate, strode over to me, and without warning snapped his right leg into my thigh.

I dropped to the ground like a doll.

Hushed silence.

I shook myself, spitting sand out of my face.

My left thigh pulsed with my heartbeat.

"Get up," Flint ordered.

I spit another grain of sand out, braced myself on my hands, and pushed myself upright. Sensation started to come back to my leg as the nerves recovered from the explosive trauma; real throbbing pain mixed with adrenaline flooded my brain.

"Well, this is different," I told Flint, breathing hard already. Nothing like getting clocked, decked, or flattened to test the cardio.

He twitched his head negatively, then I found myself back in the dirt, my other thigh exploding in pain.

Absolute, total, hushed, horrified silence.

If Flint expected me to just lay there, hell no. He'd had his chance the previous night if he didn't want me being Luna. My legs shook and tingled. I couldn't feel them so well, but my brain commanded them to move from muscle memory.

I expected a kick to the head next.

But Flint turned to the shocked audience (a few of which shot glances toward the house, expecting Gabel to appear at any moment and descend upon Flint like a Hound) and said, "Wolves, I have spoken to you of a female's courage before. And how heart and and guts," he made a fist and punched himself several times in his own stone-like abs, "cannot be taught. A good trainer knows how to push a student to their breaking point. It is only at that breaking point that we know who we are. It is mental, wolves. It is in our heads and our hearts. Observe how a trained Oracle is able to withstand what would have any of you whimpering for mercy."

Another kick swept both my legs out from under me.

He was so fast I couldn't even see the kicks or punches coming, or even as they happened. Just *bam!* and I ate dirt while my nerve endings tried to feed so much pain information to my brain I felt nothing at all, and my mind went blank from the overload.

Great. I was going to be Flint's mental discipline example for the day. Week. Month. Year. I couldn't quite hear the lecture he was giving to the wolves about signs to look for in a student who still had more to give, or what body part was giving out from exhaustion and trauma. My left thigh trembled with exhaustion, and to prove his point, Flint snapped a kick into it. I dropped, questioning how many times my leg would physically let me stand up after so much punishment.

I crawled back to my feet. Now Flint held up both of his broad palms. "You know the drill."

I was already exhausted from being pounded like sand. It didn't matter to Flint. He offered his hands, and he expected me to punch them. "Harder! More. Faster. Again. Again. Again!"

My arms burned, ached, dissolved to jelly, flopped about. I swung a final time, my left leg quaked, and I lost my balance. I dropped to my knees in the sand and collapsed forward, somehow managing to catch myself on my hands before I face-planted into the sand. I panted and dripped sweat that quickly froze against my skin.

"Hix is too easy on you," Flint growled at me. "He never pushes you as hard as you can go. Are you going to quit?"

"Fuck you, Flint." I gasped for air. I hadn't bowed to Gabel, I wouldn't bow to Flint or his little demonstration of how far and how hard to push a student.

"Haha, little wolf! Then get up!"

My battered legs shook. They were filled with throbbing-numbness and didn't want to hold my weight. I wanted to quit. I needed to quit. My body screamed at me to quit.

The song to call a Queen to war rang in my memory as my physical exhaustion eroded the barrier between my waking mind and my gifts, and the visions leached through.

Flint smiled at me, his eyes flickering green to amber in my wavering vision, and I felt half in, half out of my flesh.

"Enough!"

The song shattered, and the curtain in my mind flopped shut, snapping me back into the rather painful reality of my battered, exhausted body.

Half the wolves present plummeted to their knees.

Gabel stormed into the center of the ring, shoved his face right into Flint's and snarled, "Master of Arms. What are you doing?"

Flint didn't budge an inch, didn't even flinch or twitch. "Giving a lesson on recognizing the limits of one's students and sparring partners."

"And you are using your future Luna to do it?" Gabel circled Flint, growling under his breath. Some of the wolves present whimpered and cowered in front of his anger. Flint was calm, but for the first time, I saw the Master of Arms be wary.

"I understand your concern, Alpha Gabel," Flint said very calmly, "but all is well."

"She is here to improve herself, Master of Arms. Not be used as a tool to improve my warriors or your skills."

"I taught you in a similar way. Are you dissatisfied with the results?" Flint asked mildly.

"*She* is not a warrior!" Gabel shouted. "She is an Oracle, and *your* future Luna, and there may be my pups within her now! Have you lost your mind?!"

"Alpha Gabel, if she does have your pups within her it is so early there is no danger."

Gabel's menace shifted, sharpened, solidified into something very real. "I have no reason to trust your expertise on *that* subject."

Whatever Gabel could say to Flint, that was apparently on the forbidden list. The Master of Arm's face hardened, the calm teacher disappeared into something wrathful, and the blue-gloss tattoos squirmed on his skin, limned in a faint burning light. His growl trembled the ground under my feet. "Invoke that again at your peril, Gabel."

Gabel had made his point. "I have *never* approved of her being here. You have pushed my tolerance too far."

"No harm will come to her under my eye."

"Those bruises and pain and blood *are* harm!"

Flint didn't give an inch. "Superficial."

"*She* is out here to improve herself. Not you, not my warriors!"

Flint stated the appropriate response, "As you say."

Gabel tried to scoop me up. I shoved his hands off me. There was no way Gabel was going to carry me out of that sand ring, no matter how battered my legs were or how shaky they were. No. I was going to walk. Or crawl. But I would not be carried.

The Master of Arms wore a mysterious little smile.

"This cannot continue," Gabel growled halfway to the house, unable to keep a cork in his anger any longer. "I've tolerated it long enough, Gianna. I'm not putting up with it anymore! Those wolves having their hands all over you—"

"So what?" I snapped. "You made me go on that damn Hunt. This is IronMoon. The IronMoon can't have a Luna that's some... some... soufflé that collapses at a loud noise! There are female warriors! Warrior Lunas, too!"

"We're done with this I-Can-Be-A-Warrior-Too nonsense."

"I don't want to be a warrior, you arrogant prig. I don't want to be a fat, sitting target for our many enemies."

"That's not how it started. It started with you wanting to piss me off."

"And now I don't want to be a helpless blob!"

Gabel ground his teeth together. "You are an Oracle. Not a warrior."

"So you've pointed out."

"I will not yield on this. Flint has gone too far. I do not know why, and I do not care, but I will not let it happen again."

"You could *ask* him."

"I don't care why."

"Asshole."

"But I will trade you something of great value." He offered it like he offered a juicy rabbit.

I glared at him. "This better be good."

"I have found where SableFur sources their obsidian from."

PIECES OF THE TIDE

A pparently there were humans who dealt in large chunks of obsidian and semiprecious stones, and Gabel had located a dealer out in the middle of nowhere with several acres of rocks stretched out in old corn fields. Just browse through and select whatever one wanted, with the price based mostly off the stone's quality and weight.

The middle of nowhere being to the east of IronMoon's borders, which were a mixture of small packs with names I didn't know. Donovan was sent to scout the area for my sake, while Gabel called the Alpha of that territory. SaltPaw was next.

"The warriors might want another SpringHide," he told me in the dark of morning. We were both leaving, and the warriors who had been chosen to go to SaltPaw scurried around the front of the estate in final preparations. "I do not. It was needless."

I swallowed the lump in my throat. "You think SaltPaw will accept your arrival quietly?"

"The Alpha's words were conciliatory, his tone was not. SpringHide was butchered for no good reason." He was dressed in a dark kilt despite the cold. The scabs on his body slashed into his bronze form. "This will only take a few days. He is expecting me tomorrow."

A sly, cruel smirk, and he melted into the darkness.

"Safe travels, Lady," Flint stated. He was in charge; Gabel had taken Eroth, and I had Hix in tow. "We will see you this evening."

It was a long drive to SaltPaw—which was how Gabel and his warriors were getting there. Donovan, Hix, another warrior, and myself took a small private plane. It would prevent my presence from being announced and played into Gabel's plan: I would arrive *before* him. I'd traipse in and out of their territory.

All part of Gabel's mental warfare: *I will come for you. I can knock on your door, or I can appear on your border. I am not afraid of you. You can do nothing to stop me.*

Donovan brought a much-abused paperback of *The Divine Comedy* to read. Hix had an equally well-worn book, although the title was in Turkish.

I mindlessly stared out the window. Gabel would have gone for the SaltPaw eventually. That hourglass had just run down quicker because of the rocks. It wasn't much of a comfort.

We landed two hours later at a small airport with a single runway. I uncurled my body. Donovan gave me a doubtful look as he slid a metal bookmark into place.

"I'm fine." I tried to shake Hix's hands off as he steadied me. "I'm just stiff."

Stiff didn't begin to cover it. I felt ancient. Like five hundred years old. My muscles refused to stretch through the bruises Flint and Gardenia had gifted me. "This must be what old vampires feel like crawling out of their coffins."

Hix didn't reply. He also didn't move his hands from me. I gripped his shoulder as I gingerly put weight on my left leg. It hadn't yet woken up enough to bear my weight. That's when I realized there were bandages under my fingers. I pulled back suddenly, stumbled, and Hix steadied me. "I'm sorry. Your shoulder—"

"Not needed."

"I just didn't realize your shoulder..." Now that I paid attention, I caught the scent of bandages and antibiotic cream. It was faint, but how badly had Gabel injured him? It had been so difficult to tell in the darkness after the run, and I had seen him briefly since, but in the chaos had lost track of him. He hadn't had entrails hanging out...

"It is not serious." Hix's dark eyes warned me to not speak of it further. Concern implied he wasn't fit for duty. Concern implied weakness. He changed the subject. "Any problems, and we are leaving. If I say we are leaving, we are leaving. If you argue, I will throw you over my shoulder."

"You're such a charmer, Hix."

"Unlike Alpha Gabel, I do not believe you should be out here, especially given your battered condition. I believe it is inappropriate and not necessary. The SaltPaw are expecting IronMoon at their front door, not their back porch."

"I'm glad it's not up to you, then. If you had your way, I'd be locked into a gilded cage and spoon fed ambrosia the rest of my life."

"You object to a treasure being treated as a treasure?" Hix asked.

"And when was the last time I got treated as a *treasure*, Hix?" I snapped.

Hix looked out his window, expression hard, then told me, "Alpha Gabel has not always treated you well. Now he takes too many risks with you. I am not confident he is not trying to prove to everyone he fears no wolves and he can protect you even from a distance. He takes it for granted that he can protect you and is willing to gamble on it. This plan is foolish."

"There are only twenty-two SaltPaw, and they are miles

from here, with no extended range scouts." Donovan said from behind his book.

Hix's turned away from us to look back out his window and said nothing the remainder of the trip.

The rock farm sat on a flat stretch of acreage that stretched to the horizon without a single tree in sight. Frost clung to the withered grass. There was an old iron gate with no fence attached on either side marking the drive. A two-level house with a wrap-around porch sat on the right, and an old, ramshackle barn on the left. There was a single huge chunk of smoky quartz that stood as high as my shoulders in the center of everything, and beyond it, instead of rows of corn or soybeans, were just rows and rows of rocks.

"Interesting." Donovan's tone communicated it was not at all interesting.

"Remain here. Keep a nose out," Hix directed the other warrior with us. "Where does SaltPaw end, Hunter?"

"That row right there straddles it." Donovan indicated the boundary. "We're on the right side of it. Why? Does it matter to you, First Beta? It will all be IronMoon soon."

"But it is not IronMoon *now*. You should concern yourself with that as well."

Donovan said something in a language I didn't understood, but from his tone, I guessed it was an antique insult.

The screen door on the house swung open, then slammed shut. An older man wearing a pair of battered overalls and a flannel hustled out to meet us. "Hey there! What can I do for you folks?"

Hix said, "We have an appointment."

"We had an *appointment*?" Donovan groaned. "Moon's Eye, you stupid Beta."

"The SaltPaw do not monitor the airport, why would they monitor *this*?" Hix hissed.

"Because obsidian is valuable, and this is one of SableFur's sources?" Donovan dragged a hand over his face.

The man limped slightly on his left hip but moved with good speed. His workboots weren't laced and gaped at his ankles. He shook Hix's hand. "Right on time, Mr Demirci. I didn't catch your first name?"

"Hix. That is Donovan. This is Gianna."

The man shoved a meaty palm in my direction.

"Don't touch her," Hix stated.

The man held up his hands, "Sure thing. You're the boss. What are you looking for? You said obsidian?"

Hix didn't reply. I sighed, and said, "Preferably obsidian. Although malachite, clear quartz, or moss agate will also do. Large chunks, suitable to be made into shallow bowls."

"Scrying bowls, eh?"

Suspicious, I leaned a little closer to him. "Why do you ask?"

"Oh, get you New Age types out here all the time. Chunks of rock to make bowls or pyramids or obelisks or orbs or whatever you gonna do with 'em to align 'em to some charkha or ley line or energy field or higher vibrations." He waved his hands at his crops. "Jewelers and mystics all I ever see. Jewelers don't come here looking to make bowls, so you gotta be the mystic. I don't care, ya' know. I see UFOs out here all the time. Now I don't think they're aliens, mind you, but the government. You know. Black book. Ultra secret. That kinda thing. Weird critters around here, too. But I don't bother 'em and they don't bother me, so live and let live, I say. They don't come any closer than that part over there, and I don't have a varmint problem, so I ain't complaining. The howlin' scares anything away. Except me, but my ex-wife never said I had good sense."

What would he have said if Hix had gone war-form right there for him? Hix half-smirked.

The Rock Farmer waved his hands again. "Just askin' cause I got the pieces sorted by size, you know. Got the ones to be bowls and orbs out this way. So you looking for scrying bowls or orbs or something else?"

After a moment of hesitation, I said, "Bowls."

"Right this way." He pointed to our left and kept rambling as he walked. "Malachite, eh? Most folks come out here for scrying bowls don't want malachite. Not hard enough, absorbs too many negative energies, wrong vibrations. Prefer it for healing. Sell lots of it for folks who want to use it for healing."

He chattered on about his other customers and what they bought. Lots of turquoise. Could never keep enough lapis lazuli or large quartz spears in stock. Too hard to find natural large quartz crystals. He led us out to long rows of obsidian in varying sizes laid out on narrow strips of tarp and planting plastic.

Damn. Even if the right stones were here they'd need months of preparation to heal from the sun exposure.

"Obsidian's over here," Rock Farmer said. Another hand wave to indicate a general area many rows over. "Agate and quartz is over there. Malachite's on the other side of the property, if you don't mind a walk. I'll just pull up a seat, and you guys look over the rocks. They ain't shy and can't run fast enough to get away."

He chortled at his own joke and shuffled over toward an ancient tractor carcass.

"How entertaining," Hix muttered to me.

I chose the farthest left hand row to start. Hix followed me so closely he was practically breathing on me.

"Do you have to loom?" I hissed.

"Yes."

"Back up a few steps. It's not like you won't see anyone coming from twenty yards." I gestured to our flat, barren surroundings.

Rock Farmer sat down on the tractor's fender and reached into his pocket. He shoved two pieces of gum into his mouth.

"What are you looking for?" Hix asked.

"The right stone."

"How do you know the right one?"

"I just will."

"What do you mean you just will?"

"How does a male know a potential mate?"

"By her scent."

"Yes, but what *is* the scent from any other scent? You just know it when you smell it, don't you?"

"I suppose. I wouldn't know."

"Well, it's like that, I've been told. Blast, these are all so bleached."

"They are dark as night."

I crouched down and picked up a hunk. It felt quiet and lifeless. I rolled it in my palm. "These are all asleep."

"How can a rock sleep?" Hix picked up another rock and turned it over.

"Hix, you are so literal." He frowned as he stared down at me, watching me as he had in my jungle vision. He had been in wolf form in that vision, but it was the same expression, complete with the sunlight shining through the blue-dark of his hair. "Is Gabel sure this is where SableFur sources their rocks from?"

"I suppose. I wouldn't know. Why?"

"Because all these rocks are stored under the sun. It's going to be months to wake them. If they routinely source bowl-suitable chunks from here, why make extra work?"

Hix glared and proceeded to loom even closer as I walked up and down the aisles. Rock Farmer watched, occasionally spitting out his gum and folding two new pieces into his mouth. Hix periodically checked his watch. He had a phone, but he also had an old, antique watch he took off his wrist to wind when noon came.

"What are 'varmints'?" Hix asked.

"You must be bored to ask that. Critters. Like mice or moles."

"So these SaltPaw come hunt the vermin in his rock crops." Hix squatted down, grabbed a handful of dirt, and held it to his nose. He inhaled deeply of the scent, then threw it back onto the ground. "Pathetic. Alpha Gabel should just end them. We have no use for that weakness."

"So was Romero strong?" I snapped. "Was Gabel strong when he ripped these marks into my arm? Was he strong when he humiliated me with Gardenia in front of Anders just to prove he could?"

"Those are different things."

"No, they're not." I shoved past him.

In the middle of the sixth row of obsidian chunks was a sharp-edged, square shaped chunk that drew my attention. I dropped to my knees and grabbed it in both hands, felt a shiver course through my bones.

I turned the chunk over in my hands, marveling at how it would soon be a shallow bowl, and I could already see the form it would take under the excess rock. Even sleeping and sun-burned it shone. I flipped open the satchel on my shoulder and slipped it inside without hesitation.

"How much time do I have?"

Hix checked his watch. "Just over an hour."

I went over to where the Rock Farmer sat, content to chew on his gum and watch me. He grinned. "You find the one you want?"

"Yes. I would like to see the quartz and malachite before we settle up."

"Sure, sure."

"Lady Gianna, we should leave if you have found—"

I glared at Hix. "We came all this way. I want to see the other stones."

"Lady, eh? Got him well trained, eh?" Rock Farmer grinned at me. He clucked his tongue and winked at Hix, then hobbled off toward the quartz fields.

Hix growled to himself. "Disrespectful—"

"You're going to pick a fight over protocol with an old human who thinks aliens are in his rock crops? I've always wanted a clear quartz bowl. Don't ruin this for me by pissing him off."

The RockFarmer had a large selection of quartz spears and chunks and beautiful clusters. But it was something the next row over that caught my eye. A couple of chunks of something blue.

The stones were raw, unpolished, and uncut, the color of the ocean. One large column about the diameter of a pancake and the length of my forearm ranged from tropical green-tinged sea blue, moving to a pure blue at the other end. I clutched the blue-gradient one in both hands, hardly able to breathe at how exquisite it was.

"What is this?" I managed to ask.

"Indicolinte. Blue tourmaline."

I turned the chunk over in my trembling hands.

"It's fairly rare. That's not a true blue tourmaline. The true blue stuff with no green will cost an arm and a leg. I've got a jeweler with a standing order for that stuff. Those have too much green. Pretty, though."

"A jeweler? Not a mystic?" I asked.

"Jeweler. Makes gorgeous necklaces. Real pretty. Got some pictures in my phone if you want to see."

"How hard is it?" Soft stones flaked or shattered or cracked during the carving process.

"About like quartz. Could make a bowl out of it if you wanted, but it'd be a waste. Small little salt bowl, I guess, but would waste a lot of the spear. Most folks don't want it. Too expensive even with all that green," he mused.

I'd never heard of this stone before, or anything like it. Nobody used it for scrying, or runestones, or anything as far as I knew. But it was like the Tides. I wasn't going to leave the best pieces. If anything they'd make pretty paperweights, or maybe candle holders.

"Might want to ask the price on all that," Rock Farmer suggested.

"She doesn't," Hix said.

"Okay then. Your money, and I'm glad to take it." He hobbled back toward the house. "You still want to see the quartz?"

"We do not have time." Hix shot me a warning look. "Give me the bag."

"No." I clutched the strap. "I've got it."

"It must weight fifty pounds. Give me the bag."

"And you have stitches!"

"Give me the bag," he growled.

I surrendered the bag but scowled at him.

"It is not about whether or not you can do it," Hix put the bag over his good shoulder, "but should you. And no decent male would not insist. Stitches are meaningless."

"They mean something to me."

His face softened just a little bit.

The Rock Farmer was still writing up the invoice for the rocks when we arrived. He handed Hix the yellow carbon. "Cash only."

Hix pulled out his wallet, counted the bills for the stones, and handed them over.

"If you get a chunk of the tourmaline big enough for a bowl, contact Hix. We'll pay you better than the jeweler for it," I said as he counted the bills a second time.

He gave me a long look. "I'll think on it."

"You will be happy that—" Hix started to growl.

I grabbed his arm and told the Rock Warden. "Thank you. If it helps, I'll be happy to take flawed blue-green. I like it better."

Still twisting Hix's sleeve around in my hand, I glanced to the south. "You probably don't want to go into town for a few days. Just stay here with your rocks."

"Why you figure that?" Rock Farmer inquired.

Hix grinned at him, flashing bright white teeth. "Her future husband is conducting business here. The local mongrels may never return to deal with your field varmints."

I closed my eyes for a heartbeat, then told them we were leaving.

THE OTHER SIDE OF AN IRON MOON

Gabel >> *Are you on the plane yet?*
   Gianna >> *Not yet.*
Gabel >> *Did you find what you were looking for?*
Gianna >> *Yes.*

I did not ask him where he was. He would not tell me. It was better he didn't tell me.

Gabel was far away, the Bond stretched across a distance. I nudged my satchel with my foot, aware of the sharp, cutting obsidian lump and the mysterious blue column.

Gabel >> *Buttercup*
Gabel >> *I have a confession.*
Gabel >> *You are far away. It is not right.*
Gabel >> *I miss you.*

We returned to IronMoon later than expected.

"Seems tense." Donovan rolled down the window and sniffed the cold air as the cars meandered up the drive. "Wolves out tonight. More than usual."

"Gabel is gone. Flint is always wary," Hix said.

Donovan grunted, but his scent unnerved me. He shoved a cigar between his lips and champed down. "That's not wary I smell out there, First Beta."

He leaned over and tapped the driver. "I'll get out here. I'll walk into town and find my own trouble."

"Hunters," Hix muttered as Donovan slammed the door behind him.

Flint greeted us on the front terrace. He took one sniff of Hix and insisted he summon the doctor to deal with his injuries —there was blood on his shirt and dark circles under his eyes. Hix grumbled something and headed down the hallway to his rooms.

Dinner was long over, but I knew how to shove some meat between two slices of bread. I was halfway through gobbling it down when I noticed Flint was still there. He also was in a kilt. Flint normally was in jeans and a shirt after dinner, and in his rooms by ten. "You're on edge."

"I am responsible in the absence of both Betas, the Alpha, the and Luna," Flint said. "What have I said about always being ready?"

"This have anything to do with the trouble Donovan said he smelled in the woods?"

"It may. Things came to my ear. There are wolves who are not pleased with how the tone of the pack has changed." He shrugged.

I was not even slightly fooled. I forced myself to eat the rest of my food.

"Threats will come and go, Lady," Flint added. "You will have to trust your lieutenants to—"

"Given that it is you, myself and Hix here, Flint, just tell me what caught your ear. Unless you don't think my womanly ears can bear it." After dealing with Hix all day, I had had my fill of male "protective" instincts.

Flint huffed a laugh. "No, not that. It's that many here embraced Romero's thinking."

And with Romero dead, Gabel gone, and me the Luna in all but name... if they were going to strike... "Are you talking revolt?"

Flint shrugged. "Revolt would be a compliment. Lady Gianna, this is IronMoon. Alpha Gabel gives the flawed and violent a place here if they aren't cowards. That doesn't mean they aren't idiots. You've seen that for yourself."

"I have," I agreed, hesitating.

"Shadowless never had scuffles?"

"I don't think so."

"Many packs do. Especially young bachelor packs like this one."

I ate the crust I had just peeled. "Should I sleep tonight?"

"I'd tell you if you needed to stay awake."

Right. Because I could go to sleep after being told that. But I suppose it's something that rulers had to deal with for thousands of years: rebellion, revolt, treachery, betrayal. I finished my food and bid Flint goodnight. I had been up a day and a half, my body ached all over, and if Flint assured me I could go to sleep, I'd go to sleep.

"It's not a promise, Lady Gianna," Flint advised me, "but I'll keep watch."

"Have you told Hix?" I asked.

"I have, but he needs to rest more than you or I. He can't keep ripping open that gash on his belly."

"How badly hurt is he?"

"If he keeps ripping open that gash? Bad enough. Stupid way to die. I've told him that."

I smiled. "Thank you. He is a mule."

"The best warriors generally are."

"Goodnight, Flint."

"Goodnight, Lady Gianna."

The bed felt empty and too large without Gabel. In the darkness I picked at his pillow, thinking about his scent that clung to the sheets and would be gone next wash day. It wasn't the first time Gabel had left, but I felt it more that night.

I miss you.

Perhaps he had just been trying on the confession for size, to see what it felt like.

A shattering sound tore me out of sleep.

Shouting. Male voices shouting, bodies crashing.

More things crashed, splintered, shattered. I reached for the nightstand light, realized that the glow under the door might be a bad idea, and instead snatched my phone. The racket tumbled louder, barks, shouts, a howl of fury, and a howl to wake the whole house.

Was it just a brawl, a scuffle... did I go out there? Wait for Hix or Flint to retrieve me? Hide in the closet? Under the bed? I'd be underfoot in a brawl and an obvious target.

I dropped my phone and melted into wolf-form. More wood shattered. Then glass shattered. Bodies tumbled.

And the *howls.*

Male howls summoning the enemy to face them.

My hackles rose.

Hix's song answered the challenge.

I nosed open the bedroom door. Three dark forms tumbled into the moonlit-hallway. They unfolded from their crouches and snarled at me.

"*Feeeemallle...*" One managed to growl. The others giggled.

I bared my own fangs. Their war-forms weren't familiar, nor their scents, but it didn't matter. I knew what they were. Little Romeros. Little Romeros who had waited to hatch their plan and came at a female like cowards. Just like their damned master had.

I crouched, growling, as they advanced. Below me more bodies smashed and tumbled, roars, barks, the scent of blood, fur, spit, urine, broken wood, pain.

I backed across the threshold into our bedroom. No doors, no windows, no way out except through these flesh bags. They came slowly. They liked this. This feeling of power. The scent of my terror. The clacking of my claws on the varnish from my trembling.

The Bond swelled and swam into my awareness, latching onto my terror, and offered me something else: violence, darkness, death, cruelty, and sick pleasure from it all. It flooded my system like adrenaline and braced me, cleared the blizzard of fear from my brain, and replaced it with a familiar thrum.

My Mark pulsed.

They wanted fear. I'd offer them fear.

I lowered my tail and crouched with each backward step.

"*Feeeemallleee...*" the one who still had something resembling human speech growled. "*Hollldddd still...*"

Just one chance to get this right. Flint was always yelling at me *explode!* in training. I pressed the tips of my rear claws into the floor varnish and feigned terror until one of them had his claw extended toward me.

My claws dug into the varnish and launched me forward. I shot through the middle one's legs.

They grabbed at me, their claws raking hot fire lines down my back and sides. But I slipped through.

I barked something mocking at them as I swerved around the corner to the main landing. In wolf form I was nimbler and smaller in the hallways than their bulky war-forms, and they tripped and stumbled over each other in their effort to get after me.

I shot down the ruined stairwell into a fray of fur and bodies. If I could find loyal IronMoon warriors I could make my stand with them. *If* I could identify any of them through the writhing, thrashing tangle of bodies.

Claws raked my haunch.

They were faster and more nimble than I'd thought.

The Bond surged, howling uselessly.

I didn't look back.

A gold war-form wolf sailed over my head and tackled the three wolves behind me.

Flint.

Now I looked back. Just in time to see him grab the first war-form by the neck and arm and *rip*. A dark geyser of blood shot up to the ceiling. Flesh tore, and bones snapped.

He threw the two pieces of the wolf away, grabbed the next and bit down onto his neck.

Intestines flowed under my paws. The two halves of the first wolf flipped onto the first floor.

My paws slipped in the offal, and I tumbled tail over head down the remaining stairs.

Another howl. Hix's voice, a howl of triumph.

I stood up, panting, covered in blood and sticky things that come out of dead bodies. The howl came again: the song of triumph, the song offering victory to the Alpha's glory.

Or Luna.

Flint stomped down the steps, dragging the last war-form by his head.

I threw my head back and howled the Luna's song to honor her warriors.

Okay, presumptuous, but given the circumstances, time to assert myself.

The loyal members of IronMoon answered with howls of their own.

The Master of Arms was tawny-gold, the shafts of his fur catching the moonlight in a way that gave him an exquisite luminescence. He growled something guttural at me. His war-form did not allow him to shape human speech. The rage that fueled the form did not permit words.

Only deeds.

Without pause he stomped toward the mudroom with his grisly prisoner.

Donovan slid through the ruined front doors and almost collided with me. His timber-wolf grey form was soaked with blood. Hix limped into the foyer, clutching the re-opened gash on his belly. Blood slid through his fingers. "Are you hurt?"

I was soaked in blood but it wasn't mine. I slipped into human-form. "No, but you are."

"I'm fine." He grunted at Donovan and jerked his head. "Run down the ones who are fleeing. Bring them back."

Flint returned, this time in human-form. He was still covered in gore. "Are there any other survivors?"

"For now," Hix grunted. Then, to me. "What should we do with the injured ones?"

"How many are there?" It was tempting to tie them to trees and cover them in suet and let the birds peck them until Gabel returned home, but in the bitter cold they'd die of exposure too quickly. Only one real option: the basement. Which was unoriginal, considering I had banished Platinum to it as well.

"Three or four. The rest are dead."

I looked at the blood seeping out from between his fingers. "Go deal with that."

"I am fine, Lady."

"Go."

Hix stomped off like an insulted child.

Fucking bloodbath and rebellion and Gabel was in the south and Hix was mad because *I* told him he needed stitches.

"And maybe some a kilt?" I asked after the bloody buttcheeks, but then I looked down at myself and sighed. I looked at the blood-soaked body-part-decorated foyer and swallowed as the scent and gore hit me.

Now that my heart wasn't racing, and all the endorphins leaked out of my system, I started to quiver and grow cold.

Holy hell, those three war-forms had planned on ripping open the door to my room and doing who knew what to me. They had broken into the house, turned on their own pack...

I gulped down bile.

I could not show weakness. Not for an instant.

The Bond offered a shoulder to lean on again.

I took it.

COUNTING

From what Donovan and I could piece together, the IronMoon rebels had snuck up from their barracks about two miles from the main house, broken in through the library windows, and headed up the stairs to find me.

This plan was rather flawed considering the library windows were at the far end of the house. It also alerted the night guards. By the time they'd gotten halfway to their goal the loyal warriors were on their way.

No wolves loyal to IronMoon had been killed, and there were no serious injuries. The mess in the hallway and the foyer was... extensive. The stairs were in one piece, but the banisters and railings splintered, the koi pond trashed, the marble shattered, the wood in the main hallway gouged, windows shattered, walls broken, and of course, the downstairs was littered with blood, body parts, and entrails.

It took a surprisingly long time to account for everyone and sort out the traitors from the troublemakers. I expected that kind of thing to take an hour, tops, but somehow it took hours.

Flint didn't let the filth linger. Body parts had to be scraped off walls, and the whole house had to be doused in bleach.

Debris and dust had to be cleaned up, and some basic repairs done, like a few ruined steps. A more skilled craftsmen would have to repair the floor tiles and doors. We'd already had the front doors replaced once that year.

"How serious are the injuries?" I asked the doctor from the relative safety of Gabel's office later that afternoon. The white-haired wolf dug under one of his fingernails with a scalpel and twirled the point of it against the pad of his index finger.

"Nothing but some meat stitching," he said with a little grin that sent a shudder down my spine. Not the same kind of shudder Gabel caused, just a shudder of pure revulsion.

"No more dead bodies to worry about?" I asked. The disloyal wolves had died in combat, thank the Moon. I hadn't had to deal with them personally.

"Probably not. Might need to clean up some festering. Debride some tissue."

Another shudder of revulsion. "Great. Thank you."

I gestured to the door to shoo him out as quickly as possible. The less I saw of him, the happier I'd be. Creepy old sadist. Pack doctors were difficult to acquire. There weren't many. We were lucky to have that one. At least that's what I told myself.

I cringed at the idea of him doing so much as a pregnancy test on me, much less delivering a pup. Gabel would make a better midwife.

But no time for that. I headed to Hix's room to find out if he'd been a good Beta and gotten stitches like I'd demanded. If he managed to kill himself out of pride, I'd cross the Tides to drag him back to life so I could kill him myself.

Hix's rooms were at the far opposite end of the house, on the second floor and not far from Flint (who preferred life on the first floor). Even as I stood at the closed door I caught the scent of antiseptic and blood, and a very grumpy wolf. I knocked.

No answer.

I knocked again.

No answer.

I knocked again.

"*What!*"

I pushed the door open.

A very angry male glared back at me from his couch. So angry that it took a few seconds for him to shove all that anger down and away from sight, and he moved to sit up around his bandaged midsection.

"You don't have to get up," I said.

"I am not—" he growled. "What are *you* doing here?"

"Making sure you're being a good patient like I ordered." I didn't try to stop him from wrestling himself into a sitting position. He only had on a pair of abused black sweatpants, which is not really the most flattering look for any man. But with his midsection wrapped and padded, I couldn't fault him for being comfortable. He also hadn't shaven. I didn't tell him he looked more like an angry wet cat than the First Beta of IronMoon.

But I did spot some fresh stitches on his shoulders, and that wrapping around his midsection looked better than a home-grown hack job. He also had a couple other stitches puckering his torso and arms.

"As you can see, I am obeying your order, Lady," he grumbled.

"Good. Because that is a stupid way to die." I pointed at his swaddling, then looked at his television. "What on earth are you watching?"

He clicked it off. "It doesn't matter. You have my attention."

"Were you watching the weather? You were watching the weather."

"It is very numbing." Hix glowered. "Lady, I appreciate your concern, but I am being obedient, as you can see, and I will not die. I prefer you only see me when I am at my best."

"What is the difference between you trying to nursemaid me, and me showing enough concern to come down here to make certain my First Beta isn't bleeding to death?" I asked, annoyed. "Wait. Wait. Let me guess. You're male, I'm female."

"You are learning."

"A Luna should value her warriors. You've been injured several times in my service."

Hix looked uncomfortable. His eyes moved to my shoulder, then to the muted television.

"I don't take any of it for granted. What you did last night was your duty, and I'm not going to insult you by thanking you for it. But what you did that earned you most of those wounds... you didn't have to do any of those things."

Hix glared at me. "I did, but you don't understand that. Most of the wolves here wouldn't. It'd be best if it wasn't mentioned again."

"It won't be."

He was comfortable with that. He nodded to me. "It is an honor, Lady Gianna."

Gabel arrived home the following afternoon during a snow storm. Waiting outside on the snowy front steps was very cold business.

Gabel slammed the car door as he got out. My insides leapt at seeing him, a shiver of pleasure, the Bond roiling happily at his return, and I did not feel the cold so much. His eyes locked with mine, and he strode across the snow with purpose.

He grabbed my face and yanked me to him for a hot, summer-inducing kiss.

The hungry, possessive lust curling through him was new and unexpected.

"You are not hurt?" he hissed to me, still holding my face in both his hands and looking me up and down.

"I am fine."

He kissed me again, hungry and slow this time, pulling me against his body. One of his hands released my face so it could grip the small of my back and hold me against him.

"Later." My breathing felt ragged. I swallowed, breathing hard in the cold.

"Not much later, buttercup," he growled, "not much later at all."

"Don't you want to hear about what happened here?"

"I got the details from Hix late last night."

"I would have told you."

"He is a warrior. That is the report I wanted. I know they came for you. They got to our door," Gabel growled.

"Not exactly, that's a bit of an exaggeration—"

"No! It is not an exaggeration. It is the truth!" Gabel smoldered, furious and angry that this had not been properly foreseen. He glared at me, but his anger was elsewhere. "This is why I do not have windows in that room, Gianna. They could have been upon you!"

It should never have happened, but could it be avoided in a pack like IronMoon?

His fingers dug into my skin. Without a word, he growled and took my hand, leading me into the house, just grunting acknowledgments at Hix and Flint as he passed them.

His anger only grew when he saw the foyer, which still reeked of bleach, and the gouge marks outside our rooms. He crouched down and ran his fingers over the ones my claws had made. "These are your dainty claws, buttercup. Did you fight? Did you have to defend yourself?"

"I bolted between their legs as Flint came up the stairs."

"But they had you cornered. They got our door. You were cornered."

"For a moment, perhaps."

"They should never have gotten this far." Gabel herded me into our room, closed the door.

"Gabel, you were gone. They took the opportunity."

"Yes. Yes, I now realize that. I did not realize Romero's supporters had such stubborn stupidity. They heard we were going to complete the vows and decided to act while there was time." Gabel began to yank off his clothing. He paused, looked at me. "You are not angry?"

"Only confused." His shoulder had not ripped open again. He had not shifted forms while traveling, but he had lost his bandages somewhere, and the skin around the stitches was angry and red.

"You are still in shock."

"Am I?" I asked. "Or am I just your mate?"

"I felt you call upon the Bond," he said pensively.

Was that what I had done? Gabel seemed so pensive, and I was confused as well. I didn't respond directly. "This sort of thing never happened in Shadowless."

"And it will not happen here! They must come for *me*, not you!" He threw his clothing to the ground, stepped out of his pants. He came over to me, grabbed me by my arms and inhaled my scent. "You smell of pain, buttercup."

"I have bruises, Gabel. Remember?"

He pushed my sweater off my shoulders and down my arms.

"Gabel, what are you doing?" I breathed as he kissed my neck, moving close to me, his hands sliding under my top.

He didn't answer. The Bond did: needing something, assurance, connection, to be fed, to be satisfied I was not hurt, that I was well. He pulled me over to our bed and divested me of the remainder of my clothes, his lips moving over each bruise and scratch. His fingertips explored a bruise on my arm. I whimpered and swatted at him, but it did no good.

"This is new," He growled.

"I fell down the stairs in the commotion." Like a total klutz.

"And this," he brushed his lips over a scrape on my hip, "this is new."

"Do you know every bruise?" I asked.

His hands lifted my hips, he kissed my belly, moving lower, and lower, "Yes."

"I thought warriors did not care about such things." My fingertips found his hair. I closed my eyes and bit down a mewl, the Bond sighed and warmed at his caress.

"On ourselves we count nothing. On our mates, we count everything."

SUMMONS

Gabel stared at his map. He held a yellow push pin in his fingers, uncertain where to move it.

"So the SaltPaw were a lie? It was a trap? They ran?" I asked.

"The houses were there. The territory markings were there. They had very recently been there. But they had not left in too much of a rush, either." Gabel jabbed the pin into the side of the map, having decided to not put it anywhere. "Everything important in the house had been taken."

"They abandoned their territory." I couldn't fathom that.

"No. I suspect conveniently *absent*. The houses weren't ripped up in chaos, like they had fled. They also hadn't been packed up as if to move. Save for the curious absence of anything sensitive. I sent Donovan to the south to watch for their return. I suspect they will be back."

"If they're not there, nothing to conquer, hmm?"

"Exactly. I had to return here else I could have tracked them down. Their Alpha is not nearly as clever as he thinks he is. I will remember this. Donovan will find their scent, and he will find them. I suspect they have scattered, and other packs have taken them in. These packs are all very small. Close knit. Inter-related."

"Except for IceMaw."

"Except for IceMaw." He nodded.

"It would say a great deal about Aaron if he could convince an Alpha to run away and hide," I mused.

A whole pack just... leaving their territory to avoid a war party. It was sort of clever, in a cowardly, sneaky, backhanded way: if he wasn't there to surrender, Gabel couldn't do anything. The IronMoon show up, no wolves present, territory cleaned of anything useful, and the whole of a pack just pleasantly not there to answer the door.

"And me, without my Oracle," Gabel told me.

That might be a permanent affliction for him if we really did share the same future. I didn't tell him that, though. "What are you going to do? Go find them?"

"I was tempted to raze everything. Burn it all down. But I wanted to see what would happen if I just left. I've never heard of this strategy. I want to see how it plays out." Gabel grinned, excited by the new mystery and the prospect of Aaron of IceMaw being the source of it.

"Aaron might be a worthy adversary," I needled him. Aaron was a safer choice than Magnes of SableFur, certainly.

He came over to me and leaned down, his hands braced on either side of the sofa back. "I take them where I can find them, buttercup."

"You aren't King yet, Gabel."

"As you so often remind me. Do you want me to send a group down there to raze it?"

"No." I sighed.

Gabel chuckled. "So you found what you were looking for. How long until your new bowls are ready?"

"Three full moons to purify the chunks, then whatever time

is needed to carve the bowls, then another three moons to prepare them. I still have my dreams and meditations, but scrying is out for now. I found a stone I have never seen before, nor heard of. I need to mediate on it. Gabel." I put my index finger under his chin and pushed upward. "My eyes are up here."

Before he could reply, a knock on his office door, then the door opened.

The warrior on the other side coughed and averted his gaze. He clutched a red leather folder in one hand, ancient, well-worn, with a patina that bespoke age. "This arrived for Lady Gianna."

"From who?" Gabel demanded. "Who brought it?"

"A SableFur messenger." The warrior handed me the folder, stretching out his arm and sidling toward me so he didn't have to get closer to Gabel than was actually required.

"Leave," I told the warrior.

He beat a hasty retreat out the door.

"What is it?" Gabel turned his burning attention to me.

"Elder Oracle." I flipped open the top of the binder, and peeled apart the ancient leather edges. Despite its fancy exterior, inside was just a common sheet of white paper and a note scrawled in a quivering, ancient hand.

Elder Oracle Anita had summoned me to SableFur on no uncertain terms.

"Screw the old bat," Gabel spat as I read the demand to him. "You are the Luna of IronMoon and you will not be summoned—"

"I am not Luna yet," I reminded him. "I am still an Oracle and—"

"She cannot do this!"

"She can defrock me," I said mildly. It wouldn't strip me of my gifts, or the Moon's Blessings, but I'd be a renegade. "Could you be with a disgraced Oracle? I'm not a male. I can't redeem myself through combat. I'm a female. Once we're damaged, we tend to stay that way."

"You are not going to SableFur because their old crone demands it. Withered old bitch thinks she can just summon the Luna of IronMoon—"

He wasn't listening. I slapped the binder shut and threw it aside. "I am not the Luna of IronMoon! I am the IronMoon Oracle until Solstice, and I've been summoned. She doesn't have to explain why."

Gabel fumed. "You do not have time to play handmaiden to some withered old bitch."

"Stop calling her that. Elder Oracle Anita was one of my teachers. She deserves some respect." I secretly despised Anita and had thought of her as a withered old bitch on more than one occasion. None of the students liked her, and I doubted her disposition had improved in the three years since I had seen her. She was one of those old women who expected the world to cater to her, that all her students were also her slaves, and that her will was to be obeyed.

But she was also an Elder Oracle, and had proven time and time again she was a master of enduring the Tides.

"No." Gabel's tone grabbed my spine and twisted. "I forbid it. I am going to have this folder shoved right between that messenger's teeth!"

I snatched the red folder against my breasts. "Do you want to attract SableFur attention? The SableFur probably don't know I've been summoned. This is Oracle business—"

"Unless it isn't. Has it occurred to you that the SableFur might not have liked us annexing their precious rock farm, so they are going to take my mate prisoner?" He'd sent IronMoon warriors back to the SaltPaw territory. If they'd thought they'd quietly return to their homes... they were wrong.

"*This* is an Oracle summons," I corrected. "If I ever become an Elder Oracle I can summon little Oracles here, and I'd never bother to tell you. You'd eventually find out, but I doubt you'd pay attention."

"I am sure the SableFur leadership knows you have been summoned. You think they send a formal messenger into Iron-Moon territory, and nobody knows? What guarantees do I have of your safety? Can I send an escort with you? Those rocks are valuable. SableFur is not going to let me just have them."

"There's this." I held up the red binder. "Although...I have to take it with me, as it will grant me safe passage."

"How convenient. Leaving me with no proof. And anytime she wishes, this Elder Oracle can just snap her fingers, and off you'll run!"

A summons was so rare and unusual that I didn't think it would happen again. It was also very convenient it happened *right* then. "If I don't go she'll strip me of my status as an Oracle, and I'll be disgraced."

"Some wizened old crone does not get to pull my Luna's strings!"

"I am not your Luna, and I won't ever be if you don't let me go. You won't mate with a disgraced she-wolf who can't keep her promises!"

"She is going to try to stop us," Gabel said. "Your Oracle vows will always be a string she can pull."

"I am not giving up my vows," I whispered.

"That crone is loyal to Alpha Magnes, as you are loyal to me. You will not dance on her string." His anger boiled over. He snapped his elbow back, then forward, plunging his fist into a wood column. I flinched.

Again.

Again.

Again.

"Stop it!" I shouted.

"Give me one reason why I should let you walk out of this house at all, much less without a full escort?"

"I'm not your Luna yet," I said, annoyed he would shout at me like I was the enemy. "But I am an Oracle *now*. If you refuse you're handing her my pelt, and that might be exactly what they want. If I don't go, I *will* be disgraced, and I will be dishonored. They'll poison the well."

Gabel simmered. Then, in an ugly tone, he said, "And if they murder you? Take you prisoner? If you are lured there, will it reflect badly on this crone?"

"And this might just be Oracle business," I reminded him.

He growled, deep, deep in his throat. "I will permit you to go. With Donovan. A warrior would be too hostile. If they refuse to let you in with even a token hunter escort, Donovan is bringing you back."

"Donovan is hunting the SaltPaw."

"Now he will escort you," he growled. "Do not linger with this Elder Oracle. Be wary of delay."

He snatched the red binder from my grip and pulled out the summons. "You can take a copy. I'm keeping the original as proof. Inform her I will never allow you to answer another summons again.

"You will leave tomorrow. And I expect you back in three days or sooner. If you are not back, I am going to tell that gutless birthpack of yours that they are going give me every warrior they have, and I am coming to get you."

OUTRAGEOUS REQUESTS

"How do you know this Oracle?" Donovan asked me.

"She was my last teacher."

"Last? You flunk out elsewhere?"

"No. When you have proven you have the gifts, the will, and the ability to ride the Tides, you study under one of the Elder Oracles. She decides if you can ever take the vows, gives you your first tools, finishes your training. I trained in a few different packs. Acolytes move around. Different teachers, different circumstances."

"How long were you away from your home?"

"Five years. I earned my title at sixteen."

"That's young, isn't it?"

"A little young, but many who start never finish."

"What happens to the ones who don't finish? Go home?"

"They die."

"They die."

"If you're powerful enough that you can become an acolyte, then you either finish the training or you go insane," I said. "If you can't control your gift, it controls you, and your Oracle sisters put you down instead of let you suffer that."

"And most never finish."

I shrugged. "Every Seer thinks they're going insane when the gift comes on them. You get reminded when you start training that it will end badly if you can't learn to control it, but it takes a while for it to sink in. You don't make friends with other students."

"Because they could die."

I fiddled with a piece of string tied to one of the air vents on the truck. "You start to see it happen after the first few times. Recognize the symptoms."

"Ever fear you were lost on the Tides?"

"Yes."

"How frightening is it?"

"On the Tides, you're all alone. No one can save you. No one is coming to help you. No one even knows you're gone."

Donovan leaned out the window and eyeballed the terrain. "They know we're here."

"How do you know?"

"Two too many random guys standing out by stalled cars."

"I hadn't even noticed."

"That's not your job, it's mine. That's why you're driving."

I was exhausted by the time we arrived at Elder Oracle Anita's residence: a small cottage set out in the middle of an open field. There was a small, circular, spring-fed pond around which marble tiles had been placed. I had lived in the cottage my final year of training, serving as much as Anita's personal maid as her student.

Cantankerous old bitch.

"The male must wait outside." Anita's crusty old voice stated from the door of her cottage.

"Yes, ma'am." Donovan leaned up against the side of the truck. "As you say, ma'am."

Anita gave him a sharp look and jerked her fingers at me.

With her were two acolytes. I knew those pained, long-suffering expressions well. The cottage still smelled the same: lavender, obsidian, dust, green tea.

She was a heavyset older woman now and moved with a limp in both hips. She wasted no time bringing me to the solarium overlooking the pond, and I sighed at its splendor. In the snowy winter night the pale blue, mineral-laden pond was a thing of beauty. There was nothing like it in IronMoon.

I took care to walk only where I would not disturb the wards and knelt in the familiar spot where I had received many hours of lectures (and brow-beating).

I set the folded copy of her summons. "I have come as summoned, Elder Oracle."

Anita grunted. One of the acolytes fetched the summons and handed it to her. She unfolded it and waved it. "Where is the original?"

"The binder will be returned to you once I have returned to IronMoon," I replied, careful to keep my head bowed in a respectful fashion.

She grunted. "So that dog thought I'd double-cross him, hmm?"

Obviously.

"Show me," Anita told me gruffly. She tapped her shoulder. "Show me his Mark."

I shrugged off my light coat and pulled off my sweater. The acolytes gasped in horror at the raw, cruel slashes. She, however, just grunted again and snapped a finger at the acolyte on the left. The woman scurried forward clutching a piece of paper. A drawing of the *comet* rune.

My heart beat faster, but I wore a bewildered mask. "What is this?"

"The reason you can't mate Alpha Gabel," Anita said.

"Oh?" I resisted the urge to wad up the paper and throw it

at her. She was still a powerful Oracle herself, and the Moon could have shown her anything. She was loyal to SableFur, too. She'd never violate her Oracle vows, but if there was anyone who knew how to stretch the limits, it was Anita.

"I know about the broken bowls. From a vision." She folded the paper and placed it on the little table to her left.

I didn't believe the vision part of it for a second. She'd found out, or figured it out. "And because my bowls were broken I can't be with Gabel?"

"Don't you understand he destroys everything he touches?" Anita jabbed her finger at the piece of paper.

Bitterness washed the back of my throat. And *now* Anita wanted to save me from the monster? Why now?

She gestured with her hands. "I saw you wearing a necklace made of the shattered pieces of your obsidian bowl. Alpha Gabel placed it around your neck, and then a crown of more broken pieces on your brow. On the back of your hand, as you touch the center stone, is a brand. *Balance* has been burned into the back of your right hand."

It was difficult to absorb this, and even more difficult to keep my reaction away from her. A crown? Balance? The Comet? Did it matter? Not especially. "You're six months too late to tell me you're worried about my being a monster's mate. Where were my Oracle sisters when he did *this* to me? When he humiliated me and degraded me in front of everyone? But shattered bowls and a drawing of a rune so unimportant everyone's forgotten about it, well, yes, of course, that means you have to intervene."

Anita's leathery old face constricted. "In another vision I am standing in a forest, in front of the shambles of an old hut. It has a thatched roof. It is very old. I go into the hut, and among the broken pieces, I found an old metal box. In the box was a ring. It had once been a promise ring, but the markings for Luna and Mother had been added to make it a pup-ring. In the center between the two signals was a spot for a stone, but the stone was gone. Under the band, was the ancient rune for the Comet, the destroyer."

"What does this vision have to do with the one of me?" I feigned a minor scoff. "It's not my ring."

"You must not complete the mating with Gabel. Sever the tie and walk away," she insisted.

I didn't need to be too clever to know Anita wasn't telling me everything. For all I knew, Alpha Magnes had asked a question, and the vision about the necklace was part of it, and he wanted to prevent Gabel and I from mating. That crown imagery probably didn't sit well, so he'd used Anita to scare me off Gabel.

There was no clear link between the pup-ring vision and the necklace that Anita revealed, so either she was patching together pieces of a vision to try to sneak it by me, or she was leaving out some big details. "Anita, I'm not your novice anymore. I am an Oracle, and I've served as an Oracle for years. You're going to have to do better."

"I'm giving you a reason to call off a pairing with a man who took you by force," Anita said.

I laughed at her audacity. "Are you serious? You're six months too late. Where were you this spring? You didn't summon me away from him or try to keep me safe. I don't see you offering me sanctuary now. You just want me to call off my mating. For what? Because you saw me wearing a crown and had a vision of a ring that has nothing to do with me? Is Alpha Magnes offering me safe haven here?"

"No," Anita said, like she hadn't been prepared for the question.

"Then what do you think is going to happen? Do you think

Gabel is going to let me walk away? I had to fight with him to even get permission to answer your summons."

"Gianna, as Gabel placed the necklace around your throat and the crown upon your brow, I saw packs on their knees before him," Anita said, unwilling. "It was cold and dark on a rocky island in the sea. All around were water and wolves kneeling. Gabel is a comet. He brings destruction to us all."

This had to be someone else's question and answer, and I was getting edited snippets. I rocked back on my heels, eyed her, and lied again. "A comet? I don't know that rune."

"It's fallen out of use. Back when we used to believe comets were harbingers of destruction." Anita flicked her wrist. "Comets are destroyers. They destroy everything they touch. They smash into the world and lay waste to everything without regard for anything."

"And you think Gabel is this comet? Why? That's a big jump, Anita."

"You must *not* mate with him. He will destroy everything he touches."

"Wherever I will go he will find me." I prodded around her to see if she would give me more details. We'd had the same vision—sort of—and I wanted to know more.

"You *must* listen to me," she said.

I shrugged. Time to antagonize her. "You're not saying anything very interesting. I've had the same vision of the house. I've seen the ring."

"There is a Moon's Servant in IronMoon. A gold wolf with blue-gloss tattoos," I said. "Gabel might have taken me as tribute, and he is a monster, but he hasn't acted against the Moon's design."

Anita's old eyes hardened. She had expected obedience and wasn't used to explaining herself. The acolytes shifted nervously. Anita's lips twitched in a suppressed growl, then she finally said, "The inside of the ring was inscribed with three runes. *Love, faith* and *balance*. Every time I see you in a vision, Gianna, you have the *balance* rune, very tiny, branded on the back of your right hand. Even years ago, when you were my student, you always had that rune on the back of your right hand. *Balance* is almost never used. It means all things are as they should be or are intended to be. It's not a rune Oracles find themselves using."

"You never told me it was dangerous to use," I said.

"It's not *dangerous*," Anita said, "except that when you ask the Moon to show you things plainly, it can be more than you want to invoke. There are things we shouldn't see, Gianna, and doors we shouldn't open."

And that explained why the *balance* rune had worked so well for me: I had needed those doors open to see Gabel for what he was:

The Moon's Comet.

"Why didn't you ever tell me this?" I asked. Pure curiosity, I didn't actually care.

"Why should I have to warn you about a rune like that?" she scoffed. "It's never a rune you'd use anyway. Many Oracles who try to enter the Tides using it find Her Eye closed."

I wasn't inclined to tell Anita I'd been using the rune regularly. Wasn't her business the way I saw it. "So what do you suggest I do, Anita?"

"As I said. Cancel your mating."

I gestured to my arm. "Sort of impossible. It's not like SableFur has raised their hands to help me escape. Where am I supposed to go? He'll find me wherever I am. He has Hunters, he rules most of the east. I'd have to go hundreds of miles before I was out of IronMoon, and I'll still have this Mark on my arm."

"I'm not in IronMoon, I can't help you figure it out. Ask the Moon for help."

"You think I *haven't?*" I shouted. "You think I didn't pray this rotted off my arm? You think I haven't *pleaded* with Her? She hasn't answered. It's too late, Anita. I could have my pups in his belly now. All that's left is a formality."

Her expression turned ashen. She sagged back in her chair. "No."

I snorted. "This is bits and pieces of another wolf's visions. You think I can't tell? You tell Magnes—because all this is his vision, isn't it? That's why I'm *really* here, because your Alpha doesn't like that crown on any head but his—that it's too late. SableFur missed their chance. You should have done something a long time ago."

I stood. "I've been using *balance*. I've already seen the Comet. I've looked into the abyss. My bowls have been shattered, but my gifts are intact."

Anita extended a shaking hand up to me, but she smelled of anger, not fear for my soul. "Don't do it, Gianna. Can't you see what he's done to you?"

"You had your chance. I didn't see my Oracle sisters coming to save me when he dragged me off to IronMoon and degraded me and humiliated me and carved me like a turkey! I *can't* do anything but this!"

"If you mate with him you will destroy us all!" Anita braced herself on the arms of her chair and shoved herself to her feet.

"I already have!" My voice cracked. "We lost control of the Bond and consummated it months ago! It's too late, it's been too late!"

She shoved her finger under my nose. "Figure it out, Oracle. You will destroy all of us if you do this!"

The only thing Gabel was going to destroy would be SableFur.

My Mark thrummed, and the Moon spun in my awareness for the first time in weeks. She warned me to be silent.

It was time to go.

"As you say, Elder Oracle," I said. "I will do what I must for the good of us all."

I knew the way out of the cottage. I could have found my way in the dark.

Donovan, sitting on the hood of the car, looked up from his book. "All done?"

"Yes."

"Good to drive?" He jangled the keys.

"Wide awake." I got into the cab.

"So. How many lies did the old bitch tell you?" Donovan asked.

"One too many."

FORWARD

"What did the old woman want?" Gabel asked.

"To tell me not to mate with you."

"It's a little late for that."

"Which is what I told her."

Gabel raked his fingernails along his neck, lightly itching his skin. "I'm almost flattered she doesn't like me that much."

"So you aren't going to heed her?" Flint asked over coffee.

"She didn't tell me anything to convince me," I replied.

Hix scowled. "A waste of time."

I paced over to the window of the office and stared down at the training fields. The warriors had gotten started in their regular conditioning with Eroth leading the fray. "The Moon showed her the ring and rune, Flint."

Flint sipped his coffee.

"I got snippets of a vision from someone else. Anita had permission to reveal enough to stitch together a story that would stop me," I continued. "It had to come from high up in Sable-Fur. Magnes, Adrianna, Lucas, someone. She saw the rune, too."

"What rune would this be?" Gabel asked.

Flint gestured with his coffee cup. "The ancient rune for *comet*. It's like the Death card of the Tarot."

"It has her frightened, but not frightened enough to offer me anything. Leave Gabel, she told me, but was SableFur going to give me a place to hide? No. I told her she was insane. He'd hunt me to the ends of the world onto the Tides itself." I turned around, hugging myself. "They're going to try to stop the mating. Or do *something*. I told her it's too late, we consummated the Bond months ago. She was almost in a panic."

"Excellent diplomacy, buttercup. War with SableFur," Gabel said with a quirked brow. "Tsk tsk. That ambition of yours."

"There's a spy in IronMoon." I ignored his comment. "She knew my bowls were broken. She knew I obtained new stones."

"Every pack has spies." Gabel leaned on his desk. "That doesn't concern me. SableFur didn't know we'd consummated the Bond some time ago, and we just announced our intentions. They're dealing with old information or rumors. What concerns me is why did they play their hand *now?*"

I grimaced at my own denseness. Obvious question. Not the *what*, but the *why*. Oracles didn't spend a lot of time with the *why*. "I don't know."

Gabel pondered the puzzle further. "If she's seen a shift in power that threatens SableFur, and you told her we had mated, why risk letting you live? Your death would have been simple and easy to justify. No one would have asked many questions."

"I don't know," I said. The Destroyer Next Door breeding heirs from a legitimate Moon-accepted mate sounded like a cosmic call to action. Killing me would have killed Gabel, or if it didn't, weaken him enough IronMoon could have been had without much difficulty. Yes, it would have been disgraceful, but a little disgrace to save the world? Easy trade. Once Anita had known I'd consummated the Bond, why risk letting me live?

Gabel watched me from behind his desk. He tapped his fingertips on the surface. My mind reminded me of those fingertips on my skin. I'd trade places with that desk. The Bond shivered and whispered I should do just that. "Buttercup, you're keeping secrets again."

"What she told me was from pieces of other wolves' visions. I'm not going to relay some garbled, cherry-picked mess." I said, unwilling to tell him SableFur believed *he* was the Comet.

"What did she offer you in return for leaving me?" Gabel asked.

I laughed bitterly. "Nothing."

His eyes narrowed. "Nothing you wanted, or nothing at all?"

"Not even bus fare." I sighed and leaned back on the couch.

Gabel's fingers raked at the stacks of papers, then picked up a pencil and snapped it across the bridge of his fingers. Then he ordered Hix, "Nobody knows about this. Lady Gianna answered an Oracle summons. I sent her with Donovan, she left, she returned without incident. It's Oracle business."

Hix nodded.

Flint spun on his heel and walked away. Hix followed.

The door clicked closed.

"What game are you playing now?" I asked him.

"The SableFur are dangling this like meat in front of me." His tone was as angry as the slow-broiling rage building within him.

His rage seemed to strangle me, reaching up like tentacles from the Bond, grabbing and pulling at me, snarling and lashing. Was he just blowing off steam, or was the worst of a male's protective instincts driving him to blindness and fury?

I stood up and approached him with caution.

Once within reach one hand snaked out and grabbed me by the dip of my waist. I squeaked but didn't resist, and he snatched me against him, his other hand clasping down on my hip. "Buttercup," he growled. He shoved his nose into my neck, inhaled my scent, held me so tight it hurt. I closed my eyes against it so I wouldn't whimper.

"I'm fine, Gabel," I whispered.

"You are tired. You smell of bruises and old blood and distress."

I pushed his head away from my neck, slid my hand over his cheek. He tried to snake away from me. I didn't let him. "Listen to me."

"I cannot let them hurt you," Gabel growled.

"They did not hurt me. No one has hurt me. I am here. I am whole. I am not going to do what they want."

He growled and his hands pushed under my shirt. His fingertips found each bruise and sore spot, counting them all again.

The tentacles of his seething anger pulled at me, as if he needed to assure himself I was still there. He lifted me onto his desk and pulled my shirt over my head. I didn't resist. Feral fury flowed from him, and something else I had never sensed in him: something that resembled fear.

"I am still here, my Alpha," I whispered around his hungry tongue and rough hands.

But I don't think he heard me.

STAY IN THE PAST WHERE YOU BELONG

G abel kissed me, his breath hot and ragged from exertion. The Bond slept like a contented, warm cat.

It had been selfish, and rough, and about him, but I did not mind. I raked my fingernails over his shoulders. "I am very much here, my Alpha."

He ran his hands over my breasts, ribs, hips, thighs, assuring himself once more that my body was whole. He kissed the scars on my arm, lost in stormy thoughts. "The Master of Arms will be expecting me. I have things to attend to. To make certain this... nonsense... never bothers our den again."

Never was a long time for an Alpha, and even longer for a King, but I didn't point it out. He'd take a page from Hix's book and put me in a gilded cage I'd never leave.

I slid off the desk and twisted my skirt back around my thighs. My panties were in ruins on the floor, and my bra hadn't fared much better. So much for my plan to meditate that afternoon.

Violet intercepted me in the second floor hallway with an envelope. "I was just bringing this to you."

A pang of anxiety hit me, but this envelope was cream

colored and embossed, not red. Quite formal and thick, though. Stiff enough I could have cut a finger off with it. Violet didn't normally rush the mail up as soon as it came in from town. She pursed her lips at me. I took the cue, turned it over to the front and—

"The fuck," I said before I caught myself.

It was addressed to Gabel and...

Gardenia.

I almost threw up. It slammed into me like that blasted comet coming from space right smack into me.

"The fuck is this?" I snarled.

"Shhhh!" Violet grabbed me and shushed me with her fingers. "Shhh! Shhhh!"

I snarled at her, holding it up like it was some kind of holy writ.

"Shhh! I don't know. I was bringing it to you. Not him."

I grit my teeth so hard they squeaked

And now this. Goddamn Gardenia again. The stupidest, most insignificant, pathetic problem I could possibly have coming back for round fucking...

What round was it with her? Five?

I was going to make a belt out of her hair.

Right after I throttled Gabel.

"Violet, I swear by the Moon-"

Violet dragged me into the bathroom off the hallway. "Shh! Deep breaths, Lady. Deep breaths."

I shoved it at her. "Tell me what it is. I can't look at it."

I could look at anything my scrying bowls wanted to show me, but I wasn't going to look any farther at the contents of that envelope. Violet took it, and I spun around so I didn't have to see. Every sound of the thick card stock scraping against the envelope's satiny interior was a fresh papercut on my skin.

"It's an invitation. To a Solstice party at GleamingFang."

"Gleaming Fang?" I asked over my shoulder. Alpha Anders.

"The postmark date is the day before Alpha Gabel had me send out the invitations to *our* Solstice festivities."

"Anders may not know, you mean," I said, feeling like I had gulped down some toxic brew. "He still thinks Gardenia is Gabel's BondMate. He's heard Gabel has taken one, and mistakenly thinks it's Gardenia."

"That sounds most likely," Violet offered. "Anders holds a Solstice party every year."

"Anders must have his head up his ass to not know by now," I grumbled. Or Anders didn't have a spy in IronMoon.

"Unless names were never mentioned, and when people spoke of Gabel's BondMate, he assumed it was Gardenia and said he had met her... not knowing it was um... that Gardenia was—"

I glared at the bathroom wall. "Does Gabel usually go to this party?"

"He went last year."

"Alone?"

"Alone."

I huffed a breath. Gardenia. She was no flower. She was a goddamn weed, and I was going to have to gulp down humiliation on her account one more damn time. I turned around and took the invitation out of Violet's fingers. "Well, we can either be sure Anders doesn't have a good flow of gossip, or he's being deliberately insulting."

"What are you going to do?" Violet asked.

"I'm going to put this in our room. On his pillow. Then I'm going to find something to punch."

I got as far as putting it on his pillow. Right there, torn envelope and all. He wouldn't miss it when he came in from working out. After that my plan to punch something didn't work out, because if I tried to actually work out, I'd run afoul of Gabel,

Hix, and Flint, who were not going to let that happen for various reasons. If I saw Platinum as she scurried around the house preparing for my wedding (oh, the irony) I would probably strangle her. Instead, Cook occupied me with questions about the menu for our Solstice party.

He seemed really into it, especially the matter of if we should roast four pigs or a single cow.

Gabel came in from training through the kitchen, sweating despite the cold, blood trickling from various scratches and scrapes, absolutely filthy. He was haphazardly dressed in his usual mangled, faded kilt. His stitches had pulled and bled, and the cracked skin was reddened and dried. It'd never heal at this rate, the stubborn ox. Blood wept out of the deep slashes.

"Get out of my sight," I snarled.

He gave Cook a look. "Excuse us."

Cook headed for the walk-in pantry muttering something about capers.

Gabel leaned down to be eye level with me. "So very, very angry."

"I left it on your pillow." I narrowed my eyes. "Go bathe. You're disgusting."

"Come with me." His tone pulled at my spine, willing me to follow him.

"I might hurt you," I growled back.

"Promises, promises, buttercup."

"Don't get ahead of yourself, *Romero*," I hissed.

"What did you call me?" He pushed his face right in mine with a snarl.

This time his dominance had no effect. I snarled back, aching and humiliated, and it was his fault!

"That's not very nice, buttercup."

I slid off the stool and stormed up the stairs. If the pack saw me having a tantrum over this, they'd think I was actually jealous, and it would get back to Platinum. I slammed our door behind me while Gabel went to his pillow.

He picked up the envelope, noted the address, then read the contents. His face chilled to something unreadable. "I haven't touched her."

"Oh, I'm not accusing you of that. But dear Alpha Anders of Gleaming Fang seems to think she is your BondMate. Either he's being insulting or he doesn't pay attention," I said. "It doesn't matter. I get to be publicly humiliated again on the evening of my Bonding because *you* wanted to cause a catfight, you small, petty, pathetic—"

"Gianna."

I tossed my hair. "So what are we going to do, Gabel? Show up at the party, and you tell him what? How are you going to explain this?"

"You're grumpy, buttercup." Gabel said, eyeing me sideways. "Are there pups in your belly?"

"No, there are not. Perhaps I've had enough of curs outside my door, Elder Oracles playing mother-may-I games, bitches smashing my tools, and this little relic from a time I'd rather forget. I'd feel better if I knew this was because Anders was jerking my chain, not if he actually thought that pale-haired bitch was your intended. But I think he thinks it's Platinum you chose!"

Gabel put down the invitation on the nightstand. "This is very embarrassing."

"Oh, shut up if you don't have anything intelligent to say." I rolled my eyes.

"I thought this was a matter settled between you and I."

I threw up my hands, then clasped them to my sides, fingers holding the fabric of my leggings. "It doesn't mean I won't still get angry when it crawls out of its grave, and I have to pretend it doesn't stink."

Gabel's fingertips lingered on the invitation. He stared at the wall, a frown carved into his features. Then he pulled off his kilt and headed for the shower.

I wished his backside wasn't so damned perfect. There was the large silver burn marring his left thigh and butt cheek, but that only made him more perfect in some demented way. The Bond nagged me to put the humiliation behind me and reconcile.

I told the Bond to shut up. I was so not in the mood.

Standing in the corner was stupid. I hugged myself and moved to the edge of the bed. The pack couldn't see us fighting over Platinum. Platinum couldn't know I had even flinched. I picked at the sleeves of my sweater and held myself very tight, keeping the awful memories at bay.

"You're very upset, buttercup," he said when he emerged from the shower.

"You expected something else?" I hunched over my arms and stared at the wall.

"You told me the matter was settled."

He didn't get it. The matter was settled until it crawled out of its grave to humiliate me again. I twisted my head to look at him. Did he just want it to all go away, or did he really believe that since we had settled it between us, I wasn't allowed to be angry when past mistakes came back to the door? I was allowed to be angry that I was going to have to go to some party and smile and make up some snide lie to my Alpha's vassals about how it had all be some ploy. I was allowed to be angry about that.

Gabel was just annoyed at me. "Buttercup, we've spoken about this. Sulk up here if it suits you, but do not let the pack see."

"I've never let them see it before, why would I now?"

"Don't forget that." He circled around in front of me and

bent down to my level. His warning pressed on me like a stone wall. "You should be more concerned with Anders either being an idiot, or him growling at me."

I glared at him.

He straightened. "Let's go, buttercup. We have dinner."

I couldn't let the pack see me upset, just in case anyone found out about the invitation. I had managed not to cry, so I wasn't all pink and blubbery. I could just imagine walking up to Anders, his face confused and there being some awkward, painful conversation, then everyone muttering about and thinking for the next however many years that Gabel had had a fling with Platinum.

I ran my tongue over my teeth and worked my jaw. The ulcerated pain wailed within me, and I couldn't stop it. I could only shove it deep away from the surface and endure it. The Bond wriggled and bit at Gabel, shaking him like a dog shaking a toy.

For him, this pain was an unfortunate necessity. A consequence of past actions, like an injury not yet healed and re-opened. Just like that wound on his shoulder that kept ripping open.

Gabel was Gabel, my four-form wolf, and all the marks he left.

All I had to do was go to this party, smile sweetly, and show no pain.

I paused in the hallway, remembering the jungle vision, and how Anders had barked at Gabel while the cloaked man got away.

"Buttercup?" Gabel growled at me, thinking I had balked for a different reason. "Dinner."

"Don't growl at me. I was just remembering something I never told you." The jungle vision suddenly seemed very important. It intruded into my mind, ringing like a bell. I had never finished telling him all of it. We had gotten too distracted.

"Buttercup, you and your secrets." He turned around and advanced, backing me up against the wall.

"Not a secret. It's the jungle vision. We got... distracted," I growled back.

"So we did."

"It's an old vision now." I wasn't feeling the least bit gracious. My heart whimpered and wailed. "But in the vision, Flint was there. He was dead, but then he jumped up again. You attacked him, or tried to, and while you were distracted, the cloaked wolf slipped away. Anders barked at you to keep fighting with the other wolf. Hix was also there, watching you, and when Flint escaped you, singing the song to call a female leader to war, he wanted to go after him, but didn't."

Gabel's blue eyes held mine for a long couple of moments. Then he pushed off the wall and headed back down the stairs, brooding and contemplative. "We are late to dinner."

WOLVES IN TUXEDOS

Predictably, Hix had something to say about us going to Anders' little Solstice get-together.

"It is obviously a trap," Hix stated. "It is bait. You have the perfect excuse to not go. What is a Lord-Alpha doing at this party anyway?"

Lord-Alpha? That was a new term, but Hix's meaning was pretty clear. I didn't say anything. I was still bristling with annoyance, Flint had told me training was out of the question with Gabel so rankled (because I had to babysit his emotions?), and I had had to pretend like I wasn't about to swallow a big mouthful of humiliation. So I just stood on the second floor of Gabel's office and watched the other ranked male members of IronMoon argue and growl at each other.

"It is disgraceful what you did," Hix snarled at Gabel, "and now your Luna has to be humiliated again for your... indiscretions."

"I never laid a hand on Gardenia," Gabel stated.

Technically that was a lie. I didn't correct him.

"No, you presented her to another Alpha on your arm. I care that you publicly disgraced the woman carrying your Mark.

While I am glad you are going to have to answer for this to those who should have your respect, I also know how much shame this will bring on Lady Gianna, and how it only furthers the worst of IronMoon's reputation."

Those words would have provoked almost any other Alpha into a fit of rage. Gabel was like a dark, angry void. However, he stood there, and after a few minutes of reining in his temper, he said, "I agree."

"Good." Hix didn't back down.

"It doesn't change that we have to go. I went last year. I need to appear gracious yet powerful. And because of this, Gianna has to come with me."

"No matter how dangerous it is. Do you not understand she's a target?"

"Get used to it, Hix, that won't change," Gabel said, like it had just recently dawned on him how much of a liability a mate was.

"No." Hix didn't budge. "I will not get used to it."

"Enough." Flint waded between them. "The choice has been made. She is going."

"And so are you, old man," Gabel told Flint.

"Me?" Flint never showed surprise before, but he did right then. "I need to remain here."

"You are the voice of calm experience. If things get ugly, I want you there," Gabel said.

Because Flint could tear whole war-form wolves into pieces and splatter them on walls. That sort of calm experience.

Flint folded his arms across his chest. "I do not do parties."

Anders' Solstice party was a black tie, human-style affair. I contemplated how much work it would take to wrestle the kilt-wearing Master of Arms into a tuxedo.

"You are going. As are Hix and Donovan. Eroth will have to manage things here."

"Take Eroth," Flint disagreed. "He is a bachelor. Let him meet some females."

"This is not a friendly party, Flint."

Flint rolled his eyes and wandered over to the window. That accounted for him resigning himself to the inevitable. "I am not wearing a tie. Or buttoning my collar."

"You could wear a kilt. It acceptable formal dress," Donovan said.

"No. Tuxedo means court shoes, which can be kicked off. Kilt means brogues."

"We will be a long way from here should it not be friendly," Hix said in a dour tone. "You and I and Donovan will go. Flint and Lady Gianna will remain here. If they kill you, it does not matter."

"It matters," I said from my perch. "His violent death will likely kill me. I am no safer here than I am there."

"The Bond being ripped is survivable." Hix, as usual, disagreed. "It is males who are the least likely to survive. Haven't you two figured out by now that our enemies are circling us? They do *not* want you to mate. The Elder Oracle failed to prevent it. They will move at this party."

"And what if they do kill you and Gabel? What does that leave me, Hix? The *almost* Luna of IronMoon? I'm not safe anywhere. I'm worth more dead. As violently and painfully as possible." I swore that Hix's logic at times was as blunt and dense as a stone.

Hix shifted his baleful glare to Gabel. "This is your fault."

Gabel snarled, "Do you have a point, Beta?"

Flint pushed Hix and Gabel apart again. He glanced at me as if to say *you need to deal with this*. As if I could. What could I do about it? Trying to reason with Hix was like trying to reason with a tree or stone.

I was still pissed at... circumstances... and I wouldn't have minded watching Hix rattle Gabel's teeth. That wasn't a very nice thing to think, and it wasn't fair. Gabel had admitted his mistake. It was also hard to leave the past in the past when it didn't stay dead.

Hopefully this would be the last time I had to deal with this in public. Gardenia, I meant. Not Gabel and Hix snarling at each other. That was going to continue.

Flint did not look the least bit comfortable in a tuxedo. He looked amazing, but not comfortable. I think it was also the first time I had ever seen him wear shoes. Patent leather opera flats with a folded velvet bow across the toe. Very old school. Although he wore no tie, no cummerbund, and his collar was not buttoned.

Alpha Anders' Solstice gala was one of the most formal and well-attended events in our part of the country. Even the Shadowless had gone to it, and I prepared myself in case I ran into Alpha Jermain or my father.

It was not actually held at the heart of Gleaming Fang but at a rented opera hall in a modest-sized human city towards the edge of Gleaming Fang's western border. It made getting to the party quite convenient. We were not the only wolves who chose to arrive by air. It also tended to keep hostilities down.

So one would hope.

The custom for mated females was to wear a dress that showed at least our Marked arm. Violet had chosen one of midnight purple silk with off the shoulder straps, and plunged very low on my back to show off my very pale skin. Unmated females wore something on their shoulders. Easy way to tell from a distance which females were off limits, and which ones weren't. Males... well, males, if you were looking, you just had to guess.

Hix had opted not to shave and had a shadow along his jaw, which gave him an even more menacing look than usual. He was in a rotten mood.

My stomach knotted and unknotted as we walked up the marble steps to the entrance. Adrenaline pumped through my system. Just as well the invitation had only arrived a few days before the party. If I had had to sit and be nervous for two weeks I'd have gone crazy. Gabel's forearm was tight, and his fingers clenched into a fist. He was not just an Alpha, he was the Alpha that had conquered and accepted the submission of the host Alpha, and probably a good number of other attendees there.

Scared the shit out of me, personally.

The hall was illuminated by massive overhead chandeliers, and absolutely everything was lit, from the corner where a small quintet played classical music for the people already dancing, to the tables of food off to one side. The room already hummed with chatter.

Gabel surveyed the party from the top of the stairs. He noted the faces of the wolves he already knew. His fingers flexed, causing the iron cables of his forearm to shift in my hand.

Just as he shifted to move off down the stairs, the conversation in the room quieted, and eyes moved toward us.

The IronMoon had arrived.

Gabel's forearm tightened to a steel beam. The Bond slid into the darkness as he pushed everything aside and focused solely on the wolves below him. Many of them had bowed their heads to him, but some in the crowd were not under IronMoon's control.

Yet.

It must be very surreal to be looking at your future conqueror and weighing if you dared to meet his gaze or not.

Gabel's prestige and authority hung around him in an aura, summoned forth for just this moment. To me it was glorious: his strength and authority and resolve, and his willingness to prove all of them.

As his mate, I was probably the only one in the room who found it thrilling.

We descended the stairs as the silence deepened.

A man moved from the back of the crowd with a woman in tow. I recognized Alpha Anders immediately.

His face was burned into my memories, after all.

I clenched Gabel's forearm. Hard.

Anger curled up inside me like steam building.

Anders' had a look of polite confusion when he saw me, his eyes finding my Mark. I gripped Gabel's arm tighter. Thankfully I wasn't expected to smile.

By now it was absolutely silent except for the soft notes of the quintet. Even the caterers slicing delicate portions of exquisite beef had paused.

When Gabel spoke, his voice carried through the room with ease, pitched to a note of command. "Anders."

Anders' brief flash of authority faded. He averted his gaze to a slightly different angle, his neck bowed very slightly and his shoulders bent a degree. His Luna's aura of composed command washed out under the heat of Gabel's authority.

"Welcome, Gabel." Anders dropped Gabel's title, which indicted humans were present. He paused, mouth open a bit, struggling to find words when he looked at me. This had gone off-script.

"Gianna," Gabel's voice stepped into the chasm of silence. "This is Anders. I did not concern you with introductions before. Anders, the Lady Gianna."

Anders made a sound in the back of his throat that might

have been a word. His Luna, a willowy woman of my height, saved him. "Welcome, Gianna. I am Ura."

I nodded to her. I also didn't trust her.

"Yes," Anders found his voice again. "I recall seeing you, Gianna. You are, I mean, were, the Oracle from Shadowless. Am I right? Rogan's daughter."

"Yes," I answered, my insides twisting at my father's name.

Anders hadn't been expecting me on Gabel's arm, but he seemed more flustered than I would have expected. Gabel noted it as well and bristled. The nearby wolves fidgeted and shifted, ducking heads and watching everything from the corner of their eyes. The musicians gave up trying to play.

Gabel's eyes narrowed a degree, and he gestured with his left hand to the rest of IronMoon for the benefit of the room. "Hix, Flint, and Donovan."

Anders recovered at this point and gestured to the party. He smiled for the crowds and graciously told us to enjoy his hospitality. The musicians picked up a tune, the people started chattering again, and the Gleaming Fang Alpha and Luna retreated to regroup.

I lifted my hand off his arm. Gabel caught it and clapped it back down, his fingers covering mine. The Bond jolted at the sudden touch. I had been neglecting him since the invitation had arrived. Somewhere between 'could end horribly' and 'public humiliation' I hadn't been remotely in the mood. Now that the worst was over, it seemed the Bond had its own ideas again...

"Careful." He brushed his lips along my ear and whispered to me.

I quivered all over at his touch.

"Buttercup, don't remind me how alone I have been," he whispered.

"Who's fault is that?" I tugged on his grip.

Hix cleared his throat.

Gabel's possessive heat mixed with concern, desire, power, authority. He released my hand.

I picked up a drink off one of the passing trays and moved into the crowd. I had never been to a party like this and had no idea what to do. I did not have to wait, though, because my father pushed his way through the crowds, with Alpha Jermain not far behind him.

I froze. My heart twisted, my gut burned.

"Gianna!" He reached out and grabbed my arm, then pulled me toward him. My drink sloshed.

His fingers slipped off me as Hix appeared from nowhere and slammed my father backward, sending him into Alpha Jermain.

My father was still the First Beta of Shadowless. He straightened, cricked his neck and curled his upper lip at Hix.

Hix snarled, "You do not touch her.".

"I'm her father, not some errant male," my father growled.

"I know who you are. You're the father who didn't shed one drop of blood for his daughter. I've shed more of my blood to honor her than you ever bothered. She—"

"Hix, enough." I put my hand on his trembling bicep. I muttered to him, "Your temper is going to cause a scene."

Hix growled and stepped aside.

Gabel, not far away, watched.

"Go on," I told Hix under my breath. "It's fine."

Hix stalked off into the crowd. So much for him working a party. I didn't know how to do it, but he wasn't even trying.

I stepped out of reach of my father's embrace.

He couldn't just hug me after I hadn't seen or heard from him in months. Yes, IronMoon was powerful and strong, but not even growling at Gabel, and just lining us all up that way? It still stung. Deep.

"Gianna, it's so good to see you," he told me.

I had to say something. "You say that like you didn't think I'd be here."

"I didn't know if you would. I hoped you would be, but—"

"But what?" I asked.

He looked at my Mark, then stepped closer. He lowered his tone, "We heard Gabel had taken another BondMate after you."

Anger spiked within me, accompanied by another hot jolt of adrenaline. My father had heard, and he hadn't reached out to me? He just let me rot in IronMoon? It was everything I could do to keep my voice composed and steady. "You mean after Alpha Anders visited IronMoon."

My father explained the rumors that had been circulating in Gabel's domain: he had taken an Oracle from Shadowless as his BondMate and tribute. Anders had subsequently been presented with Gardenia, and I had not been introduced, leading to gossip that I had been quickly discarded.

"Rumors," I said shortly. "I've been his since the day you saw him Mark me. Our vows are at Solstice. Haven't you gotten your invitation?"

"Gianna, listen—"

"You let it happen without a drop of blood. You left me with a monster!" I hissed under my breath. "You have no idea what he's put me through, and you think I want to *listen* to *anything* you have to say about it? Or is this where you *still* try to tell me there are things I don't understand?"

Jermain just loomed back there like a cardboard cutout. How could I have ever respected and feared him? I snorted in disgust.

My father whispered, "Gianna, I didn't want to make things worse for you, and—"

"Not possible." I cut him off again. The night Gabel had ripped my dress, made me undress for him, sleep naked next to him. Taunting me with Platinum. Mocking me. Degrading me. Using a divine gift as his personal toy because he was so damn arrogant he was bored with conquest.

I could come to love the thinking, cruel, brilliant Gabel no matter how brutal or savage he was, though, because, as I looked at my father, into the abyss itself... I was right there, too. I despised, still, with a passion, the weak, petty, worthless version of him that had sawed this Mark into my arm.

It could have been a beautiful Mark.

"Gianna, you don't understand," my father said.

"Playing the *things you don't understand* card? Things you couldn't tell me? I am about to be the Luna you will kneel to." My heart hurt. It just hurt, hurt, hurt, and I'd have given anything for him to send me even a card to say he'd been thinking of me. My soul wept. It reached down into the Bond I shared with Gabel for comfort.

It was an instinct, and not a very useful one, because Gabel wasn't exactly a comforter of souls.

"Will you listen to me for five minutes?!"

"No." I was tired of this. "You have no idea what I've been through because of whatever this thing is you say I wouldn't understand. Now *you* don't understand. I will be the Luna of IronMoon, and you have only yourself to thank for it."

I went to the other side of the party. I needed a bite of some food to get the rotten taste out of my mouth.

As I stood by the bar waiting for the bartender to pour my ginger ale, another form moved up to my side. I paid him no mind for a moment, until he said, "I was hoping to see you here, Lady Gianna."

I knew that voice.

MeatMan.

LURE-SCENT

The MeatMan smiled at me. He was very tall, like in the visions, and had the commanding presence of an Alpha. I put his age at somewhere around thirty. On the back of the hand holding his drink was a thick scar that ran from his knuckles to his cuff.

Instinct told me to back out of his immediate grasp. I held my ground, but my heart raced, and my blood shook.

The MeatMan.

The secret I kept from Gabel. The wolf who pulled the strings of the disloyal.

And I did not expect to feel something prickle over my Mark, *under* it, like it squirmed uncertainly against my soul.

"I was expecting you to be here, Lady Gianna. I wasn't expecting you to be on Alpha Gabel's arm." He sipped his own drink.

I took my drink from the bartender. "Have we met?"

"No. I am Alpha Aaron of IceMaw." He gestured for me to step toward the dance floor and away from the bar. I eyed him but decided to comply. I didn't think he was being gracious or gallant (not exactly), but given we were taking up space at the bar, it was polite to move. I permitted him to usher me a little closer to the quintet, where it was a tad quieter and not as busy.

My Mark kept squirming. My fingers twitched. I seized a fold of my gown to hide it.

He looked at my Mark, clucked his tongue. "What a shame."

"Excuse me?"

He stepped closer to me, coming exactly one step too close. He towered over me. "I came all this way to meet you. I had been told Gabel had traded you for something easier to handle."

As sharp as a kick from Flint to my belly it hit me, and another rush of adrenaline plowed through my system. He saw through my composure, picking up on the tick of the pulse in my throat and the flutter of my eyelids, his eyes marking every small reaction.

His eyes were a rich brown flecked with amber. He leaned forward very slightly and inhaled. I shifted away, appalled.

"I would do more than merely catch your scent," Aaron said, "but I see every IronMoon in this place watching me. That is surprising in itself. I thought Gabel would charge across this room and make a scene."

I didn't respond.

"No defense for your BondMate and Alpha?"

"I don't take cheap bait."

"But you did tolerate Gabel humiliating you in front of Anders. Twice," Aaron prodded.

"And that's a cheap shot," I snapped. Dammit. Aaron got that much out of me, and I wasn't giving him anything else. Especially not the 'strategy' lie. He'd press and press and push me into the lie so deep he'd bury me.

"You seem to think I have my mouth open waiting for a bite of food from your hand," I said darkly.

He curled his upper lip. "And you haven't told him."

"That was cheap bait too," I said as my heart raced in near-panic. The Petitioner Wolf *had* been a plant... sent by the IceMaw.

"Such a burden you must carry. Such a secret kept on behalf of... him," his tone flicked concern for Gabel away like a little bug.

"Are you usually so petty?"

Aaron straightened. "Apologies. Rude of me to bring up both matters. Still, from your scent, I can't let it be unsaid it is a shame he convinced you to forgive him. I would enjoy the chance to win you, not make off with you."

"So you did know I'd be here." I narrowed my eyes. "Even though you were expecting Gardenia, too."

He smiled. "That is only simple logic. I assumed Gabel would want to parade his Oracle before all of us." He gestured to the room. "I wanted to see what docile little puppy he'd selected to be Luna, and what woman was too dangerous for him to bed. *That* is a woman I would very much want to meet."

He pulled his upper lips back just enough to show the whites of his teeth, and I saw his canines flashed a little longer and sharper.

He could partially shift. If he could just extend his fangs outside of the Mark-making, he... I focused on not gulping, because he'd see my throat move. My fingers clenched my drink. The ice rattled *tink-tink-tink* against the glass.

He shouldn't even have *been* at this party. Anders had invited him just to parade it under Gabel's unknowing snout... and in front of everyone who *did* know.

Did *everyone* here know what was really going on, and the joke was on us?

Tink-tink-tink.

"I am very disappointed, Lady Gianna, that Gabel found his courage. Unless... is that a glint of intrigue I perceive?"

"No." I think I lied. I wasn't exactly sure the way my Mark squirmed even though I was as frightened of Aaron as I'd ever been of Gabel.

"I'm not sure about that. Did I overhear your vows are in a few weeks? I don't expect an invitation, of course."

"They are, and you shouldn't."

"Reconsider. Taking the vows, I mean, not the invitation. Gabel has no idea what he has, and even less idea how to keep it." He lowered his voice. "I can smell your scent. The scent of a cereus flower that blooms one night a year."

I gasped. "You're lying."

"It shouldn't be there, but it is," he all but purred. "Gabel is only death and burning. His pack is garbage no other pack wants. They will betray him in time. It is their nature. When he howls for aid those who bowed before him will ignore him."

He paused, glanced at Gabel, then returned his attention to me. "If it's him you fear, don't."

"I've heard this *don't mate him* demand before." My voice trembled, my skin quivered, and my Mark seemed to slide around my skin like oil on water.

"Yes, I know. But I am not a SableFur."

He half-bowed to me in a me in a manner like Flint and excused himself before I could even conjure a response.

My hand shook as I raised my glass to my lips and took a slow sip. My throat was so dry I almost gagged. I choked down the mouthful, then another.

Gabel had disappeared. Donovan stood in a center of a dozen wolves entertaining with stories and jokes. Hix dragged himself through the crowd like an unwilling boulder. Flint hadn't moved from his spot under the second floor balcony. He had picked that spot from moment one and stood there, watching the crowd. No drink, just waiting. We could stuff him into a tux, push him onto a plane, but we couldn't make him mingle.

I tried not to stagger over to the safety he offered and hide my shaking. Aaron knew about Anita. He knew about SableFur. We might be in a hall full of traitors.

And I couldn't tell anyone.

I attempted to make some small talk and pretend everything was normal. "Not even going to pretend, Flint? Or are you playing Cyrano for some hapless bachelor?"

"No to both questions, Lady Gianna." Flint glanced at me. "I would complain about my tuxedo, but I believe your dress is more constricting."

"I am firmly supported at all angles," I said with a trembling sigh.

Flint's green eyes slid toward Aaron. "Hmm."

"He thought I'd be unattached," I commented worriedly.

"That is not the look of a male who finds your Mark a barrier. Be wary of him."

Oh, I was more than wary. I was scared to death. "He said he can smell my scent."

"That's impossible. You are Marked. He must have been lying. Regardless, that is a wolf who is after you."

"To what end?" I glanced around the party again, trying to stop the trembling in my hands. I scanned the crowd for Gabel again, saw Aaron talking with someone—

I froze.

Moving through the crowd was another wolf I recognized: the MeatTaker.

There he was, wearing a tuxedo, shaking hands with some other male from some other pack I didn't recognize. But it was the MeatTaker. Somehow in his human form I recognized him. I stepped backward until I pressed against Flint's bulk, because otherwise I would have crumbled into flakes and sequins.

"Lady Gianna?"

"Who—who is that?" I asked, then tore away so I wouldn't be staring at him.

"Alpha Marcus of MarchMoon."

Sweat patched between my shoulders, and a trickle traced my spine. MarchMoon was a traitor. They belonged to Aaron of IceMaw.

And I couldn't tell Gabel.

Flint cocked his head to the side and didn't say anything, but those green eyes saw right through me. Instead, he said, "Back to your Alpha, Gianna. You've scolded an old man for being a curmudgeon long enough."

"Yes." I nodded dumbly, mind blank. I somehow managed to find Gabel in the press of wolves.

Gabel glanced Flint's way. "No luck drawing him out?"

"You know what he told us. Doesn't do parties." Aaron's gaze burned into my back, and I felt the weight of Marcus on my soul.

Gabel lifted his eyes past my shoulder, noted Aaron, then returned his attention back to me. Very deliberately, he picked up my right hand and placed it on his forearm. He said nothing, but our Bond bristled and growled, rattling like a snake's tail.

I enjoyed the steel and iron under his tuxedo jacket and shirt, the familiar lines of his body. I held tightly to him and whispered, "Don't trust him."

"The way he is looking at you, buttercup?" Gabel growled, the snarl sliding between his clenched jaw. "No risk of that. Did he say something to you? You seem very upset after speaking to him."

"Not here." I shook my head. "I can't tell you..."

Aaron smiled at me, *daring* me to tell Gabel and break my vows.

Gabel reached up with his other hand and slipped his

fingers under my chin, compelling me to look up at him. The Bond rattled and trembled.

He moved, his fingers holding my chin, and kissed me gently.

A DIRTY PITCHFORK

His tongue grazed my lips, very gently. I melted. Where had this sweetness come from? Where had this tenderness? My lips parted for him, just enough for our tongues to meet. Just a brief glance of heat, but it was enough to spark more. I wanted to throw my arms around him and kiss him hard and feel his hands rip the confining dress off me and wrap my thighs around his hips.

For a moment, the past just didn't exist. Just him and the sweet, delicate kiss.

Clap.

Clap.

Clap.

The crowds melted back for Aaron, conversation stopped, music once again dribbled into the background. The IceMaw Alpha straightened the ring on his right pinky finger. "Lovely performance. Lovely."

Gabel dropped his hands and turned his full attention to Aaron.

"I'm not impressed, Gabel," Aaron said. "You think a sweet kiss and your Mark on her shoulder proves anything to me?

That Mark didn't mean anything to you when you had another woman on your arm. What was her name... Gardenia. When you had Gardenia on your arm."

That name struck my insides.

Aaron went on, smug. "To be honest, Gabel, no one was surprised when you were spotted with her. She seems like your type. Pretty, stupid, and very, very easy to handle. An Oracle is more than you can manage."

"Gianna has always been the one I chose," Gabel said. "Gardenia was a decoy. It worked well."

Aaron didn't buy it for a second. "A decoy? For what? To draw me out? I'm not going to hide my interest. That kiss just now? That kiss was for me, for this room. Because Gabel wanted to prove to everyone who Gianna belongs to. Oh, and remind her who she belongs to."

Gabel's shoulders bunched under his jacket.

"Ladies and gentlemen, this is the man who rules you, to whom you have knelt." Aaron gestured to Gabel and laughed. "You must be pleased to know he takes his obligations so seriously that he uses females as pawns. The Moon knows what else happens back home, considering what he's willing to parade in front of us."

I gripped Gabel's forearm as hard as I could.

Aaron gestured to the marble floor, "Perhaps you will take her in front of us, Gabel. Prove to me, beyond a doubt, who owns her. So far, you haven't convinced me I can't win her from you. Maybe if I hear her pant your name?"

Gabel's anger spiked, splashed my insides like acid, roiled within him, building. "She carries my Mark, Aaron. You have already lost."

Aaron didn't look away, and his eyes seemed more gold than brown. "I only bothered to come to this little party to meet her. I intend to have my chance with her. Step aside and let the woman choose!"

"She has already chosen," Gabel growled.

I hadn't really chosen any of this.

Aaron growled at him. "Impressive that you found your balls and chose the Oracle, but not impressive enough, Gabel. Go back to your dogs and rejects. I and mine will never bow to you!"

Gabel pounced, grabbed Aaron's shoulder, and yanked himself against the other wolf. His other fist smashed into Aaron's belly, lifting the man off his feet. Aaron shoved back, snatched free of Gabel's grasp, and slammed his fist into Gabel's jaw with a crack that startled me.

Aaron shot forward, Gabel met him, they crashed into each other, Aaron punched Gabel in the floating ribs, Gabel ate it, threw an elbow, Aaron dodged it, ducked inside and as fast as Flint, snapped a kick into Gabel's thigh. It actually staggered Gabel for a breath.

Gabel's enjoyment slid over my spine like hands stroking a cat. He grinned at Aaron, fury and the thrill of combat building. The two of them crashed together again, I flinched at the sound of a bare fist hitting flesh, growls and snarls. Gabel managed to snake around Aaron and get the IceMaw Alpha's head in a crank, but Aaron somehow got a hold of Gabel and ankle-tripped him.

Flint snorted, unimpressed.

The crowd scrambled backwards to make room.

Aaron slid out of range of Gabel's grasp, moving like a fluid dancer.

Gabel dropped back, reassessed, a cruel grin smearing his face, along with a trickle of blood from a cut just under his eye.

Aaron had first blood. He grinned himself and continued his smooth half-circle pace around Gabel. " You've gotten arrogant feasting on small wolves. I cut myself into an Alpha on the bones of my own family. You're a blunt object."

Gabel laughed. "Come feast on me then, IceMaw."

Aaron didn't decline the invitation. His shin snapped into Gabel's knee with a *crack!* And Gabel's leg buckled for an instant. Gabel grabbed Aaron behind the back of the head, yanked the IceMaw's face to his own, and then cracked Aaron's nose with his forehead.

Aaron punched him in the jaw and *shoved*, sending Gabel backward.

Flint rubbed his chin.

Gabel burst upward and plowed into Aaron. The force drove Aaron back, and Gabel's leg snaked around Aaron's ankle in a glorious trip, sending both Alphas crashing to the marble. Gabel snarled as he delivered a punch square to Aaron's jaw. Blood splattered. Aaron bucked, shrimped, exploded upward, Gabel snatched a handful of Aaron's hair and held him down. Aaron fought to stand, managed to get one knee off the ground despite Gabel's pressure.

Aaron spit out a tooth, blood pouring from the cut over his eye.

Gabel's hand clutched the back of his neck, bearing down on Aaron's spine. "You will kneel, Aaron. Both knees."

Aaron spat out another mouthful of blood. "Never."

"When it suits me, I will come for your pack, and you will bow or watch me rip everything you love into small. Little. Pieces." Gabel shoved Aaron forward, but Aaron's defiant knee did not bend. With a growl of disgust, Gabel snapped his knee into Aaron's ribs and flung Arron onto his back, then jumped on him. Gabel pinned him with a knee in the belly, leaned over him, pinned Aaron's neck to the marble floor with one hand. The other hand elongated, extended, fingernails shaping and sharpening into yellow claws.

Aaron's whole body moved with the effort of breathing around Gabel's weight and the fingers clenching down on his neck just enough to weaken him. Gabel grinned at him. He didn't crush Aaron's throat. He wanted the IceMaw Alpha to be aware of how powerless he was, and how he, Gabel, could have killed him.

Gabel's darkness choked me, squeezing upward from my belly and shoving my lungs out of the way. It flowed from him like lava. It was so much worse than anything I had felt with his fight with Romero.

Aaron's off hand twitched as he wheezed, and through blood, grinned. Laughed. His fingertips sharpened, and with a final, huge effort, stabbed three of his claws deep into Gabel's thigh.

"Gabel!" I gasped as blood pooled up around Aaron's claws. The IceMaw Alpha pushed deeper and rotated his wrist a few degrees.

Gabel grinned at Aaron, his face darkening, and for a brief instant Aaron's face flashed with shock and horror as he saw the Alpha of IronMoon. Then it was replaced with an iron mask. The IceMaw wheezed, "Bleed, you Moon-damned monster!"

"Pain." Gabel's tone was low and guttural as his rage melted his humanity away. "Amusing. More."

He savored it, drinking in the challenge it was, gathering it around himself like he owned it. Aaron snarled at him, fear shaken off, and Gabel slid a claw down Aaron's cheek. A wafer-thin slice of skin separated and folded down. Gabel repeated the process over and over as if Aaron's face was a holiday ham.

Aaron didn't make a sound, and he struggled to twist his claws as deep and tight into Gabel's thigh as he could manage. He wheezed, disgusted and defiant, and *twisted*.

Gabel's body jerked in pain as Aaron tore chunks out of his flank, but it didn't stop Gabel from carving another wafer of flesh off the IceMaw's face. He shifted his shoulders and neck in a fluid, inhuman way. There was something about it that caused many of the onlookers to back up, pale and horrified.

His claw finished the final slice, then traced a thin red line of blood from the final slice, down the line of Aaron's jaw, over the soft spot under the chin and down the throat until it rested on Aaron's Adam's apple. He grinned at Aaron and pushed down.

Aaron jerked his chin up and hissed. "Do it, or be a coward."

Gabel pressed harder, snarled, and when Aaron didn't yield, contemplated death. Aaron was not broken. If he would not break, he must die. Aaron tore another hunk out of Gabel's thigh. Blood pooled under both of them.

Gabel's body began to shift under the human clothes, the dark magma rage increasing, melting, burning away his human awareness.

"Gabel!" My voice cracked in the hot silence. "Gabel!"

Gabel turned his head to look at me, a growl in his throat. The Bond pulled and twisted under his rage, stretched taut, as if he were very, very far away. He growled a warning at me.

"Gabel." I tried again. "He's beaten. It is done!"

"Minnneeeee." Gabel growled at me. "Minnnnnnnnnneee."

"He's beaten." I repeated, trying to sound firm and not sure if I succeeded.

Something flickered in him. He snarled at Aaron in frustration, but clicked his teeth together. He removed his hand from Aaron's neck, swatted Aaron's hand away from his thigh, and got to his feet. The tide of rage receded back from whence it came.

Aaron got to his feet, chunks of Gabel's thigh hanging off his fingertips. Flaps of skin dangled from his face. I shuddered but didn't look away.

"You should have killed me, Gabel." Aaron said.

Gabel snarled something inhuman at him and bared his teeth.

"You are a brute," Aaron grinned through his broken mouth, "and nothing more. You will never defeat me again."

He turned and walked back into the crowd. Gabel pulled against Hix's restraining hand.

Flint leaned over to me, "I think it's time to go."

Gabel would want to stay and prove to everyone he wasn't fleeing (nor injured), but he was also on the borderline of feral rage to the point he had lost the ability to speak, even if he held his human form. I didn't trust him to keep hold of his temper, or maintain human form, or be containable if he shifted.

Gabel growled over his shoulder, still looking for Aaron.

Aaron hadn't gone far: just to the bar for a drink. He saluted Gabel with the crystal tumbler, then sauntered off, presumably towards a restroom to mop the blood off his face The humans present tried to step around the blood, and the musicians picked up an uncertain tune. The wolves were less frazzled by the sudden violence.

"We can't leave," I whispered to Flint. "Aaron will still be here spinning things his way."

"Aaron might have lost, but we have an angry lupine with chunks missing from his thigh," Flint whispered back.

We left the opera hall. Gabel still wasn't limping, but he was pouring blood out of the puncture wounds on his thigh. His soaked sock squished each time his foot moved within his shoe. leaving bloody footprints, although I heard a wet squishing sound as his soaked sock moved in his shoe. In the back of the car, I took the seat across from Gabel, and as soon as the door was shut, Flint ripped the torn pant leg even further and examined the injury. "We have to get this looked at."

Gabel grunted something negative.

"It is deep puncture wounds." Flint stated. "Donovan. You scouted. What are our options?"

Hix, however, agreed with Gabel. "We can't linger here."

"He is still bleeding." Flint told the Beta as blood pumped out of the three puncture wounds on Gabel's outer thigh. It had soaked his pant leg and sock. Gabel poked at the wound curiously, Flint shoved his hand away.

Donovan scrolled through his phone, and his thumb moved as he texted. "There's a sketchy veterinarian somewhere around here."

"He is the Lord of this territory, and we're taking him to a sketchy veterinarian?" Hix asked Donovan.

"I'm thinking discretion," Donovan retorted.

"Hix, take Gianna and go ahead." Gabel's rage had melted enough that he had regained his human speech. "I will—"

"We are staying together," I told him.

"No, we—"

"We're staying together, and we're going to the veterinarian," Flint cut him off. "Donovan?"

"Yeah, yeah, I got it." Donovan leaned over the backseat and passed the driver his phone.

Flint took off his jacket and ripped off both arms. He tied one of them around Gabel's thigh above the holes, then the other one around the holes themselves.

The vet's office was part of a run-down strip-mall half an hour from the opera hall. The parking lot was empty this time of night, there were no parking lot lights to speak of, and the strip mall itself seemed largely vacant. There was a cheap shoe store, a discount clothing store, and a few other random places. It wasn't dangerous looking, but it was seedy, and nowhere I'd want to hang out. Especially wearing an evening gown.

Hix oozed so much disgust he practically left a slime trail behind him. Going to a hospital would have been inconvenient, though, and appealing to the sketchy Anders for help wasn't worth it. Aaron of IceMaw was the MeatMan, and my money said that his hand was the one on Anders' collars. He was the wolf the SpringHide had been expecting, and he had advised the SaltPaw to run.

It was genius when I thought about it. Instead of challenging Gabel directly, Aaron slid tentacles into the IronMoon extremities. Small deals. Small movements. Like a parasite sipping from the intestinal wall. Gabel could sense it, feel it, knew it was there. The vague sense of disruption and the battles that didn't go well, or weren't satisfying. The victories that were too small to feed those bellies. The intrigue and maneuvering the likes of Romero had no patience for.

Gabel growled at Hix outside the car, his eyes darting to me.

"She's fine. Try not to bite the vet." Flint grabbed Gabel's arm as Gabel's torn up leg threatened to buckle. Hix pulled Gabel's arm over his shoulder and pulled him toward the vet's office.

The vet lived in an apartment behind the main building, caring for the hospitalized animals instead of leaving them unattended at night. It also saved on rent and made her available for late-night patchwork. Cash only, no names, no questions.

She had on jeans, flip flops, and a tee-shirt despite the cold night. She looked at the bloody footprints Gabel into the office and asked, "Rough night at the ballet?"

Donovan actually chuckled. "*Petrushka* got out of hand."

The backdoor led to a long rectangular room lined with glass-front cabinets, two metal exam tables, and an assortment of other devices, none of which looked especially welcoming.

"Just the leg?" The vet sized up Gabel's battered face.

"Yes."

The vet bent over and untied the makeshift bandages. She peered at the three puncture wounds on Gabel's leg. In the bright light of the room, it was much worse than I had expected. "Gunshots?"

"Pitchfork," Flint said.

"It helps if you tell me exactly what did it."

"A dirty pitchfork," Flint amended.

The vet shrugged and rolled her eyes. She retrieved a pair of scissors and clacked them at Gabel. "Hope it's not a rental. And that you're not shy."

"He's not," I said without thinking.

Donovan pulled up one of the chairs and made himself comfortable.

The vet had Hix help Gabel shrug off his jacket, then snapped off his suspenders, and proceeded to cut his pants and boxers off him. For good measure they pulled off Gabel's shirt as well. The doctor noted the scar on his hip, and the one burned into his haunch, then patted the metal table. Hix had to help him up, Gabel's leg had turned a hideous shade of purple around the three holes.

"Swelling," Flint told my worried expression. "Muscles are so engorged they can't move. Probably not actual damage since he walked out."

"Progressive loss of function is either dying nerves or swelling," the vet agreed as she pulled Gabel onto his side. "Swelling, from the looks of this. You going to faint, Purple Dress?"

"No."

"You look pretty pale."

"I am always this pale," I replied.

"He belong to you?"

Donovan chortled, and I half-laughed. "Something like that."

"Something like that? Buttercup, I am offended." Gabel propped himself up on his elbow like he was posing for a demented life drawing class. He pointed at the three holes in his leg. "I believe this was all over you."

It was a good thing he had regained his human speech and sense of humor, even if the situation wasn't funny.

The vet pulled on a pair of gloves and asked me, "Is he good with pain?"

"Yes," Gabel told her.

"I did not ask you. All men say they are studs. They can please any woman, and they can take any pain. I'm asking your woman about your pain tolerance. She'd need another kind of doctor if you leave her thirsty."

Donovan snickered again. Flint sighed in his general direction.

"Thirsty?" Hix asked the room in general.

Donovan supplied the more common meaning. Hix winced and rubbed his head.

She began to examine the three holes in Gabel's leg, taking care as she examined them. Then she pulled off her gloves and told us, "This is a mess. Thousand, cash. Up front."

"Cunning one, this one," Gabel told me, "she cut me out of my clothing, gets me on the table, and then names her price."

Hix, still refusing to see anything the least bit entertaining about the situation, took his billfold from his breast pocket and counted out the bills. The vet re-counted all the bills, tucked them in her coat pocket, pulled a little metal tray up to her counter, and began to place implements on it.

She didn't offer him anything to numb the pain. Gabel stared off into the distance, unflinching, as she flushed the holes, then pulled the margins apart and peered into them with a little thin light, and generally fished around. Blood kept bubbling up from his thigh and forming a little puddle on the metal tray. She explained it wasn't much blood (relative to Gabel's weight), and it was better to let it bleed to get the toxins out anyway. "Not really any major blood vessels on the outside of the thigh," she explained as she worked. "Well, there are, but they're by the bone. He's got so much muscle it's just meat bleeding."

Hix glowered as the minutes ticked by. Flint excused himself and returned with a change of clothes for Gabel. Nobody went anywhere without a change of clothes.

"Pants too much for you, old man?" Donovan asked as Flint shed his attire.

The doctor turned around, whipped back to the front, then looked at me. "Is there a naked, tattooed man behind me?"

"There is," I confirmed with a sigh.

"Excuse me a moment," she told Gabel. She turned around and drank in an eyeful of Flint.

Flint gave her a look of polite inquiry, as if he had no understanding how a woman might be distracted by his nudity. And he was now absolutely naked, holding a kilt in one hand, and making exactly zero attempt at modesty.

She indulged herself for a solid thirty seconds. "I'd have given a ten percent discount for the peep show."

Flint's polite inquiry turned to something less amused. "How fortunate payment was not an issue."

"*Burn.*" The vet turned back around. "Well, just saying, if you don't want looksies don't randomly undress. A whole lot of man is worth appreciating. Normally it's just the unwashed weirdos nobody wants to see naked stripping down."

Flint sashed his kilt around his hips in record time. "Do you normally grope clients?"

"If I'd groped you you'd have known. Trust me."

"With your eyes."

"Do you normally get naked in front of strange women?" She threaded a needle.

"Nudity is not sexual."

"Never said it was. It's the ink that turns me on."

"My tattoos are religious," Flint informed her, affronted.

"Oh, yes, they are. Praise the Lord." The vet licked her lips and bent over Gabel's thigh.

"Have some decorum," he scolded her. Her response was just to snicker under her breath.

Decorum was probably not a service sketchy vets wearing flipflops sewing up holes at three a.m. for cash provided.

The vet seemed harmless anyway. Just a woman trying to make some money. No different from any other kind of hunter on barren land.

The vet finished stitching, bandaged Gabel's leg, and once Gabel had wormed his way into a spare set of pants (which required cutting the leg seam for the wound wrap), she hurried us out the door. Not because she was scared—there was another client stumbling in clutching a bloody arm.

The whole thing had taken two hours, and I slumped against my seat and tried not to turn into an exhausted puddle.

"Buttercup."

I lifted my head. Gabel seemed a little paler, and tired, and I knew his leg hurt like hell, but his blue eyes were human again.

"You recognized Aaron."

COLD PAWS

Guilt and anxiety slammed into me. I admitted, "Yes."

"Does he have some claim on you?"

"Of course not. I've never met him."

"I know you recognized him, and you weren't happy to see him. Don't give me the run-around, buttercup. You're not good at it, and I'm not in the mood."

At least he hadn't picked up on Marcus, and Flint hadn't betrayed me. "Can we talk about this later?"

"And give you time to get your story straight? No."

Every moment I balked at answering him I dug myself deeper. "I saw him in a vision. It wasn't your question. I can't tell you more than that."

"Before or after you came to IronMoon?" Gabel asked.

I squirmed. "After."

"The petitioner wolf," Gabel muttered to himself. "It was his vision."

"I can't say more." I'd already said too much.

Gabel sat up a little straighter, pinned me with an ocean-colored stare. "You *knew*."

My voice trembled, "Knew what?"

He glared at me, jaw working.

"So what if I saw Aaron?" I asked, voice still trembling. "You don't know what the question was."

"I have three damned holes in my leg on account this question."

"You don't know that, but we both know you'd have gotten those anyway."

Gabel glared at me.

I withered into my seat at the impossibility before me. Even the most loyal underling might have a compromising question, and use my vows against me. I had deliberately not thought about it, but now it was front and center, and it seemed like I couldn't be both. This is where it broke.

"You knew what I am," I whispered.

He turned away from me and didn't say anything the rest of the trip.

I offered to sleep in my bedroom on the other side of the house.

"No." Gabel pulled off his shirt. We were alone now, in our room, and I did not fancy the idea of being caged in with a wounded Gabel who was trying to decide if I was a traitor. I knew what IronMoon did to traitors.

"I don't mind. If you want the bed all to yourself."

He cricked his neck. His back had bruises on it. "I know you won't tell me what you saw, Gianna."

"Then why are you angry?"

He flexed his bruised knuckles. Something popped into place. "Tell me this, then, how much should I *not* discount Aaron?"

"I don't need to be an Oracle to tell you you already know the answer. He's very dangerous."

"Does he tempt you?" Gabel gave me the side eye.

"Are you jealous?"

"No. You're a female. If you responded to his prestige and authority even through the Mark, I want to know."

Clever. I rubbed my Mark. Interesting way to ask two questions at once.

"Buttercup," he warned me, "tell me the truth. I saw you with him. I *felt* you with him."

"Felt me? What did it feel like?" I asked.

"Like there was a door between us. I could hear you, and smell you, but you were apart."

A jealous Gabel was better than the one trying to ferret out secrets I couldn't tell him. "I felt my Mark squirm like oil on water."

His spine tightened as he drew back a bit. His eyes clouded, his whole body hardened over. "The vows must do more than we realized."

"Perhaps," I murmured, rubbing my Mark thoughtfully. "He told me I still have my lure-scent."

"Impossible. That's a lie," Gabel snapped.

"That's what he told me."

"So what do you smell like to him, buttercup? Did he tell you? Cinnamon, perhaps? I've heard that's a popular one," Gabel said sarcastically.

"Cereus. The night-blooming flower."

His lips stretched back over his teeth, revealing gleaming white that shifted dangerously. Fury erupted between us. I scrambled backward and bumped into the wall.

Under the fury was something that resembled fear. No. Anxiety. A crush of anxiety.

"What?" I asked blankly. "So what? He didn't say the Moon, at least. You said the Moon."

Gabel snarled, "Yes. You smell like the Moon. But your *lure-scent* is the cereus."

That couldn't be true. Females lost their scent with the Mark. "You must have told someone."

"No. I never mentioned *that* to anyone," he hissed.

"I—"

"The Moon had best not cross me on this. She will regret it," Gabel growled.

Paralyzed with shock I watched as he slid into bed, careful around his heavily bandaged leg. The Moon—had left my scent? And *Aaron* could smell me? I scrambled to understand it and failed. It didn't make any sense. Had the Moon chosen to punish Her Comet—if that was what Gabel truly was—for going too far? Was She trying to teach him even the strongest could be undone? Was it a clever lie by Aaron? Who was Aaron he could smell my scent?

Was *Aaron* the Comet?

Gabel hadn't said a word to me since the previous night, and he had retreated into a pensive silence that was unlike him. It seemed prudent to make myself scarce before he dragged more deductions out of my non-answers, so I retreated to my workroom.

I turned one of the smaller pieces of tourmaline over in my hand, marveling at how it seemed to catch and hold the sunlight like ocean water. Even if Gabel no longer wanted to finalize our mating, I would still be the IronMoon Oracle, unless he threw me out.

Gabel would almost surely go through with he mating, because if he didn't, Aaron would use it against him, and say he was too weak to handle me. The IceMaw would probably make off with me, and I'd be a war-prize once more.

Gabel would go through with the vows. He couldn't afford not to.

What a fitting end to the entire thing. Caught in his own trap.

"How it was always destined to end. Except I'm locked in here with him," I told the blue stone.

The stone had no answers, but it was beautiful to look at. Maybe this was why I had never heard of it. Beautiful but useless. A pretty trinket for my shelves.

Gabel didn't come to dinner, leaving me in the unenviable position of making excuses for him.

Hix didn't approve of Gabel being in his office needlessly, and he said as much to me after dinner.

"He is licking his paws," Hix grumbled to me.

"I don't know what he's doing. I haven't seen him all day," I retorted. I didn't know what he was doing, but I did know that prodding a brooding Gabel was as smart as poking an angry badger with a stick.

"You're going to let this continue?"

"You think me going in there and trying to get him out of his burrow is a good idea? No thanks."

Hix frowned. "You fear he would strike you?"

He'd rage at me, and the punishment I'd feel from his fury was something I would have rather not imagined. I knew how much pain even his anger would cause. He didn't have to hit me to hurt me.

"Has he hit you?" Hix lowered his voice.

"No."

"Are you sure?"

"Am I sure? Of course I'm sure. I know what it feels like to get hit. You've hit me, remember?"

"In training!"

"Don't get so offended, Hix. You know what I meant."

Now I had an angry, rankled Hix glaring at me conjuring all kinds of stories to himself. Suddenly being locked in with Gabel didn't sound bad. Trying to reason with Hix once he got his mind stuck on something was like shouting at a rock. I sighed. "I will go deal with him. Go to bed, Hix."

I did knock, however, before entering Gabel's office.

As always he was staring at his map, but I don't think he actually saw it.

His dinner was untouched on his desk and had gone cold long before.

"Holed up in your burrow, Gabel?" I decided to go right for the throat.

"You don't have to be here."

"Hix sent me. You skipping dinner to lick your paws is not allowed. I made your excuses. You are very busy working."

"I am very busy. I have had a great deal to think about and do not need distractions."

"You should not be standing on that leg."

"I am not going to lie on my back like some goddamn corpse."

"No, but you giving a damn about healing quickly might be nice!"

"I will heal fine."

"Then I'll report to Hix you are not lying dead in your office. Be at breakfast in the morning. I don't care if you come to bed or not." I was in no mood to deal with him. I was not the enemy. I wasn't the one who made my Mark move in the presence of another male he despised. "Go howl at the Moon if you're angry. If you're going to punish me for all *your* bad choices over the past six months, you can go fuck yourself."

I slapped away the Bond's whimper. It could keep on whimpering. It couldn't force me to love Gabel. It could do a lot of things, but Bonds were possible to kill off, and if Gabel was going to start blaming me for his mistakes, that would wither our connection very quickly. A petty, weak, selfish Gabel wasn't one I could love or even respect. Not even a little.

"Buttercup," his voice pulled at me, "was Aaron the cloaked man?"

"I don't know. I never saw his face or caught his scent. I'm leaving now."

"Do you think it's strange, buttercup, that the Elder Oracle tried to warn you off me, and Aaron wants you?"

"Anita told me you would destroy everything you touched. Aaron seemed miffed he hadn't got a chance with me. Those aren't the same reason."

"Unless there was some reason for Anita to want to help Aaron."

"I don't know what that could be." I needed to get away from this conversation before he went back to the petitioner wolf, because it didn't exactly take a monumental mental effort to see the connection.

"What did he say to you in private before he started spouting off in public?"

I glanced at the door, then sighed. "I'm not going to talk to you if you're standing up. You have to get off your leg."

Gabel muttered under his breath but limped over to the couch. "Happy?"

Not really, but it was a start.

"What did Aaron tell you?" Gabel asked.

"Aside from making a pass at me and telling me I smelled like the a flower?"

"Besides that."

"He told me you have no idea what you have, and even less idea how to hold onto it."

Gabel's chuckle surprised me. He rubbed his chin, staring out the large window, and nodded to himself.

"So now you're not jealous?" I asked.

"I was never really jealous," he corrected. "Unsettled by this thing that should not be, from a wolf I had not expected to see, nor in a mood to deal with."

"Don't take Aaron lightly." I bristled with annoyance at his arrogance.

Alpha Magnes hides behind his Oracle, but Aaron comes right for me, and Anders tries to play both of us." Gabel smirked. "And Aaron comes for my mate. How desperate must he be?"

It wasn't just Anders trying to play both sides. "Aaron's offer to me was serious, Gabel. Serious enough to make my Mark shift against my soul."

"How flattering, but it changes nothing. You are mine. I simply can't take my eye off you, even for an instant. You bite, claw, scratch, kick, howl, and then disappear for days on end to places I cannot track you. The risk of defeat makes every victory worthwhile. Every day with you will prove a battle to be won."

Damn, this Gabel I could come to love. I shifted onto my knees, shimmied across the middle of the couch, and kissed him warmly.

He hadn't shaven since the previous night, and I liked it under my hand. What would it feel like against my—

"You were thinking so many naughty thoughts last night, and here they are again." He slid his hands into my hair and lifted large handfuls.

"You have holes in your leg."

"So?" He pulled me down to him and whispered, "You smell of desire. That is all I care about. That desire, and fulfilling your every wanton need. Including the ones that maidenly you doesn't yet realize she has."

He tugged me against him with one hand, and the other slid up my thigh, under my skirt. I twitched and squirmed, his hand slid higher until his fingertips grazed the seam of my panties.

It was his leg. If he wanted to risk popping a stitch—

"Fine," I breathed hard as I spoke, "but I get to be on top."

SO-HOT-FOR-INK

T en days.

Ten days until I'd see if our enemies would ruin our Solstice. Ten days until I'd affirm my Bond with Gabel under the Moon and before the pack.

Ten days until I would be the Luna of IronMoon.

Ten days until history will hold me as accountable as Gabel.

Ten days until I had to decide if I could remain an Oracle.

That last one was the crux of it: if I remained an Oracle, it would always put Gabel and I at odds. It would leave me subject to the whims of Elder Oracles. It would leave a huge open door with a neon blinking sign inviting all his enemies inside.

I stood out in the freezing cold. It was a miserable overcast winter day, it wasn't snowing, and everything was just sort of frozen brown mud. supervised roasting pits being dug out of the frozen ground.

Two men walked by carrying something that looked like a large sawhorse, but the middle beam was covered in a sheet of metal to form a strange sort of pointed saddle. They disappeared into the house.

Odd. There weren't any repairs going on in the house. The foyer had been cleaned up and basic repairs done, like fixing stairs and spackling over holes in walls. Actual craftsmen would have to come at a later time and repair the ruined tile and floors. It wasn't going to happen before Solstice, so the foyer had just been cleaned up as much as possible. Because we were going to have guests in the house and of course... we meant to make this mess.

One of Gardenia's little pack of females tip-toed out to me and murmured, "Alpha Gabel needs you. He is in the...basement."

The basement. Gabel had finally decided what to do about the traitors.

Those wolves had sat and rotted in the basement since the night they had been locked down there. Gabel had been conjuring some especially horrible punishment for them. There hadn't been any pressing reason to interrogate and punish them earlier. As if being in that basement for all this time wasn't punishment enough.

Come to think of it, it wasn't.

Noises from the basement, and the stench of crippling anxiety, but not so much fear. I gripped the banister. Damn, I hated going down there. These wolves deserved whatever horror Gabel conjured for them, but I didn't take any enjoyment out of *watching* it.

Hix and Eroth were there, as were a few other males, along with Gabel. Gabel had on dark pants and a pale green shirt, with the sleeves rolled over his forearms and first button undone, like he was overseeing some board meeting.

"Gianna," Gabel greeted me as I stepped off the last stair. "Sit."

As before a single chair had been placed for me. In the center of the aisle between the two rows of cages was the sawhorse, which was much, much taller than I had originally thought. Not a normal sawhorse. Next to it were several large, very heavy kettlebells, and thick nylon ropes. The neon pink of the nylon was the brightest thing in the basement.

I took my seat, which was set a bit back from things.

"She does not need to be here for this," Hix said. He firmly believed this sort of practical torture was appropriate only for males. For him this was no different than slaughtering pigs or cattle. It was dirty work to a female.

The Bond slipped beneath my awareness. All of Gabel was darkness and focus. "Which one should I start with, buttercup?"

Um... Sawhorse, kettlebells, nylon rope... what was I going to condemn one of these traitors to? And more importantly, how to choose?

Gabel picked up the nylon rope and wrapped it in a neat, slow coil while he waited for my answer.

The wolves were all unshaven and filthy. They all seemed beaten down, like the fight had been bled from their bones. Every single one looked between Gabel, myself and the sawhorse, trying to figure out what the hell was going to happen to them.

Well, what did these idiots *think* was going to happen when they attacked their own packmates?

"That one." I pointed to the one I remembered best. I couldn't recall exactly *why* he stuck out, but he did, and since I had to choose, I chose him.

Gabel snapped his fingers. Two of the warriors yanked open the rebar cage, grabbed the wolf, and dragged him out while he struggled and mewled. They cut off his filthy clothes and left him completely naked. Then they pulled him over to the sawhorse. Each one grabbed an arm and hefted him up, while another warrior grabbed his left leg. They lifted him over the point of the sawhorse, and a fourth warrior slid the sawhorse forward. When the wolf was middle over the sawhorse, they carefully lowered him. His feet didn't touch the ground, and the point of the sawhorse's metal saddle—

Let's just say no female would have wanted to sit there, and a male even less.

The wolf grabbed the front of the saddle and lifted himself so that his privates weren't bearing all his weight on the metal. Nobody moved to stop him. Eroth attached chains on the sawhorse's legs to rings on the floor. It would rock a little bit but couldn't be toppled.

Panting and whimpering, the traitor looked up as Gabel approached him, already streaming tears and blubbering from fear.

Gabel separated out two lengths of rope. One he looped through a ring on the front of the sawhorse, then tied a noose around the wolf's waist, and fed the tail back through the ring, tying it off like he was tying off the rigging on a sailboat. He repeated this with a ring on the other end of the sawhorse. The end result was the wolf being tied by hot pink nylon cord around his middle to the front and back of the sawhorse.

After giving the wolf a few minutes to appreciate the severity of his plight, Gabel asked, "Did you believe you would succeed in killing Lady Gianna?"

The wolf breathed hard through his mouth and didn't answer. He focused on trying to rock himself into some kind of position that wouldn't punish his privates. Gabel let him squirm until he heaved and panted and his body shone with sweat. Only once the wolf stopped squirming so much did Gabel repeat the question. And repeated it, and repeated it, impassive and patient, dark and still, but now with a warm flicker of growing anger, like he was a banked coal.

"No," the wolf finally sputtered, "we weren't going to kill her!"

"Interesting. Then what were going to do to her?"

The wolf shook all over, his attention on keeping his tender bits off the saddle.

Gabel picked up one of the kettle bells. He looped some pink rope through the hoop at the top, then tied the kettlebell to the wolf's ankle. He did this to the other ankle as well. The wolf howled and whimpered as the weight of the kettlebells pulled him square onto the saddle's point.

"I'm disappointed." Gabel leaned close, "You had the courage to attack your own pack member, your future Luna, and you can't even face this with a little dignity? You can't even spit in my face? Spit in my face at least. Tell me how much you hate me. You *hate* me."

The wolf sobbed like a child and whimpered some pleas.

"Excellent choice, buttercup. You chose the coward of the group."

"I chose the one I remembered most clearly." I corrected, feeling unwell.

"Then the others aren't going to be very interesting." Gabel shoved a kettlebell with his foot. The wolf howled as his leg swung back and forth, grinding his bits into the saddle. "Do you know what this is called?" He directed this at the wolf.

The wolf shook his head, sputtering and bubbling around his lips, eyes bulging. The pendulum forced his leg to swing back and forth, grinding his tender bits and punishing the tiny muscles of his inner thigh.

"It's called a Spanish Donkey. Variation of the Judas Chair. The human Spanish Inquisition was so... unrestrained in their torments. Something about punish the flesh to save the soul? That's what they believed. What were you going to do with Lady Gianna?"

The wolf just blubbered and sobbed and whimpered for

another half hour before Gabel, still impassive, decided he had other things to do.

The prisoner's screams to not leave him like that followed me up the stairs until Gabel closed the door to the basement.

Eroth looked a little shaken. Hix was a stone. Gabel, an impassive hot coal, focused and perfectly calm.

I was as white as if I were about to start puking from the stomach flu. "What are you going to do with him?"

"See if he's feeling more conversant later tonight. And if he's not, if his friends are more motivated to talk."

"Only if he knows something." I licked my dry lips.

"They didn't want to kill you. So what did they want? To use you as sport and some kind of trophy? Ransom you, perhaps? With what else has happened, I have to consider that it's all related. I also have to make sure it never happens again."

Hix nodded once.

My lips felt so cracked and parched. The tip of my tongue found a crack. I had bitten myself while down there. "You don't think maybe just... revolt? Sport?"

"Of course I think that could be it. In their mind they think, 'we'll attack Gianna, defile her, weaken Gabel, overthrow him, and turn IronMoon into the pack that Romero promised us.'" Gabel's eyes were the same color as the tourmaline. "I'd rather have that problem. That's an easy one. If Aaron's got his paws in my den, that's much more concerning."

"Don't focus just on Aaron. Don't lose track of Anders, Salt-Paw, SableFur. Need I go on?" Aaron wasn't the only problem out there. I wasn't even sure he was the source of all of them. I worried the crack in my lip, and reconsidered Anita and I were wrong: Aaron was the Comet.

"Aaron would like to think he has all my attention, but he doesn't. There is still plenty of me left for you."

"Did you deliberately ignore my point?"

His smile had a cruel twist to it. "Yes."

Going back outside to supervise the digging of roasting pits and playing lady-of-the-manor sounded *much* better than dealing with the aftermath of the Spanish donkey. I left the males to whatever else they had to do.

Much later in the evening, the doctor came by our rooms to change the dressing on Gabel's thigh and examine the healing puncture wounds. Changing the dressing was a twice-a-day thing. The swelling had gone down a fair amount, but not entirely, and his leg was a mottled purple and magenta. The discoloration had also started to travel down the back of his thigh and made it to his knee.

"Why is he bruised down there?" I asked worriedly.

"Just gravity pulling the bruised blood down," the doctor grumbled. "His body will clean it up eventually. I'm working, stop bothering me."

I glared at him, but he ignored me and squirted saline over the holes. Gabel pulled at one end of a stitch.

"Don't do that." I chided him. Why did he do that? He had an injury and *poked* at it like a child poking something in one of those pet-the-wildlife aquariums.

He pulled at it a bit more. "Does it make you squeamish, buttercup?"

"It's just not right, Gabel."

Gabel released the stitch and smirked at me.

"He doesn't need you babying him," the doctor said. "And I don't need supervision. You can leave."

"I don't think me telling him not to pull his stitches is *babying* him. I'm the one he'll bleed on," I snapped.

"She will remain if she wishes it," Gabel informed the doctor with calm authority.

The doctor huffed but didn't say anything, and finished wrapping Gabel's thigh. When he finally got out of our rooms, I slammed the door after him and told Gabel, "If you told me he was conducting horrible experiments in his house and doctored IronMoon on the side, I'd believe you."

"Don't like him, buttercup?"

"I have *never* liked him and cringe at the idea of me ever needing him," I said, annoyed. "He's fine for dealing with rough warriors who need rough handling, but did he just tell me to get out of my own *den?* Where did you *find* him?"

"Literally, or what's his past?"

"What's his past? How did you acquire him? There aren't a lot of werewolf doctors." Many pack doctors were actually humans who had been brought into the fold.

"The story is that a she-wolf spurned him, so he lured her into his office, drugged her up, and proceeded to carve his name all over her back with a silver scalpel."

My jaw went *twhunk.*

"He hadn't gotten as far as the whole, *how will I not get caught,* was branded and thrown out. That scar on his neck?" Gabel pointed to the place. "It's where he burned himself almost to death trying to hide it, but if you look very close, you'll spot it. I found him stitching up drunks and scumbags in a mining town."

"His pack didn't *kill* him?" I asked. "They just set him loose?"

Gabel shrugged. "I don't know those details. This was thirty years ago. I only know what he told me about him, and I don't believe he lied, and I don't believe he cares that anyone knows. I gave him a chance to get back around wolves, and he took it."

"You will be my midwife. I'm not going to let that man perform so much as a pregnancy test on me!"

"Buttercup, do you—"

"I mean in the future." I glowered.

"Find me another doctor." Gabel shrugged again.

"Let's recruit the vet." The suggestion popped out of my mouth.

"The *vet?* You mean Doctor-So-Hot-For-Ink?"

Now that I had said it, it sounded like a great idea. She was already comfortable working beyond the fringes of the law. Vets made perfectly good pack doctors too, assuming they were willing to learn some human anatomy, and that vet already had some experience. Stitching up wounds and setting broken bones weren't too different from animals, and the basic knowledge and techniques were all there. If I had to choose between Doctor-I-Carve-Up-Females and Doctor-So-Hot-For-Ink, I'd choose her.

"I am going to go tomorrow and do this, because the Moon save me if I need that doctor anytime soon," I decided.

"There aren't things here that need your attention?" Gabel asked.

"When was the last time we had sex?"

"Last night."

"Exactly. I don't know when I'm going to need my own doctor, but I know I *never* want him. This is my highest priority."

I also didn't want to do another day in the basement with the Spanish donkey. Recruiting a new pack doctor so that the females of IronMoon didn't need to have Doctor-I-Tattoo-In-Blood touch them needed to happen *right* away.

Besides. It would distract me from the crushing weight of what I was about to become.

STUDENT LOANS AND HAM

I took Eroth and one of the other hunters, Renzo.

Gabel shut down Hix's insistence that he be the one to go and sent me on my way with the Second Beta and hunter.

"This is more depressing in daylight." The night we had been there it had been vacant, which seemed normal. In broad daylight it was slightly-less-than-vacant with a few beaten up cars, and only three occupied businesses: the vet, a seedy mattress store, and a laundry mat.

"Fewer witnesses," Renzo said.

"You're only here to make sure I get back home in one piece." I reminded him.

He held up both hands and nodded. "Yes, ma'am."

The vet's waiting room was empty, and she sat at the front desk with her feet up, tapping madly on her phone. "Don't know why you're here, Purple Dress, but I thought it was clear I don't like to see my nighttime patients in the daytime. If he's dead or infected, not my problem. I stopped the bleeding. That's what you paid for."

"No daytime clientèle today?"

"Have you seen this place?" She gestured. "It's depressing,

PurpleDress. People around here can barely afford to feed their pets, much less care for them. And you know, that's not what pisses me off. You want to pay me with a ham? That's fine. I can't pay rent with a ham, but I can eat a ham. It's that people are assholes. They come in here with some dog that has a mangled back leg that's been rotting for five days and act like it's a huge problem that Fido had the audacity to get hit by a car. But you know, they couldn't be bothered to secure the dog so somehow it's the dog's fault you're a horrible caretaker. When folks come in distressed and frantic and paying me in hams, that doesn't make me mad. I'm talking about the assholes. And I see a lot of them. Oh no, kitty is diabetic and needs one shot a day and it's too much a pain in the ass to bother with."

She twirled around in her chair, kicked the wall as she passed, then gave me a look that could have melted glass. "What do you want, Purple Dress?"

"To offer you a job." Given her bad disposition to-the-point seemed best.

"I don't know what you're into, but I probably don't want any part of it."

"It's not illegal." I hesitated. Well, it actually was, and humans would have something to say about it if they knew. "Mostly. It's *mostly* not illegal. But it pays well."

"How can it be *mostly* legal and pay well?"

"Are you interested? Because if you're not interested, I won't waste my time."

She chewed on her cheek, then said, "Might be."

Better make sure she didn't know Anders and the GleamingFang first. Wait, who the hell cared if she did? That would make things so simple. "Unless you already know Anders and the GleamingFang."

"The Gleaming what? I told you I've got my limits. Organized crime is not my thing. You can come by and I'll stitch you

up, but I ain't joining up. Nope. I am an independent contrac-
tor. Free agent."

"That's not what I'm talking about. GleamingFang isn't... a
gang or crime ring."

She eyed me, very sharp, shrewd, chewed her cheek again,
twirled around in her chair and said, "Okay. Let's go in the back,
and you can tell me all about the money and how much crap I'm
gonna have to slurp down to get it. Because student loans.
Goddamn."

The back smelled of disinfectant and dogs. She took up a
position behind the largest metal exam table. I gestured to Eroth
and Renzo to stand back and just relax while we spoke. Now
that I had time, I noticed the peeling counters and paint, the
way everything tried to stay clean but was dirty with the grime
of age and disrepair.

I had never told anyone about wolves before, and I wasn't
sure the best way to go about it. That was a conversation we
usually avoided having.

"Spill it, Purple Dress."

"My name is Gianna. You remember that dirty pitchfork?"

"Bullshit story. Who the hell runs around stabbing people in
tuxedos with pitchforks? That should at least make the weird
crime section of the newspaper, but let me tell you, I've been
waiting for it to show up, and it hasn't." She wagged a finger
at me.

"It was claws."

"From what? A fucking bear running loose in the city? Also
not in the weird crime section."

"No, a werewolf."

"Right. Are you high? Because I don't have any really good
drugs here, and I ain't gonna help you get them. That's more
than 'slightly' illegal."

So not the best start. I weighed my options, then decided

she just needed a demonstration. "Eroth, can you handle being in war-form without destroying everything?"

"Yes, Lady."

"Demonstrate to the doctor what we're about."

He started to remove his clothing, neatly folding each piece and placing it in one of the plastic chairs.

"Well, okay then," the vet said, eyeing him up and down as more and more skin was revealed. "No ink, but still nice. Very nice. So can you pick up a dollar bill with those pert butt cheeks?"

Eroth grinned. "Show me the dollar."

She reached into her pocket and pulled out a few crumbled bills. "What will three bucks get me?"

Eroth was about to say something when I intervened. "Show her what you are before she spends money on you."

With the frightening speed required of all IronMoon warriors, Eroth melted and stretched into a dark brown, shaggy war-form, smaller than one might expect but with vicious fangs and wild, yellow eyes, his breath echoing off the walls of the room. His claws cracked into the cheap linoleum and under-lying cement pad.

The vet yelped, scrambled up onto the counter, and tried to crawl into the cupboards before she realized she was not the size of a mouse. She turned back around, but Eroth was already back in human form, looking rather smug. I told him to get dressed while I coaxed the vet off her perch.

"You won't outrun me," Renzo informed her when she tried to squirm down the length of the counter away from me.

"You aren't helping." I half-pulled, half-coaxed the shaking vet off the counter.

"The fuck—" she sputtered. I let her babble to herself. After a few minutes her color had halfway returned. She went to the ancient fridge, pulled out a bottle, and downed large slugs of it.

She wiped her sleeve on her mouth, then, panting around the burning liquor, said, "So. Um. Yeah. Um. Wow. Yeah. And it ain't even the full moon."

"We don't force-shift on the full moon. And if we bite you, you won't turn into one of us."

"So everyone I saw the other night was a werewolf?"

"Yes."

"Wolves in tuxedos at the ballet." That required another shot.

"Sort of."

Her shaking eased a little with each word. "So... what do you want with me? Did I pass some werewolf medical board exam?"

"I don't like our pack doctor and don't want anything to do with him."

"I'm a vet."

I shrugged.

"And you call the shots? You're the boss? Because the big guy with the holes in his leg seemed like the boss to me."

"He is a... Lord Alpha." I said. "I'm going to marry him in about a week. Well, what a human would call marry."

"So if Boss Wolf rules this territory, what the hell were you doing here for mending, and why was he cut up at all?"

If Hix had been there he would have commended her shrewdness. But Hix wasn't there, so I glossed over it, since it was a complicated question. "We were down here at a Solstice party hosted by the Alpha of Gleaming Fang and an Alpha from another, distant pack who picked a fight."

"Over what?"

"Me."

This made her laugh, "Oh my gawd. Put wolves in tuxedos and they'll still brawl over a woman. Testosterone doesn't vary much between mammal species. So who won?"

"Gabel, of course." I said like it was stupid.

"Gabel being the one with stab wounds in his leg."

"Yes."

"Didn't look like he won. Guess I should have seen the other guy. And you didn't really answer my question."

"It's not relevant." I tried to pull my best high-handed tone, but I think it mostly failed. Or she was a tough mark.

She tinked her fingernails on the metal exam table. "How much are you paying, what are the hours, and how much will it suck? Because you're gonna have to convince me to leave all this. I mean, who wouldn't?"

I told her what she'd be paid, which instantly made her eyes light up. "And the hours are on-call, and I don't know. Almost all of IronMoon are male, and most of them are a rough lot. Sometimes enforcement of order is... brutal and fatal."

"So it's like working at a late-night dive bar that has illegal, no-rules, bare knuckle matches in the basement after two a.m.."

I didn't know much about late-night dive bars or no-rules, bare-knuckle brawls, but it sounded like it a good approximation.

"Am I going to get molested?"

"No. Not allowed. Gabel doesn't have many limits," I thought of the donkey and collars, "but he doesn't let females be abused."

"Do they all look sort of like that?" She pointed at Eroth. "I mean the body. I can always put a bag over ugly faces. Or turn the lights off. I mean, there are options if the face is ugly."

Eroth smirked, and Renzo flipped him the finger.

"Physical strength and ability are requirements of virtually all IronMoon males," I said.

"But they might be idiots. I can live with that. What's the catch? Aside from the fact that I'm a veterinarian practicing on human bodies without a license, and there may be the occasional dead body? That's the slightly illegal part, right? So what's the legal but crappy part?"

"You can't tell anyone, you can't have guests, and the Iron-Moon are mostly made up of those who have been driven away from proper werewolf society. The other doctor carved his name into the back of a female who rejected his affections."

"Nice." The vet leaned on the table. "Nice. I promise I'm not into carving my initiations into junk. Branding 'em like 'mine' or 'Ana Was Here' isn't my kink. So what did you do to mix in with this lot?"

"I was tribute. My birthpack surrendered to Gabel, and he took me as his mate."

"That's old school hardcore." She frowned.

"That's not how it's usually done." It still stung.

"Is that what this was?" She touched her arm. "All cut up there? I noticed you two have matching scars."

"It's a Mark," I said, unable to not sound bitter. "The male—with the female's consent—carves it into her bicep, and the mirror image appears on his arm. It is supposed to be a beautiful pattern. I did not consent. I resisted. He ripped into me."

"So I should just file that shit under, 'it's complicated.'"

"Are you interested in the job?" I was no longer in the mood to coax this vet along. She had all the information she needed. There wasn't anything complicated about this.

She tossed back another gulp of her drink, then put it back in the fridge. "When would I start?"

"Right now. Plane is waiting for us." I checked my phone to see the time. The bright white-blue overhead lights reflected in the surface and flitted across my mind. Something dark fluttered in my awareness, shadows moving across a strange surface I didn't recognize, then the sensation of asphalt against my cheek.

"Lady Gianna?" Eroth yanked me from the pull.

I pointed at Renzo, and then the door.

We waited while Renzo slid into the front of the office, bolted the door, and turned the sign to closed. Didn't mean anything, but if anyone was coming through the front door, they'd be easy to spot. It only took him a minute but it felt like forever.

Technically speaking Anders should protect us if there was a problem, but Anders might have been the problem.

Renzo slipped back into the room and clicked the door behind him. He pointed at the ceiling, then out the front. To Ana, he whispered, "Back way out?"

"How many?" I asked.

"Three. Two coming from outside, one on the roof."

"GleamingFang?"

"I don't know."

Ana rolled her eyes and told Eroth, "You better be able to tie those dollar bills in a pretty bowtie."

She took us to the far end of the long room and opened a little door I had thought was a closet. It opened onto a very narrow, steep set of stairs. We hurried up the stairs into a tiny, one-room apartment with one window overlooking the back of the lot and an ancient fire escape. Renzo sidled up to the window while Eroth herded me away from it. The vet scurried around, grabbing a few things and throwing them into an old army duffel bag.

I squirmed through the small window onto the ancient fire escape, which wobbled under our weight, but mercifully didn't make much noise. I couldn't see over the edge of the building, but nothing peered back at me.

"He's facing the front," Renzo whispered.

"And nobody is on the back?" I whispered back.

"Yet."

I carefully tip-toed down the two flights into the back lot. It was bordered by a crappy chainlink fence and apartment complex on the other side. Eroth moved down the ladder after me, swift and silent despite his size. There were no trees and no cover for a hundred yards. A moment later the vet crawled out the window and came down the steps with her bag in tow. Renzo carefully closed the window, then crept down the stairs.

"Hell yeah." Ana grinned with a twinkle in her eyes. "Who are those guys?"

"Not GleamingFang." Eroth said.

"Probably IceMaw, then," I said. "Aaron must be the one controlling Anders."

"Who's Aaron?" Ana poked me.

"The Alpha who put those holes in Gabel's leg."

"Stabby-stabby!"

"Are you normal?" I asked her.

"I'm going to go be a werewolf doctor. No, I'm not normal, Purple Dress."

Renzo led us down the back lot to the far end of the strip mall. He peeked around the corner. "They've busted into your office."

"Sweet. Insurance money!"

Ana was really not normal. Since she was taking this so well, she could take the point. "Give her the keys, Eroth."

"Why?" Eroth asked.

"They aren't looking for *her*. She can go get the car and drive it around here. You want it to get back to whomever sent them that we fled the scene?"

"But—"

"We're not fleeing. We were just leaving. Advancing on our base!" Ana snatched the keys out of Eroth's hand and sauntered around the building.

"I think I'm in love," Eroth muttered as we craned our heads around the building.

We had parked a bit away, and she was able to walk to the car, get inside, and pull away without us hearing shouts.

"Flawless victory," Ana chortled as she crawled into the passenger seat. "They came by car. Cruise by, I'll snap a plate."

"I don't want them to see us," Renzo said.

"They're tossing my apartment. The glass is all shattered."

I piled into the backseat and squished down against Ana. Eroth cruised back around, and Ana snapped some pictures on her phone.

Gabel was not going to be happy about this, and Hix was going to have a kitten. Or a whole litter of kittens. Angry kittens.

Gianna >> Vet acquired. On our way to the airport. They were expecting us.

Gabel >> Who is this someone?

Gianna >> Don't know, but we have a truck plate. We were not seen leaving.

I could feel his anger, even from a distance.

Gabel >> Come home, buttercup. We shall compare notes. We may have a very serious problem.

RELATIVE SAFETY

I thought Ana would have a ton of questions once we were on the plane, but she grabbed a bottle of liquor from the kitchen, took out her phone, and began tapping wildly on it without so much as a word. Eroth slid into the seat next to her, and she ignored him, engrossed in whatever game she had been playing before we showed up.

"So what's this Second Beta stuff," she asked Eroth about half an hour into the flight. "Like there's an Alpha male, and I guess that makes you some kind of not-quite Alpha?"

"Yes," Eroth said with measured pride, while leering down her blouse.

He leaned a little too close, she planted her hand on his face and pushed him back, eyes never leaving her phone.

"And who's Gianna? She's like your queen or something?"

"She is an Oracle, and she will be our Luna soon. A Luna is a female Alpha."

"An Oracle? Like seeing the future?"

"Yes."

"Baloney."

"Her powers are very real," Eroth said with mild affront that reminded me of Flint.

"If you say so." She tapped faster. "Awwww, yeahhhhh, almost a high scoreeeee... allllllmossssssttttt!"

This continued for the remainder of the flight.

I wanted to get Ana settled into IronMoon, but one of the warriors was waiting at the front steps as soon as we arrived, and told me Gabel wanted me in his office as soon as I got back. I asked for someone to round up Violet to show Ana around, and get her squared into her room (hell, to find her a room), oh, and I mentioned maybe not next to Flint's. Then on to Gabel.

"Gabel?" I closed the door to his office behind me.

"Up here. Good hunting?"

I came around the stairs to the second floor of the office and found myself licking my lips.

By the Moon, Gabel was good looking.

Gabel had an open spiral-bound book in one hand, and his lips curled into a smirk that made my panties moisten. "You missed me."

I bit my lower lip and tried to tell my privates to calm down. Gabel clapped the book shut and shoved it onto the shelf. He gripped my arms and pushed his face into my neck. I arched as he inhaled, then bit me lightly. "Desire, buttercup. You are nothing but desire."

"I... we have something to discuss." I floundered, trying to stay on task. Gabel had said it was serious, but his scent... so much power, so much prestige...

"It will wait." His lips moved over my neck. His hands slid over my rump and lifted me against him. "You cannot expect me to think of work when you need my attention."

I tried to protest, but I only breathed his name.

He kissed the hollow of my throat, then another kiss below

that. And another. Each kiss left a burning mark on my skin, stoking a heat within my core.

He pulled off my top, and cupped my breasts in each hand. His thumbs moved across my nipples through the satin of my bra. I reached for something to steady myself that wasn't him. My fingers found the spines of some books. I grasped, pulled them down, and found some purchase on the sharp edges of the shelves.

His lips found mine again. I greeted his tongue with abandon, struggled to pull myself back from the edge. My skirt became his next victim, then his hand slid between my thighs.

"Wait." I tried to catch my breath, but all I could do was moan once he slipped two fingers inside me.

He growled as he sampled my wetness. I clawed the shelves. Nerves raced, his scent consumed everything. I moaned as he moved within me, and when he withdrew his hand I whimpered in protest.

Another rough-edged laugh. His fingers teased me a moment, then his grip clenched. The heel of his palm ground into my jewel, and I gasped, jerked, arched against him. The seam of my panties ground into me along with his palm, blending raw abrasion with the pleasure of his skin.

"Enough of these," he said with a sudden snarl. He snatched my panties and bra away with his other hand. Then he stepped back to admire his work: my flushed body, hard nipples, wet thighs, my scent.

He couldn't mean to leave me like this. I panted, despising him for the threat dancing along the bond, and the cruel glint in his gaze. He pulled of his own clothes, and took me in his arms again.

His cock shoved against my thigh, and his ashen scent rose cruel and hungry around me. I bit his lower lip. "No games, Gabel."

He seized one of my thighs and hooked it over his hip, then other other. His cock pressed along the entire length of my wetness. I arched, and gasped, and he groaned into my neck. I clawed at his shoulders. He couldn't mean to do this to us. His hands held my ass, guiding me against his length as we both shuddered, and my body pleaded for more.

"You must learn to ask," he rasped.

"No."

"I could finish like this," he bit my ear, "and leave you aching. I'm so close, buttercup, there isn't even time to taste you, and I so love your taste. Perhaps I should punish you for your stubbornness."

"When has that ever worked?" I growled back.

Another rough laugh. He shifted me in his grip, and slowly, so slowly I cried out, he lowered me onto his cock. Pleasure burned away every intelligent thought I had. Everything became a hot, hard-edged pleasure as he drove into me, over and over and over.

One final thrust finished me, and I couldn't even gasp, or breathe, or do anything except rasp his name. I shuddered on his body, dripping wetness along him, flinching with the pain/pleasure of his touch. He sank deep one last time and rasped a tearing groan as a quake wracked his spine from end to end.

I panted. I would have collapsed if he hadn't been holding me.

He shifted, lowering both of us to the ground, still joined, and tumbled me onto the floor amid all the books.

My hand lazily felt the outline of a book. Hard cover, thin pages. I pulled it within my field of view. Some dry treatise on government.

"Such a mess, buttercup." Gabel kissed my shoulder. "Pulling my books everywhere."

I looked up at the shelves. "Not all of them."

The hardwood floor was not very comfortable, but I didn't yet feel like moving. Gabel's kisses moved down my arm, to the tender spot on the inside of my elbow. I shivered, and he moved lower to my wrist and my palm.

He released my hand with a final nip, then got to his feet. He extended his hand to me.

I kissed him, enjoying his naked skin against mine.

"Buttercup, did you miss me?" He cupped my jaw in his hand, bit my lower lip very gently.

"I just wanted some attention." I dodged the question.

Gabel smiled. "Maybe you should say what you mean."

"You understood, didn't you?"

"Oracle, perhaps some enjoy your riddles, but I would prefer to hear that my Luna," he lowered his lips to my ear, "wants my body inside hers, and my lips upon her flesh, and that she is clawing her desire into my skin, hmm? Or is that too obtuse? Perhaps my Luna wants me to—"

I blushed and skittered backward at his choice of words.

"Ah, there is that maidenly affront again." Gabel smirked as I bumped into the book shelves.

I blushed a furious red.

"Your brain protests, but your body... I didn't know a male could sense his mate's mood that way." Gabel approached me. "I know when you are unhappy, I know when you are angry, when you are pleased, and I most certainly know when you," he slipped his hand over my thigh, across the front, sliding upward. I gasped, and his expression was so smug, "You need... attention. But I suppose that before anything else makes sense. Tell me, buttercup, do females in human form go into heat?"

"No." I swallowed, breathing hard, ignoring his fingers teasing the tender parts of me. "No. Only if I stay in... wolf form... long enough..."

"So you need to stay in one form for us to have pups."

"Um... I think so..." I couldn't think straight. I tried to squirm away. My body was so raw and sensitive that his touch was pleasure/pain, and I whimpered. The Bond squirmed. Shouldn't Gabel know humans didn't go into heat? What a strange question. "Stop it, Gabel."

"Why?"

How could there be something I wanted so much, it was painful? My body was so raw, even if the spirit was more than willing and the Bond goaded me. "Later."

"Hmmm, making me wait? I'd rather not, but I enjoy the game." He watched me as his fingers teased and moved, in no hurry to free me. I squirmed, the Bond rushed in my ears, and Gabel leaned closer, smug and fascinated by what he could invoke.

Beast.

Then he backed away, freeing me, and I stood there panting as he picked up the books as if nothing had just happened.

I picked my clothing up off the floor as he put the books back on the shelf, smoothed my hair and, on somewhat trembling legs, went down to the main floor of the office, all the time aware of Gabel (still naked) smirking at me, gloating over everything.

"You know," he informed me, "I win either way. You act the shy maiden, I corrupt you. You act the frosty bitch, I melt you. You act the passionate mate, and well... that should be obvious."

"I will let you have your victory, Gabel," I told him.

He laughed.

My ears burned. I had spent so long fighting him, I wasn't sure how to deal with wanting him.

Especially since Gabel was determined to watch me squirm like a salted slug until I stopped squirming. Now this was his new game, and either way, he was going to win.

Dammit. Still playing games.

It was very dark outside, and dinner would be in about an hour. I was already hungry, having missed lunch. So now I was hungry, my lady-bits were tender, and Gabel swirled around me like a smug cloud, gloating on the game. But I had brought back the vet, and as I sat down in the chair at his desk, I gloated a bit myself.

"That's my chair," Gabel told me.

"And I'm sitting in it," I replied.

"Territorial."

"You told me that we had something serious to discuss."

"Buttercup, we're having a lovely evening." He went over to his map, touched one of the spots, and traced a line between it and a more southern spot.

I suppose we were. There was a list of names scrawled on a notepad. I had never given it much thought before, but Gabel's handwriting was atrocious. His scratched letters looked more like runes than letters, but they were letters... sort of. Could anyone read this? Even doctors would win better penmanship prizes than Gabel. There was bad, really bad, Doctor, and then there was Gabel.

It was a list of names.

"The basement wolf started to talk today."

That was a mood killer. I dropped the notepad.

"They were supposed to kidnap you." Gabel tapped a push pin into the map to mark something.

"For Aaron?" I asked.

"Perhaps," Gabel said. "For the wolves we banished back in autumn. For the two I let run. The two that went to IceMaw but were seemingly chased out."

"That doesn't make sense. What would they do with me? Kill me? Ransom me? Try to sell me to someone?"

"Exactly," Gabel agreed. "I'll start on the second one tomorrow and see if he is anymore forthcoming."

I shuddered.

"I find it strange," Gabel cocked his head and looked at me out of the corner of his eyes. "That they refuse to answer questions. They know I will kill them eventually. They know telling me what I want to know will end their suffering sooner. Who are they more afraid of than me?"

There was a challenge waiting for him somewhere, and he wanted to find it and test himself against it. He hungered for it in a dark, terrifying, and yet enthralling way that made my soul shiver with delight.

My Lord-Alpha, my four-form wolf, who had dared to test himself against the Moon.

She had swatted him for his conceit, but what was the swat of a goddess? It was flattery She found him worth punishing.

"Does that bother you?" I goaded him anyway, just because his rising ire enticed me so much.

Gabel grinned at me, feral and a little wild, smoldering with the thrill of a challenging hunt, and my undeniable approval of it.

"They also might just be idiots who don't realize who they should really be afraid of," I prodded even more.

"That would be so disappointing. You have already denied me a second round of pleasure, buttercup. Don't deny me entertaining this thought."

The dark sensations coiled up within me from him, and made me laugh.

"My theory is those runner wolves are just middlemen for a chain that ultimately will lead me to Aaron or Magnes. Anders was a distraction, but he's someone's pawn—I'm not sure he's realized it yet, though," Gabel mused, once again entertaining the thought of Aaron as a previously underestimated but now fascinating challenge. "Both have a vested interest in seeing you torn away from me, although I am inclined to believe

Aaron is behind this. Perhaps today's little encounter will lead us close."

"Maybe it wasn't about getting me to IceMaw. Maybe it had been about using me to get you out of the south." The attack had come while Gabel had been dealing with the missing SaltPaw. I shifted in his chair and walked my fingers along the arm.

"Aaron arranges for the SaltPaw to disappear, so I won't be entangled in a fight, hoping to divert me back to the north to rescue you?" Gabel clicked his tongue. "But what would he hope to accomplish?"

My Mark squirmed for a moment. I gulped and thought about what Gabel would do. "Proving to himself he can manipulate your actions?"

It was flimsy, but I could see Aaron jerking Gabel's chain just like Gabel jerked everyone else's chain. Proving to Gabel he could play that game too.

If only I had my bowls, I might have been able to catch a glimpse of something! I had no idea if I could scry for Gabel, but Hix or someone else could ask a question. Questions that shared a common interest weren't forbidden. If the Moon decided I was too entwined, She just would close Her Eye.

Gabel's gaze reminded me of the tourmaline. "You're thinking, buttercup. I can sense the shifting."

"Have you considered MarchMoon?" I ventured with care, knowing I was dangerously close to betraying the petitioner wolf's question.

"That is too obvious, buttercup."

"Just reminding you."

"I didn't need the reminder. I hope you enjoyed your outing today, buttercup. Because it is the last one you will have for a while. First the SableFur want to come between us, and now one abduction attempt too many, Aaron making a public bid for you, and a possible traitor in our den." Gabel shoved a final pin into his map. "You are in too much danger to leave the safety of IronMoon's heart."

The safety of IronMoon.

Oh, the irony.

BELLY OF THE MOON

Ana got a proper werewolf greeting at dinner, although with more applause and less howling since she was human. Still, the addition of another doctor (even if human) was a huge upgrade for IronMoon, and the present warriors preened and clapped each other on the back. To them it was a sign the pack's status was increasing. They didn't care about the details, just that the pack had enough prestige to add a second doctor-type to the group. And a female to boot.

Even Hix was moderately pleased with this.

"Going to tell me she will make fine pups?" I asked him.

"She is human," Hix said, unamused at the suggestion. Interbreeding was highly frowned upon, and human-werewolf pairings usually produced questionably sane humans, not were-wolves. It was one of those ill-advised risks, with the most likely outcome being a child who didn't fit in with humans (and was probably violently unstable) and wouldn't find a place within a pack. They would be driven to compete for status while physically inferior to a purebred.

Gabel, however, got the joke, and curled his lips in a grin.

"I meant it as a compliment when I said it, Lady Gianna,"

Hix stated. "Would you prefer me to say you would produce weak pups?"

"I would prefer you not to talk like I was a baby factory, and my only value is as a garden for Gabel's seed."

A few of the wolfs coughed on my choice of words. Gabel looked sidewise at his Beta, highly entertained.

Hix, however, remained nonplussed. "But that's not all that I said. Simply because I say one thing does not mean I would not say other things."

This was a losing battle. I suppressed a sigh and tried one last time. "But it's the first thing you said. Oh, after 'a fine choice.'"

"But you are a fine choice," Hix stated. "I do not understand your offense. Just as I don't understand why you object to being in a gilded room being fed ambrosia from a spoon."

"What is this about?" Gabel asked me, "Gilded room? Ambrosia?"

Hix straightened just a degree, realizing he had said something that might not come off well.

"The First Beta and I had an argument over how I was allowed too much freedom," I said, choosing my words with care. "I told him if he had his way, he'd lock me in a gilded cage and spoon-feed me ambrosia, as if I were a bird and not a wolf."

"You would chew your way out of that cage, buttercup." Gabel grinned.

Hix glared. "A treasure should be guarded as one, no matter how much she chews."

I rolled my eyes, Gabel chuckled, and the matter was dropped in favor of conversation about the wolves who had broken into Ana's office. Ana had already gotten a phone call from her landlord, and the police were crawling over it looking for fingerprints. It was a matter for the humans and the hunters now.

After dinner I saw her hold up three crumpled dollar bills and flick them at Eroth. "After today these better be in a fancy bow by the time you're done with them."

"What the hell is that about?" Gabel murmured to me as Eroth trotted after her like an eager puppy, clutching his three dollars.

"I don't think I could explain it even if I tried. But if you need Eroth tonight, I know where he'll be..."

Gabel raised his brows. "I see she wasted no time moving on to the next piece of prey. She will do well here with such predatory instincts."

He was as bad as Hix...

I cradled the lump of tourmaline in my hands.

The blue stone still fascinated me. I refused to believe it had no use.

Obsidian was volcanic glass. It began as magma in the darkness of the earth. Tourmaline, if it was like the ocean, always saw sunlight, and it always saw the night.

I needed to know something about the tourmaline, so I'd decided to mediate over it. That was relatively safe, although I threw in *balance* and the little bag holding the RedWater fangs for good measure. They'd been with me in other visions. Perhaps they'd help reveal something useful about the strange stone.

Tension slipped from me, and I focused on the stone, the rune, and the little pouch in my cupped hands. This I understood, this was familiar, this I knew. The quiet, the stillness—

~*~ *Through The Tides* ~*~

Water rushed past me, tossing me around and sucking me down through illuminated blue-green darkness.

I pawed at the currents to reach the surface as the sucking water pulled me deeper and deeper.

I couldn't scream.

I couldn't scream.

The pressure built on my ribcage, trying to squeeze all the air out of me and replace it with the Tides. My ribs creaked. Every joint stretched and popped.

The air in my lungs was all I had. I would not let go.

I was drowning in the Tides.

I could not scream.

The sky was farther away, I was going farther away, I don't know where, everything was blue-green froth and light, but I was moving, the current dragging me.

Gabel.

The Bond. If I held onto it, I could pull myself out of the Tides.

Something yanked the Bond out of my grasp and slammed me deeper.

What have I done, Moon? What have I—

I woke up face first on a beach that was more rocks than sand. I sputtered and pawed pebbles from my face, spit them from my mouth. My lips were torn and bleeding, my skin bloody and raw, and my ribs... every breath was punishment.

But I was...

somewhere?

I crawled to my knees, holding my right ribs. Blood dripped

out of my torn lower lip onto the grey-white pebbles below. In front of me was a lush green meadow, and beyond that, an evergreen forest. There seemed to be no sun, but it was not night, and there seemed to be no moon, but it was not day. The sky was fully obscured by silver-bellied clouds, and although the tops of the trees and grasses ruffled like a storm was coming, I felt no breeze.

Behind me was an ocean, perfectly still and perfectly blue-green, seeming to shine with its own mild light.

Like the tourmaline.

I staggered to my feet.

This was no vision.

I was... *somewhere.*

And Gabel was very, very far away.

I was alone. So very, very alone.

And no one knew I was here.

I hugged myself, although it wasn't cold (nor was it hot). I took stock of myself. I was battered and torn, and my ribs ached from the pressure the Tides had exerted. Pieces of my skin had been stripped off my forearms, my lips were split and cracked from the salt. My feet had been battered to bloody ribbons on the rocks, but I could still walk.

I grimaced and reached under my breast. In the fold where my breast joined my chest was a hard oval item.

The *balance* rune.

Despite my injuries, I didn't limp, even though I hurt.

The rocky sand gave way to soft green grass.

A sound. A growl, a bark.

To my left a small, perfectly round pond had appeared, incredibly dark, but the still water seemed to have a silver sheen. I crept closer and saw that the pond was not a pond at all, but a massive obsidian scrying bowl implanted into the dirt.

Slow-creeping panic started to slide up my spine like insidious tentacles, daring me to look, daring me to contemplate.

I heard a grunting sound again.

Beyond the pond, perhaps twenty feet in the distance were two wolves: one a dark grey, clearly of very high prestige, the other a tawny silver-brown. The grey courted her with barks and tenderness, she resisted him, unenthused and unwilling, but his forceful nagging eventually eroded her resistance. She capitulated. He clamored atop and mated with her.

I watched, bewildered by the scene and distracted by the silvery pool and *balance* burning in my palm, almost vibrating and humming like a little bird.

The male finished his business and cavorted away, while the tawny sat down and waited for him to return. He did return after a time, but he danced around her as if mocking her, as if to say *did you really think it was anything but fun? It was nothing more than a tryst, silly female.*

She snarled and barked at him. She spun around, and on her right shoulder was the rune for Seer.

He snarled back, barking and chasing her away. Their casual fun had conceived pups, and the Seer was not his mate, and he did not want her, or the pups she carried. They were young wolves. He was a male of prestige that had had his fun and now wanted nothing to do with the consequences, especially not a litter of ill-conceived lupines. He couldn't afford it and was in a position to make sure she didn't make him pay.

When she growled and tried to pass him as if to return to the pack and force him to do the right thing, he raked his teeth across her belly and his claws across her Seer rune.

She fled into the forest, and the grey turned back toward home, the secret forgotten and buried.

The bowl-pool's silver surface quivered, then the silver shifted into a half-crescent shape, spinning around the perimeter of the bowl. It waxed and waned from new to full as if it were the moon itself, and the *balance* rune vibrated in rage.

The obsidian bowl-pond's surface shimmered a final time, the silver film pulling back like a membrane across an eye, and the water pushed into the center and formed into stairs leading down to the bottom.

There couldn't be much more of an invitation than that: stairs that would lead me back to my world, back to my life, to the IronMoon, to Gabel.

DREAMS OF SILVER AND SABLE

The watery step shifted a little under my weight. I took the next and the next, and kept going down into the bowl that seemed to have no bottom. When I looked up the sky was gone, and there was only darkness.

Oh shit.

The silence hurt. The emptiness hurt. It hurt the way the basement hurt.

A hundred thoughts crowded into my mind to keep me company, but I shoved them all away. I had to focus on what was real, and my goal: which was to keep moving down these watery steps.

A pin prick of light ahead of me grew with each step, and I could finally make out the mouth of a cave that opened onto a forest.

I burst through it.

There was no cave behind me.

I was back in the forest, the same one I had seen before, and at the other side of the little clearing was a ramshackle old shed, gutted and decaying under weather and years.

Anita's vision. My vision.

No scents on the trees, no markings, no paths, and nothing to indicate anyone had ever been here, or if this was a place within the physical world at all. I approached the ruins with caution, looking for any clues of civilization: a garden bed, garbage, anything.

There was nothing.

The door fell open when I touched it, exposing the ruined interior I had seen before. The box was where it had been before and contained the same ring.

A ruined house, and a ramshackle, blasted ring.

In the back of the shack was a door.

The smells came to me first, the vivid, subtle shape of the world that told me I was in wolf form.

I rolled onto my chest and instantly regretted it. My chest ached. My whole body ached, worse than Flint beating me up, falling down the stairs, and then being run over by a herd of angry rhinos. My brain sloshed in my skull, my eyes wandered in various directions, and my head wobbled back and forth.

I fell over onto my other side and whimpered.

A form blotted out the daylight, and a snout pushed into my ruff.

Gabel stood over me, also in wolf form, and there was nothing comforting about his leathery-hided, oily-furred body nuzzling me.

I struggled to right myself, but my limbs weren't obeying me just yet.

"*You are awake,*" he observed, peering down at me.

I moved my eyes in my skull. My workroom. I was in my workroom, laying on my rug, and I was in wolf form. So was Gabel.

What the hell had happened?

The question caused a flood to crash from the back of my mind to the front. I closed my eyes and went limp on the rug, everything spinning until the memories and visions retreated from the shores of my mind.

Gabel's claws had shredded the carpet, and little bits clung between the pads.

When the sea-sick feeling in my head abated, I rolled back to my chest. I wanted to be in human form. It was easier to talk that way, maybe it'd be easier to think without all these smells crowding my nose and noises in my ears.

Gabel steadied me as I wobbled on two legs, not four, and pulled me back to my knees. "Slowly, buttercup."

"Why are you here?" I pawed at him, my fingers caught his strong shoulder. I wasn't even sure where I was. It was all such a mess in my head.

I knew I was back in my world, but—

"Buttercup." Gabel pushed me back down. "Hold still. It can wait. It's been waiting for days."

I sank back down onto the rug. Gabel's fingertips touched the bruises on my arms, touching each one in turn, his face far away. I felt far away, maybe I was even drooling. I don't know. Then Gabel got up, went to retrieve a robe he had brought up to the room, and placed it over my shoulders. When I didn't move, he pulled each of my arms through the sleeves and drew it around my waist. I watched him put on a pair of sweatpants. The holes on his thigh were still ugly and bruised. The slashes on his shoulder were still a little crusty and—

"What..." My voice was hoarse and thin, and it hurt badly to talk. I looked at my arms. Battered and bruised.

"Where did you go, buttercup?" Gabel placed his hand under mine, lifted it in his palm, and traced the outline of each bruise.

"I—I don't know." I looked at my other arm, which was also bruised, and I pulled apart my robe. I was mottled all over, and I had a raw red welt under my left breast where *balance* had been in my vision. "Was I... gone? Not here?"

"Your body was here, but you were not here," Gabel said. "You were somewhere else. Where did you go?"

"I... I don't know." My brain wobbled in my head.

"I felt you slip away the morning after you returned from getting Ana. It is the afternoon of the second day. I was beginning to get worried."

"Beginning?" I wheezed a laugh. "Beginning?"

Gabel game me an arrogant, little smile.

It was so hard to think. I was so tired, and woozy.

"Come, buttercup." Gabel gathered me up in his arms. "I was afraid to move you from here, but now that you are back, you should sleep in a proper bed."

"I can walk." I squirmed and swatted at him.

"I have not had my hands on you in nearly three days. Let a man enjoy himself."

"Sick, Gabel, sick," I mumbled.

He chuckled.

"Well, you are regular fucked up," Ana said the next morning. Gabel had summoned her, and I woke up at dawn to her pulling back the blankets.

"What are—" I pushed at her hands, still in a partial stupor.

"So I guess this Oracle business isn't total bullshit." She lifted one of my arms and looked it up and down. "Wowee.

Looks like you got dragged behind a truck over a dirt road. Except your skin is still attached. Okay, so you got dragged through a ball pit at high speeds. You know the ones at those kiddy play zoo places? Damn scary things."

"What are you talking about?" I whined.

"I am totally a morning person. And you didn't tell me I'd have an all-I-can-eat man-meat buffet around here. I thought there'd be some competition, but you've got a major population imbalance. It's fish in a barrel, and they are packed in tight."

"All packs have more males than females," Gabel said from the far wall.

"Is that for a biological reason or something else? Like your veg there make more boys than girls?" She gestured at Gabel.

"Considering I have never heard of a preference, I would guess it is biological."

"I am so gonna spin some down and find out."

"Spin some what?" I asked her.

"Little swimmers. The girl ones are heavier than the boy ones, sink to the bottom if you put them in a centrifuge." She made a twirling motion with her hand.

I groaned.

"I told you, morning person."

Gabel, however, leaned forward slightly, and asked with far too much interest, "Do they survive the spinning?"

"Sure do." She grinned at Gabel. "They sure do. Why? Sound like something you two are in the market for?"

"Oh no," I said, "Oh no, Gabel. No, no, no."

A coughing fit seized my raw, throat and I hacked a few times. All this craziness in my bedroom that morning, and I had only been awake two minutes. It felt like an ambush.

"It's not fair to tease you," Ana said as I wobbled in bed. "Well, I'll just have a look, not that I'm an especially good human doctor, and I don't know a thing about Oracles who go off to la-la land with the Moon. But I guess I better pretend to do something for all that sweet, sweet cash you're paying me with. So you can really see the future?"

"Sometimes. This time I saw the past."

Despite her tone, she was gentle. She seemed more fascinated by my bruising than concerned. She finished by peering at the back of my throat. "There's nothing serious here, except it's ugly. Throat's raw like you inhaled a lot of salt water or something."

Maybe I had.

"So much excitement leading up to a wedding." She tucked things back into her bag. "Ohhh, drama! Anyway, you're fine. Sleep it off. Have him give you some massages, soak in salts, the usual."

Gabel closed the door after her. I closed my eyes for a minute. I was awake (oh, achingly awake), and the pack needed to see I was alive and in one piece. And also, my enemies needed to know (because. spies) I was alive and well and not easy pickings just now.

"What are you doing?" Gabel asked as I sat up and moved my legs off the edge of the bed.

"Getting up. Breakfast." I wasn't hungry. Gabel had made me eat some mushed up strawberries in the middle of the night, but a few mushed up berries verses several days of not eating was nothing. The idea of being in the noisy dining room at breakfast, though, did make my wobbly brain feel even more wobbly.

"No," Gabel said. "You should stay in bed."

I ignored him.

Seeing I was determined, he grudgingly fetched some clothes out of the closet while I dragged myself into the bathroom.

"Damn." I pulled at my cheek. I looked like death warmed

over: grey-pale, huge bags under my eyes—one eye was a real black eye—and I had scratches on my cheeks. Whatever had beaten up my body hadn't spared my face.

"We can eat breakfast in the sun room," Gabel said.

The sun room was a rarely-used room at the far end of the house, not far from Flint's quarters. Sounded like a fair compromise to me. After looking at my face, maybe it was better the pack didn't see me until the black eye had faded a bit. I didn't want people to think Gabel had beaten the hell out of me, and I wasn't prepared to talk about what had actually happened. It would also be quiet, which I needed just now. There was enough of an ocean rocking back and forth in my own skull.

We passed Flint on his way to breakfast. "Lady Gianna."

Gabel nudged me down the hallway, and said to Flint, "We'll be in the sun room for breakfast. Tell the pack."

It was very quiet. I waited at the little table against the windows, which gave me a look at the front of the property. Everything was still covered in snow. Gabel set my plate in front of me and took the chair opposite. The sun shone off the ocean-blue of his eyes, illuminating their depths like the blue-green hues of the tourmaline.

I had to look away to the dawn light-tinged snow.

He poured us both a cup of coffee.

I didn't touch mine. "You're a lupine."

Gabel paused, bewildered by the sudden statement. "Yes."

It explained so much about Gabel. He had been born a wolf, raised as a wolf.

I reached for my coffee and tried to figure out the next question that wouldn't cause an explosion of his temper or the swirling mess in my head to drown me. It was like visions were still trying to crowd into my awareness. When my gifts had first started to awaken and develop it had been like that, things intruding into my mind and slamming into me like endless waves on a shore.

He mistook my silence for disgust. "Does that bother you?"

Compared to what had happened since I had arrived? "No."

His lips curled. "You are shocked. Don't lie. Why? Lupines aren't forbidden."

Not forbidden, but a very bad idea. The one lupine I had met before had been a twitchy, rabid wolf in a human body. No one had ever been sure what would set him off and what wouldn't. Even our oldest texts warned of the difficulties lupines faced, and that the short-term benefits of birth numbers and faster maturity weren't worth the risks.

I wasn't going to insult Gabel by saying "not a good idea," or "they all end up crazy," but even if I knew my litter would end up like him... was that a good idea? My instincts said it wasn't, but it wasn't an argument I wanted to have. How did you tell your mate that you valued him the way he was but didn't want his children to be just like him?

My heart hurt at the thought.

Gabel expected me to say something.

I fished around, and settled for, "They're very rare."

"True," Gabel agreed.

Was even asking him how old he was rude? Had he been raised in a wolf pack, or a werewolf pack? Just him and his litter-mates? Wolves first shifted sometime around the very start of puberty, so for most lupines, that meant around a year to a year and a half. That would have made him (as a human) about ten to thirteen. At that point the accelerated aging of a lupine flipped to the human maturity curve.

By now he could be maybe... fifteen or sixteen, by the human measure. I had never asked him how old he was. He looked mid twenties or so. For all I knew he could have been five hundred years old and an original King-Alpha and I'd have believed him at this point.

In fact, that would explain everything and I laughed to myself.

"What, buttercup?" Gabel asked.

"Oh, just thinking," I said. "About everything that's been happening, and now this strange... vision, if that's what it was. I was thinking you might tell me you are an original King-Alpha from five hundred years ago. Well preserved."

Gabel chuckled.

"Are you?" Werewolves didn't have supernatural lifespans. But Gabel? I was clearly messed up in some weird divine politics.

"Not that I am aware of, but I will take that as a compliment." His eyes were warm, pleased that I thought he had the bearing of a King-Alpha.

"Well, I'd expect you'd have made a little more progress on being King by now if it were true."

"What have I told you about your ambitions? Patience, my Queen. Patience. I will bring you your crown."

The Bond prodded me with his teasing. "It's not like I could convince you to settle for less."

"No, you could not," Gabel agreed.

"So how old are you?" I asked.

"I don't believe you and I have ever asked that of each other. I have been on this earth twenty-six years. Now I have a question."

I picked at my toast and decided it needed jelly. I fished through the small selection that had been set out and waited for him to speak.

Gabel watched, noting every small movement and every bite I ate. When he spoke, there was restrained anger in his voice. "What were you doing scrying? You told me it was too dangerous without your bowls to protect you."

"I wasn't." His bristling anger poked me from within. "I was meditating. I can have visions while I meditate. I just—"

"You were on the Tides."

"I know! I was just meditating over the tourmaline. I wasn't trying to enter the Tides. It just... pulled me in and—" Suddenly I tasted salt water and heard nothing but the thunder of water rushing past me, and a force pulling me down. I dropped my toast.

I bit my lower lip so hard my tooth sank past the skin, and blood bubbled up instantly.

A drop hit my plate. I stared at it, then lifted my napkin to my lip.

"Wherever you were, you were far away." Gabel did not relent.

"It was on the other side of the Tides." It sounded like madness, because no such place existed.

"The other side? You mean the next world? The land of the dead? Is that what is on the other side of the Tides?"

"I... I don't know." I set my napkin down and looked at my battered arms. "I didn't disappear, did I? My body was here?"

Turbulence from Gabel, his face clouded, and his eyes chilled. "I felt you slip away. Where did you go?"

"I told you I don't know!" I gestured to my head. Just when I thought I had made sense of everything, it sloshed around, and I realized there were pieces still missing. "I washed up on this shore, and there was a scrying bowl, a huge pond that was a bowl, and there was a film on the top that moved like... the Moon, and there were two wolves. A high prestige male, and a Seer female, and he bred her, and then chased her away and..."

I stopped, my mind sloshing, and as it slowed, I focused on Gabel. The expression on his face was indescribable.

By the Moon.

He knew this story. He knew it because—

"It was your mother. I saw your conception."

Gabel's eyes narrowed a tiny fraction. "It sounds like what she told me. She was a tawny wolf and a Seer. She never told me of my father except that he had driven her away."

The warning note in Gabel's voice and the coiling within the Bond warned me off like the rattling of a viper's tail. I took a bite of my toast instead. "That is how you knew so much about Oracles."

Gabel nodded.

I gulped down some toast. "Have you ever met your father?"

"No. My mother never spoke about him, or her life before."

The memory of what I had seen crowded back into my head, and I fought off another wave of wooziness. I rested my elbows on the table and put my head into my hands.

"Does it bother you I am a bastard lupine of unknown pedigree?" Gabel asked me, his voice steady but the menace real.

"No, no, I don't care about that!" I cared that suddenly the Moon thought this was so important She had pulled me into some weird Land-Beyond-the-Tides and shown me that shack again. A vision so important she had also shown to Anita at least once as well, and Anita had been so upset she had summoned me to demand I walk away from Gabel.

What was so goddamn important about that shack and that ring? The ring. Moon, Luna, Mother, a pup-ring that hadn't been meant to exist and cobbled together after the fact and some ancient rune marking the Moon's vengeance and—

I breathed, suddenly realizing everything as it all crystallized into one fine point in my mind. One tiny scrap of knowledge that explained everything.

That the Moon needed me to know.

Needed Gabel to know.

That Anita already knew.

The secret Anita kept.

The secret Anita could never risk escaping.

Balance. Justice. The point on which light and dark turned.

"What?" Gabel turned the full force of his attention onto me.

My skin burst into painful prickles, I trembled all over, my thoughts tumbled and sloshed in my head, but I knew what I was about to say. I knew it as clearly as I knew anything else.

Gabel leaned over the table. He reached out and grasped my wrist with his hand, fingers curling into me.

"I know who he is," I breathed.

"My father? Who cares?" Gabel growled.

"The Moon cares." My voice rasped out from my abused throat.

Gabel released me. "I don't care."

The Bond lashed under his anger. I held my bruised ribs, unable to deal with his dark emotions, and what I knew. "Gabel, it's too much for me to carry alone."

Gabel tapped his fingers on the table, and the tapping changed slightly as his fingers tapered and extended under his rage. Had Gabel's littermates died? How had his mother died?

I held my aching sides and waited for Gabel's anger to pass. I had to tell him, and he had to hear me.

Because the future of IronMoon depended on it.

The future of *all* of us did.

He forced out in a low, guttural tone edged with a feral growl. "Buttercup, I do not make much of my past. I have very little of a past, and there are parts of it that I am not proud of, and have left in the past."

"When I tell you, you'll understand why." I whispered.

Gabel's anger flared again, and he growled at me, "Tell me."

"Alpha Magnes of SableFur."

EVERYTHING WILL BE FINE

Dark, roiling fury slammed into me. I couldn't breathe, there wasn't enough room for my lungs to expand.

The geyser of rage burst upwards, and the table went with it. It shattered into a thousand splinters. I screamed and snapped into a little ball. Glass shattered, liquid splashed, silverware hit the floor, splinters bounced off me. I heard—or did I feel?—a beast breathing, deep and angry, like something from the shadows of the Moon, when Her rage came upon us all. Heavy footsteps crunching over the debris, moving away from me.

Then it was still.

Inside me still burned: a sea of dark, smoldering magma laced with shocks of red and yellow.

Trembling, I peaked over my hands.

Gabel stood rigid in the center of the sun room, hands clenched into fists, quivering all over with a fury his skin could barely contain. Blood stained his pant leg from the holes ripping open, and his left hand was not a hand, but a claw, elongated fingers curled around and the yellow talons digging into the flesh of his forearm. Blood trickled onto the carpets.

Did I dare move?

I barely dared to breathe.

He was the son of Alpha Magnes of SableFur. The oldest son. And an heir to the SableFur crown, a threat to Magnes' two other sons and his Luna.

Anita was in her sixties. She had to have trained Gabel's mother, or at least known her when she had been in SableFur. She had to have known when Gabel's mother disappeared.

Anita knew what I now knew: Gabel was Magnes' son.

Those visions hadn't been Magnes'. They had been *hers*. The Moon warning the old Oracle that Her vengeance was upon the world.

Magnes owed his son. He owed for the loss of a female, and if there had been any littermates who had not survived to adulthood, he owed for those, too.

The saddest thing was that up until the moment Magnes had chased her away, no crime had been committed. There was no prohibition against what had happened. A young unmated male knocking up a young unmated female with a litter of lupine pups was a massive scandal, but it wasn't a crime.

It wasn't even as if Magnes had been the heir to SableFur, and the pack had moved to protect the honor of the ruling family. His Luna, Adrianna, had been the one bred and raised to rule.

After a very long time, Gabel's left claw dissolved back into human flesh, and he asked in a very low, forced tone, "Does Magnes know?"

I steeled myself for another explosion of rage. "I cannot imagine he does not."

"That is why Anita summoned you." He spoke very, very slowly, shaping each word with effort, teetering on the brink of a terrifying rage that kept me cowered in my chair. "But it does not make sense."

"Why not?" I ventured.

"You do not have to be my mate for the Moon to reveal the truth to you. Anita offered you nothing from SableFur to win you to her side. What assurance would she have of your silence if you found out?"

I knew the answer to that. "If I believed you were a monster, I'd have sided with the dishonorable Alpha. The lesser of evils."

"But I am not a monster?"

"Six months ago I might have believed her and asked no further questions."

"Yes," he said mostly to himself. "Yes, you would have. But not now."

He cricked his neck one way, then the other.

Very carefully, I uncurled my body. Every joint and tissue protested. Gabel turned all the way around. I froze.

He kicked the debris out of the way with his bare feet. Little pieces dug into his skin and pricked it so that drops of blood welled up around them. He offered me his hand. "You should know by now, buttercup, that my violence isn't for you."

"What are you going to do?" I looked at his hand doubtfully. His rage had gone to low tide, but it was still there.

"Nothing," Gabel answered. "You and I will tell no one."

His fingers curled around me and pulled me up, less graceful and more harsh than usual.

"Nothing? You aren't going to do anything?"

Gabel drew me away from the splinters and glass. "Aaron is a bigger problem. Magnes cannot move against me openly. It will draw too much attention. He needs me disposed of quietly."

Maybe my brain was full of wool and exhaustion, but how could Gabel just do nothing? He was the son of Alpha Magnes of SableFur, who had condemned his mother to a life of exile, robbed him of his birthright and family, and possibly killed his littermates. And Gabel was going to do nothing?

"Ignore it?" I laughed, without humor. "Ignore it? Like my father gave me to you without a fight? Why is it males are always so eager for a fight, and then when a real one comes along, they wither? The Moon didn't show it to me so you could ignore it."

His tide of anger rose and flooded the banks. His hands caught me as I crumbled, my brain swimming in dark magma, and he growled, "I am not withering, Gianna. I am also not charging off into a fight like an enraged bull. Do you really think I can just waltz into SableFur and announce I'm Magnes' son?"

I couldn't think at all with his anger suffocating me. Perhaps he should tell Magnes he knew the secret to keep Magnes at bay! Mutually assured destruction. Maybe he should grab for SableFur, or try to draw Magnes out. It all swirled around in my head, caught in a whirlpool of anger.

"IronMoon isn't ready to take SableFur, and when we are, we'll only get one chance. I will not waste it. Only the mindless monster they believe me to be would charge off like a bull," Gabel snarled. "Leave the war to the warriors, Gianna."

"You mean to the males."

Gabel gripped my chin between his thumb and forefinger. Blood dripped down his wrist from where he had punctured his skin with his own claws. "Patience, my Queen. Magnes is a bear in spring, and if we do not plan the hunt carefully, he will turn on us. You are so wonderfully bloodthirsty under the refined Oracle pelt of yours, but you will have to be patient for now."

He kissed me lightly. "I will take my anger downstairs. Perhaps the wolves in the basement will better appreciate their predicament when I am not feeling reasonable. You go upstairs and rest. In six days time we will have our unreliable vassals here, and I do not want them to think there is weakness in either of us. You may be angry. Let them think your claws are at my throat."

He left, and the waters of anger retreated after him, focusing on a different shoreline.

Blood on the carpet, coffee and water splattered on the floor, smashed jars of jelly, food, ruined plates and cups, the splintered remains of the table. There were even pieces driven into the ceiling.

I did the best I could picking up the worst of it, but I was forced to find Violet and show it to her, as I didn't know how to get stains off walls or blood out of carpets.

"What happened?" she asked as she absorbed the destruction.

"Gabel's temper." There wasn't any further answer for it.

But she did give me a very sharp look, noting my black eye and battered face. My heart sank. I had fallen down stairs twice, beaten up Gardenia, had Flint use me as a training dummy, and everyone's first thought was Gabel beat me.

Violet surveyed the damage again, then put a hand on my arm. She hit a bruise, and I flinched, which she also misread. "I'll clean it up."

"I'll help." I hadn't summoned Violet here to clean up the mess, just to tell me the right way to do it. Blood soaking into antique carpets and splatters on ceilings weren't my forte. Baking soda? Club soda? No idea.

"No, it's fine. You go have a nice, hot shower. Did you get to eat breakfast before it ended up on the walls? I'll have something brought up to your room."

She meant my rooms at the far end of the house, away from Gabel's rooms. My heart sank even lower.

"Yes, just didn't get that third cup of coffee." I tried to sound cheerful. "I should go see how the Solstice preparations have been going."

"Oh, they're fine," Violet assured me. "Gardenia has it under control."

"That's what worries me."

"Macy and I are watching her." She sighed. "I tried to tell Gardenia this is a chance for her to start over. Start fresh."

"How do you mean?" I frowned.

"Everything being publicly explained as her being a decoy. Just say yes, she was willing to play a part, serve the pack, plan the party. It's a chance to start new. Change things."

"You mean change her reputation."

Violet shrugged, then sighed again.

"Has she tried to cause trouble with the party?" The last thing I needed was for Gardenia to wreck the IronMoon Solstice. If we couldn't even command respect in our own den...

Maybe giving Gardenia the party had been too hasty on my part. But what the hell did I know about planning huge parties on short notice? Or any notice.

"No, we're keeping an eye out, but she's too busy figuring out how to pull it together to figure out how to ruin it." Violet grinned a little bit.

Small comfort? My stomach squirmed and shuffled the toast inside it. How had Violet ended up here? But that was a rude question in IronMoon, even though learning Violet had some background as a super cunning, bank-robbing grandmother type would have made me feel better.

"Don't worry. Your wedding will be beautiful, and everything will be fine." Violet shoo'd me out of the room. "Everything will be fine."

Six days to go.

PIECES, PUZZLES, PANTIES

G abel was still in an utterly vile mood the next morning. Vile enough that when someone knocked on his office door, his snarl of "What?" shook the windowpanes.

Hix, Donovan, and Ana were on the other side. Hix came right on in, while Donovan eyed the destruction, and Ana looked downright skeptical. She made sure to stay behind Hix. Their timing, as far as I was concerned, could not have been worse. Gabel snarled, then clicked and growled in his throat. I found my own voice, since his would fail him just then. "I didn't realize you were back, Donovan. Good hunting?"

"Informative hunting." Donovan scratched his beard.

Hix, never one for small talk, got right to the point. "We have information on the wolves who came for Ana's office."

This instantly mollified Gabel.

Ana handed over a wad of papers. "I'm claiming I've never seen them before and don't know a thing. Here's the police report. We got the name of the guy that the truck is registered to. Donovan did a little scouting, and we found two mug shots. There were three guys, but I recognize these two faces."

Gabel was still not inclined to speak, so I asked, "Do we know what pack they're from? GleamingFang?"

"No," Hix said, "MarchMoon."

Gabel roared his fury and ripped several books in half. Ana squeaked and hid behind Hix. Smart girl.

Hix flicked a piece of paper off his chest.

"What were the MarchMoon doing in Gleaming Fang?" I asked, trying to sound completely innocent while Gabel slashed at the bookshelves, fingertips talons and splintering the wood.

Ana watched him, transfixed with fascination and horror.

"It's all IronMoon territory, technically," Donovan said. "The borders are all very porous now, Lady, and the low-status wolves move freely. The other Alphas are glad for it to be someone else's problem for a while."

Relief started to loosen all my joints. MarchMoon had over-played their hand. Now Gabel could deal with the traitor Marcus, independent of the Petitioner Wolf's question. No one would ever link Marcus' downfall to a violation of my Oracle vows.

Donovan handed me two more pieces of paper. "I think these guys were also involved. They weren't there, but known associates, as humans would say."

I looked at the two printouts. I didn't recognize either face, nor the names.

A growl by my thigh. I looked down, saw nothing, heard it again, like a memory from a dream.

The world hazed over as if someone had thrown a sheet over my head, my insides burned from Gabel's rage and the singed Bond, and my own brain wobbled from the painful vision. The growl came again, closer this time, and I saw in my mind the two RedWater wolves pacing at my feet. They were growling and their ears were slicked back.

"Lady Gianna."

The wolves circled, and in my mind, one jumped and snapped at the papers, whining at me under their growls.

Gabel's fury sucked back from the shore. His hands caught my arms as my knees wobbled.

"I'm fine, I'm fine." I tried to push his hands off.

"You were supposed to be resting," he said, as if he hadn't realized I had been there at all. "What are you even doing in here?"

I steeled myself for the geyser of pain his rage would cause. "RedWater. They're the RedWater wolves."

"Who is? Which ones?"

I pointed to the papers. "Two of the ones who fled and left the others to die."

"How do you know? We didn't see their human forms."

I shook my head. Seeing visions of ghost-wolves wasn't within the usual scope of an Oracle's powers. Especially not waking ones where their souls came forward to growl about wanting vengeance against the packmates who had abandoned them. "I just do."

"Well, well, well," Gabel said, and I choked as the tentacles of his malevolent anger curled all around my insides. "Perhaps they were hoping to use you as a bargaining chip to reclaim their lost honor."

As far as I was concerned, there was no reclaiming lost honor for what they had done. Abandoning a packmate, running away like a coward, that was eternal damnation.

Hix's face stretched into a slight scowl, and his voice dripped contempt. "Or they know how careless you are with her."

Gabel snarled at Hix. "How careless I *was*, First Beta."

"I warned you we would pay for your games." Hix didn't back down. "This is your fault."

"If you want something from me, Hix, come and take it," Gabel growled.

Ana, proving her excellent survival instincts, carefully tip-toed behind Donovan.

"I want you to treat your Luna the way she should be treated, and not some toy or some lure dangled in front of everyone just to prove you dare do so. Flint warned you this is what happens when a male behaves like a fool. This is your fault, and you are tearing up books and punishing her with your anger as if you have any right to be angry with anyone but yourself!"

"And they are not mistakes I intend to make again."

"Enough." I pushed between them. IronMoon couldn't afford for Gabel and Hix to be at each others' throats. "You both agree with each other, you just want to snarl. I don't want to hear it. I am too tired."

The "tired female" card wouldn't do much for Gabel, but it'd make Hix retreat instantly. And it did: Hix grumbled something, gave Gabel a final snarl, and Gabel growled back, and that was that.

Donovan tucked the papers into his vest. "We don't know that Alpha Holden of RedWater even knows these wolves were disgraced. RedWater isn't part of IronMoon, so why would they admit any of what happened to their Alpha?"

"Then why were they back in MarchMaw or whatever the hell the name is?" Ana asked. "If they were there trying to make themselves look good, then this Holden or whoever *told* them to do it. Which means how did he know she'd be there at all?"

"They were an hour behind us, and not prepared for where Lady Gianna was going, so that means they were already in GleamingFang," Donovan said. "But you're right. Someone authorized trying to kidnap a Luna."

Hix frowned thoughtfully.

Gabel chuckled.

Ana *eeped* like a woodland creature.

"You're overthinking this," Gabel's voice was low, rough, something out of a nightmare. "Are you forgetting that the goal of the little rebellion was to kidnap Gianna? Not kill her. Now the MarchMoon has wolves in GleamingFang—wolves who are known to associate with the RedWater cowards—waiting for an opportunity. Anticipating I will go there for Anders. Knowing," Gabel looked at at Hix, "that I have been careless and arrogant. SableFur failed in their effort to use Anita to get Gianna away from me. The world knows we have consummated the Bond. Why kidnap her, when killing her would be more expeditious?"

"Because killing her instead of you is disgraceful," Hix said.

"Exactly." Gabel smiled unpleasantly. "These are Aaron of IceMaw's machinations. He is pulling all these strings."

I almost trembled with relief. The MeatMan *and* Meat-Taker tied up in a neat little bow that had nothing to do with the Petitioner Wolf.

"A worthy adversary." Gabel growled low in his throat, practically gleaming with pleasure.

Ana fanned herself, "Wow-ee, excuse me, but all this medieval male posturing is really hot. Mmm-mmmm-mmmm. Gonna melt right into my panties. Oh wait, I'm not wearing any panties!"

"This is serious," Hix grumbled at her.

Donovan, suppressing a sideways grin in Ana's direction, said, "So are we going after MarchMoon or IceMaw?"

Gabel's smile sharpened. "MarchMoon. There's no reason to alert Aaron we are onto his scent. I've suspected March-Moon's disloyalty for some time. Now I have the proof I need to act. And demonstrate to the IronMoon I do not suffer promises made in bad faith."

"So what are you going to do about it?" Hix asked.

Gabel's cold, cruel malice curled over my spine like tentacles. "Tell the IronMoon there will be an offering of blood and flesh at Solstice. In keeping with the old ways."

NOBODY LIKES WEDDINGS

Solstice dawned grey and extremely cold.

"Don't trust her?" Gabel asked.

"Would you?"

"No."

I sipped my morning coffee and watched the final preparations from the window in Gabel's office. The pack was in understandable chaos that morning. We had brought our breakfast up to his office so we wouldn't be underfoot. The scent of roasting animals had started around midnight, and now Gardenia stood in the center of the backyard, directing an army of assistants like a queen bee directing her hapless drones. The trees were decorated with the blue and silver paper lanterns of the Solstice, and with the red lanterns of a pair-vow ceremony. They danced in the breeze. The sky hung overcast, but supposedly, it was not going to start snowing until after midnight. It wouldn't matter if the paper decorations were ruined then.

Long tables had been set out to receive the food Cook had been preparing for the past four days. Four pigs and two cows hung on spits over pits dug into the yard

Better safe than sorry, Cook had decided.

Tradition dictated the color and decorations. Due to the short time we had, Cook had chosen the menu based on what he could pull together. There would be the traditional run through the woods for males, and since the party was outside, dress code was... functional.

Even being in human form was optional. "Traditional attire" on a werewolf party invitation meant you could wear fur if you preferred.

Even me choosing my dress had been easy. The traditional color was bright red, and since I owned two dresses of that color, I had just chosen one. There had not been time or mental energy to spare on dresses or fittings, especially since I knew someone was going to die that night, and odds were good I'd be close to the blood spray.

The oldest of the old traditions, back from the darkest days of our kind, was that an Alpha welcomed his new Luna by vanquishing an enemy. Proof of his strength and prowess, that he would keep their den safe.

Alpha Marcus of MarchMoon had unwittingly volunteered.

I watched the activity below, fully expecting to see Gardenia trying one last, sneaking mistake, but I had to admit, she seemed too busy to have pulled any sneak attacks. Things churned around her.

"Too bad she is convinced her only option in life is to attach herself to a male like a parasite," Gabel observed. "She is not stupid. Just low quality."

"Would you want her if she suddenly developed some quality?" I asked, feeling more than a little prickly at his backhanded compliment. We *were* discussing a traitor, although I didn't like to think of Gardenia as a traitor. Traitor implied some conviction. Gardenia was just a flea, hopping from male to male looking for the next feast.

"She is not fierce enough to suit my tastes. She only thinks she's bloodthirsty. Unlike you, who thinks she is not blood-thirsty until the scent of a challenge comes to her snout."

"I think that's a compliment?" With Gabel you could never be quite sure.

"I think it was." He observed the scene below with just a sharp a gaze. Hix and Eroth had been set to make sure nothing snuck through to the heart of IronMoon, which put the other-wise restless warriors to task. Orders had been given that had sent the young, most restless warriors out to the perimeter of the immediate territory, with instructions that anything that wasn't where it was supposed to be could be killed.

They were pleased at the orders that gave them discretion to kill whatever they saw. They just needed to bring back a head, or hand, or paw, or some teeth, or whatever else would identify the wolf's origin.

"Nervous, buttercup?"

"Not really." This wasn't exactly a day I had been looking forward to, and it was one I had actively tried to avoid. I had surrendered to the inevitable more than summoned it to my side.

Would I have changed any of it? I didn't know. I tried not to think about what I would have done or what could have been, because none of that mattered. For better or worse, I was about to become the IronMoon Luna.

And perhaps the force of Balance that kept the Moon's Comet from destroying everything he wasn't supposed to destroy.

Or help him destroy everything he looked at.

"Are you?" I asked him.

"No," Gabel said.

"You don't even care," I said.

"You and I are already Bound together, buttercup. We sealed it months ago, and we made our own promises that night in the garden," Gabel said. "We are just doing this for everyone else. Tonight is about IronMoon, not you and I."

"Come for the wedding, stay for the bloodshed?" I asked dryly. I opted not to remind him the way my Mark seethed like oil on water sometimes.

Gabel's presence roiled and swirled next to me. "How morbid, buttercup. Will you reject my offering?"

"No, Marcus betrayed you."

"Us. He betrayed us."

"And Aaron? Are you worried about him and what he wants? There's no assurance the vows will erase my scent."

Gabel grinned. "I find that most intriguing, but not disturbing. There is always a wolf who wants what is yours."

"And you want what every other Alpha has. You want their power." Gabel didn't want their groveling or their wealth or their lives. He just wanted their authority and their power under his hands, as if they were carriage horses, and he was the whip.

"How sage of you, buttercup."

"Well, if we're allowed to take intangible things, I can think of a lot of things I want."

"Like what?"

"Knowing why Alpha Jermain showed his belly." That still sat badly with me. Jermain wasn't gutless, so why had he acted gutless? Maybe I had been in IronMoon too long and had become too paranoid.

"Ah, an apology of sorts." Gabel nodded.

I clenched my teeth. I didn't want an apology. I just wanted to know *why*.

"Does it still sting?"

"I don't know. Maybe."

Gabel sipped his coffee, "He hasn't done anything to violate our treaty. Punishing him for giving me what I demanded isn't fair. But you know how I feel on it."

He had a chewed up shoulder, and Hix had a gash on his belly. It was impossible to not warm a little to how they had tried to make up for Jermain's cowardice.

"Tonight may be very bloody, buttercup," he added.

Calling Marcus out for his disloyalty may bring Aaron to the surface as well.

People could argue Gabel was a monster who had to be destroyed, but they had knelt and sworn loyalty. They could have fought to bloody defeat and been conquered. Some had chosen that, but many had simply surrendered. Violating that surrender later was betrayal.

But I had seen how gutless most of those Alphas and packs had been at Anders' party. Most of them had seemed to just want the scene with Aaron to be over, and not get involved.

Everyone was going to be put on notice tonight.

This was IronMoon.

The guests started to arrive around moonrise. The overcast skies obscured the moon's light, which was unfortunate. Snow was on the wind. So were the scents of burning torches, food, and roasted livestock.

The lanterns shone in the barren trees, and the IronMoon laughed and chattered in the garden. Many of the local males had been put on scout or guard duty, which suited them fine. They didn't want to be at a party where manners counted and women were in short supply. The promise of leftovers and brawling afterward were more than enough.

All the perks of a fancy party with none of the actual party.

All of them were in kilts and barefoot. The males would run before the ceremony, howling to the Moon. The bitter cold was held at bay by large torches throughout the terrace. Torches. Actual fire.

Was it wrong my first thought was what Gabel would do with one?

"Why do I get the feeling some shit is gonna go down?" Ana asked.

Not caring to stand on ceremony or reverence, she had found a kilt (somewhere) that fit her, hacked off half of the length, and wore a white button-down knotted under her breasts. Over that she wore a lab coat and had a stethoscope in her pocket.

"Because it's an IronMoon party," I replied.

She waved it off. "You know what Flint told me?"

"Aside from no, never, and not happening?"

Ana laughed again, "Can't help looking." She craned her neck about. Flint, his tattoos seeming to move and shift in the unsteady torchlight, was chatting with a wolf about twenty feet away. Ana sighed. "I must limit myself to admiring him from afar. Oh well."

I smiled, and prodded, "What did he tell you?"

"That I'd have to leave my human sensibilities behind."

The same thing Gabel had said to me. Interesting. So perhaps Flint had tamed Gabel? They both did love books an inordinate amount.

She patted me on the shoulder and bid me have ever so much fun, then skipped off to amuse herself somewhere else.

The guests passed through the path that wrapped around the house (I think Cook would have brained someone with a ladle if we brought guests through the kitchen), and as they arrived, they greeted me. Gabel was out front, greeting them as they arrived. Hix loomed nearby, the barely-healed gash on full display, wearing a plain black kilt. He looked ready to rip some-one's arm off.

"Don't you like parties, Hix?" I asked him.

"You don't seem to be having a good time," he retorted.

Well, fair. This was more work than party.

"Blood may erupt at any moment," he added.

That possibility did exist.

Alpha Anders' arrival with his Luna, First Beta, and a few other high-ranking males made a familiar nausea curl in my stomach. "Lady Gianna."

I stretched my face into what I hoped passed for a warm smile. All I could think of was how mortifying our first meeting had been, and how he was also a pale excuse for a traitor.

I knew Shadowless had been invited and would attend, but I still wasn't prepared when they rounded the corner of the house.

My heart burst into a rapid pace, fluttering and flipping in my chest. My stomach roiled.

Amber was with them, walking just behind Jermain's shoulder.

She was as beautiful as ever, sleek as a lioness, and even Hix gave her a brief glance.

"Lady Gianna," Jermain greeted me.

My father embraced me, pulled back, a damp sheen in his eyes, "Gianna. Gianna, you look beautiful."

"Thank you." His words didn't reach where the stinging ache resided.

"Hello, Lady Gianna." Amber's voice pulled my attention.

I had always thought I would be the one addressing her by title. The reverse caught me off -guard for a moment.

"How have you been?" she asked.

The question rubbed me the wrong way. But what other

sort of small talk was there? We hadn't been especially close friends. It had been more me in awe of her.

Besides: how did I answer that? I almost laughed. How *had* I been?

Things happened. More things happened. Chaos ensued. Gabel threw books around. The Moon dragged me beyond the Tides. Hix growled at everything. Flint spoke in riddles.

"Busy." I decided on an honest answer that didn't answer the actual question.

How do you think I've been? You watched him make off with me. You've heard the rumors. How dare you ask me that.

No matter how my life with Gabel ended, I would always remember how it had begun, and part of me would never forgive Shadowless.

Admitting that lifted a huge burden from me.

I sighed with relief.

My father hesitated moving to the party. He lingered as if he had more to say. Jermain tugged on him.

"Should I have them kept at a distance?" Hix asked me.

"No, no. They're my family."

"So?"

"Hix," I sighed.

The parade of guests continued, and I was relieved when Gabel came up the walk with the last of them, smiling and nodding to whatever they were saying.

He could be so charming when it suited him.

"Gianna." He slid his arm around my waist. "All our guests are here."

His touch, with the Moon overhead, veiled as Her eye might be, knowing we'd make promises that couldn't be broken soon, flustered me.

And what would come afterward...

"What have I told you about those thoughts?" he whispered,

his lips grazing my ear. He bit down very gently, just a soft pinch that made me gasp.

"I will be more disciplined." Or at least I would try. We had been so distracted that the Bond roused from its sleep to tell us it was more than a little neglected of late.

He nipped me again, then pulled away.

My father watched the scene, quickly looked away, but not before I saw the flash of distress on his face.

Gabel and I moved through the crowds, trying to head toward one of the roasting pits, but constantly distracted by guests.

Ana sidled up next to me. "The blond bimbo is talking shit."

My stomach smashed into my knees. Did I ignore it? Maybe I should. Platinum wanted attention. Carefully, I asked, "What kind of shit?"

"Something about she's the real thing and not a decoy."

Gabel went rock-still.

I bit the inside of my cheek. Platinum wasn't going to sabotage the party or spike the punch, she was just going to flat out ruin it.

I couldn't ignore it. I wanted to, but I couldn't let her go blabbering that sort of thing to anyone who would listen, and everyone there would listen. I'd have to go at her again, and give her the goddamn fight she wanted so badly. Nevermind she was a pale shade of a traitor, too.

Ana led me (with a very concerned Gabel) to the scene, where Platinum (who, I must confess, looked beautiful) stood, chatting with Alpha Anders.

"Gianna," she greeted me cheerfully, her eyes gleaming daggers. She had dropped my title deliberately. "Alpha Gabel. Are you enjoying the party?"

"You did an excellent job," Gabel said.

She smiled prettily. "It's what I had planned for our—I mean, my wedding."

Gabel's lips bent downward in a frown.

Anders and his Luna seemed more than a little uncomfortable.

If she couldn't have Gabel, she was going to force me to acknowledge her as a once-rival. Unfortunately for her, I knew what she'd done.

I had never hated her before. Now I hated her with a burning, dark passion.

Still, composure. Within an hour I'd officially be a Luna, and better to get started sooner than later. I gripped my emotions and said, as blandly as I could manage, "Yes, it's quite lovely."

Her beautiful face tightened a few notches. "I was just explaining to Alpha Anders about what happened a few months ago. That meeting where I was presented to him? That subsequent ugliness with Romero over you?"

"You and I already had this conversation," I said in a cold tone.

She smirked at the tiny triumph. "Oh, that bit about the decoy to protect your feelings? We all know Gabel grabbed you in haste and regretted it."

"And you're the one he secretly wants?" I didn't even hide my sarcasm.

"I know what he wants," she said mildly. "It's been clear to me more than once. He made a mistake with you and regretted it right away. He told me that."

Maybe he had to put Gardenia right where he needed her to be to bait me. Not because he meant it.

"You think Romero didn't know?" Gardenia prodded. "Oh, he knew. He knew you were a weak Luna, and Gabel didn't see what was right in front of him."

Now she was dangerously close to insulting Gabel. I snorted. "Romero didn't want to behave properly. Like you."

"Oh really? Is that why you told me you didn't want Gabel, so I could have him? You didn't care? Such a nasty thing to say. No wonder Gabel regretted it. No wonder Romero wanted you out. You don't deserve Gabel's loyalty!"

"Gabel Marked me without my consent," I heard people inhale as I confirmed the rumor for anyone who had thought, perhaps, it had been an exaggeration. "So, yes, I was angry. It doesn't change Romero being a weak fool, or that you were anything but a cheap pawn. But if Gabel actually wants the likes of you, he can have you. I won't shed one tear. Not one. There are no chains on him. Take him if you can."

I spat the last word. Because I meant it.

Gardenia faltered.

A dark violence like I had never known seeped into my bones. This bitch. Now it wasn't just embarrassing, and now it wasn't some private war between Gabel and I. It was her humiliating the Alpha, the Luna, and undermining the IronMoon's status in front of the whole court. I had given this horrible little mutt a chance to have some damn dignity, which was better than she deserved.

"But I know what you're really about." I smiled at her. "I know you're a spider stumbling along a web. You've served your purpose, Gardenia. To both those you spied for, and for me. Hix!"

The First Beta melted out of the shadows.

Gardenia backed up. "What are you talking about?"

"Pretty little spy," I said sweetly. "Pretty, pretty little spy. But not a very good one. Hix, put her somewhere the Moon cannot find her."

Hix grabbed Gardenia by the arm. She shrieked and smashed her fist into his jaw. Another collective gasp at her harpy antics. Hix rolled his eyes, tossed her over his shoulder, and walked to the house.

"He doesn't love you, Gianna!" she screamed. "He was fucking me the whole time! It's all a lie! I know where he'll be tomorrow night! He'll have his tongue between my legs!"

Anders coughed.

She flailed and pounded Hix in the kidneys and shrieked, but punching Hix was like punching a very large rock. I hoped she broke her fingers, and I vowed after this party, I was going to deal with her once and for all.

"Crazy biiiittttcchhhh." Ana shook her head.

"Traitorous bitch," I replied coldly.

"Oh well, you know how it is. Every wedding has at least one crazy relative, and one drunk person sobbing in the bathroom," Ana consoled me. "So, we've got one down."

Gabel said to me, "On that note, I believe it is time for the run."

When Gabel returned, he would kill Marcus, and we would make our vows. I had asked him just to make Marcus' death clean and quick, and not to play with his prey. I frankly would have preferred to make the vows before the offering of blood, but it didn't work that way.

Gabel turned his attention to Anders, "Come, Anders. Bring your First Beta, and we will run."

"I—" Anders hesitated.

"It is tradition," Gabel said. "You do not wish to honor the tradition and honor the Moon with praise?"

Anders balked again.

Gabel grinned, grabbed Anders, and hauled him off. "Come, man, you will enjoy it! I promise to return you to your Luna in one piece."

IN BLOOD AND BONE

"Wolves!" Gabel shouted. "We run to the Moon!"

Howls from the IronMoon.

Ana and I went to get something to eat before the hungry males returned. They'd strip everything off the bones. But before we got halfway there, Amber came to my side.

"I have to speak with you," she murmured.

Ana tugged my wrist. "Na-uh. Come on, Lady, Gianna. I see tits, and where there are tits, there's drama."

Amber sighed.

"It's fine, Ana. She's from my birthpack. I'll be along in a moment," I assured her.

Amber led me off to the side, where the shadows were the longest. She took my hands in hers. "Are you really going to take the vows?"

"I'm wearing red, aren't I?"

Her grip tightened. Her hands were deeply calloused from training. "Come with me, Gianna."

"To where?"

"Shadowless."

"Are you insane?" I asked bluntly.

She tugged harder. "We can leave now. While the males are gone. We can be out of scent range in twenty minutes!"

I pulled back, she held on. She tugged again. "Now's your chance, you idiot! Come on! There's a car waiting,"

"I'm not leaving." She clearly thought I was being held against my will.

"Yes, you are. This has gone far enough!"

"What are you talking about? This was the deal. You were standing right there. Me for Shadowless!"

"Just come on," she growled.

I yanked back. "Gabel and I are already Bound. I could have pups in my belly right now. You think I can just leave?"

"Let's go." Amber's voice cracked on panic.

I permitted her to tug me a few steps. "This was the deal, Amber. What's going on now?"

All these months later and the first rescue mission. Now I didn't need rescue.

"It will be fine," she crooned. "You don't have to be afraid of him. The Bond can still wither and die. It isn't permanent or forever."

"He'll come for me like wildfire ripping across dry grass."

... *or a comet.*

"He won't get you," Amber promised in a whisper. "You never wanted to be a Luna, Gianna. You're an Oracle. Forget this. It's gone far enough. You don't have to stay!"

"IronMoon will destroy Shadowless to get to me." I couldn't believe what she was saying. This didn't seem real. Even months ago I wouldn't have let her drag me away like this. I knew, better than anyone in the world, what Gabel was capable of, and what he would do.

I had expected SableFur or IceMaw to crash my wedding. But *Shadowless?*

She shook her head yet again. "SableFur promised to help us get you back. Now move!"

I yanked back. "What are you talking about?"

Realizing I was not moving, and if she created a big scene, I'd have Hix and Flint on me in an instant, she grimaced, stood close, and whispered, "Before you were taken. SableFur told Jermain to give up without a fight if IronMoon came to us. Their Oracle predicted that he'd take a Shadowless female, and when he did, they'd help us get her back in return for our loyalty."

Oh Anita, what have you been up to? So you've been spying on Gabel for a long time now. How long have you known he was Magnes's son?

"So there are SableFur here?" I whispered.

"No, it's only Shadowless. We just can't let this happen, so we're going to force them to do what they promised. Now let's go—"

"Which Oracle had the vision?"

Amber paused while she searched for the name. "Anita."

"And she saw me with Gabel?"

Amber hesitated, then said, "She saw me with him."

Balance: the point on which light and dark turns.

"I'm not jealous. It's not like that," Amber hissed. "Please, Gianna, let's go. Please! It was never supposed to be you. It was supposed to be me!"

"And you were supposed to kill him," I said with sudden understanding.

"Wouldn't you have, if you could have?" she whispered, eyes bright.

Anita lied. Had Anita lied to Magnes, too? Did Magnes know Gabel was his son?

It didn't matter. The SableFur hadn't kept their promise, and they never had intended to. The Mark would never have allowed Amber to kill Gabel. But it was a nice lie to tell her. I smiled grimly at her. "SableFur isn't going to keep their promise."

"Come *on!*" She tugged.

"I was in SableFur three weeks ago. Anita summoned me. She told me to leave Gabel. That I *must* leave him. But they didn't offer me sanctuary. Even when she told me Gabel will destroy everything he touches, and when I told her my Bond had been consummated, and Gabel would hunt me to the ends of the earth, she told me to leave anyway. But she offered me no help."

"What?"

I yanked my hand free this time. "You have been played and lied to. SableFur will never keep their promise. Not now, not ever. They never meant to. I doubt there was ever a vision at all. Just a way to play Shadowless into doing their dirty work."

She lunged forward, grabbed me, and pulled. I twisted my wrist, ducked under, and wrestled myself free. She tried again. I slid left, jumped backwards.

"Come on!" Amber snarled.

A gold shadow brushed past me. A large arm yanked me behind a male body.

Flint's other hand seized Amber by the throat.

He squeezed, his fingers finding the blood vessels on either side of her neck. She clawed at his wrists.

"While the IronMoon value females such as yourself," Flint said, "this is a party. Please do not abscond with the hostess. That would be very rude."

He released her. She sagged and gulped down air. "Gianna, please, come—"

"No." I had no idea what was going on outside of IronMoon, but I was certain I wanted to stay with Gabel. Gabel's cruelty was simple. Gabel did not lie, and he did not break his word, and he did not abide by dishonor. That was more than I could say for anything beyond our warped borders.

The Comet indeed.

"Lady Gianna," Flint said, "your guests await."

Not that any of it was Amber's fault. She hadn't known.

"Gianna, please!"

Flint raised a hand to Amber. "You are a warrior, she-wolf. As am I. She is my Luna. I will strike you to defend her."

Amber sobbed and crumbled to her knees.

At least my wedding was not dull.

Gabel and the other males returned, his nightmare wolf-form crushing terrace slate, the hunt rising off him, and fierce glee singing in our Bond.

As promised, Anders was unharmed and in one piece.

"Buttercup." Gabel nuzzled my neck, gloriously naked and pressed against my hip. I shivered with delight. "You smell of ferocity."

"I have a gift for you," I murmured as I handed him his kilt. I did not want him to move, the press of his skin on mine... but that would make our guests blush. I would have run my fingers along the outline of his abs, trailing lower to—but best think of SableFur now. And not let their little Shadowless spies (or Anders, or Aaron, or anyone else) think I was enthralled with Gabel. Let them think I was a prisoner of the Bond.

His blue eyes warmed, and the Bond pulled on us both. "Where is this gift?"

"I can't tell you yet."

"Pups in your belly, perhaps?"

"No, not quite." I winked at him and moved away.

Through the crowds I spotted Amber gesturing to my distressed father and a frowning Jermain.

Gabel sashed his kilt around his waist and sprang onto the

short stone wall separating the garden levels. "Wolves of IronMoon!"

The crowd hushed, and slowly eyes turned to him. Hix and Flint moved to stand closer to me, Hix right behind my shoulder, Flint a few feet away.

Gabel gestured to the crowds. "Many thanks to all who have come to join us on our Solstice, and to welcome our new Luna."

He gestured to me. No few wolves bristled at the word *our*, meaning *their* Luna... when they had one of their own.

But their grumbles were drowned out by the howls of celebration that struck the sky. Through the layer of winter clouds, the Moon's light shone.

Gabel waited for the songs to end, then continued. "Iron-Moon is a pack that honors the old traditions and the old ways. Tonight, I will prove to my mate that I will spare no pain for her, that I will bleed for her, that our den is safe from all harm."

A soft buzz of conversation.

"Alpha Marcus of MarchMoon. Come forward and assist me in this."

The MarchMoon Alpha stepped forward, and the guests around him pressed backward into a semicircle.

"Alpha Marcus," Gabel said in the hushed quiet, "a year ago, you knelt before me and pledged loyalty to IronMoon. In return, I did not permit the destruction or abuse of your pack. I have left MarchMoon as I promised I would, under your direct and complete stewardship. I have not asked more than that which you agreed to."

Marcus did not say anything, and he didn't understand. He stood there like a nonplussed sheep.

"When the MarchMoon wolf came here to petition Gianna, his question was honored. I did not ask after it, she did not offer. I have kept my end of our deal. You have not."

"It offended you that one of the MarchMoon petitioned an Oracle?" Marcus' voice had contempt in it.

"Not at all. Your betrayal offends me. I know you collude with Alpha Aaron of IceMaw. You are not nearly as cunning as you may think."

"I have done no such thing!" Marcus shouted.

"I know about Aaron. I know about the wolves you had in Gleaming Fang ten days ago." Gabel grinned at him, the glint of cruelty in his ocean-blue eyes, the hunt rising off him again. "You are incompetent, or a traitor. How do you want to be remembered?"

The only sound was the crackling of torches.

The Bond sung with Gabel's bloodthirst and sharp-edged anger. I suppressed a whimper of pain, just as it filled me with its own cruel delight in the next heartbeat. Marcus would get what he deserved, hot, swift justice at Gabel's claws. There was no hope for him, and I would enjoy watching Gabel dispose of him, even though it caused sharp pain to feel it within me.

"Your pet Oracle betrayed me!"

I gasped in horror, but Gabel laughed it off. "Gianna betray her Oracle vows? Never. She cannot be bent, nor broken, nor manipulated, nor intimidated. She has fought me every step, every breath. She did not consent to the Mark and still growls at me. She has hardly been tamed, and after all these months, I cannot take my eye off her for a breath. It is a glorious thing to keep such danger so close. To have her skin against mine, taste her pleasure, and know that she could do something most terrible to me."

Gabel, my father is in the crowd, and I'm sure nobody here is interested in what we do in private...

Marcus spat on the ground. "The Alpha Kings of old are dead, Gabel. They are dust and have remained dust. Your pack of dogs will never succeed!"

Gabel grinned. "Now you will be the offering of blood and bone for my Mate!"

He sprang off the wall with a curdling howl, his body twisting into the familiar, leathery nightmare, yellow talons and immense yellow fangs. Marcus, for a split second, was so transfixed with horror he did nothing.

Hesitation, even for a split second, was a death sentence for anyone faced with Gabel.

Gabel tackled him, flattened him, slashed once, and before Marcus's shift was even complete, Gabel twisted his head and clamped down on Marcus's throat. Marcus made a horrible noise. Gabel's fangs slid deep, hooking around the windpipe and delicate tissues.

Gabel yanked back, and Marcus's throat came with him.

Gabel spat out the rope of flesh and tissue, then raised his face to our guests and growled.

It reverberated through the air, the ground, through bones and hearts and brains.

Many of the guests dropped to their knees. The rest, after a pause, followed, either because compelled or just out of good sense to play along.

Gabel uncurled, melting back into human form. Blood darkened him into shining blackness in the night, as if he were a shadow passing before the Moon's eye. "Gianna, Oracle of the Moon and my chosen mate, I have removed the danger from our den. Do you accept it as proof of my worth?"

"Yes," I answered.

Gabel flicked gore off his hands. He was smeared from face to thigh in blood, his teeth stained red and his hair copper. Several IronMoon scurried over to clean up the mess he had left behind.

"You," Gabel pointed at the MarchMoon First Beta, "crawl back to your hovel. I will expect MarchMoon's affirmation of loyalty or writ of war within two days. On the third day, I expect your proxy here to swear loyalty, or you can expect First Beta Hix for breakfast."

Gabel stood in front of me, reeking of blood, death, and hot, dangerous triumph. "I will wash. Then, you are mine."

I took a breath.

There was no doubt in my mind I would go through with this, or that Marcus had to pay the price he paid.

The looks of bewildered pity from the crowds of guests told me everything. Flint came to stand next to me, and Ana actually took over the duties of stirring the party back up. "Goddamn! So this is a fucking werewolf wedding? Holy shit! It's not as crazy as my nutty cousin's wedding where her girlfriend brought a shotgun and tried to take out the groom, but hey, hell hath no wrath, right? Hey, do you guys believe in Hell? Like with devils poking you in the butt with pitchforks for eternity?"

"She is... a strange human," Flint muttered to me, watching the crowds try to resume some normal flow and motion.

"Very," I agreed. "Do you think she's actually a full human?"

"I would not be surprised if there was a hybrid far back in her pedigree," Flint agreed. "A peculiar find, but this is a pack of peculiar finds. Perhaps she was just tired of the human world."

Gabel returned in half an hour, clean, smelling of soap, his hair mostly dry and roguishly askew. He wore only a clean kilt, not even shoes. He gripped my bicep. "Come, buttercup. We will not delay further."

"Pull me a bit. For show," I murmured to him.

He yanked me against him. "You want to play rough?"

I suppressed a naughty gasp as his skin sent jolts through mine, and the Bond quivered and squirmed with desire. "For the guests. I can't seem too willing."

"Why not?"

"It's part of your gift."

Gabel's expression didn't change, but his eyes smiled for him. He stepped back, pulling me after him and over to the stone wall.

In modern times, mated pairs spoke their own vows. Promises for whatever the pair wanted to promise each other. The vows were a formal, public declaration of what they already knew. Gabel had made it clear we would use the old vows specifically for Alphas and Lunas.

Gabel held my hands in his, lifted them between us as his ocean-colored eyes churned in the firelight, his breath warm on my cold fingers. "Will you rule justly and wisely at my side?"

"I will," I answered.

"Will you bring pups to our den, and they will be ours to raise and value?"

"I will."

"Will you temper my cruelty with wisdom, and goad my fury when required?"

"I will." I did that already... I liked to think.

Next, I removed my hands from his placed my left hand at his throat, and squeezed. He lifted his jaw and eyed me from his height. According to some old texts, I was supposed to grab his most tender bits too, and threaten to twist them off, which I was tempted to do.

"Do it." Gabel's whisper was hoarse around the pressure on his throat.

"You'll get too excited," I told him. It wouldn't have the same effect if everyone just saw he was enjoying the danger more than he should.

Gabel tried not to grin.

"Will you protect our den, our pack, our pups with every drop of blood and fiber within you?" I asked him.

"I will."

"Will you accept the pups I bring to you, that you will raise them and love them as the Moon expects an Alpha and father to?" There were records of old where Lunas had pups from previous mates, and the vow expected the Alpha to accept all of a Luna, pups included.

"I will."

"Will you cherish me and love me so that I know no other male will ever be worthy of my glance?"

"I will."

I released his neck. He recaptured my hand, grabbed my cheek in his other, and pulled me against him, roughly, for an equally rough and hot kiss.

The Bond swarmed over my awareness like crashing waves, and the Moon saw, even through the clouds and first flakes of snow falling around us. The IronMoon howled around us, songs of victory and greeting, and the song to welcome a Luna.

Gabel released me, and we turned to face the crowd. Ana flung rice at us and laughed like a maniac.

Gabel did not release my hand. He glanced at me, a smirk on his lips and mischief curling in the Bond between us.

A hot desire burned within me. I gasped, and the Bond curled around my brain, whispering to me all the things that needed to happen very, very soon. I shifted on my feet, my body so tender and poised for him that I was going to do something rather embarrassing if I didn't keep a hold on my mind, keep it above the hot surface of the Bond's churning waves.

Gabel's smirk intensified. Then he gestured to the crowds. "Thank you, IronMoon, for welcoming your new Luna. The party we leave to you, but in keeping with tradition, Luna Gianna and I have something else to attend to."

"Gabel!" I gasped in shock.

"Shall we do it here?"

I was so taken aback (because if I had answered yes he

would have ripped off both his kilt and my dress, and taken me right there on the ground) I couldn't answer for a second. He just grinned, grabbed my bicep, and hauled me after him.

"You did tell me to play rough," he reminded me in a hot whisper as he herded me toward the house.

"I was done with that party anyway," I whispered back, every stride sending jolts through my lower body.

"You were done with it before it even began, my Luna. Now we shall celebrate in private. That will suit both of us better." His voice was low against my ears, tripping up and down my veins and nerves. "Buttercup, the scent of your desire is more than I can stand."

His fingertips pulled over the silk at my spine as I walked, making me stumble as the heat between my thighs spiked higher.

"Up the steps, buttercup." His fingers slid lower, cupping the curve of my rump as if to help me up the stairs, but he was not helping at all, drinking in my almost incoherent hunger, his enjoyment of that giving him as much control as it robbed from me. "That's it. Don't trip, my darling."

"I... hate... you." I wanted Gabel's fingers to slide under the silk, between my thighs and—

"I know," he all but purred.

"My wrath... will be... terrible." I managed to crawl to the top of the stairs, my skin burning from the desire. I needed my dress off right then. I didn't care, it had to come off.

Gabel pulled the zipper down over my breasts, my hips. He ran his hands over me. "Do your worst, buttercup." His fingers slid back down my spine, over my rump, caressed my thighs, slid upward. "And then do it again."

THE DAY AFTER

The backyard was a disaster scene. A wild after-party had happened after Gabel and I had cleared out. There was blood on the snow, but no obvious bodies, and nobody had come rushing to our rooms to inform us that somebody important had been injured or killed.

The pigs and cows had been stripped, even bones were missing (no surprise, probably being gnawed on somewhere), and not a single scrap of food was left. I'd have to organize getting everything cleaned up, but that could wait. There was no reason to rush out the morning after.

"So tell me about this present," Gabel said, amusement on his voice. "If it isn't pups in your belly, I'm not sure I care."

"Shadowless is in SableFur's pocket." I poured myself a fresh cup of coffee. No formal breakfast that morning. Most of IronMoon was still asleep, save for a few members who were on duty. Gabel and I were alone in the kitchen for the moment.

"How do you know this?" Gabel asked.

"Amber told me."

"Amber. Amber. The she-wolf they had with them. That Amber."

"Don't pretend you don't know who she is."

Gabel thought for moment, then said, "I remember her face, but not so much her scent. All I can remember from that day is your scent."

"I was freshly bathed."

"It makes no difference to a male. So tell me how you acquired this gift."

"Anita told Shadowless she saw you taking Amber as a mate, and to let it happen without protest. They promised to help get her back, but she was to try to murder you," I said.

"That was why Shadowless went so quietly." Gabel's eyes narrowed to sated slits, his voice a warm growl.

"Amber had no idea I'd been to SableFur. Anita lied to Shadowless. Now, the question is, does *Magnes* know you are his son? Because Anita knows you are. It doesn't mean Magnes knows."

"Interesting." Gabel mulled it over, then dropped the train of thought. "So. We know Shadowless negotiated in bad faith. That is why you wanted me to handle you a little roughly. You don't normally enjoy a harsh touch."

"Aren't you tired and chafed yet, Gabel?" I asked him.

He smirked. "I fear no pain nor exhaustion, buttercup, save yours."

I was indeed quite delightfully chafed. Gabel's ocean-eyes smoldered, the Bond shifting and rocking like the Tides themselves, seductive and inviting. He had been very determined the previous night to create those pups he wanted so keenly. I kept my attention on the matter at hand: his gift.

"I let Amber think I was trapped here." I had no regrets about the fib. Shadowless had sold me. They had made a vow of loyalty to IronMoon in bad faith. "And not that I stayed of my own accord."

"You would have made a false promise before the Moon."

"It seems you and I are the only ones who are disgusted by false promises."

"I wonder if Anita lied or not," Gabel said. "I had met a dozen, two dozen females who I caught the scent of before I met you. I felt as though the Moon were dangling females in front of me giving me false choices."

I said dryly, "And I was so different?"

"Fishing for compliments?"

"Perhaps I am."

"You were the night-blooming flower," he said, then changed the topic. "I wonder if Aaron is also a SableFur pawn."

"If he is, it's only because he lets SableFur think that."

"Why would you say that?"

"I don't know how I know, I just do. He's brilliant. The SableFur could crush IronMoon if they wanted to. If I were Aaron, I'd be asking why the SableFur asked me for a favor."

"SableFur and IceMaw will come for IronMoon one day. I think it is time to insert some spies into both. Buttercup, when did you become so cunning?"

"Oracles can't be stupid." And as long as I was an Oracle, the door to IronMoon remained open.

Gabel would never ask me to give it up. I knew in that moment he would never demand it, because he expected me to know if I needed to walk away.

A cunning Alpha like Aaron would continue to use it to his advantage. As an Oracle, I still had to humor Anita, but would Magnes risk invoking the ire of the IronMoon Luna? There were no Lunas that were also Oracles that I knew of.

And no Queens.

Gabel set his coffee cup down. "For Aaron, it is also personal. He wants you. He wants you as surely as any lone male trailing a pack wants to challenge the Alpha for his female.

He will come for you, and he will be willing to kill me to win you. It is only a matter of *when* this happens."

Gabel smoldered, then said in a low tone, "And if he succeeds in dispatching me with IronMoon intact, you would give him a very fine empire. One to even challenge SableFur. Those two things are more than enough reason to drive him."

"You cannot think that I would betray you."

"Of course not. But he could smell your lure-scent. I told no one you smell of the cereus. If he kills me, but Marks you soon after, your chance of survival would be much greater."

"Perhaps I should just see if I could manage both of you. I do have two shoulders," I retorted, angry at the thought of another male daring to handle me as Gabel had that first day, furious Gabel would even contemplate letting me fall into Aaron's grip.

He glared at me, sharp and prickly with hot anger. "No."

I snorted. "Do you even still want this empire?"

"I have to do what I have to do.

He had been born under an angry Moon. She had shaped him to carry a dark, burning banner under Her eye. He was the Comet. He had no choice. It was how he had been made.

"Shall we turn our attention to heirs?" he inquired instead. "Not that we have not been giving it some attention, but some... focus."

I eyed him. "You spent all night working to that end."

"And what is one night if you weren't ripe? I do believe you made certain promises to me to provide me with pups."

I had, but I also hadn't promised him a schedule.

"Buttercup, if it's infants you worry over, I am proof lupines can be civilized. Winter is here. We could have a spring litter. Think about how easy it would be. I will eagerly sire pups on you in any form."

It was impossible to tell if he was joking or serious. "Hmph,

Easy for you, perhaps." I decided to treat him like he was joking, because I was not going to entertain the idea of having lupines. "I think you should keep your mind focused on making sure we don't invite traitors to the Naming. Bloodshed at a Naming is very bad luck."

Gabel's smirk deepened. "Speaking of traitors, I have dealt with Marcus. What are you going to do about Gardenia?"

The discipline and management of the she-wolves now fell squarely on my shoulders.

I knew what I was going to have to do about Gardenia. She had been given every chance at redemption.

The scales of Balance tilted toward darkness.

I only regretted that I felt no regret.

"What happens to traitors in IronMoon?" I asked him.

Gabel smiled.

ABOUT THE AUTHOR

Merry is an independent author living in the Bay Area of San Francisco, with her husband and two cats.

She enjoys coffee, combat sports, casual games, low budget disaster flicks, and the very occasional 10K. In addition to writing novels, she also posts free serial fiction on Wattpad.

The second book in the IronMoon series, *Iron Oracle*, will be out in late 2018.

———————

www.merryravenell.com

ALSO BY MERRY RAVENELL

The IronMoon Series

Iron Oracle - *coming soon!*

Ice & Iron - *coming 2019*

Obsidian Oracle - *coming 2019*

The SnowFang Series

The SnowFang Bride

The SnowFang Storm - *coming 2019*

Other Titles

The Nocturne Bride

Made in the USA
Coppell, TX
23 June 2021

57946686R00288